Praise for *The Drum Within*

"First of a welcome series." —*Kirkus Reviews*

"Nothing makes me happier than the debut novel of a brilliant new writer, and I was wowed by Jim Scarantino's *The Drum Within* ... Best of all, his main character Detective Denise Aragon ranks as one of the most fully-realized, strongest female characters I've read in crime fiction. Aragon powers her way through this twisty plot, racing after one of the most lethal and credible villains you'd ever want to meet, serial killer Cody Geronimo." —Lisa Scottoline, *New York Times* bestselling author

"*The Drum Within* is a gritty police procedural that will make you rethink everything you know about justice. A tour de force of good guys and bad guys." —Robert Dugoni, #1 Amazon and *New York Times* bestselling author of *My Sister's Grave*

"*The Drum Within* keeps many ducks in a row through a maze of gritty encounters, bitter confrontations, and some very clever red herrings."
—*Santa Fe New Mexican*

"A thrilling police story." —*Suspense Magazine*

COMPROMISED

JAMES R. SCARANTINO

A DENISE
ARAGON MYSTERY

MIDNIGHT INK
WOODBURY, MINNESOTA

FIRST EDITION
First Printing, 2017

Book format by Bob Gaul
Cover design by Lisa Novak

Midnight Ink, an imprint of Llewellyn Worldwide Ltd.

Library of Congress Cataloging-in-Publication Data
Names: Scarantino, James, 1956– author.
Title: Compromised / James R. Scarantino.
Description: First Edition. | Woodbury, Minnesota: Midnight Ink, [2017] |
  Series: A Denise Aragon mystery; #2
Identifiers: LCCN 2016039126 (print) | LCCN 2016045344 (ebook) | ISBN
  9780738750408 | ISBN 9780738751665
Subjects: LCSH: Women detectives—Fiction. | Santa Fe (N.M.)—Fiction. |
  GSAFD: Mystery fiction.
Classification: LCC PS3619.C268 C66 2017 (print) | LCC PS3619.C268 (ebook) |
  DDC 813/.6—dc23
LC record available at https://lccn.loc.gov/2016039126

Midnight Ink
Llewellyn Worldwide Ltd.
2143 Wooddale Drive
Woodbury, MN 55125-2989
www.midnightinkbooks.com

Printed in the United States of America

*To the men and women in law enforcement
who lay it all on the line for us every day. They go
where we never want to go except in the pages we turn.*

ONE

Lily Montclaire needed these cops to believe her. That or, what did they say, three stacked jail sentences? What was left of her fashion model looks wouldn't do her any favors for the next twenty years.

"That thing you do with your hand, laying your fingers against your neck, showing your long lines, what a fine thing you used to be. You're going to want to stop doing that."

Detective Denise Aragon talking now. Short, brown, solid forearms. Montclaire didn't know there were that many muscles between a wrist and elbow. Black eyes that didn't blink, that took you apart and let you know how bad it was going to be without her saying a word. Hair cut so close to her scalp you could see scars. Without the badge, Aragon could be like the women waiting for her if she couldn't make this work.

But the pretty-girl face on top of the thick neck. The buzz cut making her big brown eyes even bigger. The lips, no gloss, probably never lipstick—this close they were beautiful, even cracked from the drought and crazy heat all around them this summer in Santa Fe. Montclaire was wondering about the scars when Aragon spoke again.

"Start over. Convince us we should help you."

"What else can I tell you?" She got no answer from Aragon's dark eyes.

She looked past Aragon at Detective Rick Lewis, hoping for something in his face. He had his chin down, showing her the part in his yellow hair, the shelf of his shoulders. What was he doing, texting someone while she was giving them more than anyone could believe?

Five times already she must have told them about the judge and the girl. Andrea had said she was eighteen, but no way was she old enough to drive.

"I picked her up at the Pizza Hut on Cerrillos. Then I drove her to the judge's house." Now giving the detectives a little more, the transportation details, something to help them believe. "I took her back there. She wouldn't let me take her home."

They wanted her old boss, the lawyer she'd worked for serving subpoenas, finding and talking to people, handling evidence clients turned in. Marcy Thornton. Her and the chief judge, the Honorable J. S. Diaz—pretty much the two of them running things in Santa Fe's First Judicial District Court. And the woman she saw in her mirror, Marcy's salvage project, the gofer with the crow's feet and sun damage who helped them keep it together.

The judge and the girl, a gift from Marcy to say thanks. A little more to help them along: Yes, she'd followed Andrea once. Lost her cutting across a lot behind the Walmart. By the time she drove around, she'd lost her in the dark. Marcy had wanted to know where she went. Andrea could be a problem if she realized who she'd been with.

"Following people. Was that something you did for Thornton?"

Lily Montclaire started to lay her hand against her neck, then stopped, remembering what Aragon had just told her.

"When I had to," she said.

"You ever follow me?"

Was that a ridge of muscle growing between Aragon's eyes? Who had muscle between their eyes?

"Yes. Well, no. I was following someone else and they met up with you."

"You'll tell me about that later. Back to Andrea. She knew the house," Aragon said. "She could figure it was Judge Diaz's."

"It was always dark. Those skinny streets off Acequia Madre, at night you can't tell where you're going until you come out on a bigger street."

These detectives wanted to believe. Maybe she should have given everything at the start, not making it better bit by bit when they interrupted and told her to start over. Why hold anything back? Like she had chips to bargain with.

But that's how Marcy played it. She'd watched her a hundred times never putting it all on the table, knowing she'd need something at the end to push the deal through. *Always keep something in the bank*, Marcy said. *Late withdrawals are worth the most.*

"She did see the license plate." Montclaire gave a little more.

"How many Aston Martins in Santa Fe?" Aragon spread those stubby, square hands. No nails. Not bitten, clipped down to nothing. "It wouldn't take long to find out who it belonged to. Thornton. So Andrea knew she was riding in a big-time lawyer's car. Come on, she knew where she was going. You ever tell Andrea straight out who she was partying with? Try to impress her?"

She remembered Marcy sitting right there with her not so long ago. Before she'd agreed to talk to the police. Marcy wanting to represent her, not leave her alone with these detectives. *No charge. Don't say a thing. Let me handle this.* Wink. *They've got nothing.* Wink. *Nothing to worry about.* Another goddamn wink and Marcy's hand on her thigh under the table.

Nothing for *her* to worry about.

Marcy had tried to keep her from reading the memo Aragon had waved around. All her mistakes when she thought she'd been so smart, doing what Marcy wanted to make problems for clients go away. All the bad news laid out in five pages, with tabbed attachments stapled at the end.

They've got nothing. Wink.

Marcy, you're fired.

It had felt so good. Marcy Thornton going stiff, flipping her hair over her shoulder the way a person blinks when they hear something they can't believe. She could still hear the sound of Marcy's heels clacking on the floor outside the door as she stomped away down the hall.

"Lily, it's still your word only." Aragon turned her head to hand the questions to her partner and Montclaire got a good look at the scar above Aragon's ear, a lightning bolt in the skin running toward the back of her head. What could have cut her like that?

"Give us some tangible evidence," said Lewis, shirt too small for his big shoulders. He'd been standing against the wall. Now he came to the table and looked down on her. "This keeps getting richer every time you tell it. I believed you more before you added the judge and Andrea to your story.

These two, Aragon and Lewis, bodies that made you back up when they came close.

"What's that mean, 'tangible'?" Montclaire asked.

"Solid, physical evidence to corroborate what you're telling us," Lewis said. "Look at it. Why should a jury believe someone like you talking their way out of jail? The chief judge, she'll have her story. Not just

4

judge, chief judge. She's the boss of the nice man in the robe who swore them in, instructed them on their solemn duties. Diaz will say she never met this girl. Never had her in her house with you and Marcy Thornton. Never poured tequila for a minor, did the rest you've been telling us, even harder to believe. Chief judges don't do those things to girls."

"Gran Patron Platinum," Montclaire said. "Marcy brought it. Expensive stuff."

"Jose Cuervo, Everclear, Walmart wine out of a box, whatever," Lewis said. "Look at it—a former *Cosmo* model saying Marcy Thornton gave the judge this girl as thanks for throwing a case. The first words that come to mind are 'yeah, right.' We'll check about *Cosmo*. Everything you tell has to be absolutely true for us to keep our end."

"I was in it. Not the cover. An inset about a beach resort."

"Name it. The resort."

"It was years ago. I can't remember. We flew into Miami. They had me in a long flowered dress on an old bike with the fat tires. It was hard pedaling in the sand. Another one, I was on a seesaw staring at the sun, trying to keep my eyes open. I hated that shoot. I looked great but felt dead."

"Everything will be a lot harder at Grants." Aragon talking again, that ridge of muscle between her eyes pushing toward what passed for a hairline, little black dots on brown skin.

"What's Grants?"

"The women's correctional facility on I-25, surrounded by something called the Malpais. That's Spanish for badlands. Lava that cooled, nothing grows on it, big tubes opening under your feet, everything for twenty miles black and scary. You wander in there you don't get out. Perfect place for a prison." Aragon leaned across the table, slapped down a palm. "Think Clinton and the blue dress. That's the kind of evidence you need to give us."

Montclaire wanted to point out maybe Aragon hadn't been listening close enough to who exactly was at these parties.

A smart mouth wouldn't help. She said, "Let me think about that."

It was cold in this bare room. Bright as flashbulbs, bare lights bouncing off the linoleum floor, the one-way glass. The detectives wore long sleeves with cotton tees underneath, jeans. Montclaire wore a short skirt, tank top, sandals, toenails red today. Ninety degrees outside and still morning. She'd seen smoke from the fire in the dry forests to the west of the city when they'd brought her in. No rain for months, everything on the edge of burning.

They'd planned on making her miserable so she'd want to get this over with. They hadn't been wearing long sleeves when they came to her house.

"Can you turn down the AC?" She made a show of hugging herself, looking from the doll face on the thick neck to the guy who was all chest and shoulders, getting only stares as cold as her hands.

Lewis said, "Give us something that can't be made to look like you were working overtime to pull off a plea bargain."

Tangible. It sounded like a French perfume. She saw the ads, dark, smoky background, a little cut-glass bottle on a pedestal, a model, breastbone under skin, red lips parting, a tongue peeking between white teeth.

She had it. "Judy bit her."

"Judge Diaz bit this girl." Aragon cocked her head, raised an eyebrow. "Andrea."

"Yes. On the shoulder. Well, sort of a nibble."

"Here?" Aragon reached across her own chest and laid a hand on top of a shoulder. Montclaire wondered if Aragon hit the weights before interrogations to bulk up.

"Closer to the neck."

Aragon slid the hand up her traps.

"About there," Montclaire said.

"When? How long ago?"

"There was a party Friday night."

"Forty-eight hours plus," Lewis said.

Montclaire felt this finally moving forward and added more to keep it going.

"Marcy bit her, too. You can match teeth marks, show who did it. Both Judy and Marcy with the girl. And there's DNA in saliva, right?"

Aragon should be happy. But the fire in her eyes made Montclaire try to inch her chair away, put more room between them. The chair didn't budge. It was bolted to the floor.

"Where did you bite her, Lily?"

"I didn't."

"We've got you on aggravated arson, multiple counts of destruction of evidence, conspiracy to obstruct. All worse because the client you and Thornton were helping, your buddy Cody Geronimo, only killed, what, fifteen women? If Andrea has your teeth marks on her skin and you don't 'fess to it now, we add another ten years to your tab—a child molester. The women you'll be with, when they look at you, they'll see the person that did them when they were kids."

Montclaire sat on her hands to keep them from shaking.

"Maybe," she said. "Not hard."

Aragon sat back, gave her room to breathe. "I might believe you." Montclaire felt her heart jump. She was getting close. Then came, "Problem is, teeth marks are too unreliable, especially with this much time passing. And you said nibbled, not a bite to leave a bruise mark. Saliva on the girl's skin is probably lost. I don't know any teenage girl who'd go this long without washing. Back to square one. Time you told us about the handcuffs."

"How do you know about them?"

"The night you brought Andrea to Judge Diaz's house, I was at the end of the drive, under the trees, watching. I almost shot you. That gun you had on her, was that Thornton's? We know she's got a concealed carry. You don't."

"You were watching? Were you there the other times?"

"What other times?"

"Get Marcy's court calendar. Whenever she won a motion or something, she'd tell me to find Andrea and bring her to the judge's house."

"The handcuffs, Lily."

"Marcy's idea. Something different for the judge. Andrea thought it was funny."

"'May it please the court'—I heard you say that when you walked Andrea to the door. And Diaz saying back, 'I'll be the judge of that.' You all started laughing. Andrea, too. She hadn't laughed, we might not be having this conversation. It would have gotten bad right there. Where are the cuffs?"

"Marcy's office. There's a dressing table, bottom drawer."

"We're a million miles from probable cause to search a lawyer's office."

Lewis's phone buzzed. He stepped outside.

"With what I saw—" Aragon pointed one of those stubby fingers without nails. "Cuffs, a gun at Andrea's back. I can charge you with kidnapping. Maybe Andrea was nervous, laughing out of fear, thinking that was the best way to defuse the situation."

"But you heard her."

"Maybe Andrea won't back your story. Maybe she'd say you abducted her at gunpoint. We still haven't found her, and you dribbling information, wasting our time here." Aragon folded arms across her chest. Fists under her biceps made them look huge. "Tell me what happened inside the house. About the cuffs, now they're in the picture."

"I was getting to it. Inside, in the living room, Judy said, 'She looks good enough to eat.' She was giggling."

"Stop." Aragon was back on the edge of her chair. Montclaire saw something different in her eyes. "Andrea had her shirt on. You had to unlock the cuffs to get it off."

"Judy couldn't wait. Andrea was squirming. I couldn't get the key in the cuffs."

"They started in while Andrea was still dressed?"

Montclaire saw where Aragon was going and nodded, maybe more than she needed to.

The door opened and Lewis stepped in, filling the entrance with his size.

"They left saliva on her clothes," Aragon told him. "We get DNA for Diaz and Thornton, this thing starts breaking open. With Thornton's calendar, we can tie the house parties, whatever you want to call them, to Diaz throwing cases. We get their phone records, their e-mails. Imagine that girl's testimony. Wait. Lily, were the cuffs part of it two nights ago?"

"Judy liked Andrea coming in the door wearing them. 'Remanded to custody,' she said. They bit through her clothes."

"Bit? Before, it went from bit to nibbled," Aragon said. "Now we're back to bit."

"I meant, nipped. Love nips."

"We have to find Andrea."

Lewis didn't return Aragon's confident smile. He said, "Maybe someone did. Dumpster off Jaguar Road."

TWO

THEY CAUGHT THE CALL, the only Violent Crimes detectives on duty today. They left Montclaire in the interrogation room with the promise a sweater would arrive. The two-mile drive gave Lewis time to explain why he thought this might be Andrea. Montclaire had given them hair, height, and weight and described a tattoo on the girl's hip. All four matched the information he took over the phone.

Patrol cars blocked both ends of the dirt alley. Thirty yards from where Lewis parked, people in white suits were building a platform over an open dumpster. A mobile home park fronted the alley, with single-story stucco homes on barren lots beyond that, most without garages, all with windows closed. Air conditioners and swamp coolers running full blast laid down a white noise backdrop to the crackling of police scanners.

To the west, black smoke lifted into the sky from fires in the mountains above Los Alamos. At night a red glow defined the horizon. The wind was keeping the smoke out of the city, blowing it west across Bandelier National Monument and the forests that had been burned every summer for the past decade, making people wonder how there could be anything up there left to burn.

They showed their badges and followed a pathway between yellow ribbons weighted with stones. The dumpster had the phone number of the disposal company under a warning that unauthorized use would be prosecuted to the fullest extent of the law.

"We make an arrest," Aragon said, "we add illegal dumping. Don't let me forget."

Lewis recorded the telephone number and said he'd call for when the dumpster was last emptied.

Sergeant Ralph Garcia ran the show. He had the person who called 911 waiting in his car. Aragon and Lewis wanted to see the body first. Lewis asked how Garcia and his people had walked to the dumpster, where they had left their footprints. Garcia pointed to a board put down by residents of the mobile home park to avoid stepping in mud.

"Back when we used to have rain," Lewis said. "Wet stuff falling from the sky. I think I remember that."

Garcia raised his eyes to the fire on the mountains, something everyone was doing that week in Santa Fe.

"It's gotten bigger while we wait for you," the sergeant said. "Crown fire now. It'll be moving on Los Alamos tomorrow."

"Let's see the body," Aragon said. "Then we'll talk to your witness."

Forensic technicians on ladders around the dumpster set braces holding scaffolds across the opening. Nate Moss from the Office of Medical Investigator, dressed head to toe in a white cleansuit, waved them closer, directing Aragon and Lewis to use the board across the dried mud.

"I want to photograph the body *in situ* without trampling the articles around her," he said. "We'll try to lift her straight up. Your forensic folks can do their archeology on the trash afterwards."

"Is this thing safe?" Aragon tested the scaffolding. "It looks like junk you ran out and bought at Home Depot."

"Lowe's. Don't touch the dumpster."

Aragon pulled on latex gloves. She climbed a ladder and stepped onto a wooden plank. The smell below her made her catch her breath. She lowered herself to hands and knees then lay prone, her nose even closer to what was cooking inside the dumpster's steel.

A teenage girl's body lay two feet below. Face up, naked. The corner of a stained mattress covered one leg. Styrofoam packing covered her head. Red roses, dozens, were piled to one side and Aragon thought of cleanup after a wedding or *quinceañera*. An arm lay under black plastic garbage bags that appeared to hold lawn cuttings, the other under an empty beer case. Bags leaked orange peels, vegetable cuttings, moldy bread, coffee grounds, soiled diapers. Aragon saw bruising on the left breast. Her eyes traveled down the girl's torso: a bloated stomach, dark pubic hair shaved into a pencil-thin line, a clear bite mark on the inside of a thigh, the leg bent allowing her to see it.

The tattoo on her hip was an automobile, a sports car of some sort. What Montclaire had told them to look for.

"I want to see her face."

"Use this." Moss passed up a set of barbecue tongs. "Lowe's has all the latest in cutting-edge crime scene supplies. Let me get up there and photograph the process."

Aragon waited for Moss to clamber onto the platform opposite her, the opening and body below and between them. His weight bent the plank as he lowered himself to one knee.

"Wait till I'm off," she told Lewis, who'd started to climb up. "I don't think these boards can hold all of us."

Moss aimed his camera and nodded. Aragon tried the tongs. She had to lift Styrofoam packing to see that the girl's head was inside a reusable Whole Foods shopping bag.

"I'm going to slide it off her head," Aragon said, and Moss nodded behind his camera.

She grabbed a corner of the bag with the tongs and tugged, slowly, trying to keep the head in place on its pillow of garbage. She saw twisted long black hair, bruising on the neck. A word from high school came back to her: "hickeys." Then a smooth chin emerged, lips, the tip of a nose. She left the bag where it was, still pinned under the back of the head, and lifted enough to see the whole face.

"She's absolutely … " Aragon swallowed, gathered herself. "She's beautiful."

———

"Federal Bureau of Investigation. How may I direct your call?"

Special Agent Tomas Rivera was in court in Albuquerque. His cell would be in a lockbox near the lobby. Aragon asked the FBI receptionist for voicemail, got it, and waited for Rivera's recorded voice to finish instructing callers to leave a message.

"Hurry back to Santa Fe, Tomas. The witness we've been looking for, the one that makes the case against Thornton and Diaz, we're pretty sure she's dead. Add homicide to the predicate acts we've got for you. Time your office formally took this on. Call me. We need help."

"We'll have more federal help than we want," Lewis said when she'd ended the call. "No more talking to Montclaire alone. Let's interview Garcia's witness before we have a crowd."

Sergeant Garcia had taken his own turn on the scaffold and was climbing down the ladder, his face the color of ash.

"May we use your car, Sarge?" Aragon asked. "Find out what this person knows."

Garcia pressed the heel of his hand into his brow, closed his eyes for a second, and his color returned. "You think the dumpster smelled bad. Better roll down the windows."

"What's wrong with your car?"

"My car don't stink. It's the witness."

"Name?"

"Gray," Garcia said.

"Gray what?"

"Just Gray." Garcia lifted his shoulders and let them drop. "Says she's a St. John's student. Too busy reading old books to wash, I guess. Check out her feet. She's like the little people in that movie, The Rings. The furry ones don't wear shoes."

"Hobbits?" Lewis asked.

"A hobbit girl. First I thought she was wearing those shoes that look like gloves pulled over feet, where the toes slip into little sleeves or what you call them. I thought hers were black high-tops. It's dirt. She's caked in it."

Aragon rarely stepped on the campus of St. John's College, the school of great books where kids who didn't need a job out of college, might never need a job, burned up more per year in tuition than the average New Mexico family supporting four kids.

"What's she doing here?"

"Looking for something to eat."

Aragon had seen what was in the dumpster. Nothing she'd feed to a starving dog.

14

"I'm not kiddin' you." Garcia caught the look on her face. "She was hungry. Been up all night. Some guy made her get out of his car, she was gonna hitch from the corner of Cerrillos back to campus. Decided to dumpster dive. She lives in the dorm." Garcia paused. "Where I guess they don't got showers."

"We'll talk out here," Lewis said. "Let's see this … Gray."

"Sergeant." Aragon pointed to the mobile home park. "Could you start your officers on the door-to-door? We're interested in anybody seen throwing anything in the dumpster during the last twelve hours. It's a long walk across open ground with a body over your shoulder, so especially vehicles backing to the dumpster."

"Roger," Garcia said. "We know this place. We're here a lot."

Aragon wished she'd worn a hat. She kept her hair buzzed to nubs so no one could grab it in a fight, and nails clipped to nothing so she wouldn't draw an excessive force beef for scratching someone. Going around in the sun she'd get a wrinkled scalp, friends told her. When you see me with long hair and painted nails, she told them, you'll know I'm retired.

They crossed open ground to Garcia's black-and-white, the gold stripes of the Zia symbol down the side and *America's Oldest Capital City* printed below. Lewis opened a door and waved a hand in front of his face.

"Miss, would you step out? We'd like to ask a few questions."

"Rick." Aragon spoke as the door cracked open. "I'm sure Gray is hungry, maybe thirsty." The door swung wide. A short young woman got out, bare filthy feet coming first. She had the sour smell of street people. Aragon caught herself stepping back. "There's a Blake's not far from here. We could call in for Lotaburgers."

"I won't eat anything from there," Gray said, an edge in her voice. "That place is full of pain."

15

"It's a hamburger joint."

"I hear screaming every time I go by one of those. I don't have an appetite right now, anyway. Who are you and what do you want from me?"

"First," Aragon said, coming back with some edge of her own, "I'm Detective Aragon and this is Detective Lewis. What's your real name? We need that information."

"I choose Gray."

"For us to take your statement, subpoena you later—this is a homicide and we cross our T's—we need the name you didn't choose. What's on your driver's license?"

"Chelsea Brinnon. But that's not *my* name. It's an oppressive fiction society uses to plug me into its imposed narrative. *I* am Gray."

"Right," Aragon said, pulling out the notebook she carried in her jeans' rear pocket. "Is that with an 'a' or an 'e'?"

A few more questions and the girl gave a DOB for Chelsea Brinnon. And one for Gray, born eighteen months ago.

"Any plans to legally change your name?" Lewis asked.

"That would be surrender to the system from which Gray has freed herself."

It was his turn to say, "Right."

"Why don't you tell us how Gray came to be here and what you saw," Aragon said.

That approach, as though they would be talking about someone else, seemed to relax the hobbit girl. She squatted on her haunches and dragged a finger through the dirt. Aragon got low, too, so she could watch the girl's eyes. Lewis remained standing, giving them shade.

"I saw a bag of tortillas, corn tortillas, no refined flour. I was reaching for it, holding my nose against the smell, worse than any other dumpster, and I saw lots of roses under a sheet of cardboard.

They looked fresh. What a waste. When I moved it so I could grab one, that's when I saw the legs. I fell in then, did everything I could to get out without touching her. It was horrible."

She'd called 911 on her cell. A police car came right away.

In exchange for a ride back to the St. John's campus, she provided her parents' address and her cell number, saving them the trouble of getting it from the 911 operators.

They put Gray back into Garcia's unit and went to their own car to talk things over in cool air.

"I couldn't see what killed her," Aragon said as she handed Lewis a bottle of water. "We'll have to wait on Moss."

"Thornton and Diaz know Lily's been talking." Lewis's shirt had turned dark with sweat. He chugged half the bottle while Aragon cracked one open for herself. "They've been circling," he continued, "trying to find out what she's saying. If that's really Andrea in the dumpster, we need to worry about Lily. She's in danger. Thornton and Diaz have much to lose. I don't know about Diaz, maybe she only sees them in court. But Thornton, she knows lots of very bad people."

"Agreed." Aragon picked up the thread. "A judge with everything on the line, a lawyer who gets her jollies turning killers loose. I could see them doing it together. It took a lot of strength to lift a body that high, a hundred-pound standing military press. I don't think Thornton or Diaz alone could do it."

She liked this part, kicking ideas back and forth, trusting each other enough to try out paths without being held to owning them.

"You see the bite marks?" Aragon asked.

Lewis nodded. "We need to get back with Montclaire, ask who chomped who where. I'm not convinced she never hurt Andrea. She was able to run interference for Cody Geronimo, not too bothered by what he'd done. She thought nothing of almost burning down west

Santa Fe to destroy a table with blood evidence and other stuff when we were onto him. How much further to trying her hand at killing and using everything she learned as Thornton's investigator to steer us wrong? She's been in on police interviews, she's watched testimony, learned where Thornton's clients or our side slipped up. Are we letting our hots for Thornton and Diaz blind us? Lily was the last person we can put with Andrea. That makes her our top suspect."

"Thornton and Diaz have motive. I don't see it for Montclaire. Killing's a big step from the other stuff she pulled. It crosses one huge line for most people. Especially killing a girl."

Lewis pinched his sweaty shirt and lifted it off his chest, fanning himself with the damp fabric.

"Maybe Lily's one of the other ones," he said. "Seeing a line that's nothing to step over. Or seeing no lines at all."

———

The SFPD crime tech, Elaine Salas, arrived. She was the sole civilian who ran the department's Crime Scene Auxiliary Unit. She had the help of several officers, but it was her show, no one else permanently assigned to CSA.

They discussed what she could possibly learn from a dumpster and the hard-packed soil. Salas had her own ideas, and it was going to be archeology as Moss had said. She'd catalog the contents of the dumpster, their depth and position in the trash, and see if that told her anything. She was doing prep to lift latents off the dumpster when they asked her to get Gray's.

With Gray's fingerprints in Salas's mobile reader, they took her to the St. John's dorm, AC blasting, windows down the whole way while Gray told them about the Fregan lifestyle, the reason she ate out of dumpsters and didn't wash to minimize exploitation of resources and build her natural resistance to bacteria, bacteria having a right to live like everything else. They got no more, except questions about how could they not hate themselves, killers of young men of color, tools of the one percent, serving oppressors of the weak. Aragon asked if eating garbage could cause brain damage. The dead girl in the dumpster, she look like an oppressor to you? And, excuse me, Chelsea Brinnon, screw this Gray bullshit, this campus looks damn white and one percenty to me. And take a damn shower. You know how many poor people of color dream of being clean and smelling nice? Your stench is an insult to their aspirations and damn oppressive to this working-class Latina.

Lewis said, "Working-class Latina? I thought you were a pig like me."

They dropped Gray at her dorm and kept the windows down to air out the car, driving out of the hills away from the St. John's campus. They came along a green patch in the drought-brown of the city. Girls in yellow and blue uniforms ran across a soccer field, holding a line, charging forward, back, to the left, now right.

"Pull over," Lewis said. "For a minute."

Aragon parked outside the chain-link enclosing the field. A coach's whistle penetrated the roar of the city.

"There's one of my reasons for being a cop," Lewis said. "Katie, over on the other side, sixth from the end. Mind if I watch my daughter for a second?"

"First a minute, down to a second. We'll sit here long as you want."

They did. Not saying anything, the car getting hot, neither noticing. Lewis looked away, out the window. Aragon saw him raise the back of his hand to the corner of his eye.

"I'm ready," Lewis said and faced the windshield, his cheeks wet. It wasn't sweat. He reached across the seat to lay his hand on her shoulder.

"You alright?" he asked.

Aragon looked down, to her left, making like she was searching for the button to bring up the window and dragging a fist across her eyes so Lewis wouldn't see.

"She was beautiful."

"She was," Lewis said. "No kid deserves to be thrown out like trash."

"The one that did that to her …"

"A dumpster's too good for them."

THREE

Walter Fager in court, in the witness chair without a tie, a black mock-turtle under his pin-striped Hart, Schaffner, and Marx jacket. And slip-on canvas shoes instead of wingtips telling them he was done with the past twenty years, the old-school jacket left over from those days. No longer a lawyer. Now a civilian and having fun.

Not telling them much else.

"Mr. Fager, I order you to answer Ms. Thornton's question."

Marcy Thornton watched him lift his chin to meet the scowl of Judge Judith S. Diaz, black robe matching black hair and eyebrows, and even blacker eyes above bony cheeks. Her face had grown hard, lost anything girlish, the eyes and mouth getting the worst of it. But still she had a good figure inside the folds, and was proud of it.

"You're ordering me to answer," Fager said. "If I don't?"

"You know I'll hold you in direct contempt. The bailiff will lead you off the witness stand and through that door that your former clients used to enter this room. But you're going the other direction, to the elevator, downstairs to a holding cell. The bus to the detention center leaves at six. I'll schedule a hearing to reconsider upon notification you're prepared to purge yourself of contempt and comply with this court's orders in every respect."

"You're ordering me to answer truthfully, not simply say what you and Ms. Thornton want to hear?"

"You have failed to appear at three depositions and ignored a subpoena. You have not answered interrogatories and have disregarded requests for production. I issued a bench warrant to bring you here for a deposition under my supervision so I can rule on objections on the spot. The whole purpose of the long, extended process you have forced upon this Court is, yes, to get the truth out of you. Word for word."

Fager lifted a wrist to shoot his cuff, then caught himself. No starched cotton with onyx links at the end of his jacket sleeves.

"The truth is"—a hint of smile like he'd just won something—"that you've been throwing cases, giving Marcy Thornton favorable rulings not supported by law or evidence, cutting her clients loose, generally debasing and corrupting justice because you enjoy intimate relations with her. Oh hell, why not say it: you and Marcy screw. It's been going on ever since you two had your law school study group and it's gotten worse now you're Chief Judge and think you're untouchable. Untouchable except by Marcy Thornton and the underage girl she gave you in appreciation for derailing the Cody Geronimo prosecution. A lot of touching going on there."

"Your Honor!" Thornton charged the bench, spike heels hammering the floor, short legs scissoring fast to cover the distance from the counsel table.

"I have this, Ms. Thornton." Judge Diaz pointed at Fager. "I find you in contempt of court. You will be taken into custody immediately. Bailiff."

"What?" Fager lifted his hands, palms up, his collar riding higher on his neck. "Let's review: you said give us the truth. Ms. Thornton's question was, what did Lily Montclaire tell me. I objected on grounds of attorney-client privilege. You overruled. I am a disbarred lawyer, you reminded me. That means not a lawyer, which means fifty percent of the requirements for that privilege does not exist. Ms. Thornton then digressed, asked if I had accepted any compensation from Ms. Montclaire, hoping to prove unauthorized practice of law. I said there was no charge, didn't utter the words *pro bono* since that sounds like I was providing legal advice but for free. I said we just talked, Ms. Montclaire and I. That brought us to the next question, or rather, the original question. What did Ms. Montclaire tell me? You ordered me to answer truthfully, which I just did. So why hold me in contempt?"

"Because—" Judge Diaz's square chin shook. "Because. Because your testimony is willfully false. A further discovery violation, compounding your overall display of disrespect for the rules of civil procedure and this court."

"May I say something else?"

"I've heard enough."

"Your Honor." Thornton now at the bench, reaching up, gripping the polished edge, fingers near Diaz's gavel. The judge not telling her to remove her hand. "We finally have Mr. Fager under oath and talking. We might as well hear it."

Diaz straightened her robe, shiny black fabric sliding over her breasts, Thornton thinking, Jesus, she's not wearing anything under there. Fager could probably see it from his chair, maybe a little more every time Diaz leaned over to lecture him.

"Mr. Fager, answer the question."

"I told Lily Montclaire she should report everything she knows to the police. It doesn't sound right, wouldn't you agree, a judge having sex with a lawyer appearing before her, corrupting her office in exchange for a few orgasms, even lots of orgasms. And illegal thrills with a minor? It's Ms. Montclaire's duty as a citizen to report all she knows."

"That's it. Bailiff."

"One minute, Your Honor. May I?" Marcy Thornton came around to stand in front of Fager, not waiting for a ruling.

"Were Detectives Denise Aragon and/or Rick Lewis present during your conversation with Ms. Montclaire?"

"No." Fager, done pouring out the words, reverting to trained witness mode.

"FBI Special Agent Tomas Rivera."

"What's the question?"

"Was he present?"

"When?"

"During your conversation with Lily Montclaire?"

"No."

"But you've met with him and Detectives Aragon and Lewis?"

"Yes."

"Why?"

"They were investigating your client's murder of my wife and over a dozen other women. If you hadn't obstructed the first investigation years ago, my wife and many of those women would be alive today."

"Did you meet with Ms. Montclaire in the offices of any law enforcement authority, state or federal?"

"No."

"Where did you meet?"

"My office. Well, my space."

"Your law office on Paseo de Peralta?"

"I don't have a law office anymore. It's just my building, next to yours. That's where we met."

"What more did she tell you?"

"She started getting into details. Something about handcuffs and teeth. I told her stop, go to the police. Oh, and I told her one thing more."

"What was that, Mr. Fager?"

"That I hope you and Judy Diaz rot in hell and I'll do all I can to send you there."

Thornton jumped at the crashing of Judge Diaz's gavel.

"Bailiff!"

"Right." Fager leaned back and linked fingers behind his head. "You wanted it word for word."

————

"What's with Walter?" Judge Diaz asked back in chambers, in a wingback chair, sitting on her feet with her robe partially unzipped, a cross on a chain between her breasts. "He danced a jig shuffling through the door, like he loved wearing cuffs and shackles."

"You gave him what he wants," Thornton said, passing Diaz a cup of tea poured from the judge's electric kettle. The robe fell open farther when the judge lifted her arm. Thornton had guessed right—Judy was naked under the fake velvet. "We need to figure out exactly what that is."

"I wish you hadn't taken the Geronimo case. I know, defending the man who killed the great Walter Fager's wife, how could you pass it up? Him your mentor, you the next generation, phoenix from the ashes. Where does this end?"

"I represented Cody for years. You know that. And you're right, how could I pass it up? Walter used to brag he taught me everything I know. I don't hear that anymore."

"You taught him something new, for sure. Provoking him to choke you in front of cameras as you laid out your case for him being the murderer instead of Cody Geronimo. Nobody teaches that. But the way you went after him. Everything that made Walt a lawyer to be feared, he's using it to come after us. Maybe you went too far, admit it."

"Don't worry about Walter." Thornton sipped her tea, nibbled at a cracker. "He can't use the Disciplinary Board against us. Not a lawyer, not a client. Sorry, Walt, you're out of the game. This lawsuit I filed on behalf of the Geronimo estate, it lets us keep tabs on what he's up to. I've got Aragon in deposition later this week, your courtroom again. We'll find out where they've got Lily stashed."

"But this time we don't invite the world to watch, okay? A closed hearing?"

"I need him back after Aragon, to get into how they coordinated efforts. That's the key to the suit, so I can reach those deep taxpayer pockets. I have to prove he acted under Aragon's direction. I prove he's their agent, Aragon setting things in motion, losing control, Cody getting killed, it's on her."

"Fager didn't actually kill Geronimo. That was Sam Goff." Diaz shifted position, untucked her feet, leaned forward to rest her cup on the table next to her chair, one breast almost spilling out of the robe. "The retired detective trying to pin it on Fager, getting revenge for, what was it?"

"Defending too well the drunk driver who wiped out Goff's children. Walt did a hell of a job on that case. He was something to behold."

"A minor factual shortcoming in your claims against him, don't you think?"

"Facts not in the record don't count. Here's how it's going to work: You enter a default judgment against Walter for willful discovery violations. He's blown off my requests for admission. You deem them admitted. That means my story and only my story is what gets in the record. My proposed findings make Aragon vicariously liable for everything everyone else did. You approve my claim for damages. Risk Management settles. We can get this done in six months."

"You're ignoring me," Diaz said. "Fager's happy to go to jail. Why?"

"Walt wanted to vent in open court. He knows a regular deposition can be sealed before anyone sees it. He calls us names behind closed doors, it's a waste of time. He had an audience today."

"You couldn't help billing this as a big show. That reporter from *The New Mexican* was in the back. And the blogger who does *Santa Fe Sentinel*—the rumors about us drew that one in. He's a vile homophobe."

"The Our Lady of Guadalupe shirt, second row from the back?"

"Get used to reading his stuff. Every Catholic in Santa Fe watches his site. I'm positive courthouse staff have been feeding him dirt. Some of the old timers. I get the looks."

Thornton helped herself to hand lotion on the judge's dressing table, right there in chambers. It was something Diaz had picked up from her, a dressing area off to the side of the mahogany desk. Past the wet bar, but the judge couldn't show bottles of liquor where she met with lawyers and held settlement talks.

The door in the dressing table was cracked open. A big bottle in there. Thornton nudged the door open wider. The old male judges would keep bourbon in a desk drawer. You could tell they'd had a taste before the lawyers came back to wrangle about objections away from the jury. The smell would be hanging in the air but no one would say anything. Diaz had a half-gallon bottle of Absolut in here.

The bottle was nearly empty and Thornton wondered how often the judge was hitting it. This morning she'd come to the bench carrying her own glass of water when the bailiff had a pitcher with ice waiting for her, next to her microphone and gavel.

In the mirror behind jars and bottles she saw a face doing much better than Judy Diaz's. Still cute, a tight body she worked at, black silk making her look thin.

"I need another subpoena," she said. "For Leon Bronkowski, Fager's investigator. He's not talking since he drove his Harley into an underpass. Any failure to answer my questions, I get to argue the facts I want."

"Yes, you can argue negative inference."

"Mr. Bronkowski, did you and Mr. Fager conspire to kill Cody Geronimo? May the record reflect the witness declines to answer. You later rule the negative inference in my favor, meaning yes, they conspired. Did Mr. Fager shoot Mr. Geronimo and then you attempted to dispose of the gun, but were interrupted when your motorcycle crashed into the highway overpass? May the record reflect the witness declines to answer. Negative inference for me, again. You get the picture. I can tie everything up with one deposition and dump it all on Fager, without any inconvenient true facts getting in the way. Walt's in jail, so he won't be shouting objections or yelling at the stenographer to pack up. I'll have Bronkowski to myself. A helpless lamb staked out for the wolf. That would be me."

"Bronkowski? He's in a coma, isn't he?"

"It will be a very short deposition. And I'll be doing all the talking."

28

Walter Fager stood at the back the courthouse with other men in cuffs and shackles. He still had his business jacket over the mock tee, but his pants lacked a belt. The other men wore baggy prison red with blue plastic slippers over white socks.

"I miss the old courthouse," he said to the prisoner next to him, a Black man with hunched shoulders and short neck. "There were bullet holes in the crash doors."

"Wild West shit," the prisoner said. "Shootout at the O.K. Corral."

"I was there when it happened," Fager said, the man now looking at him, his head nested on his collarbone, the shoulders up by his ears. "That was my client with the gun. A child custody case, the last I ever did. I went strictly criminal defense after that. He lost custody and attacked the judge with a knife."

"I thought there was guns in this story."

"I'm getting to it. His wife's lawyer blocked him, saw his necktie get sliced off, but knocked the knife out of his hand with his brief-case. My client, Jerry Jaramillo, that was his name, jumped onto the court reporter's table and pulled a revolver from the back of his pants. He stood up there shooting lights, blasting photos on the wall. The judge ducked behind the bench, the court reporter frozen, big eyes under big hair. Jerry had time to reload, digging one bullet at a time out of his pockets, before deputies arrived. He escaped through the judge's chambers into the hallway. They shot him in front of the rear door."

"He lost custody, huh?"

"There's bullet holes behind the witness stand in the Gallup courtroom. That's another story."

"From long ago and far away. Before metal detectors. You can still get a knife in, fuck those machines. I done it."

"Me too. Forgot it was in my pocket."

"I know you, man."

Fager studied the prisoner's face, trying hard to remember if he'd been on the raw end of one of his plays in court, wondering if a client had killed a gang brother or a family member. Wondering how much length there was in the chain that held him to the man in front.

"You choked that bitch on the TV. We saw it in the pod. We was all cheerin' you, get it done. She suppose to be my zealous advocate. Feisty, then your money runs out. Jury screws me, I say to her, 'What the fuck? You said I'd walk.' She says back, 'You didn't ask where. You'll walk, round and round a gravel path for the next eight years.'"

"The other guys screaming—was Marcy Thornton their lawyer?"

"You want to call her that. We call her 'the law whore.' Get it? Law-yore, law whore, like some little brown Mexican sayin' it through his teeth. We don't need no stinkin' law whores."

"I'm a lawyer. Was. Maybe there's something I can help you with, an appeal, a habeas petition."

"For an old white dude in a nice jacket, you don't look sorry 'bout where you gonna lay your head. Maybe you got no appreciation for what's coming. You won't find any of your, what you call 'em, your peers waitin' to discuss the morning Wall Street report. But it's the dead time that's the worst, ask me. Watching the clock, waiting for the meal, couple hours yard time, sun on your face, lining up for the shower, getting that done quick. You know it's a week when the Bible people come. Then you roll it over and start again."

"I doubt boredom will be an issue. Now, getting back, when did you retain Marcy Thornton and what were your charges? And tell me every way in which you believe she failed to provide you the representation you deserved."

"I got ten to twenty to tell it. How long you got to listen?"

FOUR

"LILY, I'M SPECIAL AGENT Tomas Rivera." Black hair fell across his forehead when he bent forward. He extended a hand. Montclaire, seated in the steel chair bolted to the floor, had been hugging herself and unfolded a long arm. "You look cold," he said.

"I'm freezing. They've kept me in this ice box for hours."

"Please, take my jacket. We have some things to discuss after your conversation with Detectives Aragon and Lewis. I'll sit over here and listen for now."

"Lily." Aragon standing, nearly face to face with Montclaire she was that short. "Give me your phone."

"Why? I need it."

"We need it more."

Montclaire fished a Samsung out of her purse.

"Turn it on, bring up your texts," Aragon said.

"I know you need a warrant for that."

"Smart girl. We'll get a warrant. We'll serve it on you in jail, where you're waiting trial for aggravated arson, conspiracy, the

31

whole ticket. Oh, snap. Your phone will be confiscated when you're booked. We could drop by jail for a quick look and not bother you. We wouldn't want to interrupt your getting acquainted with your new pals for life."

"Here." Montclaire brought up her texts. "What do you want to see?"

"We don't have a problem with prostitution in Santa Fe County. The sheriff said so, right in the newspaper. Not like Albuquerque on Central Avenue, the girls beating the streets middle of the day, hoping a car stops so they can get out of the sun. It's not an open meat market here. That story you told us—rushing around, looking for a girl to fit Thornton's order, you find Andrea on the cruise. Inside or outside the mall, you've been vague on that. You sold her on a four-by-four with grown women, got into Thornton's Aston, drove across town to the hills where rich people live. We could check video at the mall, have you walk us through it, talk to everyone for a week and come right back here, the same chairs, these same bright lights, to say you're lying. Save us time. Was it Craigslist or Backpage? Pull up the texts where you traded pics."

Montclaire scrolled through her files and showed the phone to Aragon. Lewis leaned in. Rivera rose from his chair to look over their shoulders.

"That's me to her. This is the head shot she sent me. I don't remember how we first hooked up. Craigslist or Backpage. I was checking both."

Aragon pulled up a photo on her own phone and compared it to the image on Montclaire's screen.

"That's her," Aragon said, Montclaire craning to see but Aragon keeping the screen turned away. "Tell me again where Marcy bit her."

"On the thigh and the breast, the left."

"This was the last time, two days ago?"

"We were drinking. Things got out of hand. Marcy was acting strange."

Aragon gave Montclaire paper and pen.

"You billed your time when you worked for Thornton, right? I want you to fill out time sheets for the last week. From when you woke to when you went to bed. Where you went to bed. Who was in it. We'll be back after the three of us talk."

Outside in the hall, Lewis shook his head. "Everything out of her mouth is bent."

Aragon said, "I know this is frustrating but we're getting there. Thornton and Diaz alone are worth it. Thinking of nailing them fills me with patience."

"For me to consider witness protection," Rivera said, "I have to be convinced she's absolutely truthful. Just two minutes in there, and I know I can't take this to the U.S. Attorney yet. She's the center of the case against the Chief Judge, but a nebulous center at best."

"Nebulous," Lewis said.

"Hazy. Vague. Cloudlike."

"As in nebula," Lewis said. "I'll try it in one of my reports, see if my sergeant says anything."

"I repeat," Aragon said, "if I hadn't seen her bringing the girl to the judge's door, I wouldn't believe any of her story."

"I'm fed up dragging it out of her in pieces." Lewis cupped a hand on the glass and looked through the little window into the room where Montclaire sat. "Either she unloads now, one hundred present true and verifiable, or we charge her to the hilt. No more nebulous bullshit."

Aragon gave him a look, then said, "She's not scared enough about being charged. Hanging around Thornton, maybe she learned never to take a prosecution too seriously. I think there's another way to go at her."

Back inside, Aragon pulled a chair next to Montclaire and showed her own phone, the photo she'd taken of Andrea in the bottom of the dumpster off Jaguar Road.

"Let's end the games, Lily. We could have protected Andrea if you hadn't wasted our time. We can still protect you. Play by our rules once and for all. Or play hide-and-seek with the person who did this."

"There's one way to stay alive, Ms. Montclaire," Rivera said. "The federal government can provide a new life, in safety, all of this behind you. The price to you is small. It's called the truth."

Montclaire stared at the image on Thornton's phone.

"The bed of roses," she said. "They were beginning to stage shots like this when I was getting out of the business. I helped with one session, in abandoned buildings in Detroit. Powdering skinny girls, darkening their eyes, posing them like they were dead. Then spreading flowers around them. We did rose petals instead of whole blooms. Dead girls were in."

"Roses," Aragon said. "That's what you see?"

"Girls worked hard to get that pallor. You got it right, it stayed, and cost you all kinds of other jobs." Montclaire uncrossed and crossed her legs, hooking one ankle behind another. Aragon was impressed with how long they were, like vines. "Backpage dot com. That's how I found her. 'Dreams *al instante*,' that was her ad. I guessed she was Latina. Didn't know if she did women. Her price went up when I told her, kept going up each time, but I think that had more to do with seeing Marcy's Aston and Judy's house. She was trying to see how high she could go."

"How many times?"

"Six, the last one when I told you. And it *was* Marcy doing the biting then. It kept getting weirder. But Andrea was okay with it. She said this was the best money she'd ever made. It made me wonder about the cheap men she'd been with. You'd think they'd want to show off, throw money at a pretty girl." Montclaire lifted several pages of paper. "Here's my time sheets. I didn't kill her. I can account for every minute. Now how are you going to protect me? You know how many clients owe Marcy money? Maybe one got to Andrea as payment."

"This better check out, Lily. This is now about a lot more than a dirty judge and her lawyer friend."

"Last thing she said to me … " Montclaire shivered inside Rivera's jacket. "She thought it would be safer only doing women. Easier than men. Our rough was nothing like their rough."

Montclaire asked for the sweater that had been promised and Aragon hit up a female officer changing in the locker room. She came back with a sweatshirt Montclaire refused to wear.

Rivera had called in Agent Evan Tucker, who had worked with them on the Geronimo case. He'd helped pry Fager off Thornton's throat when Fager attacked her at the press conference where she'd accused him of killing his wife. Tucker would be working this full time now.

Aragon told Rivera to run with it. Let someone who hadn't heard Montclaire's story several times give it a fresh take. She sat back with her meal, some green stuff in seedy bread Lewis had called in to Whole Foods, a delivery service bringing it to the front desk of police HQ.

Whole Foods. They needed to look into the bag on Andrea's head.

Rivera asked Lily to go over how each night began and ended.

She chewed a nail, said Andrea waited at the Pizza Hut outside Santa Fe Place, the old Villa Linda Mall. Andrea would be in a booth, usually a tall soda and empty plate in front of her. She'd walk outside with Montclaire to Thornton's red Aston Martin, always by itself across the lot so it didn't come back scratched. Once, they used the Durango Marcy had for work. Montclaire had been using it to serve subpoenas outside Taos and was running late. They always drove straight to Diaz's home in the Acequia Madre neighborhood. Andrea joined in the drinking, but Diaz didn't let her have much until after her job was done. Montclaire drove her back to the Pizza Hut, always closed, Andrea always refusing offers to take her home. She worried about the girl alone on the streets at night.

"Nice of you to be concerned," Rivera said. "Did you learn where she lived?"

"No, and I got the feeling Andrea wanted it that way."

"And no idea about her last name?"

"Hispanic, I'd guess," Montclaire was saying. "A couple times she spoke Spanish with Judy."

"I'll check store cameras," Tucker said. "They should cover the entrance, maybe the booths. The mall's exterior cameras probably take in the Pizza Hut, definitely the parking. We can see Andrea coming and going. You, too, Lily, smiling for the cameras once again, after all these years."

Aragon wished Tucker hadn't said that. She would rather let Montclaire unload it all, check video, then hit her with inconsistencies. Let Lily talk without thinking there was any way to check what she said.

"Rolling up in a big expensive car nobody else drives," Tucker continued. "Your walk across the parking lot, not exactly the cat walk, but the show's all you this time."

She wondered why Tucker was laying it on. She watched Montclaire, couldn't tell if he was making her angry mocking her lost modeling career. He didn't stop.

"Coming through the doors, scanning the room, there she is, against the window. Do heads turn as you walk to her booth?"

But Montclaire was in it, the scene. Aragon saw her going somewhere else, her eyes not really focused on Tucker, looking past him. Seeing Andrea, in that booth, watching her approach. No, seeing herself just as Tucker painted it. The camera following her again after all these years. There, her hand went up to her neck, long fingers flat against her skin, her favorite pose.

Rivera brought her out of it. "Tell me what she said during the drives back and forth."

Montclaire drank coffee, took a moment to think. "She'd laugh at boys cruising in Honda Civics. She really liked Marcy's car. Touched everything, opened all the compartments, played with the stereo, always looking for rap music."

Aragon knew everyone was thinking about recovering fingerprints if they could get inside Thornton's Aston.

"She had a friend." Montclaire finished her coffee, folded the plastic lid, pushed it into the Styrofoam. "Maybe we wanted to include her. I said sure, until she introduced us."

This was the first time they'd heard about a friend. Maybe Tucker's mistake was no mistake at all. Montclaire was giving something new.

Rivera caught Aragon's eye. She nodded for him to keep going.

"Where did this happen?" he asked.

"At the Pizza Hut."

"This friend. Did she have a name? Describe her."

"Skanky. Stringy hair, pinched face. I didn't understand why Andrea thought we'd be interested."

"Age, race, eyes, hair, something for us to go on."

"Older than Andrea, but still a teenager. Hispanic. Brown eyes, brown hair. And metal in her face. That did it for me. I hate girls hanging hardware off their nose."

"A nose ring?"

"The worst."

"Name."

"One of those romantic names you know's a put-on. Like names strippers give themselves. I didn't catch it."

"We'll find her on the video." Tucker stepping in; you could see he knew mentioning video got Montclaire talking. "Was she there each time?"

"I got the feeling she was always there before I arrived. It looked like two people had been eating pizza. Two sodas. I met her only the once, though."

After going through each of the six encounters, Montclaire reconstructing as best she could dates and times, she asked for time out. They let her stretch her legs in the hallway. Cops stopped to watch, this tall, elegant woman so different from the usual cast. Then they brought her back.

"That brings us to where you sleep," Aragon said, speaking for the first time in the past hour. "It's too early in the process for Agent Rivera to get you into the program. We're not comfortable letting you return home alone. Whoever killed Andrea might come after you. We don't have personnel for a guard on your house."

"So I'm screwed." Montclaire bit her lip. "I'm not exactly impressed with this arrangement."

"We could charge you. You'd have a place to sleep."

"What's my alternative?"

"How are you around animals?"

"I love cats and dogs, when they belong to someone else."

"I'm thinking a lot bigger."

"Rick and I will take Lily by her house for clothes," Aragon told Rivera outside the interrogation room. "We really need the U.S. Attorney to get cracking. Will she have to plead to federal charges to qualify for the program?"

"No way around it. I must say she bothers me. You show her Andrea dead and she talks about roses. That woman walks in a very dark light. What if she turns out to be Andrea's killer?"

"Lily couldn't have put the body in the dumpster. Those skinny arms.

Lewis said, "A man wouldn't have any problem getting Andrea into the dumpster. It could be a john who found her ad. Or one of Thornton's clients, like Lily said, trading services."

"Maybe another woman we don't know about," Tucker said. "What is it we call women who use prostitutes? Junes? Joans? Shit. I'd keep seeing Joan Rivers rolling down a window, calling to a high-assed girl in hot pants, 'Can we talk?' There's got to be a word for women who do this but it's not coming to me."

Aragon pushed away from the wall. She was ready to get moving. "Listen to Montclaire talking about what they did with Andrea. Spend a minute with photos of her in the dumpster. Some words will come real quick, and you already know them. You don't need to make anything up."

"Monster?"

"That works."

Aragon called Moss at OMI before they broke up. He'd been able to raise Andrea from her bed of garbage. Cause of death was obvious once he turned her over. Two small caliber bullet holes, contact wounds, behind her ear. He estimated she'd been dead thirty hours, but it was tough with the heat building in the dumpster. For now he put time of death in the pre-dawn hours the day before. He'd move the autopsy up his list and give them a definite time for the cut.

Aragon called her brother to see if he had room for a guest at his hunting lodge. Elk season was months away. The kids were at grandmom's, just Javier and Serena right now at the place in the pines. The round trip would take two hours. Back in town, they'd visit the dumpster company. Regarding the bag covering Andrea's head, they'd hit Whole Foods. A meeting to coordinate the new joint task force would end the day.

"Who's the *flaca*?" Javier Aragon nodded at Montclaire as she leaned against the department sedan. Above them, ravens cawed in ponderosa pines. This side of the mountains the air was clear and cool, the last hint of the Los Alamos fire disappearing when they'd come through the pass at Glorieta. As they'd rolled along the dirt road to Javier's house, a plume of dust from their car had coated trees that looked as dry as match sticks. Aragon hoped the flames stayed far from the city and mountains she loved.

Her brother brushed a dun mule while Aragon explained her need to park Montclaire.

"I don't have a place for her in town. Your trailers are empty," she said. Javier and his wife ran Lobo Loco Outfitters, taking hunters into the Pecos Wilderness for elk and a rare bighorn sheep or antelope on ranches they leased on the eastern plains. Summertime, after fire season, they did drop camps for people wanting to experience wilderness, ice and beer, fresh eggs and bacon replenished every two days, Serena cooking if you wanted her to stay around for an extra charge.

"Your kids are with Serena's mom," Aragon went on. "You have tons of room. The city will cover your expenses. Maybe pay some rent."

"I'll put her up for free if you'll scout," Javier said. "When was the last time you got out of the city?"

"Fifty minutes ago, and I'm headed back as soon as we're done here. She's got clothes, toiletries. She'll need bedding."

"She in danger?"

"Maybe. No one will look for her out here. Without a car, I don't have to worry she'll take off."

"She'll be safe. Not even a mountain lion can come close without my dogs letting loose. Serena made killer stew out of the last cat to bother my mules."

"You want a hand?" Lewis stepped up and patted another mule in the corral. Lewis was linebacker big but Javier was taller and wider, a head of wild black hair to match the beard, triceps like sycamore limbs growing out of his sleeveless jean jacket, open in the front and showing a carpet of black hair across his chest.

"Run it by Serena," he said and shoved one of his big fists into a bucket of soapy water. He came up with a wire brush and tossed it to Lewis.

"I'd like to borrow your truck for the night," Aragon said. "I know I'm being a mooch."

"Anything for little sister." Javier tossed her the keys to the Ford SuperCab 4x4 parked by the barn. "Finally moving out of that shoebox you call an apartment?"

"I wouldn't need your truck for that. I can fit everything I own in my trunk."

"You need a hot ride for a hot date. Tell me that's it."

"I'll have it back tomorrow."

Serena, Aragon's height without the muscle but a lot more hair, was under trees on the other side of the homestead's clearing. She had a Broncos sweatshirt pushed above her elbows as she scraped an animal hide stretched on a rack. Behind her stood their house, two double-wides welded together, where they were raising five kids. Aragon motioned for Montclaire to join her. She needed to pass Serena's inspection.

The hide had belonged to a coyote. Serena dragged a blade across the wet inner side, then wiped membrane and blood on her pant leg.

"*Hola*, stranger. Who's your friend?" Serena pointed the knife in Montclaire's direction. Montclaire had dropped behind to watch Javier.

"Lily," Aragon called. Montclaire looked her way, then back at Javier. "Come here. Someone you need to meet."

Montclaire's feet turned in Aragon's direction, her eyes coming around last like she had to work to take them off Javier. Serena watched her approach as she scraped the hide. Aragon made introductions.

"Lily's an important witness for us. We need to keep her out of the city until the Feds take her. I thought you might let her stay in your bunkhouse."

The knife left a band of gore on Serena's pants as she wiped it clean and then felt the edge with her thumb.

"I'm not running a homeless shelter."

"Keep your receipts. I'll take care of it."

Serena sheathed the knife, never taking her eyes off Montclaire. She reached into a Tupperware tub and came out with something mushy and white that she rubbed into the hide.

"Coyote brains. The old fashioned way to tan a hide. Want to try?" She held a dripping hand toward Montclaire. "No? If you stay, you have to work. Everybody works here. Denise, too, if she hangs around another five minutes."

"She'll work," Aragon said. "But find something else for her to do."

"You need this?"

"I do. It's important and we're stuck."

"And she's an angel?"

"Not exactly. Lily's got her own problems we have to work out. I don't think you have anything to worry about from her."

"Five days. Then we start scouting. She can't be here alone." Serena took a step toward Montclaire. "My husband. He's a good looking guy."

"He is."

"You go anywhere near him, I'll be rubbing your brains into animal skins." She emptied her hand in the Tupperware tub, wiped it across her Broncos shirt. "She can put her suitcase in Upper Pecos."

"Which bunkhouse is that?" Aragon asked.

"As far as you can get from our house."

————

Lewis led the way back to Santa Fe, Aragon in her brother's truck, talking about Montclaire on their phones. They were sure Montclaire wasn't going anywhere. She'd taken only the Pikolinos she'd been wearing—woven sandals with a four-inch heel, all wrong for hiking nearly twenty miles through forest and rocky canyons. Besides, on the way out, she'd said she was scared of staying in Santa Fe. Hanging out in mountains would give her a break from all the stress of doing what

Marcy wanted done, destroying evidence, buying off witnesses to keep a serial killer in business. Now the stress of selling her out.

Doing the right thing, why is it so hard? Montclaire had asked Aragon this and got back, that's what we do every day. We and most of the world manages, Lily. Most of the time.

Aragon called Serena and heard how she already had Lily cleaning the bunkhouse she was staying in. Aragon asked her to bag a glass and silverware Lily used without her catching on. Serena said, what aren't you telling me?

She left the truck in the SFPD lot and together they took their department car to Whole Foods. Lewis knew this store on St. Francis. His wife, Sandy, sent him here for things they could get for less at Smith's. Aragon said the Dollar Store was even cheaper, where she bought the little she didn't get from living on Lotaburgers.

"What's celeriac?' she asked as they passed a produce display. She'd never been in a Whole Foods. Seeing the prices on organic grapefruit, she said it might be the last time.

Lewis led them to where he said they sold reusable shopping bags. The store offered four kinds, including the one on Andrea's head.

"We need to get a last name for her," Aragon said. "I don't like calling victims by first names."

"You do it all the time."

"So do you."

"We need to stop."

"We won't."

"The most expensive model," Lewis said, holding up a bag of lined nylon, printed brightly with pictures of fruit and vegetables. "Not what the Lewis family uses."

At checkout he asked the cashier, "Is this bag sold only here?"

The young man had dyed black hair done like the early Beatles. He'd worked the Whole Foods off Logan Circle in DC, he said. They had the same bags there, probably in all their stores.

"Leaving with an empty bag feels strange," Lewis said after he'd paid. "Do you mind?"

While Lewis shopped, Aragon wandered the front of the store looking at people eating grain salads, tapping on keyboards, reading paperbacks. She got coffee, went back through the line, and paid. Shoving change in her pocket, she saw a display of flowers for sale. No roses. It had just been a thought, that maybe the roses in the dumpster were purchased here along with the bag. She saw only flowers she didn't recognize.

Lewis was waiting at the car behind the wheel. An open box of protein bars sat on his lap. He tossed one to Aragon.

"I've got the address for the waste disposal company," he said. "Down Agua Fria. They haven't been notified yet of what ended up in their dumpster."

"The warning that unauthorized use will be prosecuted to the fullest extent of the law? I don't think they had this in mind."

FIVE

"WHAT'S WRONG WITH PEOPLE?" Benny Silva asked Aragon, standing across the counter in the office of E. Benny Silva Enterprises. "I'm not even getting paid for that drop. I give him a dumpster, the guy goes to jail. I got his lawyer giving me the song and dance. Now I get to talk to police."

His nephew, Abel, watching the security cameras in the back, had buzzed him cops were coming through the gate. Silva had his metals book out when they entered the front door. The identity of everyone selling him copper, their driver's license, home address, source of the copper, weight, what he paid per pound. But that wasn't what had brought them.

The short Latina with the arms and shoulders, biceps that don't belong on a girl and none of the hair that should be there to go with the pretty face, the big Spanish eyes, lips you could say were sexy. But those muscles and that thick neck. What was going on with this one?

Detective Denise Aragon. He knew Aragons who used to live by Miller Park. They had a daughter had a bad time once with the

Locos using her as bait to pull her brothers into a fight. Raped, he remembered. And the boyfriend running to save her gunned down. Right there on the basketball court outside their house. That park, it had been called Killer Park ever since.

She had the Aragons' square build, all of them looking like cinder blocks on legs, taking after their father who'd been a hell of a football player at Santa Fe High. Yeah, this was her. And here she was with a gun on her hip, showing a badge, asking about a dead girl in one of his dumpsters.

She wanted to know when the dumpster was delivered and when it had last been emptied. She wasn't interested in sharing family history. A big white guy next to her taking notes, Silva didn't catch his name. Anglo names sounded the same to him. He had to write them down to keep them in his head.

He explained they don't empty dumpsters like the city does garbage cans. You park one, it's empty. You take it away when it's full or the customer calls, come get it. This one had been dropped off some weeks ago. It was for the mobile home park, Plaza Contenta. Guy said he was bringing the place up to code, needed to clear furniture, toilets, heaters, moldy linoleum out of the tin cans he rented to Section 8 tenants. It was on the news. City shut him down and locked the front gate. Rats. Not mice, but rats. No water fit to drink. Tenants could try boiling, but the gas company cut off service when the lines were red tagged.

The work stopped. The guy disappeared. Then someone stole all the copper out of the mobile homes. Didn't mean people weren't living there. Some of the tenants cut the lock, moved back, this time living rent-free, filling water jugs at the gas station a half mile away. Now that particular dumpster was full of other people's garbage, people who don't pay for E. Benny Silva Enterprises to haul their junk away.

"And a dead girl," he said. "I'm not in the human body disposal business. I got a contract with Game and Fish and animal control. The highway department. The remains of poached elk. Cows, dogs, deer hit by cars. Horses they put down. Dead people isn't my line of work."

His company basically turned the dumpsters upside down and shook them out, big machines for the job, then separated the metals and cardboard they could sell to recyclers. The leftovers a bulldozer loaded in dump trucks for the city's landfill. He didn't think she was interested in any of that.

He gave her the name and telephone number of the client who had ordered the drop and told Aragon to call anytime, anything else he could do to help her get the guy who killed a girl. The parents. He couldn't imagine losing a child.

"Hey, when can I get my dumpster back?" he asked. "I need it for Fiesta week. I got the contract."

Aragon pulled out a cell phone and turned it toward him.

"This is the girl we found. Can you identify her?"

A very pretty Hispanic girl, the camera so close he couldn't see anything but her face. Her eyes were closed. She could have been sleeping.

"Never seen her. Who would do this?"

The white guy asked for the can. Silva told him there were porta-johns in the yard by the crusher, out the door, keep turning right. E. Benny Silva Enterprises provided portable toilets to construction sites, outdoor concerts, the Zozobra burning, the Fiesta parade. After his family marched they took off their conquistador helmets and went to work. Did he know those are E. Benny Silva Enterprise crappers at the Police Academy where they're building new barracks?

"Keep the door open, no one here cares," Silva yelled after the big detective slipping outside into the white sun. "Hot as hell in those things."

There was a nice bathroom behind the wall, inside the air conditioned walls. Silva didn't mention that. He didn't want cops any deeper inside his office.

Aragon waited in the car, making calls with the engine running the air conditioner. It had been Lewis's turn to ask for the head and get an extended look-around. She conferenced Elaine Salas and the FBI's Evidence Recovery Team manager about how to sift through the contents of the dumpster. They'd be lucky to find Andrea's clothes, purse, maybe her phone. It would be nice to find a gun but she wasn't counting on it. The garbage that could rot would be bagged and placed in cold storage. Already they'd found syringes and ampules and a broken scale.

Cool air rushed out when Lewis opened the door and got into his seat.

"Busy place," he said. "There's a mountain of crushed glass, cardboard in bundles the size of cargo containers, bins with copper wire, and a city of plastic shithouses."

"Enterprising guy, E. Benny Silva."

"Coming back I walked along the building, looked in through a window, the shade was up. Security monitors on the wall, lots of them."

"He's got that copper to protect. Already stripped, ready to melt or whatever they do, a cash-and-carry operation if you can get in. Easier boosting here than pulling it out of light poles and transformers, worrying you'll be electrocuted."

"And a big flat screen playing *Forensic Files*," Lewis said. "Two guys, could have been father and son, watching. For a second I thought the older one was the guy out front. But this one was heavier with no mustache. Instead he had a zipper. On his face. This scar running from his ear across his lips. You see it, you'd know what I mean. It was strange, how fixed they were on the show."

"Hell, everybody watches that program."

"Yeah, but these guys were taking notes."

"What's wrong with you?" Silva said to the man tied to the chair in the windowless room at the center of his building, not far from where the detectives had been standing minutes ago.

This one sat straight. But that was the copper wire holding him up. He was a sloucher, Benny was sure. Undo the wire, he'd slide to the floor. He had the pants below the hips, a yard of denim loose below his balls. Not even laces in his shoes. No wonder he was easy to catch.

"I didn't know," this one said. He had a metal safety pin up by his eyebrow. Those teardrop tattoos used to mean you'd killed some-one. They meant nothing anymore, just face graffiti.

"What are you, Indian?"

"Acoma."

"You'd have a good casino, but all the semis parked outside, com-ing right off the interstate? The buffet's okay. I like Cities of Gold better."

"I'm sorry, mister, whatever I did."

"You don't know?" Silva said. "First you cut power to San Isidro during a funeral, the church going black, scaring old ladies, making the priest trip trying to light more candles. Now you took wire for lights on my street. People in the dark. Meat going bad in freezers. Swamp coolers stop and it's stinking hot. Hit the museums, the streets in the hills with big houses where the people really live in California, those parking lots at the casinos with hundreds of light poles. That's not enough for you?"

"I didn't know."

"You and who else? You couldn't pull all that wire alone. I don't want my ice cream melting again." Benny looked up at the air vent, thinking he smelled smoke from the forest fires, wondering if the wind was bringing it across Santa Fe. It was bound to happen soon.

His brother, Rigo, and his son, Abel, leaned against the wall watching him lecture this idiot. Abel was the Indian's age, but Benny never had to ask him, what's wrong with you? Three kids at home, their dad making a good living using skills taught by his father, not like families where the only knowledge passed on was how to shoot the heroin. Grandparents giving grandkids their own needle, like sitting around at Christmas figuring out a new toy under the tree. Here, kids, you hold the spoon like this over a candle. Don't burn your fingers.

He and Rigo were twins. Both in light blue short-sleeve shirts, tucked in, not sloppy and disrespectful. Pressed chinos with elastic belts sewn in. Ventilated SAS comfort shoes, ugly but they felt good. Benny kept a mustache, white now. Rigo couldn't grow one because of what happened to his lips when he was a kid. They both still had their hair up top, thick and dark, a straight part on the side, trimmed every week in the barber's chair at the Chop Shop while watching the traffic, talking about new boxers coming up. New Mexico turned out tough fighters. The rest of the country learned that in the ring.

Rigo had been a wrestler, too short for football. The other teams' coaches had to get their boys ready for the face that met them on the mat. That was long before he'd heard about anybody getting their game face on. Rigo had that face all the time. He'd kept up with the weights. He had a bench and dumbbells in a corner of the warehouse. Benny, he'd been good with numbers, liked history, especially the conquistadors, how a couple dozen men kicked the shit out of empires with huge armies. There was a lot to learn from those men. Too much had been forgotten. None of these Lunas, Trujillos, Madrids, C de Bacas, De la O's—Aragons, like the detective—remembering what it took.

Five hundred years, they'd say. We've been in New Mexico since before the Pilgrims. Anglos in Massachusetts freezing, begging corn from Indians, when the Spanish already had a Palace of Governors in Santa Fe with Indians doing the cooking and cleaning.

So what do we have to show for it? Mexicans now pushing us out of jobs. Anglos buying up the land, telling people back in New York, Los Angeles how *they* discovered Santa Fe.

And this idiot in the chair, trying to sell him copper ripped from his own street. He'd been watching the local PBS with Millie before the lights went out. About Don Juan de Oñate coming into the territory at the end of the royal road from Mexico City, leading a band of conquistadors, going after the Indians Coronado had fought a half-century before, who got it together to push the settlers back across the Rio Grande. Oñate did his job, and the Spanish built Santa Fe, Albuquerque, Taos.

Don Juan, he'd taught the Indians a lesson, never had problems when things were done his way.

Now people were trying to make him a bad guy. This thing with the statue the Indians wanted in a Santa Fe park, Oñate holding a foot like a baby in his arms, saying he killed kids and their mothers when all he did was chop the left foot off Indians who killed Spaniards. Not even all Indians, just the men and boys left alive after he took over the pueblo where his men had been attacked. The Indians started it. The soldiers only wanted food and blankets. Instead a shower of arrows and spears and rocks, killing good men come all this way from Spain, up from Mexico, trying to build something here.

Eight hundred Indians killed, they say. That couldn't be true. Acoma pueblo was still out there, high on its rock like a castle in the desert. They were buying up ranches with all the gambling money, coming into Santa Fe in new pickups, tribal leaders making bids on downtown real estate that Don Juan's men had fought and died for.

That statue they wanted: spit in the eye.

The Indians could put their own statues outside casinos anytime they wanted, no need to make trouble, insult our customs and culture. Millie, his wife, was going to hearings, taking carloads of friends, organizing on the phone. We're going to win back New Mexico again, she was saying. Put down this Pueblo revolt for good. These Indians, thinking money makes them better than us. Nobody would be here to feed their slots if it weren't for the Spanish making this land into something, she said, going out the door to the hearing at City Hall, her flabby arms shaking, worked up.

"Where's the copper this one, this Acoma, wants to sell us?" Benny asked Rigo, the Indian staring at Rigo's scar.

"Out back in his truck. About a quarter ton."

"Abel," Benny said. "Move it inside and have the guys unload."

"Hey," the Indian with metal in his face said. "You said you don't buy west-side copper."

"Who said I'm buying?"

Benny bent to open a tool box, came up with a hack saw, trying to remember, was it the left or right foot?

Wait.

53

Don Juan didn't have hacksaws. He would have used a sword or an axe.

"Abel, the wall behind my desk, the sword I wear for Fiesta days. Let's see how real it is. Bring an axe from the tool shed just in case."

————

Benny sat at the desk cleaning the silver safety pin he'd pulled from the Indian's face after deciding there wasn't much difference, right or left leg. *Don't pull copper on Santa Fe's west side.* The message would get out when the Indian was found by the transformer he'd gutted.

And the sword worked just fine. It was the real deal.

Rigo and Abel had insisted they put down plastic first. The chair the Indian had been in, they washed it with lye and set it outside to dry. Then they'd spray paint it. Something about skin cells they'd learned from *Forensic Files* had them worried.

This silver pin, he might send it to his daughter in California. He'd heard Mirelle had another baby on the way. She hadn't called to give him the news. He'd had to learn it from Abel. The only daughter he had left outside New Mexico, not interested in carrying on the business, women content to let their men provide. She didn't even come for Christmas and Thanksgiving, said she was in New York, all the way across the country, when he took Millie to Disneyland, not far from where Mirelle lived.

His other daughter, he didn't even say her name in his own mind.

Abel had a son carrying his name. Abel Junior, in ninth grade at Camino High. And a new baby girl, Benita. It was close enough Benny could say he was the godfather of his *tocayo,* his namesake, yet another honor given him by his hardworking nephew. He and Rigo would talk how this salvage business, the dumpster company they owned together, the portable toilet service and the little grocery store, La Tiendita, still in the neighborhood where they had come up, all should go to Abel when it was time.

So should this silver safety pin. Abel could give it to his wife for Benita's diapers, saying it was from Uncle Benny, a sign of his love for their family. Passing along something good to the next generation. What life was all about.

Benny Silva picked up the phone and dialed the other number that was on the slip of paper with the information for the guy who had ordered the dumpster for his mobile home park. He had not given that number to Detective Aragon.

He was seeing Detective Aragon as the girl who came into his grocery store with her father. Before the muscles. Beautiful, long black hair back then. It shined in the light. He knew some of the hard-working people she'd put away since she'd turned cop. They were only doing what they'd always done, making a living, providing, in the world they'd been handed, and taking it from there. She was the one seeing a problem with the way things were.

He called that other number, the deadbeat's lawyer, and left the second message with her receptionist, a polite girl, called him sir. First time he'd called, they'd talked about more than the money he was owed. He knew her grandmother, a Gabaldon from the Pueblo Alegre neighborhood, not too far from La Tiendita. The receptionist sympathized with him. He took a person's word, provided a service, held up his end of the deal, and now he's not getting paid.

She had asked, what's wrong with people?

That's what he wanted to know.

After that call he took a prepaid cell phone from his desk and called another number he kept to himself. It rang eight times before he got an answer.

"This is Judge Diaz."

He knew the girl in the picture Detective Aragon had showed him. Judge Diaz did, too.

"Time you did the rest of what we agreed," he said. "Your little friend, she's dead. This can get worse fast unless you make it better quick."

SIX

MARCY THORNTON READ THE note from her receptionist. Mr. Benny Silva had again called, wanting payment for the dumpster delivered to Narciso Morales's Plaza Contenta mobile home park. Thornton and Associates had been representing Morales since he got popped using empty mobile homes as addresses for social security checks for dead people. Then Santa Fe code inspectors found living tenants, senior citizens, giving Narciso their checks to cash, pay rent and utilities, buy groceries, their medicine and stool softener, sharing their rooms with rats.

Morales had told Silva his lawyer would take care of things while he was in jail. But he'd left no funds to cover bills. He hadn't even paid his own legal expenses—postage, the copying charges for briefs she'd filed trying to keep him at liberty while she appealed his case. Thornton had stopped giving him copies. If he wanted reading material to fill his quiet hours in jail, he could get her paid up. Certainly no way she was covering his dumpster service out of her retainer.

She'd win his case in the Court of Appeals, where classmates from the University of New Mexico Law School sat on the bench. Then he'd tell her she'd had an easy job because he'd been innocent all along and he'd want a refund. He was that kind of client.

She kicked off her heels and leaned back in the big chair, her feet on her mahogany desk. Across the room the sofa was empty, a bottle of Montclaire's nail polish still there on the coffee table. The cops had her somewhere, prying information to bring down Judy Diaz. She should be filled with fury, her mind busy working on ways to destroy Lily so she'd be laughed off the stand when it came to that. Instead, she wished Lily was filling that sofa, her skirt pulled up her long legs, long arms reaching for her feet. What would be today's color? Lily changed toenail shades constantly. They'd chat about last night. Maybe it would have been a celebration here in the office, getting drunk over kicking the DA's butt again. Lily finding someone to include in the fun. At the front end of middle age, Lily still scored some beautiful young men. One or two maybe you could call boys, no facial hair yet roughing their cheeks. And the girls. Lily always found them, even on short notice.

Like Andrea.

There had been lots of parties. The practice had taken off after the Geronimo case. Sure, he got killed. But since he didn't live to be tried she could still brag she'd never lost a case. Bad-ass Marcy Thornton: the worse the crime, the more she shined. Clients had poured in. She'd robbed two lawyers from the Public Defender to help with the caseload.

It wouldn't last beyond this week. When word got out her investigator was talking to police, business would dry up. How could you trust a lawyer when her staff, people listening when you told it all, were spending their days in interrogation rooms?

Her secretary, a bright young thing out of Northern New Mexico Community College, brought in a message that Judge Diaz was holding. Maybe it was time to test the Bright Young Thing's views on office parties while there might be something left to celebrate. Thornton tried to see her on the sofa in Lily's place but it didn't work. Too much sunshine and innocence. She said close the door behind you, and picked up the phone.

"I need to see you," Diaz said.

"I was just there. What's up?"

"Not chambers. Our park. Now."

Thornton had seen the judge's docket. She had motion hearings until five. She should be on the bench right now.

On the way out, she instructed her secretary to cancel the day's appointments. This might take a while.

———

Her Aston was parked in the lot she'd once shared with Fager. Since he'd been disbarred he hadn't needed the parking. He kept one space for his black Mercedes and leased the rest of his share to the Tamarind Wellness Center of Acupuncture and Oriental Medicine with its back doors the other side of the alley.

Thornton pulled onto Paseo de Peralta, her driveway directly across from the Roundhouse, the Capitol building, and swung east. She detoured to drive past Montclaire's home on one of the smaller hills overlooking downtown. Lily's BMW was in the drive in the spot where it had been yesterday. A newspaper lay on the door step. The landscaping, sparse by design, was dying, turning the same brown as the cracked adobe townhome.

She drove on past, wondering where the police were keeping Lily.

She took residential streets to the ball field, empty except for kids tossing Frisbees. When Judy had said "our park," Thornton knew she meant this place, Old Fort Marcy Park, the site of a US Army outpost during the war with Mexico, now acres of grass ringed by trees.

Choosing this place meant something.

They had come here their first year in a law school, three carloads up from Albuquerque for the burning of Zozobra, Old Man Gloom, the opening of the Fiesta since the 1920s now morphed into a mad, drunken blowout. Thornton had never seen anything like it. Nighttime, the mountains a black silhouette against the stars, a figure of wood and paper and cloth three stories high swaying and groaning, a tape recorder pushing a deep male voice through hidden speakers. A couple thousand drunks spread on the lawn. Dope hung in the air. A flare sparked, flames climbed the figure's robe, the groaning grew louder, someone somewhere amping the sound. The crowd was crazy before. Now they went insane, leaping to their feet, punching the air, screaming "Burn him! Burn him!"

Flames licked the monster's head, its eyes ignited, the skull exploded in a fireball.

Judy Diaz was all over her, pulling her down to the blanket in the grass, legs and feet all around them, an empty bottle digging into her kidney, Judy's hands moving under her shirt, lips smashing hers.

They discovered they liked getting drunk and screwing. They still did. It was just more complicated now.

Diaz rolled up. Thornton knew she would find her. The Aston was hard to miss.

"Let's walk," the judge said when she opened the door to her car. She popped an Altoid in her mouth.

They moved toward the ball field. Diaz caught her foot on something. Thornton steadied her. They stopped under cottonwoods ready to dump their fluff.

"I'm being blackmailed," Diaz said. "I thought I could handle it. I was wrong."

"Say again. You're being blackmailed?" Out of Diaz's mouth it had been "*backmailed*." The "let's walk" had been "*lezz* walk."

"I got Andrea killed, thinking I could handle it. Now they're tightening the screws. I got a call. On this cell phone they told me to carry. I don't know who they are." Diaz looked around the park.

Thornton followed her gaze. "You think you're being watched?"

"I think so. I don't know."

"Judy, you've been drinking. Middle of the day."

"I'm scared."

"We need to sit down."

They found a bench under a tree, no one nearby. Diaz ate another Altoid. Her hand trembled as it opened the tin.

She said, "There was a photograph of Andrea inside my car, on the seat. And a cheap cell phone."

"Today?"

"Months ago. A phone number on the back, a note saying I'd better call or this girl would be on television talking about me. I called. All they wanted was my personal e-mail. I started getting pictures of Andrea and me. Video clips. I got another note on my car seat to call on the cell phone. I didn't. Then the pictures and videos started showing up in my office e-mail. Right there between e-mails from judges wanting another clerk, to switch from civil to the criminal docket—an attachment with Andrea in handcuffs."

She'd been doing well until she said, "civil." It came out "*shivil*." "Attachment" was "*attashmun*."

61

"These pictures, is anybody else in them?"

Diaz shifted on the bench to face Thornton. "You, Lily. The three of us in my home with Andrea."

"Judy, you weren't going to tell me?"

"I thought I could handle it."

"You said that."

"I gave them a little. It stopped. Then they killed Andrea because I was dragging my feet."

Thornton was up, pacing, ignoring her heels sinking in the gravel path. She came back and sat next to Judge Diaz, now meeting her eyes, lost, helpless. Bloodshot. She took Diaz's hands in hers. "Tell me what they want."

"I didn't want to involve you."

"I'm in these home movies. They'll be coming at me next."

"Maybe they don't know … who you are."

"Maybe this is Lily working around the police," Thornton said. "Playing them while she's running her own thing. She met my clients. Car thieves who could get into a Lexus with no problem. A guy fighting with another guy over a porno website. This woman who ran an escort service who hired me on a consult. Shit, maybe that's who set Lily up with Andrea. I want to see these videos. I want to see Andrea's eyes—was she looking directly into the camera, like 'are you getting this?'"

Now it was Thornton scanning the park.

"If they got into your car," she said, "maybe they got into your house, planted cameras. Was there sound on these videos?"

"I deleted them."

"What?" Thornton up again, her heels flipping under her, cursing, ripping them off, standing in nylons on the gravel.

"I didn't want them on my computer."

"You dumb bitch. Oh, jeez. I'm sorry." She touched Diaz's cheek. "Judy, the delete button doesn't wipe them permanently. They're in your computer, but not where we can learn anything from them."

"I don't want to look at them again."

"You know what's coming next? They sent it to your e-mail for a reason. You've got kiddie porn in your computers, especially your State of New Mexico computer in your office. They could have left photos, a zip drive, a CD, in your car. They wanted it on your computers."

Thornton pulled Diaz to her feet and caught the cinnamon heavy on her breath. "We've got a lot to go over," she said. "Let's go to my house, not my office. You don't want to be seen going in there right now."

"You got anything to drink, or should we *shtop shumwhere*?"

"We'll stop at Starbucks."

———

"I throw them one case," Judy Diaz said, on the sofa in Thornton's living room, nursing a twenty-ounce cup of black coffee. "They'll be back for more. They'll own me."

Thornton put more cold cuts and cheese on the plate at Diaz's elbow. She'd started feeding her as soon as they got in the house. It had helped sober her up.

"Tell me about the case."

"It was civil. E. Benny Silva Enterprises against Jeremiah Kohn Productions."

"Shit, I know the plaintiff. He's been calling me about a dumpster one of my clients rented."

"Has he said anything about, you know?"

"No. What's he suing Kohn for? He picked a fat target."

"He's done suing. He got a nine million dollar jury verdict. A fire started in Kohn's construction site and spread to a building next door that Silva owned. Inside was his daughter, sleeping. She was killed. The building destroyed. The claim was Kohn's company hadn't secured welding equipment. Some kids broke in and started the fire. The cause was undisputed, but the kids were never caught. Kohn didn't put up much of a defense. Hardly any witnesses, and his case collapsed. The jury didn't have a difficult job with the evidence."

"What's this have to do with the blackmailers?"

"I'm getting to that. Kohn filed a motion for a new trial, based on why his case collapsed. Witness intimidation, allegations a key eyewitness, a security guard, was murdered to keep him from testifying, destruction of evidence, jury tampering, etcetera."

"Pat Caudill presided. I remember it now."

"They wanted me to get Caudill off the case. He was troubled by what went on. He said a lot from the bench that showed he'd lost any impartiality. I was to persuade him to recuse himself. Mostly they wanted me to prevent him from entering findings of fact that couldn't be overturned on appeal."

"They used those words, 'findings of fact that couldn't be overturned on appeal'?"

"They did."

"Go on."

"I got Pat to step off the case. He stands a good chance being appointed to Court of Appeals and doesn't need the fireworks. If the evidence of tampering is as strong as he believed, another judge will reach the same conclusion. I assured him that's how I would rule."

"Would you?"

"Pat needed to hear that."

"What happened to the motion?"

"I haven't reassigned the case yet. They want me to take it and find it baseless."

"You're on the criminal docket."

"When we're short judges, I can fill the gap. And we're short judges. That's how I got your case against Fager."

"You heard from them today?"

"I'm sure they killed Andrea to force my hand. The video makes me a prime suspect. It comes out, I'll be at the top of the list, a prominent public official with a motive to eliminate the witness who could bring her down."

Thornton had been writing questions while Diaz talked. She had one circled near the top of the page of her legal pad.

"Was it Benny Silva who called you?"

"I heard three voices. All men, different ages, if I had to guess. They disguised their voices, talking low and high, something over the phone, maybe a sock. The last call, telling me 'your little friend is dead,' that was an older man. Definitely Hispanic. Northern New Mexico. Not Mexican. He didn't say *lee-tool*."

"Listen," Thornton said, "you have to get rid of your computers. Office and home. Smash them, bury them in the desert. You don't want what's on there discovered by anybody."

"Court administration loses things all the time. But how do I explain losing a desktop? Something else just occurred to me. What if Fager's behind this? Say he put one of his clients up to it. What he said in court today, he knows about Andrea."

"If Walt was blackmailing you he wouldn't give out that information for free. He was just throwing mud. He got it from Lily, I bet."

Thornton dug a note from her purse, picked up her phone, and dialed.

"Who are you calling?" Diaz asked.

"Time I returned Mr. Silva's calls. Maybe pay my client's bill in person to see who we're dealing with. Judy, you're worth it."

Diaz got to her feet and brushed crumbs off her clothes. "What makes you think you can handle this any better than me?"

SEVEN

RUGER MUD FLAPS, GUN rack in the back, country music blasting on Javier's system. Aragon enjoyed the look as she drove her brother's F-250 SuperCab 4x4 onto St. Francis from I-25. Sitting high above other cars, looking down into windows, she saw a beer can squeezed between a driver's thighs. She dropped back, read the plate, and called it in to the Drunk Busters hotline.

Her phone buzzing told she had voicemail. She played a message from Sergeant Noah Jennings, who ran SFPD's Crimes Against Children Unit, notifying her that Andrea's photo had been sent to school security officers and juvenile probation workers. They should have her full name soon, unless she was a runaway from out of town.

A Blake's, there by the light. Not exactly fast food. They cooked every burger from scratch, then loaded them with green chile, cheese, lettuce, tomato, and pickle. She never minded the wait. It was part of the ritual.

Usually she'd pull in, but not today. People were waiting for her. She found a strip of beef jerky in the bottom of a cup holder. She brushed off grit and tried to tear off a piece. Her teeth would come out of her gums before she had anything to chew. The jerky went out the window as she parked outside the FBI's territorial-style office building.

Somebody had been thinking of her. Red, white, and blue Blake's bags clustered on the table in the conference room. Lewis was there, talking with Evan Tucker. Tomas Rivera entered behind her, his hand brushing hers as he walked to the head of the table.

"Lotaburgers," Rivera said. "It's what's for dinner."

"Out of my way."

"I saw the truck," Rivera said and held her eye for a second. "Later?" She nodded, then he passed out food.

"These all the same?" Agent Tucker asked, holding up two bags.

"All perfect," Aragon said and took one from his hand. "The complete food pyramid in a bag."

"Let's get started, people." Rivera left his burger untouched. "We're all in. With the murder of a key witness this is now much more than a public corruption investigation. Denise, Rick, you've been closest to the facts. What is required to do this right?"

"I was thinking." Aragon chewed, swallowed. "We need to dig into all the cases that correlate with the times that Montclaire says Thornton provided Andrea as a reward to Judge Diaz. Maybe the judge did something subtle that doesn't jump out, but did the trick in tanking a case against a Thornton client. We'll need experienced lawyers to tell us that."

"DOJ has a few lawyers. How about the prostitution angle? We certainly must eliminate Andrea's other clients as suspects. Was her phone recovered to get us started?"

"Not so far," Lewis said, a mouthful of burger tucked in a cheek. "They haven't sifted through everything in the dumpster. But since she was stripped, I'm not holding out hope the killer tossed her phone in for us to find. Great if we do. It would show who else was auditioning for a date."

"Auditioning?" Tucker asked.

"Sending their photo for Andrea's approval. That's how her Backpage hook-up worked."

"How did she get around?" Aragon dug fries out of her bag. "She must have lived close enough to the Pizza Hut to walk."

"How about taxis?" Tucker asked. He got a look from Aragon telling him, you're not from around here, are you?

Lewis answered for her. "Forget finding a cab down there the hours she worked. But the politicians haven't managed to kill Uber. I'll see if they had any pickups from the Pizza Hut. They've worked with us before."

"Montclaire insists Andrea walked." Aragon shook her bag, wanting to hear the sound of something inside.

Rivera was writing in a notebook and looked up. "Did you get anything on the neighborhood canvas?"

"The trailers in that park," Lewis said, "are occupied by squatters. The few who talked said everybody used that dumpster, not just the mobile home park. People would pull up and empty pickups. It's a good bet stuff was thrown on top of Andrea before Gray found her. That causes problems doing anything with tire tracks, what little there are in that hard ground. Something I want to bring up ... "

"You have the floor, Detective."

"Andrea's tattoo. A sports car on her hip. It's too badly done to tell the make and model. Maybe a Corvette. I'm wondering what it says about her. My girls want tattoos, which isn't going to happen. They want words, Japanese symbols for life and joy, a flower."

He brought up a close-in shot of Andrea's tattoo on his phone and let Rivera and Tucker look.

"A convertible of some kind," Rivera said. "Generic."

"It's an old Jag," Tucker said. "The long nose, the slippery lines. I had a girlfriend who liked classic Jags, said they could drive right up inside you. A twelve-cylinder dildo."

"Thanks for that," Aragon said.

"I don't know." Rivera squinted at the picture. "Those classic Alfa-Romeos had the same look."

They talked for another hour and agreed to focus on four avenues of investigation, pending any change in direction when they got OMI's report. Aragon and Lewis took lead on identifying Andrea. Rivera said the FBI would handle the science. They had the resources and would not have to wait on the backlogged State Crime Lab. The FBI would also tackle Backpage. The agency's Child Exploitation units had lots of experience with that company, enough to know it was going to take a grand jury subpoena to shake anything loose. They needed to know how long Andrea had been running ads, how she'd paid, what contact information she had given. Any current ads, they could grab with screen shots. Expired ads would require Backpage's files.

The FBI would also work on getting Andrea's phone records using the number from her contacts with Montclaire.

Tucker would run down video. He took copies of Andrea's photo—the head shot she'd sent Montclaire—and left for the Pizza Hut to catch the evening staff. He'd get the photo to the National Center for Missing and Exploited Children in the morning.

Lewis left next. It was his turn to cook for his girls and wife. He'd work late at home, taking care of paperwork, making what calls he could. "I'll sleep when I'm dead," he said on the way out.

"I must get e-mails to DC so we're rolling first thing tomorrow," Rivera told Aragon when they were alone. "Meet you in the truck?"

She crumpled empty bags and cleared the conference table, knowing he was waiting for an answer.

"Twenty minutes, max," Rivera said and headed to his office.

Aragon spent those minutes behind the wheel making calls. First to Sergeant Garcia asking to repeat the canvas, this time showing a photo of Andrea to the squatters of Plaza Contenta. Next she texted Noah Jennings to make sure he was forwarding a photo of Andrea to State Police and all New Mexico police and sheriff departments. She was texting Moss about the autopsy schedule when a tap on the passenger window turned her head. Rivera stood outside and she unlocked the door.

Rivera climbed in. He fit a bottle of wine in the console's cup holder.

"We could go to a hotel room," he said.

"We've never gone to a hotel room."

"Was it really bad? A girl in a dumpster. I'm sorry you've got that to carry in your head. It's my job tonight to drive those images away."

"Nobody can do that. It's a gift for life. It always is."

He put his hand on top of her hand hooked inside the steering wheel. His skin was warm, his palm soft. Softer than hers.

She said, "I cried. Both of us, Lewis and me, but I turned away so he wouldn't see. We stopped at a soccer field, watched girls practicing. Beautiful girls, like the one in the dumpster with roses all around her."

"Did it strike you that the killer was saying something, throwing her out like trash?"

"The flowers made it worse. The contrast. You look at the roses and think about some happiness, love in someone's life. And then you come back to the body."

She lifted her hand, turned it up so her fingers laced with his and let the weight bring it down into her lap.

"On Backpage and Craigslist," Rivera said, "did you know roses stand for money? 'I love roses,' or 'Three hundred roses for a cute sexy girl.' It's a price. Maybe her date actually showed up with roses instead of money. She got mad. It went downhill. He threw the roses in after her. There's your roses, bitch."

"I don't need to hear voices like that. The visual and odor were enough."

"It really got to you." He released her hand and stroked her shoulder, the inverted triangle of muscle under her shirt. "Maybe we need something more than a truck this time. A place where you can relax, take your time. All the time you want." He slid his fingers down her arm until he was stopped by the wine bottle in the console. "Let's go to my place."

"I don't know, Tomas. I'm not ready for that yet, spending a night in your bed."

"Okay, your place."

"You're not ready for that. You don't want to know how I live."

"Try me."

"There's more room in this truck."

"Okay. Put this thing in gear and let's get to our place."

"How can I say this?" She brushed her hand over the stubble on her head. "I like you. Very much. But when I look at you, I need to tell you I see someone else." She waited for a response, felt Tomas listening, not needing to say anything. "A boy I loved," she went on, "when I was a girl. You look so much like him." Her hand moved behind her ear. Her fingertip found the smooth patch of the lightning bolt where the hair didn't grow. She got quiet.

Cars rolled past them in the parking lot, FBI workers heading home. Lights blinked out in the office building. Rivera waited.

She blew air from her lips, pulled in air through her nose. "I still haven't said what I want."

At the edge of the parking lot, a sagebrush shook. A coyote stepped into the pool of light cast by a light pole, then backed away when the door to the office building opened. A security guard set the lock. The door closed.

Rivera reached across the space between them. He put his fingers on her hand, where she was touching her scar.

"We background everyone coming onto a joint task force. Some New Mexico jurisdictions hire rejects from other departments, people with disciplinary problems, psychological issues. We need to know. Your assault came up. We obtained hard copies of the old reports. I know what they did to you. I know about Miguel Martinez getting shot trying to save you. I know about the gangsters getting off, how the police botched the case, the indifferent judges. It makes me admire you more. You got strong, fought back. You're fighting for others so it doesn't happen to them."

"You didn't hear it from Lewis?"

"I read about it. Those reports are in my desk. No one else has seen them."

"What I wanted to say." Her hand met his, fingertips brushing fingertips. "When we're making love, I wonder if it's Miguel I'm holding. Then I feel guilty for feeling that. And then I feel guilty for not saving him. I'm on my back on the sidewalk, those bangers on top of me, Miguel bleeding where I can't reach him."

"When we're making love, I see a beautiful, powerful, brave woman who needs what we're sharing, as much I need it. I'm not anywhere else. But I've sensed you are, some of the time. That's okay. I understand."

"Well, I don't. That's the problem."

Rivera cracked his door. The dome light came on. One foot went to the running board.

"Tonight's not a good night. I was hoping we could kill those pictures in your head for a little while. You did it for me last time. I thought maybe I could do that for you."

She turned the key in the ignition.

"Get in," she said and put the truck in gear.

————

"Who owns this land?" Rivera asked, the truck's headlights out, a nighttime desert beyond a darker arroyo, the lights of Albuquerque on the bellies of clouds sixty miles away.

"We do, whenever we're here." Aragon undid her seat belt and climbed out, then back in through the rear door to the SuperCab and its full bench seat. Rivera stepped out the passenger door, peeled off his suit jacket and left it on his seat.

When he got in the back with Aragon, she said, "Touch my head again," and she brought his fingers to the scar behind her ear.

His kissed the stubble on her skull, stroked the hard shoulder under her shirt. He let his hand slide down her arm to her ribs, found her belt buckle, pulled it loose, opened her pants. He started lowering his face, following his hand.

"No." She pulled him up. "I want you in front of me. Close."

They helped each other undress, pulling off pants, shirts, their teeth touching through open lips, his breath on her cheek growing warmer, faster. Aragon laid back across the bench, her head on a door handle. Rivera swung his legs on top of her. Her hand found him, helped him, led him into her.

She closed her eyes. Miguel was running across the park toward her. The concrete sidewalk tore at her ass, one of the gangbangers on top, already inside her. Miguel vaulted a fence, his football legs pounding, his black hair parting from the wind his speed generated. She heard the shot. The face above hers smiled. Miguel crumpled by her feet, his hand reaching, falling to the concrete.

They took turns, passing the gun around. Then they took turns with her.

She forced her eyes open. Rivera was above her, his lips on her forehead.

"Tomas."

"I'm here," he said. His face was warm under her palm, not a boy's smooth skin but the sandpaper of a five o'clock shadow.

"Me too," she said and locked her ankles around his legs, pulling him deeper.

———

She returned Rivera to the FBI parking lot. He was heading home. She headed for the office. First she called Serena to check on Montclaire. Lily had joined them for dinner, then taken a walk in the woods. Serena had followed, caught her testing locks on gates, peering into the windows on their pickups, maybe to see if keys were in the ignition. Aragon told her to keep an eye on the ATVs. Lily could ride one of those to town.

"And next time she eats, save the glass and silverware she used. Put it aside in a bag for me."

"You already asked. It's waiting for you."

They would have to charge Montclaire soon. Her arraignment would make headlines: Marcy Thornton's investigator charged with setting fire to a Santa Fe neighborhood to destroy evidence implicating the city's most famous Indian artist in the murder of Walter Fager's wife. Repeating the crime at Geronimo's ranch, trying to destroy a table where he'd butchered women to "harvest" art supplies. They wouldn't be able to keep the expanding investigation of Thornton and Judge Diaz under wraps.

Montclaire would be taken into custody. They'd have to isolate her. A snitch wasn't any safer among female prisoners than men. She'd be at risk until the US Attorney could file federal charges and move her out of state. That would slow everything down. Interviews with Montclaire would require approval for travel expenses, negotiations, tripping over lawyers every time they wanted to talk. An afternoon of questioning would take days away from doing anything else.

A note taped to her computer told her to call Elaine Salas.

"A mess," Salas said. "That dumpster's a petri dish. You've got female hygiene products, used condoms, snotty tissues, bloody Band-Aids. Your girl is swimming in DNA even though she may have been washed before she was dumped. I smelled shampoo in her hair. Nothing under her fingernails. No signs of intravenous drug use. She was in good physical condition. Well-defined muscles for a teenage girl. Maybe she was an athlete. Moss will know more. As for those roses…"

That's what Aragon wanted discussed. She'd already reached the same conclusion about the forensic nightmare posed by the dumpster. Those roses kept coming up. Lily zeroing in on them, Tomas educating her on how roses were Backpage code for money.

"How fresh were they?" she asked. Gray had said it was a waste to throw away good flowers.

"The heat in the dumpster was up by the time we got to them. But I'd say they hadn't been out of water long. The stems were still quite resilient."

"People in that neighborhood wouldn't throw out fresh roses. Even from a funeral. They'd keep them until petals started falling."

"I sent six to the FBI. A long shot, but they might identify them genetically, tell us something. Maybe nothing. I took a few to my cousin's shop. She runs it with her folks. They're sweethearts."

"So they're nice people. You can't be giving away evidence like that."

"The roses, sweethearts. That's the variety. They're sold in large bunches at retail. Florists buy through wholesalers, then break them down into separate dozens. It's hard to tell where the particular flower was grown just by looking. This time of year they could be domestic. If it were winter, they were probably imported."

Aragon doodled a picture of flowers as she listened.

"Is there a way to time-stamp them, find out how long ago they were picked, how long they've been out of water?"

Salas said she'd get back on that.

"You're doing great, Elaine. A one-woman army. Please send what you've got to your FBI pals. We've got a strong commitment on this one."

Her cell phone buzzed. She put Salas on hold. It was Lewis.

"That was quick," he said. "Andrea was in ninth grade at Camino High. But her name is Cassandra Baca. The school resource officer knew her. He can't release contact info for parents but lined us up a meeting with the principal. Chest and triceps tomorrow, right?"

"Can we make it six thirty? I'm still at the office. I'd like to visit my bed before I hit the gym."

"Roger. And get this. Fager's in jail. He really ticked off Diaz. I heard he said what all of us think about her. His one call, he called to ask me for a list of Thornton's clients in detention right now."

"To think that guy wanted to switch sides and sign up with the DA. Like changing into a clean shirt without showering. You're getting the list?"

"Done. And he wants a stack of legal pads. Jailhouse lawyers, he said, aren't required to be in good standing with the New Mexico Bar Association. Something about carrying a full caseload again."

———————

Aragon had one more stop before heading to her efficiency apartment on the city's west side. She drove down Cerrillos and turned off behind the Walmart onto the dirt street that had been blocked with crime scene tape this morning. No lights from nearby buildings reached it. She was a hundred yards in before her headlights picked out the spot where the dumpster had sat until Salas's team removed it on a flatbed to a police warehouse. Cadets from the Law Enforcement Academy would be doing the grunt work of sorting through garbage, Salas behind them, calling out if she saw anything interesting.

A strip of yellow tape blew out of the darkness across the beams of headlights and back into darkness.

She got out to listen to the night. Traffic sounds reached her. A plane descended on its flight path to Albuquerque. Dogs barked in every direction.

A gunshot. Another. She turned to the sound. Maybe a half mile off. She called it in while another shot ripped the night. It sounded louder, larger caliber. Too hard to tell. Soon sirens wailed. She called the watch commander and learned there had been a drive-by, shots fired into a home. The shooters circled back and met the homeowner in the yard with a rifle. Witnesses blocks away saw a young man limping from a Honda Civic, holding a bloody hip. The Honda took off toward the Interstate. The Christus St. Vincent ER and urgent care facilities had been notified.

The sirens ceased but dogs continued barking. They would bark all night. Aragon faced west. The fires above Los Alamos glowed in the night, showing the mass and ridgeline of mountains. She smelled smoke.

Her phone buzzed in her jeans. Lewis's personal cell number showed on the screen.

"Would you talk to my wife? A little problem with me in the van in the garage looking at prostitution ads on Backpage."

"I thought that was your arrangement for working at home. You don't want your girls to see the files, so you move into the Caravan. Your home office."

"I closed the laptop when she brought me ice cream. She said, what are you hiding? Would you talk to her?"

Sandy Lewis got on. Aragon said she'd be looking through Backpage hooker ads herself when she got home and explained the case.

"So that's it," Sandy Lewis said. Aragon pictured her, a professional woman, Public Information Officer for the Game and Fish Department. A job talking about elk licenses paid more than her husband would ever make chasing murderers. "Rick wouldn't stop putting his arms around our girls tonight. They got mad at him, said he was acting weird. It's seeing that girl in the dumpster. Denise, I know you and Rick will get him, the man who killed her. But I'm glad he doesn't want me knowing more about this."

Lewis came back on.

"I haven't found her yet. A lot of these women are older. Listen to this ad, not even trying to hide what's going on: 'Kink friendly. In, out calls. Donations required. Quick, eighty. Half hour, a hundred. An hour, one eighty. Serious inquiries only.' This is all caps: 'I don't do anything illegal. Law enforcement not welcome.'"

"So she doesn't do cops," Aragon said. "Good thing she makes that clear right up front. You're looking at the photos to get ages?"

"The ages are right there on the index, I guess you call it. The menu. I have no clue how Backpage verifies age, if they bother. Here's one, says nineteen years old. She's dressed up like a business woman. Makes her look older. Here's one, forty-one years old. She's dressed like a teenybopper. I'm going through the escort ads now. There's categories for strippers, body rubs, dom, and fetish, something called 'ts' and adult jobs. Scratch 'ts.' I just clicked it."

"Chicks with dicks."

"Roger. This is pretty depressing. I'm wondering who these women are. Maybe state workers, the nice lady at the bank, teachers. Shit, look at this one, 'highly educated, intelligent, quick wit, I'll teach you all I know. Eager students only.'"

"But Santa Fe doesn't have a prostitution problem. Have you forgotten?"

The breeze picked up. Aragon felt it on her face. The fire on the mountains looked like it had grown since she'd arrived. Directly overhead the sky was clear, only hints of smoke in the air. She wondered how long that would last.

"Hey," she said, "where you are, can you smell it?"

EIGHT

WELCOME TO THE JUNGLE.

The banner greeted them at the entrance to Camino High School. Aragon and Lewis identified themselves to the armed school resource officer and were escorted around the metal detectors down a hallway to the principal's office. They entered during classes, the hallways quiet except for a few students filming others climbing in and out of lockers.

"For the school movie," the resource officer said. "Portals to the future where everyone gets along, there's no poverty, no crime, no bullies, and nobody gets sick. I wish the kids could find that here."

"Weren't you Albuquerque PD?" Lewis asked. His tag said *Mr. McRae.*

"Twenty-seven years, finished as a sergeant. Moved up here to retire, escape the mean streets. Found the streets were just more expensive. So I'm back wearing a firearm. I like this job. Kids need one place they know they're safe, and it's not always home." They reached the principal's office. McRae held the door. "We're keeping the Sureños

81

under control, turning the corner some weeks. We lose ground the next. But it's not getting worse. You need anything, here's my card. I knew Cassandra. Knew some of her friends."

"You know why we're here?" Aragon asked.

"The memo with Cassandra's photos didn't say she was dead. But you're homicide cops. I checked you out. I want to know who's on my campus." Shouting echoed down the hallway and McRae turned his head to the sound. "Gotta get back. Barbarians at the gate."

Lewis took the door from him and they stepped into the principal's office.

"'Welcome to the Jungle.' How's that square with creating a safe place for kids?" he asked. They had to wait for a Fed Ex guy in shorts to get a signature from the receptionist.

"Comes from the school mascot, the jaguar," Aragon said. "The gym is called The Jungle. You don't know that? Where do your kids go?"

"Arts and Sciences. Outside the jungle."

"Private, nice. The other side of Jaguar Road. And very white. I went to Santa Fe High. Home of the Demons. 'Welcome to Hell,' we fired back when this school first sent over its teams. There didn't used to be anything out here."

The Fed Ex guy left. They stepped up, showed badges, and said they had an appointment with the principal, Ruth Mead. The receptionist spoke into a telephone, then pointed at an open door deeper into the suite.

Inside, a short, wide woman with salt-and-pepper hair came from behind a desk and shook their hands. She did not greet them with a smile. She introduced a lanky man, half her age, as Phil Ulibarri, the assistant principal. She directed everyone to sit at a small round table.

"Thank you for your time," Aragon said. "Cassandra Baca was found murdered. We need to contact her parents and see everything you have on her. Possible gang contacts, disciplinary problems, behavioral issues, all that. We need to learn who she was."

Ulibarri opened a file and withdrew the top sheet. It had a photograph of Cassandra Baca stapled to a lined sheet of paper.

"This is what we can give you until you obtain parental consent for more information."

The sheet of paper was handwritten, providing a DOB, home address, and the name of a Dolores Baca as "responsible adult."

"Legal has advised us," Mead said, "to wait until we receive written consent from the responsible adult. I'd like to help, but my hands are tied. It's terrible what happened to her. I was afraid that's what you'd come to tell us. When you return with this signed"—she pushed across a typed sheet of paper—"we can have a longer conversation."

"Notification of Parental Consent for Release of Student Information," ran across the top of the page.

"Time is critical," Aragon said. "We have so little to work with. Anything, please. When was the last time she came to school? Did teachers observe injuries? Was she using drugs?"

"Here's a photo of her in the school paper. A rally for the Jaguars before the game with the SFHS Demons. That's her in the front row." Ulibarri gave them sheets of folded printer paper.

"I'll have to prepare the students," Mead said. "When will this become public?"

Aragon folded the consent form. "Please don't release news of her death until we speak with her mother."

"Of course," Mead said. "We're happy to cooperate.

"Sure. You've been a big help."

"At least we've got a home address," Lewis said as a secretary from Mead's staff escorted them to the front door. The halls were crowded now, students between classes, a roar building in corridors of steel lockers and linoleum floors.

They saw McRae talking to a group of boys and stood to the side until he was done. He noticed them and came over. They moved away from the river of teenagers to talk.

"Get what you needed?' McRae asked.

"Brick wall," Lewis said. "School lawyers in the way. You said you knew Cassandra, some of her friends."

"I didn't get the memo about not talking to police. What do you want to know?"

"Did she run with a gang, for starters?"

"Not that I saw. She had some trouble with bullying, the receiving end, but that stopped. I don't think she was a bookworm, I never saw her reading during free time. But she seemed to have it together, like she knew where she was going. No truancy problems. She was always dressed nicely, unlike some kids, the boys showing their asses from the top, the girls from below."

"Was she on the lunch program?" Aragon asked.

"Few of these kids aren't. This is a poor school. Pushing ninety percent Hispanic, same percent in poverty. She brought food. Sometimes she'd go off campus for fast food if a friend had a car. So I guess her family has a little more money than most."

"Drugs?" Lewis asked.

"Those boys I was talking to—I wanted to get close, see their eyes, smell their breath. I hate to be suspicious of every kid, but it's for their own good. They're clean. Cassandra was, too, far as I knew.

She was very pretty, I want to say, but I don't remember her with anyone I'd call a boyfriend. We've got girls kissing, holding hands. The Straight-Gay Student Alliance. How things have changed, huh? But she wasn't part of that. She walked her own path here."

Aragon thought of the indistinct tattoo on Baca's hip. "Do any of these kids drive what you'd call an expensive sports car?"

"There's chopped Beemers in the parking lot."

"I don't suppose you've seen parents dropping kids off in an expensive convertible, very sharp and fast-looking?"

"Convertibles don't last in this area of town. Knifing a soft top is too much fun. I'll keep an eye, but I don't think so."

"These kids all have lockers, right?"

"I'm ahead of you." He pulled a slip of paper from his shirt pocket. "Here's her locker number. I checked. It's locked. I'll keep an eye, make sure administration doesn't reassign it until you get your warrant."

Aragon gave him a card. "Shoot me a list of friends, anything else comes to mind. Use the e-mail at the bottom."

"On its way as soon as I reach downtime."

———

Cassandra Baca had lived in a low-slung frame stucco house on a cul-de-sac off Agua Fria. A cell tower behind the house soared above the roofline. The landscaping was dirt and weeds. The little windows above the garage door had been replaced with plywood. Three cars squeezed into the concrete driveway. Dust and cottonwood fluff lay deep on two Chevy Impalas, old models with V-8s, covered in bird droppings, gashes in the bodies like wounds, tires flat. The faded

Nissan Sentra showed hand prints in the dust on the doors. It was parked closest to the street.

The screen on the top half of the storm door was pushed in. The glass on the bottom was cracked. The doorbell hung on one screw. No answer came when Aragon pressed. She reached through the torn screen and knocked. A television played inside.

Aragon knocked again while Lewis leaned over a dead hedge and looked through the open front window. No screen, the drapes hanging outside.

He pulled his phone off his hip and spoke their address. "Send an ambulance. We've got a woman down, condition unknown. We're going inside."

"What is it?" Aragon came to the window. A woman was sprawled half on, half off a battered sofa, face-down on the cushions. The room around her was a mess, plastic cups and plates scattered across the floor, fast-food bags and pizza boxes on the sofa, empty beer bottles, dirty clothes in corners and under a table.

Lewis moved to the door. The handle was locked.

"Take it," Aragon said, and the cheap frame split under his heel, the door jamb tearing away from cracked stucco.

The woman had slid off the sofa, her shirt caught on the cushions, pulled up to show a black bra. Aragon and Lewis turned her over. Pinprick pupils looked at them from under lidded eyes. She took air in shallow breaths. They straightened her legs and eased her to the floor with her back against the sofa.

Lewis held up her arm. A drop of dried blood sat on skin laced with purple veins and healing puncture wounds.

"She's OD'ing.

"I don't think so. Her lips aren't blue. Hey, you." Aragon snapped her fingers in front of the woman's face. "She's just on a long, sleepy cruise."

Lewis called in the additional information on the woman's condition and gave her description: thirty to forty years of age, five four, one hundred ten pounds, Hispanic.

"They say keep her warm. EMTs are five minutes out."

"She doesn't need to be hotter," Aragon said. There was no air conditioning. No shade trees above the house. The sun bounced off the concrete drive through the open window. She now noticed the sink, flies on dirty plates. A yellow jacket buzzed against a peeling ceiling.

Lewis found an EBT card on an end table.

"I'd guess that's Dolores Baca."

"Let's look around."

They moved down the hall. Aragon glanced in a filthy bathroom and decided to leave that for last. The next door opened to a bare mattress on the floor, clothes draped over chairs, milk crates with sweat pants, shoes, an unplugged television. Nothing on the walls except a calendar two years out of date.

The second room had a television on a low table, two vinyl chairs, more trash, more loose clothes.

The door to the room at the end of the hall had a double-hasp hinge lock installed on the outside. One plate of the hasp was unscrewed from the frame and the door was partially open. Aragon pushed it the rest of way with her toe. The room beyond was almost immaculate. A dresser supported a mirror, with photographs of teenagers wedged in the frame. The windows were clean, with curtains pulled back to let in sun. Aragon ran a finger along a sill. No dust. The bed was made, a sheet turned neatly back at the top over a thin blanket. She pulled open a dresser drawer. Underwear, bras, and socks in tidy piles. Below that, jeans folded perfectly. Sweaters and T-shirts in the bottom drawer.

But the closet had been tossed, clothes ripped off hangers, shoes pulled onto the floor. A gym bag had been unzipped, its contents—sneakers, shorts, tights, a towel, hair brush, hair dryer, soap dish, shampoo bottles—spilled onto the floor.

"Cassandra's room," Aragon said. "But look at the posters."

"My girls have horses, heart throbs on their walls."

Cassandra had sports cars. Several could match the blurred tattoo on her hip.

They heard voices and footsteps in the hallway. The EMTs had arrived. Aragon and Lewis went out to meet them. They checked vitals and reached the same conclusion as Aragon. No overdose. A hit of naloxone would do. An EMT applied it through the woman's nose, a syringe attached to an atomizer inserted sequentially into each nostril. As she awoke they stretched her out on the filthy sofa. The EMTs needed to take off for a more serious call, a dog attacking a child, and Aragon and Lewis agreed to stay until she came to. They had a valid reason to be inside the house with no one watching. They weren't going to waste it.

This time Aragon forced herself to enter the bathroom while Lewis entered the first bedroom, which they guessed was Dolores's. She opened the grimy medicine cabinet with a square of toilet tissue for a glove. She found empty prescription bottles in the name of Dolores Baca, mostly pain killers and a few antibiotics. Nothing with Cassandra's name.

"Needles, a tiny bag of dope," Lewis said when they met in the hall. "There's an empty magazine for a nine millimeter by the bed, but no gun. A couple loose twenty-two rounds in a plate with pennies and nickels. I'll check the other bedroom and meet you in Cassandra's."

Back in Cassandra's room, she looked through every drawer, finding nothing but clean, folded clothes. She was glad to see a plastic pink hamper in a corner, full with other clothes waiting to be washed. They'd show them to Lily to see if she recognized anything Cassandra had worn at the parties with Diaz and Thornton. With luck, they'd have a shirt with saliva in the threads. She'd ask Dolores Baca for consent to take the clothes when she came to.

Under the bed, shoes were arranged in straight rows. Aragon stripped the mattress and turned it over. Nothing underneath, but she found a tiny slit in the fabric encasing the box spring, and, barely visible, what looked like a prong of a safety pin. She reached inside the slit and undid the pin. A scrap of plastic was speared on the tip. It had held a plastic bag containing something Cassandra wanted to hide.

Lewis came in, palms turned up and empty.

"I'd say Mom tossed the closet." Aragon dropped the mattress back on the frame. "Everything else but that gym bag is in order. She found what she was looking for."

"Money for a fix?"

"Let's ask her."

Dolores Baca was still on her back on the sofa, coming awake, rubbing her face with her hands.

"Who you?"

Aragon showed her badge. "Where's Cassandra?"

"School."

"No. When was the last time you saw her?"

"I'm thirsty."

Lewis brought water. Together they sat Dolores Baca up and propped pillows between her and the arm rest to keep her from falling over.

"When did you last see Cassandra?" Aragon repeated.

Baca looked between them, drank more water. "I don't know. Last week? What's she done now?"

Baca nodded off again. Aragon unfolded the parental consent from her back pocket and used a pen found among the debris on the little dining table.

"She has terrible handwriting," Aragon said. "Obviously not a Catholic school product."

She showed Lewis the parental consent form, signed, an illegible scrawl in the signature block. "Did you want to wait for her to straighten up?"

"I'm good with it. Let's talk to neighbors. We can tell her later her daughter's dead."

"I won't want to leave her alone with that. Let's get someone from the DA's Victim Assistance for when she gets the news."

Aragon went down the hall and returned with the pink plastic hamper.

"Mom said we could take her daughter's dirty clothes," she said. "You were in the other room."

———

A frail Hispanic woman in a housecoat and slippers answered the door at the house to the right of the Baca residence. Cat hairs clung to the black fabric around her neck. She'd been watching them as they walked to the door.

They opened badge cases and asked if she'd seen Cassandra recently. Had there been any trouble next door? Loud noises? Did she ever speak with Cassandra, her mother? What could she tell them about her neighbors?

Her name was Perla Gallegos. She lived alone, her husband gone. She'd lived here all her life, raised three sons, two daughters, right here. Yes, she did speak with Cassandra when she went out to water her flowers and move the sprinkler, it was so hard keeping grass alive in this drought. Cassandra was nice. She couldn't say that for her mother. No, she'd heard nothing unusual next door. It was always quiet over there, the mother hardly ever came out the door.

Did anyone come for her in a car, to pick her up? Did she ever see Cassandra getting dropped off?

No, she walked all the time, coming back with groceries from the Safeway even when it was a hundred degrees.

Boyfriends?

That girl was so pretty. But no, Perla Gallegos said, she never seemed to have boyfriends. Maybe she wasn't missing anything, look at these boys today. I wouldn't want them taking my daughter out, she lives in Albuquerque, a dental assistant. She got out of here. Cassandra was going places, too, learning a skill.

Aragon said, "This skill," wondering if the woman had any idea how Cassandra Baca was making money.

"Working on cars," Perla Gallegos said. "She was always under those heaps of her mother's trying to get them running."

Nobody answered at the other houses on the cul-de-sac.

Lewis got a response to his request for a records check on Dolores Baca as they headed back to their desks and some time with air conditioning. She had prior convictions for possession, shoplifting, fraud, and prostitution ten, eleven years ago. She'd spent part of that decade in the county jail, on a sentence one day short of the full year that would have bumped her up to a state correctional facility.

She used three a.k.a.'s with different last names. But the first name was always the same.

Andrea.

NINE

"Mr. Benny Silva to see you."

He must want his money bad. It hadn't been long since Marcy Thornton had told her secretary to deliver the message he could pick up his money at her office.

For a guy dealing in dumpsters and Job Johnnies, she thought Silva would be bigger, at least have large forearms and a gut, scuffed Wolverines, with a smell to let you know his line of work. Instead he was a little guy in a nice blue short-sleeve cotton shirt tucked into Sansabelt slacks, a guinea tee showing underneath. On his feet, those ugly shapeless shoes old men wear with air holes in the arches.

What's that in the air, Aqua Velva?

"Mr. Silva." Thornton had an envelope in her hand, drawing his eyes down to her waistline. She crossed her arms, the envelope now up near her face. It brought his eyes to hers. Odd that he had white eyebrows but a full head of thick black hair, just a few strands of gray. Short sideburns. A neatly trimmed mustache, white like his eyebrows. She'd seen him pull up in a bronze Oldsmobile, probably 200,000 miles on the odometer, beaded seat covers, grandkids' stickers on the dash. He'd been wearing those big goggle sunglasses while he drove.

When their eyes met she saw something else. A deeper chamber in there, darkness behind soft brown. She was glad she'd come out of her office to talk to him in the waiting area—her secretary, a telephone nearby, the day's only client in the waiting room to the side. Behind a closed door, Benny Silva could be someone else.

Something different in his face now, there for a second, like he'd seen her before and was glad to see her again. She gave him the envelope to get his eyes off hers.

"What will it cost to remove the dumpster," she asked, "so we may terminate your service? My client's out of business and I don't want to be paying to handle other people's garbage."

"Nothing. The police did it yesterday." There it was again, that look. What was he saying with it? And what was this about police?

"Why would they take the dumpster?"

"Something about a body in there," he said. "Took it away on a flatbed, wouldn't let me do it for them. I notice you're using curb cans, busy place like this. Here's my card. We got all sizes. We can give you a lock, keep people from throwing bodies in. Your client, Narciso, he went cheap. And lookit, now I have his unit behind a police gate. His bill keeps growing till I get it back. You don't have to mail the checks. I come see you, like this."

This old man was blackmailing the chief judge. He had liver spots on the hand that held out his card.

He opened the envelope, read the check, and nodded. She expected that would be it, he'd head to the door and leave. But he stood there, smiling, teeth yellow under that snowy mustache except the front top two and one on the bottom. New white caps. It made her think of white and yellow corn mixed together. She turned to go to her office and call Diaz. You won't believe the guy shaking you down. Five steps toward her office, she looked back over her shoulder. He was still there.

Smiling: I know you.

————

He wanted to say it out loud, "I know you." He was looking at an ass under a black skirt he'd seen in Cassandra's movies. He'd seen everything this lawyer had to show.

He wanted to tell her, "You got a birthmark like a sunburst, the New Mexico state symbol, down there below your waist, sliding into home."

"Land of Enchantment." Rigo had said it first when they'd all seen the birthmark at the edge of her dark patch. The state symbol, the state's nickname, the Land of Enchantment where this lawyer's legs met and told you that the hair on her head was dyed. Walking away, the good muscles in her thighs disappearing under her dress, silk, expensive. He didn't have to imagine anything.

Thinking what he could do with things he knew kept him smiling as he stood in line at the bank to cash her check. They had names for two of the three women in the movies with Cassandra Baca, who'd done a good job aiming the camera in her purse. The judge, of course, and now this lawyer. Four movies she'd turned over. He wondered what it had been like the first time, before he'd heard about her customers and gotten her working for him.

No more movies now. Cassandra's film career was over.

He reached the teller's window, turned over the check, signed, and handed it to a heavy-set Hispanic woman with too much makeup. The plastic tent said her name was Julia Rickard.

"You're Manny Archuleta's daughter, aren't you? I guess you got married."

She lit up, a pretty girl in there under the fat and eye liner. But he was back to thinking about Cassandra's movies.

Who was the older one, all legs and arms, tall like the models you see on television walking the plank at fashion shows and looking hungry?

————

"I've slept worse places, eaten worse. At least the food here doesn't move around on your plate." Walter Fager at the stainless steel table in area five, pod three of the Santa Fe Detention Center, a crowd of men come to see the lawyer in a red jump suit like them. "But I understand why guys like you paid me to keep you out of here."

He was the only white man, the rest Hispanic, Navajo, one Black, the man he'd met coming on the bus from court. The Hispanics were ganged up with the Mexican Mafia. The oldest was in his seventies, his name Yago, written on his neck. Right away he told Fager he'd lived through the riot at the Santa Fe Penitentiary in 1980, thirty-three prisoners killed, something like two hundred cut, beaten. He'd delivered snitches' heads on shovels, held a guard while they shoved his night stick up his ass, got him ready for the *carnales* in line in the shop, c-vises holding the guard's arms across the work bench close to the tin press. Thirty-five years later, the guard was just getting compensation. He'd read it in the *Santa Fe New Mexican*, the legislature taking that long to pass a law. *Mother still walks with a rod up his ass.*

In that time, Yago said he'd killed two men, fucked a lot of women, had a million beers, beat heroin, found the Lord, lost the

Lord. What stayed real were the memories of those days, still worth something in here, people knowing who you are.

You got people on the outside who can get to your money? The old gangster had leaned in close, Our Lady of Guadalupe in blue on his forehead, her eyes staring straight ahead, spaced wide, knives drawn inside her eyes. *People who can keep it from getting hard on you in here?*

That's when Fager had asked Yago to call a meeting. He had something to announce. Yago said, I gotta hear this. Then you start making calls.

"Since I've got time on my hands," Fager said to the men around the table, "I thought I'd see how I can help you out. I'm open for business. Motions to reduce bail, dismiss for speedy trial violations, appeals, habeas petitions, discovery motions. I'll polish all your *pro se* pleadings, impress the judge you're not a crackpot scrawling 'I'm innocent, the motherfuckers framed me' a hundred times on toilet paper."

Fager looked across the table at the old gangster standing behind everybody, a wolf prowling at the edges.

"You've got me on retainer, all of you. All I ask is you get my back. If I can't work, I can't help you. It's in all your interest, collectively, to keep me healthy."

"Tell me again," said a square-headed man, drooping mustache like horns turned upside down. "You called a judge a cunt? To her face?"

The story's gotten better, Fager thought. Why not run with it?

"She said, 'Tell me, Mr. Fager, exactly what you're thinking. Word for word.' So I told her."

Leave it at that. They'll fill in the blanks.

And they did. High fives, fist bumps. The old gangster, Yago, seeing how this was going.

"Another thing," Fager said. "Ineffective assistance of counsel. That's when your lawyer fucks you. You have a right to competent, zealous representation. The system depends on that, justice in the balance, a level playing field. If one side lays down, it's not only an unfair fight, it fails to produce the truth. The adversary system depends on both sides giving it all they can."

"My lawyer—my mom gave her a mortgage on her home." The square-headed man again, taking the lead, the others waiting to see how this goes, but already showing they were warming to this white man with skills they needed. "Now she's out on the street. The lawyer had the bank take it when she missed a payment. Is that what you're talking about, my lawyer fucking me?"

"Certainly it casts the lawyer in a bad light. We need to examine how she executed her obligation to represent your interests. You said 'she.'" Fager paused, hoping he'd hit it. "What's her name?"

"Marcy Thornton."

"Me too." A man with a long face, giving him room on his cheek for a cascade of blue ink teardrops starting at his right eye. The ones closest the eye, the earliest, looked professional: neat lines, clear shapes, done outside the walls at an ink shop. The ones at the bottom had been added in prison with a needle inserted through an empty pen casing. They were smudged, different hues. "I told her go around the hood, ask people about me. Character witnesses, right? She said that would open the door or some shit. Fuck, I want to open her door. Tear it off the hinges."

"We can look into that. I need to know the facts of your case and obtain statements from the witnesses she failed to call."

"Two would say I wasn't even there."

"Now we're talking."

The old gangster stepped to the table, a different look in his eyes. "I stay down for my third felony, I die here. I want to see my grandkids one more time, but my son won't bring them."

"I'll need to know where the case stands in terms of what relief to seek. Do you have your files? Your lawyer should be copying you on everything."

"Not if I don't pay for the copies, twelve cents a page. Plus the box," the old gangster said. "And a delivery boy, fifty bucks to drive ten miles, bring it to the desk out front. I got nothing but the sheet of paper saying guilty. I had to go to court to learn what the cops had on me. She wouldn't accept my collect calls. I'm trying to see what the hell's going on, what the hell she's doing for me."

"Inexcusable. You can't possibly be assisting your defense if you're uninformed. What's your lawyer's name?"

"The one's got your eyes lit up."

————

Lily Montclaire watched from the window in the trailer, a bunkhouse for men willing to pay four figures to kill large animals. Five figures if it was a bighorn sheep. Hunting and rifle magazines in the bathroom, the furniture done in cowhide, dead deer and bobcats on the wall watching her change clothes. Across the forest clearing, Aragon's brother threw a saddle over a chocolate-brown mule. She wondered how they could be from the same family—the brother, Javier, tall and big as that animal, Aragon, squat like a fire plug. You could see it in their faces, though, the same brows on ridges over the eyes, the same high cheek bones, the strong jaw.

Spanish eyes, high on their faces. Proud, beautiful. Both of them.

Now he was grooming another mule, this one looking like it was old and getting fat. She watched him position the animal by a pipe fence, turn it how he wanted, grabbing the harness when it got restless, giving a treat when it stayed still.

And she saw herself: her mother grooming her, putting chemicals in her hair, training her how to walk, how to stand, how to smile, even. A kid's smile not good enough, she had to work on a knowing smile, a playful smile, a naughty smile. How to carry shoulders her mother said were an asset even before other assets took shape in her body.

Parading her for competitions. Claiming victory for herself when she was the one up there, her face hurting from smiling, trying to forget the touches from a smelly judge behind the curtain before she went out in front of people.

Fourteen years old, her mother taking her to a studio in New York. Bright light inside an umbrella, everything else dark, the man with the camera moving in and out of the white places, telling her to put her feet higher on the stool. Wink. Higher. Wink. There, oh that's good. I'm going to teach you so much. And squeezing both eyes shut like a contented cat.

Marcy grooming her years later, when she had nothing else. Too old to stand in front of cameras, now moving furniture for young girls to lay back on, running out for flowers to spread next to them, bringing the photographer a Martinelli cider, and going home alone, no one at the after-shoot party interested when look what else they could choose from.

"I'm going to teach you so much." Marcy had used the same words. Cruising a Santa Fe night in the Porsche convertible Marcy had then, the air cold but the heater full blast keeping her legs warm. Marcy pretending to reach for the bottle of wine between her thighs when her hand slipped.

"That's my girl." Wink. Marcy pleased with how she handled the first job as her private investigator. She'd brought Marcy the gun the police were looking for. Interviewing the jury after the not guilty, they heard how important it was the prosecution couldn't come up with the murder weapon. Marcy told her to find someone for a celebration in the office and tossed her the keys to her car. A teenage boy it was then, in his white hoodie, looking at condoms at Walgreen's. She stepped right up and said she knew how he might use a few, was he interested?

Marcy winked when she brought him back. "That's my girl."

Javier called to someone and Serena walked from the house carrying a thermos and a big packet of aluminum foil, probably a giant burrito. She'd been making them in the house. They talked while Javier cinched a saddle under the mule's belly. Serena tucked the burrito and thermos into a saddle bag. He climbed up and she watched him head down the dirt road, his dogs tagging behind like they'd done this a hundred times.

Last night at dinner—red chile in the posole that brought sweat to Montclaire's forehead—he said he would get a start on scouting for the August elk hunt. The other guides were hammering the Pecos Wilderness. He was going to try a valley outside, closer to the house, a place everybody might be overlooking.

Montclaire watched Javier and his dogs and imagined riding behind him on the saddle, feeling the heat of his back against her breasts, wondering if she could even get her arms around him, when she noticed Serena looking straight at her. She pulled a long knife from the sheath on her belt, turned to a coyote hide draped over a fence rail, and scraped, never taking her eyes away from Montclaire in the window.

———————

The files on Dolores Baca, a.k.a. Andrea Chacon, Andrea Luna, Andrea Tenorio, were no longer in central storage. They hadn't been filmed for micro fiche or digitized. But Lewis found what had been the records of a forgotten, short-lived vice squad in the basement. He came up with a torn accordion file and reports on onion skin, carbon copies of the official report that had been lost over the years.

Baca had been arrested at downtown hotels during the legislative session. She worked the bars and receptions, apparently got passed around among lobbyists. The files contained the names of three legislators suspected of using her services. She'd been offered a deal if she testified, but the penalties she faced were too insignificant to make it worth her while. She did a couple months in county, she could still work. She snitched, she'd have to leave town.

"Cassandra took Andrea as her working name," Aragon said. "She must have known mom's history."

"These are old. She would have been too young to hear about it when the arrests happened. Baca had to tell her daughter. How to inspire your kid to reach for the stars."

Aragon was reading the last file, the officer's account of observing Baca at work, following her to the rooms in the La Fonda Hotel, seeing her come down, get back to it, zeroing in on men alone at the bar. Then approaching himself, taking her to the room he'd paid for with operating expenses, haggling, the arrest.

"Maybe someone else told Cassandra," Aragon said.

"Like the father?"

"Whoever that is."

The next pages were notes about Baca's possible connection with a larger prostitution operation, the real target of the temporary vice squad. The officers had hoped to ID other working girls and find a common thread leading back to the pimp. They never got beyond arresting individual women and watching them bail out, sometimes seeing charges dismissed for speedy trial violations, the DA not very impressed with the project.

One girl, a Monica Otero, had been willing to talk. She'd been busted with heroin and a derringer in her purse. The weapons enhancement provided incentive. She told them to talk to Luke Tapia, her driver. He was getting instructions from someone else. Tapia was known to the police. He hung out at the old Tres Pistoles Bar. They waited for him, two officers stretching drinks, watching the entrance every night for a week until the bartender called them *officers* loud enough for the room to hear.

No more arrests for Tapia. No more police contacts. He disappeared. So did Monica Otero.

Aragon found something, checked the other files, found it there, too. She opened them side by side and brought Lewis over.

"Who posted bail every time?" she asked.

"Rigoberto Silva."

"I know his son. He was at Santa Fe High with my brother."

"Okay."

"There's only more Martinezes in Santa Fe than Silvas. But I'm wondering."

She did something she'd learned from Lewis when they were investigating Cody Geronimo's businesses. She went to the Secretary of State's website, brought down the tab for "search corporations," and typed in a name.

"*Eeeeeee*, Benny," she said in a sing-song northern New Mexico accent. "Rigo is vice president of Silva Enterprises."

They stood at the copier reproducing the old files, wanting to avoid handling the fragile onion skin too much. Lewis passed copies to her. She punched holes and entered them into their case book.

"Living history."

Their sergeant had come up behind them. Pete Perez was new to the department, brought in from Albuquerque after their last two bosses went down, one for getting a pal's car out of impound while his DUI charge was still pending, the last, Deputy Chief Dewy Nobles, for ordering Aragon to exclude exculpatory evidence from a case file. Perez was supposed to be a breath of fresh air, someone without political aspirations and not related to everyone in city government. He was getting a hard time from other cops, but Aragon liked him.

"I got word from city legal you have a deposition coming up," he said to Aragon.

"Thornton's suit against everybody who went after Cody Geronimo. The only people she didn't sue are the women he killed."

"What I'm learning about Santa Fe, it wouldn't surprise me." Perez shook a large black-and-white photo he'd been holding at his side. "All this stuff about Don Juan de Oñate, the Indians crying and bawling to City Council, wanting their own statue to show what an evil man he was for cutting off feet, the Butcher of Acoma. Look at this. Just in from down near Agua Fria. I gave it to Pork and Sauerkraut."

Detectives Darrel Park and Conrad Fenstermacher.

In the photo a man, Native American, ponytail sheathed in leather bindings, lay on gravel next to the concrete pad for an electrical transformer. Eyes closed, like they'd been squeezed shut. A small entrance wound at his temple, very little blood. He was trussed in what looked to be copper cable, arms bound behind his back.

"Is that bone?" Aragon asked and tapped the black and white.

"Where his left foot should be," Perez said. "OMI says it could have been a sword that took it off. Don Juan rides again."

TEN

BENNY SILVA WANTED TO know what brought the detectives back. They weren't really interested in how customers found him, his rates for parking a dumpster, what the city charged at the only landfill he could use for construction waste.

"Tell us about Dolores Baca," Detective Aragon said.

Getting to it.

"Which one?"

"You know more than one?"

"There's Bacas from Espanola. The grandmother, Dolores. Dolores Maria Baca Trujillo y Alarid, she taught me math at Chimayo Elementary. Dolores Baca at the Public Health Department, she does permits for waste disposal, my toilet rental line." He scratched his head. "Let me think, there's one down in Bernalillo, she—"

"Dolores Baca, mother of Cassandra Baca. Also known as Andrea Chacon, Andrea Luna, Andrea Tenorio."

"Now we're talking half of northern New Mexico, all those families. Five hundred years they been here. That adds up."

"Who's Rigo Silva?"

"Are you just flipping pages in the phone book?"

"Your vice president."

"You know, why ask? He's my brother, too. I'm gonna bet you know that."

"Where can we find him?"

"Out on a job. Working, like I should be."

Lewis tapped Aragon's arm, pointed to a painting behind a desk, Spanish conquistadors, Indians kneeling before them, some being whipped, some being run through with lances. A sword on the wall.

"That's Don Juan de Oñate," Silva said. "Y Salazar, the whole name. A great man. I carry that sword in the Fiesta. The Aragons came into this country with him. Your people. How come I never seen you march? You forget who you are?"

Aragon wanted to throw something back, but said, "You know everybody but the Dolores Baca we want to know about. Her daughter was the one in your dumpster. Your brother knows the mother. He posted her bail three times when she was arrested for prostitution. Have him call us."

Aragon and Lewis left a different way than they'd come in, taking a side door and a long walk around the building back to their car in front. They saw bins of scrap metal, glass, newspapers, the rows of portable toilets, a metal crusher, a metal hangar, the door partially opened, something like a huge pressure cooker in there. And unwound copper coaxial cable on the ground, by itself, looking used, like it had been pulled out of something.

"Too many coincidences," Aragon said as she snapped photos on her phone.

"I wonder if E. Benny has that copper in his book," Lewis said.

Silva was there waiting for them, the book open to the right page, showing the copper scrap he bought, from who, where they got it, where he sold it down the line. He said he saw them go the wrong way, maybe they were lost. They want a tour, just ask. By the way…

"There's a Dolores Baca in Cuyamungue, now I recall. Her husband works State Highway Department. Another Dolores Baca over in Cebolla, ranching family, and one in Ojo Caliente, the restaurant when you come off the hill. Best rellenos in the state. That's Dolores Saracino Baca, she says she's got Arab in her from when the Moors had Spain. I think of more, I've got your card."

An hour at their office playing with search engines, they found the case of E. Benny Silva Enterprises versus Jeremiah Kohn Productions. They accessed the online First Judicial District Court file and read docket entries. They understood the multi-million dollar judgment part, but not much else. Aragon called her cousin, Deputy DA Joe Mascarenas, and asked him to make sense of it. Mascarenas pulled it up on a computer in his office. Aragon put the call on speaker so Lewis could hear.

"It's been in limbo. Post-verdict motions, hearings, the trial judge recusing himself. Interest is adding up fast. The time for appeal hasn't started with the motion for new trial pending. Hold on. It's been pending almost a year."

"If there's no judge," Lewis asked, "what happens?"

"There is a judge, by default. The Chief Judge. The First Judicial Court adopted that procedure when the governor and legislature deadlocked over adding new judges to tackle the backlog. This way the Chief Judge could send work to those with the lightest or fastest dockets."

"Or keep it for herself?"

"Why would she?"

Somebody stepped into the doorway to their small office. They looked up to see Tomas Rivera holding an armful of roses.

"For me?" Lewis asked. "You shouldn't have."

"Hang on, Joe." Aragon glared at Rivera. Flowers the day after their date? Members of a joint federal-state task force screwing each other was not in the protocol.

"This isn't what you think," Rivera said.

"What is it?" she asked.

"I stopped by Whole Foods for a bite. Your Elaine Salas has been asking about collecting roses from local florists with the goal of trying to match them genetically to those around Andrea. I got these at Whole Foods. It's hot in the car. Can you put them in water?"

He only needed one for the lab. He was pushing it with a dozen. Other cops would see. The talk would start.

Shit. She'd forgotten to keep him current on the girl's identity. But it wasn't irritation that pushed an apology out of the way.

"Whole Foods doesn't sell roses," she said. "We were there yesterday."

"Someone had bought them out. A loving husband bought six dozen for his wife, all they had. They restocked this morning."

"How many roses were in that dumpster? It could have been six dozen."

They finished with Mascarenas, then called Elaine Salas and got their answer. Sixty roses. Five dozen.

Lewis and she were thinking alike. He passed around copies of the florist pages in the Santa Fe Dex and five pages of a Google search. They divided the stores and made calls. They didn't bother with FTD or Flowers.com on the assumption those outfits would merely route an order through one of the brick and mortars on their list. In all, each called nine florists. It didn't take long.

They came back with only two possibilities. Thirteen dozen red sweetheart roses had been purchased from Ava's Flowers for a bat mitzvah. They were still in the store's cooler, awaiting delivery this evening.

The other large purchase had been for a funeral at the Santuario de Chimayo the previous Sunday. They'd run that down, but it was probably a dead end.

"Let's learn who cleaned out Whole Foods," Aragon said, "and what they did with the flowers. We're one dozen short, but that's close enough. A Whole Foods bag on Cassandra Baca's head, flowers from Whole Foods around her. Just maybe."

———

Lewis headed to district court to obtain copies of the pleadings and trial transcript in the Silva lawsuit. Aragon went with Rivera to Whole Foods. He called ahead and asked to meet with the manager.

She noticed Rivera left the roses behind on her desk.

In his car she told him they'd identified Andrea as Cassandra Baca.

"Superb work." He plugged his phone into the car stereo. "You have me listening to country music. This song is about us."

She knew it, about not closing your eyes, not looking backward to another love, another time.

Rivera sang along, his voice nothing like Miguel's, the lyrics telling her what he wanted: see me, not someone else.

Brown adobes rolled by, the city historical or cultural commission, whatever it was, thinking every building looking the same was a good idea. Aragon was tired of it, all the brown, millions of dollars for a building of mud and straw, no angles, nothing new. Not a city, a theme park.

She hit eject and cut Rivera off in the middle of the next verse.

It wasn't the buildings. She honestly liked the look, was proud of it, nothing coming close anywhere in the country. It felt sometimes like a piece of Spain, or Mexico centuries ago. It was Rivera, first playing with the roses, now having fun with the hard time she had loving him. Had she told him Miguel was a beautiful singer? He shouldn't even try. It didn't help.

Did she just think that? 'Loving him'?

Not Miguel Martinez. Him, Tomas Rivera?

"I do something wrong?" He glanced at her, then back to the windshield.

"No." She wasn't going to tell him. "I was thinking about the case. I couldn't concentrate. Sorry."

"Look at this place," he said as they pulled in the Whole Foods lot. "A money factory. Always packed. I didn't ask if the flowers were organic, free trade, animal friendly, whatever."

"Fregan. I learned that from a smelly girl named Gray, whose family has more money than any Aragon or Rivera. But she won't buy food. She'll only eat what people throw away. And she won't wash."

She'd explain later if Rivera asked. They parked and entered the store. Again she saw vegetables and fruits from another planet.

"I still want to know what celeriac is," she said.

Flowers, but not roses, were displayed outside. They asked a cashier for the manager and were pointed to a young man helping another stack boxes of soy milk. He introduced himself as Simon Townsend and led them to the small floral department.

There they saw roses, dozens, their ends in black plastic buckets filled with water, each dozen wrapped in a crisp, clear plastic sheath.

They learned the roses were indeed free trade, grown in El Salvador, and distributed by an importer committed to ethical, sustainable practices. Even more, the roses bore Veriflora labels, a certification, the manager told them, ensuring equitable hiring and employment practices, safe workplace and housing conditions, access to health care, education, transportation, and the prevention of child labor.

Aragon leaned in close and sniffed. All those ethics and they forgot about smelling good.

She said, "We understand someone bought you out the day before yesterday, one person. We'd like to know who that was. Can you pull up a credit card transaction? If it was cash, we're out of luck."

"I'll check sales. Help yourself to coffee. Give my name to the cashier."

"I could eat," Aragon said. "We'll be at the tables."

They ordered from the deli section. Rivera ordered quinoa salad and got a look from Aragon. She went for a brick of meatloaf. They took seats up front looking out on the parking lot.

"We're interested in a guy named Benny Silva," she said. "His brother posted bail for Cassandra Baca's mother when she was picked up on prostitution beefs long ago. Cassandra adopted her mother's street name. She ends up in one of Silva's dumpsters. He's got a nine-million-dollar verdict hanging on a decision by Judge Judith Diaz, who, we know, was having sex with this girl. There's a circle here. They're all inside the line, but I'm not understanding it yet."

"The mother, did she know about her daughter's after-school activities?"

"She was too doped up to get anything out of her. The house is like two worlds. The one Dolores Baca inhabits, trashed out, a junkie's flop. You step into Cassandra's room, you're somewhere else." She thought of the kids at Camino High filming the class movie, stepping into lockers to reach a better world. "Neat, tidy, clean. New things. Sports car posters on the wall. I had boy bands on my wall. Lewis says his daughters have horses. Cassandra had a car tattoo on her hip. A neighbor says she tinkered with cars. Maybe Cassandra saw them as a way out, she was going somewhere, fast. Maybe a statement she wasn't like her mom with the shitty heaps in the driveway."

"Except in how she was making money. The apple doesn't fall far from the tree."

"Mom went through the room looking for money for another carpet ride. The way she went straight to the closet, leaving everything else untouched, I get the feeling she's tossed the room before and learned where Cassandra didn't keep cash."

"Cassandra had money outside the house?"

"She bought her own clothes, lunches. I don't see Dolores Baca giving her that. Maybe she was saving up for that fast car to get her out of Dodge. Rick is going to swing by the school, deliver the parental consent form, and take a look at her locker."

"Mom was too doped to talk, but read and signed a consent form?"

Aragon fluttered fingers in front of her lips, saying sorry, I've got a mouthful.

"Here it is." Townsend was at the table. He handed Aragon an index card. "Daniel Breskin. He bought six dozen roses. I can't give you his credit card number."

"We'll find him," Aragon said. "This meatloaf's great. You put in pine nuts. My grandmother did that. We'd pick them where Jack Nicklaus built those houses for millionaires."

Rivera said he'd be right back. She read texts from Lewis. He had the court files in Silva's case and was on his way to Camino High. Rivera climbed in with a small shopping bag.

"For you. Stretch your horizons." He unpacked on the seat. "Kohl-rabi, Jerusalem artichokes, parsnips, and your favorite, celeriac."

"Ain't gonna happen."

"I'll cook for you."

"I've never had a guy cook vegetables for me. Flip burgers, burn a steak, maybe. This is new."

"Can't cook in your brother's truck. It would have to be one of our places for once. I've got a kitchen I don't use enough."

"I've got one I never use."

"My place then."

"I'll bring Lotaburgers in case it's a mistake." He looked hurt. She punched his shoulder. "The rabbit food, silly. Not your place."

———————

They had Daniel Breskin with a few taps on the screen of Rivera's phone.

The top search results gave them a computer entrepreneur in Seattle with connections to New Mexico. Reports about Breskin's success with three start-ups led them to a story about the modernistic mansion he'd built above Santa Fe. They got the address with a call to the County Assessor's office.

They saw his place from a half-mile away. At the crown of a hill, sunlight bouncing off white walls. The driveway was a paved road. Halfway up, on the steepest slope, they passed through an open gate on rollers retracted into the pinyon and juniper.

They reached the house after more bends in the roadway. Macadam gave way to interlocking masonry blocks ending at a four-car garage. A path of crushed sea shells bordered by lavender led to the front door.

A woman was bending into the trunk of a white BMW. She came out with a white gym bag. Asian, thirties, long straight black hair against a white exercise bra, white stretch pants, white sandals. Strong calves, graceful back. She straightened when she saw them. Rivera pulled his car close. They got out, showing their badges and giving their names.

"We'd like to talk to Daniel Breskin," Aragon said.

"My husband is away. Can I help you?"

"May we talk inside?"

The woman bumped the car door shut with her hip.

"Would you like something to drink? It's so awfully hot."

They followed her into the house, cool and dark. A dozen roses sat in a ceramic pot on a table in the entry. Same small, tight blooms as the ones in Andrea's dumpster. At the end of the hallway they stepped into an ocean of light so piercing they winced. Floor-to-ceiling windows showed an infinity pool beyond the glass, the water line underscoring a view across Santa Fe's rooftops. Everything was sharp angles, hard surfaces, and, where there wasn't artwork or rugs, white. White leather furniture low to the ground. White blinds pulled above the glass. Built-in cabinets almost white, a very pale variety of ash or maple, Aragon guessed, not knowing how to identify much beyond pine and oak.

The Asian woman was standing at a counter with a sink and refrigerator sunk into white surfaces.

"We didn't get your name?"

"Sun-Hi Breskin. I go by Sunny."

Aragon scanned the mantle over a glass-enclosed fireplace. Small Asian figurines, cut glass, nothing with New Mexico style. On the bookshelves, volumes about localities around the world, not one on Santa Fe. She looked down another hallway, a glass wall here instead

113

of stone, a view across a courtyard to a separate building, a smaller version of this one but still larger than most New Mexico homes.

"What's that playing?" Rivera asked. She hadn't noticed the music but now that she listened, it was airy stuff, no beat, no drive. Loose, shapeless sounds. No lyrics telling stories about broken hearts and broken homes.

"It's the loop they play at my yoga studio."

"I like it," Rivera said.

Breskin smiled at that and filled glasses from a pitcher in the refrigerator. They moved to seats around a coffee table. White again. Aragon tasted pineapple in what she thought was plain water.

"From pineapple cores," Breskin said as Aragon flicked her tongue across her lips. "It adds bromelain. Good for recovery. I just finished my power-flow class. I bet you have amazing abs. May I see them?"

Rivera hid a smile behind his glass.

"I don't think so." Aragon put her drink on a white coaster on what she guessed was white marble. "Mrs. Breskin, we have a very serious case. I can't go into all the details. We're looking into purchases of large quantities of roses in Santa Fe on Monday of this week."

"Roses."

"Did your husband purchase six dozen roses from Whole Foods?"

"He always brings me roses when he comes home from Seattle." She paused. "You said six dozen?"

Aragon studied her: Quadriceps and calves filled out the stretch pants. Her bare midriff showed rippled abdominal muscles. The inverted triangles of delts topped her arms. The white top was sheer enough to see nipples and aureoles. Coal-black eyes. The light in the room bounced off her black hair.

"May I ask, how long have you been here?"

"Almost two years." Breskin got up to bring the pitcher to the table. Aragon caught Rivera's eyes following her. "We moved down from Seattle when this home was ready. Daniel maintains a condo there, where his work is."

"And you stay here?"

"His business is not my business. He spends most of his time out there when he's in Santa Fe." She flipped a hand at the glass wall revealing the large guesthouse.

"Do you work?"

"I maintain the house."

"What is your husband's business?"

"He made his money in virtual reality technology. First for medical surgery, then computer games."

"I take it you and your husband don't spend much time together."

"What's this about? Why are you interested in the state of our marriage?"

"I apologize." Aragon took a long drink of pineapple water to change gears. "I get that way, trailing one question off another. Back to the roses. Would it be too much to ask if we may have one of the blooms? I understand they may hold some special meaning for you. We can wait until you're ready to throw them out."

"You can have them. I usually get rid of them when Daniel leaves."

"Can you tell us where he was Monday night?"

"Again, what does that have to do with people buying large quantities of roses? Is that a crime?"

"The roses may be connected to a very serious crime. We need to eliminate your husband from our inquiries. If you can account for his time."

Sunny Breskin pushed silky black hair behind an ear. Aragon scratched her scalp stubble.

"We went to Coyote for an early dinner. He needed to work all night. We were done and home by seven. He went to his office in the guesthouse."

"Why would he have bought six dozen? Did he have a purpose for the five dozen he didn't give you?"

"I don't like your insinuations. Why don't you ask Danny yourself? Call his office. No, here's his cell phone." She found a pen and paper in an ivory box on the bookshelf and wrote out his number. "I'm wondering whether there's more to your visit than you're telling me."

"Why would that be, Mrs. Breskin?"

She removed a cell phone from the same ivory box and tapped numbers on the screen.

"Who are you calling, Mrs. Breskin?"

"I want my lawyer here, unless you're leaving."

Aragon gathered the flowers on the way out, water dripping from the stems on the cold stone floor.

"One dozen for me, five for someone else, that's what Sun-Hi Breskin's thinking right now," she said as they got into the car. "You were sure quiet. You really liked that music?"

"I was watching her."

"I bet you were."

The gate was open for them on the way down and started closing as soon as they passed through. Aragon stopped at the bottom of the drive to point out the cameras for Rivera.

She brought up on her phone the crime reporting map from the SFPD's website.

"We're here," she said, "where there are no recently reported crimes. Nothing. Not even registered sex offenders nearby. Down here..." She scrolled to bring up southwest Santa Fe, past Jaguar Road. "These red dots, like measles. Sex offenders, the heaviest concentration of violent and property crime. This is where Cassandra Baca's body was dumped. Two different worlds, a lot more than ten miles apart. Say those roses were his. What would a guy like Daniel Breskin be doing down there?"

"I think she's watching us."

Aragon followed Rivera's gaze. A camera that had pointed at cars entering the drive now pointed at them.

Aragon said, "She might have seen his coming and going. We need to ask if Mr. Breskin went out."

"We have his personal cell."

"Let's learn more about him. When I asked what his business is, notice she said how he'd made his money in the past, not what he's doing now? And see what your FBI mad scientists say about these flowers, whether they're the same as the ones in the dumpster."

"We've got plenty to do. I don't think tonight's ideal for you to experience celeriac and kohlrabi."

"Lotaburgers and work. I'm happy."

———————

Benny Silva telling her who she is.

You don't march in the Fiesta. You forget how your people got here?

On her knees in her efficiency apartment on the far west side of town, pushing aside coats and holding back the ironing board before it fell on her head, she pulled the suitcase from the back of her closet. Then the long wooden case her father had made, over five feet long. It took the entire floor under her clothes. Wire twisted around nails held it closed. Inside, not a fake conquistador sword like the one she'd seen on Silva's wall with his lost Spanish Empire fan club stuff. This one had markings showing it had been forged in Toledo, Spain. Nicks in the blade, her father said, from when an Aragon fought with Don Juan

117

de Oñate all the way from Mexico City to here. Four-and-a-half feet long, a foot soldier's weapon. With the hilt it was as tall as her.

A corset of chain mail was wrapped in black velvet, a couple ringlets dented and twisted where her father said it had stopped an Apache spear. In another wooden box, a *morion*, a Spanish soldier's crescent-shaped helmet, the pointed brim in front and back curving up, a ridge of tin splitting the crown. The dent over the right eye: stones hurled from Acoma's sky fortress, a city on a pillar of rock above a dry valley. An Aragon had survived the first Indian attack and returned with Oñate and cannons. They had done terrible things. But it was war on both sides. When Indians got a soldier, the Spaniard took a long time dying. The women got them at the end. Guess what they did?

That's what her father had said to the little girl watching him suit up.

She had marched with him in the Fiesta parade. She'd be in a pleated dress, usually bright blue or red, whatever her mother was wearing that year. They had matching fans and tiaras with glass stones. He father marched with the heavy sword in front of his face, point up, sweating under the chain mail and *morion*. They'd precede La Conquistadora, Our Lady of the Rosary, a four-hundred-year-old statue carried on a platform. The very same statue that had escaped the Pueblo uprising and returned to Santa Fe in the *reconquista*. An Aragon had entered the city with De Vargas and his troops.

Her parents never marched after she'd been raped on the playground across from their house. We have lost, her father said. We are not the victors here.

Her brothers were sent out of town to the New Mexico Military Academy, in Roswell. It felt like Texas down there when she'd gone to see them graduate, marching in blazing sun in military uniforms they'd

118

never wear again. Javier hated coming into Santa Fe. Her other brother, Christobal, left the state entirely, another proud export.

She'd fought to go back to school. Her parents had talked about sending her to a convent. Where else do you put a girl who's been raped? Thank Jesus she didn't get pregnant.

She'd made it through those years, always running straight at the violence, making herself get stronger, but never claiming her place in the parade, showing who she was, proud as hell of it and not making any excuses.

She marched in the shadows, her beautiful black hair gone, her armor the muscles she'd built to cover her bones. What she'd wrapped around her heart, she didn't have words for.

Aragon returned the ancient soldier's tools to the floor of her closet and lined cross-trainers and hiking boots on the boxes. She should probably donate the family treasures to a museum. She would never use them. No one would. They took up so much space.

No conquistadors left in the Aragon family.

And Benny Silva saw it.

ELEVEN

Principal Mead took the parental consent from Lewis and pushed a folder across the table.

"This is what we have on Cassandra Baca," Mead said. "Teachers complained of her sleeping in class. One teacher reported suspicion of physical abuse. He took her to the school nurse. Cassandra refused to cooperate, but there were bruises plainly visible on her neck and arms. She said they were hickeys from a boyfriend."

Inside the folder Lewis found grades, test results, and discipline reports. He didn't see something he'd been expecting. The neighbor had said Cassandra Baca worked on her mother's cars. He saw nothing to indicate she'd taken any shop classes.

Also in the file was a report of bullying, with Cassandra as the victim.

"Tell me about the bullying."

McRae, the school resource officer, was in the room this time, sitting with Lewis across from Mead and her assistant, Ulibarri. Mead nodded for him to speak.

"Cassandra got it because she was one of the pretty ones. She was knocked around good behind the gym building. Then it stopped. I saw Cassandra with Star Salazar and understood. She had a protector. Nobody messed with Star."

"Who's this Star Salazar?" Lewis asked, thumbing through the girl's file, seeing only the single report of bullying.

"One of our very real problems," Mead said. "She's older than other students because she missed time while she was in the juvenile detention center."

"For what?"

"All I know is she was an adjudicated youth under commitment. The particulars are not revealed to us."

"Armed robbery," McRae said. "I know the arresting officer. She pulled a gun on a clerk at Latinos Mundial, fired into a rack of cigarettes behind his head when he laughed at her."

"Nice friend to have watching your back. I'd like contact information for her parents."

"I'll take care of you." McRae pushed himself to his feet. "You ready to see the locker?"

"May we prepare our students?" Mead asked.

"The news has been released, now that we've identified Cassandra Baca. You'll have television reporters trying to put your students on camera. You should have them ready."

In the hallway, Lewis said, "That was bull, saying she didn't know why Star Salazar was committed."

"There's an effort to play down the crime problems here," McRae said. "It's not just a PR thing. If you're always thinking Camino High is a juvie hall with books, that's what you get. Power-of-positive-thinking sort of thing. And God forbid, don't stigmatize children as thugs. But it's my job to always see things exactly as they are. Eyes open. I know the bad kids walking these halls. Star Salazar is a very bad kid."

Cassandra Baca's locker was in another wing of the building. Students moving between classes stopped to watch as McRae positioned bolt cutters on the lock.

"Keep going," McRae told them. "In one minute you're out of class without a pass."

They waited until the hallway cleared before opening the locker.

Inside they found a sweatshirt on a hook, an overnight bag, clean underwear and bras, and pepper spray.

"Stuff gets in," McRae said. "It's like jail."

Lewis wondered if Cassandra took the pepper spray on her hookups. He reached for the overnight bag. Inside he found makeup, Handiwipes, toothbrush and paste, a mini-bottle of mouthwash, and condoms. Tucked inside the kit was two hundred dollars in tens and twenties.

He took the sweatshirt from the hook and found another three hundred dollars in the hand-warmer pouch.

With the sweatshirt out of the way he could see the back of the locker. It was covered with photos of expensive cars taped to gray metal.

"Guess I pegged Cassandra wrong," McRae said. "I thought she had it together."

"So did she. Do you have that list of friends you promised?"

"Working on it."

"Get me one on Star Salazar, too."

Lewis waited for Aragon outside Dolores Baca's house. Perla Gallegos watched him, a curtain in the front window pulled aside, weathered fingers curled around the fabric. A woman came out of the house on the other end of the cul-de-sac to put a bag in the rolling city trash container on the side of the house. He remembered they hadn't completed their ~~canvas~~ because no one else had been home and caught up with her.

She did not have much to add. She'd seen Cassandra coming and going, had noticed nothing unusual, but kept her children away from the Baca house. She and Dolores had had an argument about the derelict cars in the driveway. She was afraid a homeless person would move in. Baca told her the cars weren't going anywhere, she might need them some day. They could still run, once she got some money together.

Aragon pulled up and met him on the walk to the Baca's doorstep.

"We're under surveillance," Lewis said and nodded at Perla Gallegos's hand around the edge of drapery in her front window. "A one-woman neighborhood watch."

"Let's hope Dolores isn't zonked again," Aragon said. "She needs to hear about her daughter. We can't just leave her a note to read when she comes out of the clouds."

No one answered their knock. No response came when they shouted who they were. Lewis moved to the front window, still open, but this time no sound of a television inside.

"The Nissan's there behind the dead Chevys," he said. "She should be home."

"I'll check the side."

"Meet you around back."

He listened at other windows and heard nothing inside. A view into the kitchen showed piles of trash and dirty dishes. In the back a cracked garden hose snaked across dry ground to a dead crab-apple. The cell tower in the next lot cast a weak shadow across the yard. He lifted the lid on the garbage can. It was crammed to the top edge. Aragon came into the back yard from her side of the house.

He showed her the full can.

"Dolores hasn't been taking her garbage to the curb. For weeks, it looks."

"At least she moved some of it out of the house. We can try the back door." Aragon put her hand on the knob. "No prying eyes back here."

The door was unlocked.

"Good thing the windows are open," Lewis said as they entered. "Imagine the smell."

"But not that kind of smell. Nobody's dead."

The living room where they'd found a collapsed Dolores Baca yesterday looked exactly the same. It would have been hard to notice any changes unless it had been completely cleaned up. The rest of the house was empty. Cassandra's room still had the rifled gym bag on the floor.

"She gave us permission to search her daughter's room, take whatever we needed," Aragon said. "Remember? You were in another room and missed her thirty seconds of coherence."

"Glad you reminded me." Lewis filled the gym bag with the few items scattered on the floor, an island of order after what they'd just passed through. They left by the back door.

Putting the gym bag in the trunk, he saw Perla Gallegos still watching.

"Let's talk to her. She doesn't miss anything."

Perla Gallegos had the door open before they knocked.

"I haven't seen Cassandra," she said. "It's been days. Is she alright?"

"No, Mrs. Gallegos." Aragon took the lead. "She's not. Did you see when her mother went out? We really need to speak with her."

"No." Gallegos looked past them at the Baca house. "I thought she was home."

"Has anybody been by to see her?"

"No. Nobody. I been watching since you were here. Where's Cassandra?"

"Thank you, Mrs. Gallegos. Here's my card. If Dolores returns, please give me a call right away."

"Could you do me a favor? This smoke in the air. With my asthma, it's no good."

"What can we do for you?'

"Would you check I got a new garbage can, too?"

"What do you mean?"

"Dolores got one last night. I saw the garbage men. I was up and heard their truck. They pushed a new can around back of her place and took the old one away. Mine's cracked. I been calling the city for months. They don't do anything. Old ladies living alone, what do they care? My husband would have gone to City Hall and raised hell. Why do they need two men to deliver a garbage can? And a whole big truck. I can't get even one person to return my calls."

"How could you tell the can was new?" Aragon asked, thinking about the overflowing, faded black can behind the Baca house.

"It shined under the street light. Mine's all faded and cracked from the sun. And bounced. I could see it was empty."

"This truck, was it from the city?"

"Must have been, they do the garbage. But it didn't say Santa Fe. It had a name. I forget. Benjie's, maybe."

"Could it have been Benny?"

"That's it. Benny."

Aragon caught Lewis staring at her, eyebrows crawling up his forehead.

"Holy crap."

"No, maybe Bobby," Perla Gallegos said. "Or Bernard something. Why did she get a new can and not me?"

"The can they rolled back to the truck, how do you know it was a different can, the old one from around back?"

She scrunched her face. "I thought that, too, maybe it was the same can. Because it was shiny. I was getting mad, they're pushing new cans around in the middle of the night, what, they don't have anything better to do? But this one didn't bounce. It was full. Took both those men to lift it into the truck."

———

They called their sergeant to meet them. They wanted to declare Baca's house a crime scene, take control, treat every inch like evidence. But what did they have? An old lady with cat hair on her robe and a garbage truck in the night.

Perez arrived. They walked around back, showed him the old garbage can still there, almost spilling over, and explained what they thought was in the shiny new can it took two men to lift. In the front they pointed through the window to where they'd found Dolores Baca zonked, not knowing when she last saw her daughter. They told him of the money found in Cassandra's locker, how Lily Montclaire had hooked up with her through Backpage, how she'd used the same name Mom had used when she was tricking. How Mom had been bailed out of her prostitution arrests by Rigo Silva, vice president of E. Benny Silva Enterprises that owned the dumpster where Cassandra was found. How two witnesses in that old investigation had simply disappeared. How a company with a truck that said Benny Something came to Dolores Baca's house in the middle of the night and how she now seemed to be missing.

"We mentioned Dolores's bail to Silva when we were looking for Rigo," Aragon said. "A day later, Dolores is missing."

"We don't know for certain," Perez said.

"Her car's here. There's no place near to walk to."

"She's watching us," Perez said, and nodded behind Aragon at Perla Gallegos's house.

"That's what she does." Aragon sat on the hood of one of the dead Impalas in Baca's driveway.

"If we seize this as a crime scene, then Dolores Baca comes walking up because you were wrong about what you think happened to her, it gets dicey." Perez looked through the window into the front room. "Any other place, I'd say there was evidence of a struggle. But you say the place was a mess when you were here yesterday."

"Maybe it's more a mess today."

"Not good enough."

They went silent, the three of them burning in the sun, knowing they should do this but not seeing a way.

"Something Perla Gallegos saw," Lewis said. "Cassandra was always working on these heaps, learning a skill."

"These things are never going to run," Aragon said.

"If she was that interested in learning about cars, there's auto repair classes. But her school file shows nothing for shop. And we haven't seen any kind of tools she'd use for working on cars." He looked at the house, just a yard or so from the closest Chevy's front bumper, a window above the hood. "That's Cassandra's bedroom right there, isn't it?"

Aragon asked, "Can we search these cars, Sarge?"

"You know you need a warrant for what you can't see from the outside."

Aragon scooted off the hood and peered into the car's windows. Then she squatted low, trying to see under the Impala. She stuck her head in the wheel well, flipped on her back, and pulled herself under the chassis. In a second she pulled herself free, moved to the other side, and got down, again on her back and sliding under.

When she wiggled out she had Ziploc bags on her chest.

"We found Cassandra's bank. There must be thousands under there."

————

"They make appointments through me," Yago said, shirt off today, showing his life story in tattoos and scars. The Santa Fe riot on his chest, men up to their knees in water, cell gates swung open, guards lined up, hands tied, flames above the prison walls. "These guys, they'd fuck you up you didn't do only their cases. Then you wouldn't be doing mine. I'd have to mess you up to get you back on track."

"They'll listen to you?" Fager asked, but knew the answer. He'd seen the way the men in the pod cleared a space at the table when Yago arrived with his food tray. His skin told stories no one could top.

"You need to ask, shows you're fresh meat in here. This one." Yago turned to show his back. "An inch from my kidney. Brother of a snitch we shortened in the riot. Killing him got me back in here. I got facing manslaughter instead of walking on self-defense."

"That's a wound in your back. You were attacked. That should have been easy."

"What I thought. But stabbing him thirty times changed things a little. That's what Thornton told me. I told her, you ever been stabbed? Try counting when you're fighting back. What number you think would have worked?"

Fager sat at the stainless steel round table in the center of the pod. Like the table, the metal bench was welded to the floor. To sit down you had to park your butt first, then swing your legs over. Fager pulled closer one of the legal pads Detective Lewis had sent. On the top page he'd written the questions he needed to cover in every interview.

"I only want to see ones who had Marcy Thornton as their lawyer."

"What you call this job I'm doing for you?" Yago scratched a blue tattoo of bones on his forearm, right where his own ulna and radius lay under the skin. "I may want it on my resume when I look for work. You're getting me out of here, I need to be thinking ahead."

"Put down 'executive assistant, law office intake and screening, client interview and case establishment.' That's how we billed it."

"Get a slot at the car wash. Instead of emptying ashtrays, pulling snotty tissues from the seats, I can be the guy outside with the clipboard, handling client intake and screening. I recommend our heavy duty wash and wax, sir, and the undercarriage spray. Appears you been tearing up those country roads. Might I interest you in our deluxe detailing service? This is a sweet ride. You should treat it right. How's that sound?"

"I buy the deluxe package if you're the one selling."

Yago brought in the first Thornton client, the devil's mustache, square-head guy, black eyes crossed a little. "Ineffective assistance of counsel," he said after he covered his experience with Thornton. "*Res ipsa loquitor*, thing speaks for itself. I'm in here for a crime I didn't do. What's more ineffective than that?"

"You've been using the law library."

"I say that right, the Latin words?"

"The first one, don't say it like *rez*. The rest you nailed. Now for the reality check." Fager explained how they had to prove ineffective assistance of counsel. Wrongly convicted wasn't enough. Innocence wasn't a get-out-of-jail-free card. "Even if the trial lawyer checked off all the boxes adding up to zealous representation, you could still be doing someone else's time."

"I'll get those years back, you get me out."

"But not staying in contact with you, not keeping you informed, ignoring your questions—that gets us started."

"She called today. Well, I got a message from a guard to call her. For once she'd take collect. She wanted to know if I'd heard of a guy named Benny Silva. What's that got to do with how I been fucked?"

Before Yago brought the next Thornton client, Fager had a question for him. Seeing Yago's tattoos, he remembered something that had stuck in his mind since he'd first heard details about what happened when the guards lost control of Santa Fe's prison. Yago had mentioned it before.

"What was that about heads on shovels, in the riot?"

"The other time I was an executive assistant, I got the names in cell block 4, protective custody. I came back with proof they were done snitching. These ISIS motherfuckers, showing off, shiny big knives. Man, we had to make our tools. You learn the square shovels are best. The pointed ones can go sideways they hit bone."

"Right. Who's my next appointment?"

Three Thornton clients later, Fager decided he needed to make a call. Yago told the inmate on the phone to hang up and step out of the way. Fager dialed, called Detective Rick Lewis collect, careful to use a first name only, other men standing too close.

"Rick. Me, Walt. I don't know if you can use this. Marcy Thornton's been calling her old clients, asking if they know a Benny Silva.

I remember that name. He had a civil case being tried ahead of one of mine, back in the day. You're on it? Nine million dollars? Shit."

He shouldn't have said that number out loud. Yago was rubbing the tat of the burning prison on his chest, beating out a slow rhythm, his eyes telling Fager he'd heard.

Fager lowered his voice and listened to Lewis explaining where that case now stood with Judge Diaz. When he hung up, he told Yago, "My paralegal. He's been with me for years. I'll mail him my drafts of pleadings in your case. He'll type them, make them look professional, hand-deliver them to the court. That should send a message you're more than a run of the mill *pro se* litigant wasting the court's time because you don't have anything better to do with your own."

Yago said, "Tell me about nine million dollars."

————

Benny Silva brought Rigo and Abel to Thornton's parking lot under old elms. He stopped his Olds next to a car he wanted them to see.

"I never seen one like that," Rigo said and whistled at the sight of Thornton's red Aston.

Abel, in the back seat, leaned forward for a better look. "Be something, cruising St. Francis, racing lowriders. Are we going to take it?"

"We're after the one that drives it."

Benny drove them back to the office. Abel had the movie in a thumb drive and brought it up on his computer. They watched, again, Marcy Thornton, Judge Judy Diaz, and the woman they didn't know, the one all arms and legs, tying down Cassandra Baca.

"Does Millie like biting?" Rigo asked Benny.

"Enchiladas and Frito pies. Why are you asking such a thing?"

"They all like it," Abel said, watching the screen. "Cassandra's the only one who doesn't."

Benny focused on Marcy Thornton holding Cassandra Baca's ankles, fire in her eyes. Holding her for Judge Diaz. "That lady can keep her fat English car. She's giving us a judge."

Abel made still shots from the movie, he knew how to do that. He printed them in color, wearing plastic gloves, and folded them in an envelope that would go under the wiper on the Aston with a number to call.

TWELVE

"WE'RE A LARGE CALIBER killing ground," OMI's Nate Moss was saying. "I haven't seen this in New Mexico, two peas behind the ear."

Standing there in running shorts and tank top, Moss was doing ten miles before tonight's autopsies. He had a drive after his run, almost an hour to OMI's facility on the University of New Mexico's campus down in Albuquerque. He did this, beating pavement and dirt trails for miles, before his all-night cuts. Get the adrenaline going, some people said. Aragon always thought he ran to remind himself how alive he was before sharing the company of the dead while the rest of the world slept.

He'd been stretching while others talked and spoke up when someone commented on the small caliber bullets that killed Cassandra Baca.

Moss was in the FBI's basement conference room with Rivera, Tucker, Elaine Salas, and Phil Barone, an FBI forensic analyst who had worked the Geronimo case. And Lewis and Aragon, their clothes damp from sweat after working Dolores Baca's house. They'd brought something with them: news of finding twenty thousand dollars under the Impalas in the driveway.

Aragon sat at the end of the table away from Rivera. After the stunt with the roses in her office, she didn't want him sitting next to her, maybe touching as he reached for this or that, giving the others in the room something to wonder about.

Moss dropped the foot in his hand and passed around copies of a report limited to external observations. The full autopsy would take place tonight. His lean thighs were pale under the fluorescent lights.

"Two small entrance wounds behind the right ear. Small caliber weapon. Contact burns."

"Peas behind the ear," Lewis said. "I heard that in Pennsylvania. Mafia talk. You're saying this is a Mob hit?"

"It's unusual for New Mexico. We have sloppy macho killers." Moss bent a leg behind him, stretching his quad. "This is delicate, precise. Minute blood loss. No exit wound. The killer gives up the slugs and we can identify the make of gun. But they get a very neat, manageable kill in the bargain."

He shook enlarged black and whites out of a manila envelope. "I hate teeth mark analysis. It's a scientific quagmire and not worth my time. On the other hand, the bite on the inner thigh broke the skin. I examined the case of a girl pulled from a river after a week submerged. Buccal cells were recovered in deep bite wounds. DNA led back to her stepfather. There's a shot, even if Cassandra Baca had washed since, what do I call it, her last outing with Judge Diaz and friends?"

"I've got Montclaire covered," Aragon said. "We'll have to be creative on getting spit from Thornton and Diaz."

Moss stretched the other leg as he talked, palm flat on the wall, pulling a heel to his glutes.

"There's a fantastic quantity of biological material on all surfaces of her body. Odd, because she'd been washed recently. There's shampoo caked in her hair, like she didn't rinse thoroughly. Her hair may have dried in the dumpster. I think her killer got her good and dirty so it would be harder to make sense of anything on her skin."

"They tried washing her," Aragon said. "Then thought of something better."

"They always miss something," Moss said. "It's as though they compensated by overloading the biological information, burying us with it. She's got everything on her but semen, which would have given us a definite focus. Instead we have this curiosity."

He brought out more photos, close-ups of skin. "She has wood splinters in her back and buttocks. There's a uniform angle of penetration, as though she were dragged headfirst across a rough wood table, or sheet of plywood. I'm having a hard time seeing how it happened."

Lewis and Tucker had ideas: she'd been kept in an attic, then dragged out; she'd been abused with wooden paddles—Tucker's twisted thought; she'd been loaded in a pickup on a plywood liner, then pulled out before she was thrown in the dumpster—the most plausible but still a flyer.

"That's it for me. I need to get moving." Moss lifted a plastic water bottle from the table.

"There's smoke in the air," Aragon said. "I don't know about running."

He smiled and pulled a blue face mask from his shorts. His soles squeaked on the tile floor as he jogged the hallway toward the stairs.

Aragon said, "I'd like to hear about the scene."

Rivera turned to the forensic people, Salas and Barone. "Who wants to go first?"

"I'll go," Salas said. "Phil's still catching up. There's a million latents on the dumpster. We isolated Gray's, the college student who found her, and the first officers on the scene. But there's untold others we can't identify. We're sorting the garbage, for what it's worth. If you want to help, come to the warehouse. We'll suit you up for the fun. I can tell you right now—unless they're inside something, we don't have Cassandra Baca's phone or the gun."

"We've been pinging the phone," Tucker said. "It's off or destroyed."

Rivera walked to a dry-erase board and picked up a marker. "We have several lines of inquiry." He headed one column *Daniel Breskin and flowers*.

"I like that one," Tucker said. "I'll tell you why when it's my turn."

"This connection with Benny Silva and his brother." Rivera used *Silva* to start another column.

"Silva gets us back to our original investigation into Judge Diaz," Aragon said. "He has a case in front of her. Joe Mascarenas says her behavior appears odd, the way she's sitting on a motion for new trial. What if Silva knew about the parties at Diaz's house? His brother knows Dolores Baca, her hustling background. Andrea ending up in one of his dumpsters—what if it was a message to Diaz?"

"What kind of message?" Tucker asked.

"We don't know. If Diaz denies the motion for new trial, no reason to be suspicious. But if she hands down a ruling that's squirrely, we look closer."

"I agree we take a look," Rivera said. "What's Silva's case about?"

"About nine million dollars. Rick, you read the trial transcript."

Lewis took it from Aragon. "He had an old building by the Rail Yard. Next door, this Hollywood mogul named Jeremiah Kohn was building an editing facility so movies filmed in Santa Fe needn't be shipped back to LA. Vandals broke into the site, got hold of welding torches. Propane exploded, flames spread to Silva's building, burned it to the ground. The allegation was no reasonable person would have left welding supplies and propane tanks unsecured."

"How did the jury get to nine mil?"

"One of his daughters was inside the building. There was almost no defense case. A long witness list, but few called. The jury returned a million in property damage, two million for the daughter's life. Not much for a wrongful death in Santa Fe. That was about the only defense the jury heard, how the Silva woman was a junkie, already close to dead, washed out of every rehab in northern New Mexico. The rest came in punitives. Lawyers for the insurance company say there was jury tampering, witnesses were run off. A key witness maybe murdered, but no body to back that claim. Their investigators claim they have new evidence the fire was intentionally set. Defendants want a retrial."

"It was Thornton corrupting Diaz," Tucker said. "Now it's some garbage man. I think the roses guy is a better lead."

"Run with it," Rivera said. "You looked into Daniel Breskin."

"He's a big deal in virtual reality. You wear goggles and ear plugs that thrust you into another world. His breakthrough was using the technology to help surgeons, let them virtually walk through the body, step around a tumor, see it from all sides. His company is selling shovels and picks to the virtual reality gold rush. Every headset has his technology inside. His latest venture is a New Mexico company called the Real Deal. I'd like voucher approval to Las Vegas to investigate his company's product line thoroughly."

"What's in Las Vegas?"

"The Adult Entertainment International Expo, where he is right now. Real Deal is incorporating real girls into the imagery, photographing them from every angle, every sex position you can think of. And those maybe you can't. They've been advertising on Craigslist and Backpage for models instead of using established talent. They want a warehouse of unknown faces so every experience is new to the user."

"That could explain the twenty thousand under the cars outside Cassandra Baca's house," Aragon said. "An even twenty grand, in large bills. Not what you'd expect from turning tricks."

"Why did Breskin come to New Mexico?" Lewis asked. "Like our state needs this."

"Real Deal is bragging how its profitability will exceed California porn houses because New Mexico taxpayers are going to kick back expenses for filming here, as well as waiving gross receipts taxes. Direct investments by the state are governed by a kind of morality code. Not so for other film subsidies and the tax waiver."

"But the dumpster," Aragon said. "It's miles from his house, outside the circles that transplants travel in Santa Fe. And why kill her? Something get out of hand?"

"It's on the way to the Santa Fe airport, where his jet was waiting to take him to Vegas. The FAA has him leaving the morning Cassandra Baca was found dead."

———————

Daniel Breskin. They looked at photos on Tucker's laptop. Breskin in a sanitary bunny suit in a factory making headsets. Breskin at the New York Stock Exchange, his company going public. Breskin on the web page for the adult entertainment expo, his chubby cheeks framed between two women, naked shoulders, a suggestion there was nothing off-screen covering the rest of them. The seminar was entitled, *And You Thought The Internet Was Big.*

"Now you can explain the porn on your computer," Aragon said.

"Case-related research," Tucker said. "We can catch him if we hop the next Southwest to Vegas. I'd be glad to search for him in the private party suites."

He clicked the site's tab for *parties* and brought up a display of still shots for events labeled *no clothes*, *BDSM demo*, and *fan appreciation*, each advertised by at least one woman in very little or no clothing.

"You volunteer to go," Aragon said.

"Selfless service to the Bureau."

"Not going to happen, Agent Tucker," Rivera said. "Find out where Breskin hangared his plane. We'll meet him at the airport, where we won't be distracted."

Tucker disappeared into his computer. Aragon was glad for the break in the flood of energy pushing them at Daniel Breskin.

"This started," she said, "as an investigation of judicial corruption. We have to nail Cassandra Baca's killer. That jumps to the top of the list. But we're losing focus on what got us here."

"Fager hasn't lost focus," Lewis said. "He called again from prison. I guess we're becoming buddies."

"No one else will take his collect calls," Aragon said.

"Worth the loose change. The latest: we're interested in Benny Silva, and according to Fager, so is Marcy Thornton."

"Crap. So close." Tucker closed his laptop. "Breskin left Vegas. He's headed to Seattle. Someone else can go. I hate rain."

"Rain," Lewis said. "What's that?"

THIRTEEN

"You did a good job for my boy," Frank Pacheco told Marcy Thornton. "He paid for his dope in my car, but not the gun I forgot in the glove box. That would have killed me, him doing time because I got sloppy. Sure I'll tell you about Benny Silva. Meet me at the Railyard for the tour."

"Why can't you just tell me?"

"Seeing is believing."

None of her guys in jail would give her anything on Benny Silva. The conversation ended when they realized she hadn't reached out to talk about their own case. Frank Pacheco's kid had come to mind, a case she had taken for no cash up front. Instead Pacheco had brought a van full of guns to her office, with a gun dealer waiting to give her a price. She didn't know old shotguns and rifles could be worth that kind of money.

His son, Chucky, had been pulled over DUI. Snort in his pocket, Dad's nine in the glove box. He was looking at ten years with the weapons enhancement. Marcy had another client who once owed her money. She tore up the bill outside the courthouse when he finished testifying he'd been riding with Frankie, stuck his Glock in the glove box when he went into the post office, it being a federal crime to carry in there. Sorry, man, he said, looking at Chucky at the defense table, putting this on you.

She had Chucky ready, a friend accepting the apology, grateful tears welling up from deep inside, though the two had never met before that day in court.

She sat in her Aston in a parking lot at the Railyard, worried about leaving her car there, when Frank Pacheco arrived in a Dodge Charger. The passenger stepped out, a short, wide guy with a shaved head. He walked with his feet wide apart, telegraphing each step with his hip. He opened the trunk, Frank popping it from inside, and came over with a folding lawn chair.

"I'll be watching your car." He set up and pulled a paperback from his back pocket. He was sitting in full sun, his scalp baking. He looked perfectly comfortable.

The passenger seat was still warm. Pacheco, not taking his hands from the wheel, said, "You always had the sweetest rides. I didn't want you worrying."

On the back of one hand she read *WSL*, each letter on a different finger, not including his pointer. That was gone. The letters on the other three stood for West Side Locos, Pacheco's gang coming up. When he turned the wheel as he steered out of the parking lot she saw what was on the four fingers of his other hand: *Loko*. The graffiti moniker West Side Locos used to save spray paint. Or bullets, when they announced themselves that way.

He was saying he'd always remember what she did for his son. Chucky got out early on good time, married, and left Santa Fe to find work in North Dakota.

"Oil fields. A gun charge would have closed doors. So many guys have dope on their sheet, it don't matter long as they're pissing pure now, they can't find enough men for the jobs. He's got a kid on the way, a good wife, a *gringa*. She's been driving heavy trucks, pulling down one sixty a year. Between them they're making like a quarter mil, and living in a single wide that smells. Formaldehyde, one of the tin cans FEMA used in Katrina. The Bakken, what they call that oil country up there, so crazy that's the only rental they could find. Costs as much as a condo in Santa Fe. Here's the first stop on your Benny Silva tour."

"It's a church."

"With a graveyard. None of Benny Silva's enemies in there."

"Why show me this?"

"They're not in any graveyards. None of those funerals with everybody wearing tees with dearly departed's face, birthday, and death date. No business for undertakers, no viewings, nobody buying flowers, balloons. People bringing balloons to funerals? Sure they say something. We love you, Daddy. Miss you, Mijo. But balloons, shit."

"I'm not getting this."

"His enemies don't get buried. They disappear. No bodies turning up when the bulldozers push new houses into the mesa. No bears digging up bones in the mountains. No skull washing out of an arroyo after a good rain. I hear Benny Silva makes people disappear for a fee, but you have to approach him just right. People who make the wrong first impression ... "

He was back in traffic, now heavy, heading south away from the center of town.

"How come I haven't heard of him before?"

"He hasn't required the services of members of your profession. He's never been busted. Not him, not his twin brother. Here, look at that."

They'd turned off one of the six-lane roads carrying traffic through Santa Fe into a narrow street, chain-link fences between sidewalks and yards, statues of the Virgin by front doors of single-story stucco houses.

"Look at what?"

"I'll come back around." He drove to the end of the block, pulled into a concrete driveway, reversed. Coming back up the street he said, "The house with the Oldsmobile in front of the garage. Look close."

"I don't see anything. It's a house, like the other dumps."

"Exactly. That's the Benny Silva residence. All his life he's lived there. Nothing special, not showing off with remodeling, putting in grass, a fancy car out front. He's got a different approach to transportation needs than you with your Rolls Royce."

Aston Martin. She let it go. Pacheco said, "Go up to ring the bell, I bet you'll find 'I listen to Catholic radio' stickers on the door. '*Mi casa es su casa*,' one of those clay things you hang on the wall. But no fake ADT stickers like everyone else. You don't hit the Silva residence."

"He's not showing it, or he doesn't have it?"

They returned to heavier traffic, still moving south. He took another small street past a corner store called "La Tiendita."

"Benny's?" Thornton asked and Pacheco nodded.

After a couple miles on a busy street he said, "That lot on your left, where people leave their cars for sale with a number to call."

"Looks like a bad investment."

"Where's the next MacDonald's, the Starbucks going? Until then that lot's zoned agricultural, hardly no taxes. You see any farming happening?"

After another block he said, "That liquor store, on the right." A run-down white building, portable sign by the street, Bud on special. "In his wife's name. Safest liquor store in northern New Mexico. Never been robbed. We're getting close."

Again they were off the busy streets, two blocks back, warehouses, metal buildings, houses squeezed in here and there.

"You're seeing it now. All of this. E. Benny Silva Enterprises, he calls his business. He bought when the previous owners disappeared, a couple Jewish guys from Long Island, thought they'd buy up south Santa Fe, wait for the city to come to them. Actually, I got that wrong. He bought it right before they disappeared. Heard he got a hell of a deal. There's the corporate headquarters."

Razor wire around a scrap yard. Pickups loaded with metal and cardboard backed up to industrial scales. A cinder-block building, only the front painted, surrounded by storage bins holding tin, aluminum, iron pipe and copper wire. Through a section of fence she saw portable toilets like soldiers at attention, uniforms of blue and white, in formation, going back into the yard toward a metal building.

Another Olds in front, to the side of the front door, the one she'd seen outside her office, same tennis ball on the bumper hitch.

"He likes Oldsmobiles," Thornton said. "The other one his wife's?"

Pacheco grunted something and drove down the side of the lot to the next intersection, the razor wire out his window.

"What do you do with a dead horse, a cow killed on the road, all those deer busting windshields? Those dogs half-crushed you see on highways, somebody does go around picking them up. E. Benny Enterprises has the contract to run it through a thing called a tissue digester, mix in some nasty chemicals, suck it out of the tank, and take it in his honey dippers to the sewage treatment plant. Taxpayers built the thing, seeing the pressing need for something like this. Benny was close to some legislators at the time, like that one just got back from the federal jail in Florence, Colorado."

Thornton rolled down her window. A strong chemical smell in the air that wouldn't be tolerated in any other Santa Fe neighborhood.

Pacheco said, "A truck loaded with pigs flipped over. State police and game wardens had to shoot those that weren't killed. Like a couple tons of bacon, ribs, and hocks. A mountain of menudo. Benny's machine ate it all. Someone started calling the thing El Puerco."

"The pig."

"Thing never worked when the state was putting millions into it. Benny bought it for scrap. Somehow he made it work. Maybe he plugged it in, something they didn't think of."

"Do you know this building he had that burned? He had a big lawsuit, nine million dollars coming his way if the verdict holds up?"

"The one where he recycled his junkie daughter? You want to see that next?"

FOURTEEN

CAMINO HIGH'S MCRAE CALLED in the morning and said they should watch the new reports on Cassandra Baca's murder again. He'd been watching for Star Salazar. She'd been truant for a week. But she was in the broadcasts, in the background, behind other students talking about Cassandra, what a special girl she was, how they're handling someone they know, their own age, getting killed.

SFPD's Public Information Officer regularly Tivo'd news broadcasts. They called McRae and told him to come over. Watching the television in the PIO's office, he said, "That's her," and Lewis froze the screen.

"That is one rough-looking teenager."

"I'm wondering if that's the friend Lily described, the one sitting at Pizza Hut who wanted in on the party," Aragon said.

"What party?" McRae asked.

"Something we're looking into."

"I've been forgetting," McRae said. "Here's those lists. This is Cassandra's circle of friends. Not very big. It was Star Salazar she hung with. And here's Star Salazar's home address and friends that I know of. Right there"—he got up from his chair and touched the television screen—"is one of them. Abel Silva, Jr. Goes by Junior."

Aragon looked closely at the boy. "Who's his father?"

"Uh, Abel Silva."

"I know, stupid question. Where did we see that name?" Aragon looked hard at Lewis until he jutted his jaw and nodded. "You remember seeing it, too," she said.

"Be right back," Lewis said. "I need a computer."

Aragon replayed the videos, this time concentrating on Star Salazar and Abel Silva, Jr. They came in together and stood by a chainlink fence. There, they talked to each other. Junior had Star's arm in his hand, pulling her away.

Lewis returned and said, "Abel Silva is a director of E. Benny Silva Enterprises."

"The dumpster people," McRae said. "And the porta johns. They had a contract during construction on the school's new wing. Now that I think on it, Junior was coming to school in the trucks."

"We tackle Star Salazar first," Aragon said.

"Like I said, she's been truant for a week."

"But she came back for this." Aragon hit play and watched Star Salazar moving into and out of the shot.

———

"We should have video of Cassandra and Star meeting with Montclaire," Aragon said after McRae left. "Why's it taking so long?"

She called Rivera and caught him on his way to Breskin's home with follow-up questions for Sun-Hi.

"Where's Tucker on the Pizza Hut video?" she asked. "That's fallen through the cracks while he's looking at porn."

"I'll see him later."

"He's not with you?"

"I was near the Breskin place and thought I'd get this done. I'm here at the gate. Later."

That was rushed. And he was alone. She thought FBI agents always had to go out with someone else, either another agent or another cop, like when she and Rivera had talked to Mrs. Breskin the first time. She asked Lewis about that.

"Maybe it's new," he said. "The FBI is recording interviews now. Used to be they needed two agents to confirm the written account."

But why did Rivera seem rushed? No, not rushed. Anxious, wanting to get through the gate and up the hill to the gleaming white house looking down on mud-brown Santa Fe.

On I-25 heading to Glorieta Pass she looked for Breskin's house, a white cube against the purple and green of the Sangre de Cristo Mountains.

"You think there's anything to the Breskin angle?"

Lewis, at the wheel, shrugged his shoulders. "If your instinct about the roses is right, yes. If not, it's just face-time with some of Santa Fe's elite, the ones we only meet when we stop their Maseratis racing down St. Francis."

"I keep thinking about Daniel Breskin bringing the future of porn here. We're always talking how there's no jobs for our kids. When the politicians threw millions at the movies, funded film courses at the community college, they missed seeing this coming. How's it work, as long as they hire local talent they get taxpayer subsidies?"

"Local talent," Lewis said. "Is that what Cassandra Baca was?"

———

Lily Montclaire stood by the corral, red and black cowgirl boots on her feet, an orange hunting vest hanging off her shoulders, holding a seven-by-seven elk rack. Aragon looked closer and saw the heavy set of antlers was propped on a tripod masked as sagebrush. Serena was moving around snapping photographs with Javier's big camera. Aragon and Lewis drew close enough they couldn't miss the scoped rifle against the corral behind Montclaire.

Montclaire tried on different hats: ten-gallon, Aussie bush, a plaid ear-flap cap, a baseball cap saying *Loco Lobo Outfitters*. She was wearing a western-style denim shirt, the top pearl snaps undone, showing breastbone under skin. A Leatherman that Aragon knew wasn't hers hung off her belt.

"Look through the antlers," Serena said. "Put your face in there and give us a big smile."

"I have to ask …" Aragon stood behind Serena now, seeing what she was seeing, Montclaire's long fingers wrapped around the antlers, pulling her head into the space between the points. "What's going on?"

"We're working." Click. Serena dropped to a knee. Click. "There, give us a delirious smile, you've just bagged the biggest bull in the Rocky Mountains, you're giddy. Make sure you're not blocking the rifle. One step to your left." Click. "For the catalog. You know how many women are calling us?" Click. "I've been telling Javier we need more than beefy guys with bloodstained camos. The gun mags have the T&A girls looking sexy with an AR-15. That's not our market.

But a very good-looking middle-aged woman who reminds you of someone in underwear ads you stared at growing up, maybe kept you company in the bathroom with Mom banging on the door, someone you'd see now in a Filson's or L.L. Bean—she's perfect. Lily, get the rifle for these next ones."

"No, don't get the rifle," Aragon said. "I don't want her handling any weapons. If she were on bail, it would be prohibited. She's only here because we're holding off charging her."

Montclaire backed out of the antlers and came around, looking good in tight jeans, her long hair loose under the Loco Lobo cap. She had a walk Aragon hadn't seen before. A slow, sexy strut.

"Where'd she get the boots?"

"They're mine," Serena said. "We are on better terms since Javier went out scouting. She's been working hard, and we got talking about her career. It was her suggestion. I think it's brilliant."

Montclaire was with them now. It was the first time Aragon had seen her without a load of makeup. Lines in the corners of her eyes and mouth, skin a little too soft under the chin, a better idea of her age up close.

"Brilliant," Aragon said, "unless she's in witness protection. The idea is to, you know, to hide. Lily, wait for us in your bunkhouse. We have some things to discuss." She watched Montclaire walk away, Lewis close behind her, eyes on her rolling hips. In a softer voice, "That thing I asked, a glass, silverware she used?"

"Bagged in the house."

"Would you put it in the car while we're talking? I don't want Lily to see."

"Are you going to tell me what it is she did?" Serena removed the zoom lens from the camera. "She's nice, but different. Wanna tell me how different?"

"She was working for someone, doing their bidding. On her own, she's what you see, a washed-up fashion model with not much upstairs, someone used to other people telling her how to act."

"We talked about that. She said she's been groomed by everyone she's ever known."

"I wouldn't have parked her here if she was any danger to you."

"She's a danger to herself. You should have seen her on the wood splitter."

———————

"Why is it we can't find Andrea's Backpage ad? Tell us again what it said."

Aragon on a sagging bed in what was called the Upper Pecos bunkhouse, the one farthest from the family home. Lily's hairbrush and ear rings on the dresser under framed photos of men with dead animals: a mountain lion, blood on snow under the body, bull elk so big men sat on them, a mule-tail deer cradled in a happy hunter's arms, its neck limp, the antlers down against his hip.

"'Your dreams now,'" Montclaire said, facing her from the other bed, their knees almost touching. "'Here come your dreams.' Get it? Something like that."

"Before you said, 'Dreams *al instante*.'" That's how you knew she was going to be Hispanic."

"There wasn't a picture of a face, just like the side of legs, the top of her chest. No cleavage. She didn't have much there. Maybe I was looking around before I found hers and I'm thinking of other ads I saw."

"Great," Lewis said. He stood at the foot of the bed, a shoulder against the wall, his size blocking off the rest of the room. "You're not helping us narrow it down."

Aragon said, "Tell us about this girl that was with Andrea at Pizza Hut. First, let me ask, did you ever hear the name Cassandra Baca?"

Montclaire pushed her lips off her teeth, her way of showing she was thinking. "No."

"Okay." Aragon thinking, we'll stick with Andrea. No reason yet to let Montclaire know the girl's real name. "Andrea's friend. Describe her. What was she wearing? Tattoos, what did she say? Was she older than Andrea?"

"She was older, like a senior in high school. I focused on the nose ring. I hate those things. I don't remember tattoos. Wait, she had some writing on her hands but I don't remember what it said. Clothes were nothing to brag about, a sweatshirt pulled up on bony arms. Greasy hair, brown eyes. Hard eyes, that struck me, a young woman with eyes I'd see in Marcy's clients."

"You hear a name?"

"Sorry."

"She was there when you arrived?"

"Sitting in a booth across from Andrea. I squeezed in next to Andrea."

"Did she leave before you?"

"We left together. She paid, I remember. Or put down some change for a tip."

"Did she say anything?"

"Just nodded when Andrea introduced me."

"But didn't introduce her?"

"She would have, wouldn't she? I guess I didn't catch the name. I just wanted to get Andrea and get going."

"Detective Lewis and I are going to step outside for a second."

Under the trees away from the bunkhouse, Lewis said, "She's lying."

Aragon picked at the bark on a ponderosa. A piece broke loose and fell to the pine needles at her feet. "She slipped into that same tone of voice when she started telling us about the parties. Her voice is light when she's talking about easy things. It sort of goes back in her mouth on dark stuff, like two people in there debating which one's coming out to play."

"She's made it almost impossible for us to track down the ad that connected her with Cassandra Baca. We'd have to run through all of them, take out the elegant ebonies, thick cuties, the foxy forties ... "

"You're spending too much time with this."

"Damn, I want to say Andrea when talking about this stuff. Cassandra Baca is the pretty girl in the school photos, not the one placing escort ads."

"Me too. That was someone else in the dumpster." Aragon picked at another edge of loose bark. "We're going to ID the friend once Tucker gets video. I know its Star Salazar. I don't want to come back to Montclaire on this until we can nail it down. Meantime, let's check Star's juvie file. It should describe the writing on her hand, unless that's very recent."

"The Juvenile Detention Center does a full-body inspection when admitting kids. So that's it for Lily today?"

Aragon looked around the homestead under the trees. "I want to get her out of here. But unless I lie to Rivera that Lily's being completely forthcoming, witness protection is a ways off. Do you think it's safe to send her home?"

"Where's Dolores Baca? That's my answer."

———

At the autopsy, Nate Moss took a guess that the little lead slugs recovered inside Cassandra Baca's skull were .25 caliber. He was right. A quick ballistics analysis at the State Crime Lab confirmed it. They were now working on identifying the weapon that fired two bullets through hair and skull.

Aragon had her own guess.

"Beretta Bobcat," she said. "It's the only .25 I've ever seen. For the same size and weight you can go up to a .32 or .380. I haven't seen a new .25 on sale anywhere in a long time."

"I never liked those guns," Lewis said. "That weird tip-up barrel, it bothers me. That small round, even if you shot someone center of mass, they could still go for your gun. Grab it so the barrel can't pop up, you won't get another round in the chamber."

"But a shot behind the ear does the trick. Two, for sure. Good for sneak attacks."

They asked Salas to catalog other shootings with a .25 caliber handgun just to have the information on hand. Salas couldn't recall one off the top of her head but she'd look into it. They hadn't heard from Rivera about his follow-up interview with Sun-Hi Breskin. But Tucker finally had something other than screen shots of Daniel Breskin and porn stars.

He set two chairs before a monitor. The image had been paused. When it rolled they saw the inside of a Pizza Hut like every other in the country. The camera was pointed at the front, to the door next to the cash register.

"This doesn't help," Aragon said. "They were in a booth in the back."

"Hold on," Tucker said. "They came through this door."

And there was Lily Montclaire.

"When was this taken?"

"This is this past Monday, before the last party. Now I'm backing it up. I believe this will be Cassandra Baca."

The images dissolved, stabilized, then moved forward in time, people using the door, families, delivery men gathering orders. Then Cassandra Baca, someone holding the door from the outside. Then came the person connected to the hand on the door. A thin young Hispanic woman with a nose ring and matted hair.

"Back that up," Aragon said, "to where the door's held open. There. Can you move us closer, focus on that hand?"

Tucker pressed the remote, the shot tightened. He was too low. He moved the focus up. There was the hand on the door.

Letters across the knuckles said *Star*.

FIFTEEN

Star Salazar's mother told them get off her property, a stucco house at the back of a fenced acre lot that had sprouted additional homes and trailers through generations of the family. Lewis said housing inspectors must have overlooked this place. Aragon said, let's get out of here before those dogs climb that fence. We shoot a pit bull coming for our knees, it will be worse than Ferguson.

Using McRae's list, they ran down two of Cassandra Baca's friends. They were both pretty girls, Hispanic, dark curly hair, unblemished skin, budding figures. They got a repeat of what other kids said in front of the cameras outside Camino High. Aragon wanted to know about the fuzzy tattoo of a sports car on one girl's hip that appeared from under her shirt when she crossed her arms. She said it was nothing. Aragon made a point of asking the second girl if she had any tattoos. She said maybe, she wasn't going to show them. Can you at least tell us what it is? A Jag.

Aragon felt electricity across her shoulder blades. They were getting close to something though both denied knowing Star Salazar.

156

Aragon called McRae. He knew the girls and knew they hung with Star Salazar. Two more she'd saved from getting beat up behind the auditorium. They'd been back-to-back in a closing circle when Star Salazar stepped in and it was over.

Lewis and Aragon returned to the Salazar compound for another try. The gate was closed, three pit bulls and a Rotty running loose behind the chain-link, no one answering Lewis leaning on the horn.

"I need to look away from this for a while," Aragon said, "My Krav Maga class starts in an hour. I'll get with you later."

He took her to her car. She had her gym bag and protective gear in the trunk: shin and forearm guards, a face mask/helmet combo, and a groin protector she learned once never to forget. It wasn't only men who doubled over from a kick between the legs and still felt it a week later.

They hadn't taught Krav Maga at the Academy. She'd first heard of it from female officers in Albuquerque looking for alternatives to tasing or shooting large male assailants. Now Krav Maga was helping cops handle the growing number of criminals using mixed martial arts they saw in televised fights.

She was surprised how naturally moves illegal inside any boxing ring came to her. That's what she liked about Krav Maga, more than jiu jitsu, karate, kung fu. The moves were already inside her, in tune with her natural reflexes, including running away when that was the smart thing to do. "The Nike defense," her group of fighters called it.

She didn't need to be bowing to any sensei. She wasn't after elegance of movement. Forget the "art" in martial arts. This wasn't sport. What she needed was learning how to stay on her feet in a street fight where there were no rules, no limits, no umpires—no elegance—and any weapon could and would be used.

At five-two, even with more muscle than many male officers, Aragon needed help. With a larger, stronger man going for a choke-hold or a straight arm bar, she'd be in trouble no matter how much she could bench press. But an eye gouge would stop anyone. If he was too powerful, crushed her in a grip where she was seconds from passing out, she'd bite off his face.

Teeth were a weapon she'd always have.

Teeth marks.

Cassandra Baca's inner thigh.

Buccal cells.

Pain.

She staggered from a roundhouse kick she hadn't seen coming. An advancing side kick drove her back. A front kick to the gut had her on her toes. He did that again, she'd be against the wall. She forced everything out of her mind except the man in front, his eyes above a pink slash, the color of his mouth guard. He cocked his foot. She reached out with her right hand past the rising kick, avoiding giving him an angle to strike and stun her forearm. The kick came. She plucked it, pulling herself forward, bursting in with foot strikes. A fist to the side of his neck. He wavered backwards on a stiff leg. She angled a slap kick straight into his knee and stopped with the instep of her foot touching the locked joint.

He said, "You always make me think what it would be like not to walk. I need to put you down with the first strike."

"Not gonna happen. Unless you shoot me."

Looking away for just those seconds made her see something she'd missed.

She showered, changed back into street clothes, and drove to the dirt alley where the dumpster had been parked. She saw lights in some of the condemned trailers, people using lanterns instead of

158

electricity. In the distance, the fire in the mountains had grown during the hot day. Flames had moved down slopes and were creating their own winds. Walls of smoke larger than the mountains themselves blocked the light of lower stars. Right now, Albuquerque was getting it. Air quality alerts had been issued, soccer matches and baseball games cancelled, school recess was being held indoors.

T-bar posts that had held crime scene tape were gone. She walked in circles with her flashlight sweeping the hard ground until she found it. When she brushed her hand along its rough surface, she picked up tiny splinters on the palm of her hand.

She called Lewis.

"I found what Cassandra Baca was lying on. That piece of plywood the locals put down to avoid walking over mud. Get a van out here. This thing's too big for my car."

———————

Thornton's deposition on tap tomorrow. Thornton had sued her and everyone on the Cody Geronimo case hoping to shake loose a settlement from the state's Risk Management Division. She should get some sleep. But the rush of the fight on the mat stayed with her.

After the plywood board had been removed to SFPD's evidence room, Aragon swung by Walmart and bought a self-stick easel pad flipchart. In her apartment she wrote down everything they had in each line of inquiry: Thornton/Diaz, Silva, Breskin, and a new column for Star Salazar. The sheets went onto windows, doors, refrigerator. She took down photos of her deceased parents, Javier and Serena and their kids to make room. Where she saw connections, she drew lines across walls. The place needed a painting anyway.

One of the things she saw was the need to know where Cassandra Baca went every time she was returned to the Pizza Hut by Montclaire. The place to start was finding the route she would have walked home. Montclaire said she'd tried following but lost Cassandra crossing a dark lot.

Aragon parked at the Pizza Hut and scanned the area for security cameras Tucker may have missed. She didn't see any. She straightened her Springfield .40 caliber in the back of her belt. Then she set out.

She crossed busy Cerrillos, seeing Cassandra, drained and sore, a little drunk, rushing across the six lanes of headlights to the other side. She found what may have been the dark lot where Montclaire had lost her. On the other side was a fence topped with razor wire that didn't make sense. It didn't enclose anything. Following it to the left led to a residential street amid warehouses and small factories. To the right she came to a busy four-lane street.

Aragon consulted her GPS for the most direct route to the Baca house. It was along the busy street. Men in cars shouted out of windows at her, a woman alone where no one else walked this time of night. One car doubled back and slowed, close to the curb, four heads inside, now almost stopping.

"Get moving." She held out her badge, in just enough light for them to see. Her other hand was under her shirt in the back, hand curled around her pistol.

Men she couldn't see cursed. The car moved on, loud music trailing after it. Cassandra Baca wouldn't have driven them off like that. There were still two miles along this road before the route home turned onto quieter streets. Cassandra did not get home this way.

Aragon returned to the dark lot and followed the fence into the neighborhood squeezed among industrial buildings. She reached the end and walked a narrow street without any street signs at intersections. She reached another high chain-link fence. Dogs snarled behind a locked gate. She shined her flashlight and saw teeth and gums. Beyond were trailers and small stucco houses crowded onto the same lot, nothing marking any property division between them.

She'd seen this place in daylight. Star Salazar lived here.

SIXTEEN

Thornton didn't ask a single question relevant to her lawsuit. She used the courtroom deposition, held with Judge Diaz presiding, to ask where Lily Montclaire was.

"The witness will answer. Reread the question."

Judge Diaz nodded at the stenographer, a heavy guy in a rumpled suit, purple Crocs over Argyle socks. He backed up, past Diaz's ruling, Thornton's argument, Fager's objection. Fager, on a bring-down from Diaz, representing himself in his red jail jumpsuit.

The stenographer located the question: "Detective, do you know where Lily Montclaire is?"

Aragon scowled at the person who was supposed to be her attorney, a contract lawyer in a pants suit and flat shoes from Risk Management. She'd been doodling when Thornton veered off into Montclaire's whereabouts. Aragon had told her ahead of time to object, shut the goddamn thing down if they got to Montclaire. *This is discovery*, the contract lawyer told her. *Wide-ranging inquiry is the rule. We'll have our turn.*

She was still doodling. Fager, her only hope, was back in his seat.

"Yes," Aragon answered. She had no choice.

Thornton covered the distance from counsel table, eyes locked on Aragon's.

"Where is she?"

"In a safe place."

Thornton folded her arms. "Where precisely, using an address, a geographical location, would that be?"

"In the mountains east of here."

"The mountains 'east of here' run from Colorado to Mexico. Is she alone?"

"She might be on a mule. Is that alone?"

"She's on a mule."

"Is that a question?"

Aragon raised her eyebrows at Fager. *Come on, object. Make a speech. Something.* What was he doing? Pulling papers out of an accordion file.

"Stop dancing around, detective," Judge Diaz. "Tell us precisely where Lily Montclaire is or I will hold you in contempt. You'll get to wear the women's counterpart of Mr. Fager's attire."

"She was at the Loco Lobo Outfitters ranch, outside Pecos. I don't know any street address. It's hard to get there."

"I can find it," Thornton said. "That concludes my questioning for now. This deposition remains open while I confirm Detective Aragon's information."

"Excuse me." Fager held sheets of paper ripped off a yellow legal pad. "Other parties have the right to examine the witness."

Diaz ruled by waving for him to proceed. He pushed up the sleeves of his red jumpsuit and came forward.

"Detective Aragon, you and I spoke about your investigation into my wife's murder, is that correct?"

"Correct."

"Did you at any time instruct me to take any specific action against Cody Geronimo?"

"No."

"Did you at any time direct me to enter onto his property?"

"No."

"Was I in any manner acting as your agent?"

"No."

"Who is E. Benny Silva?"

Diaz knocked over her glass. Water flowed across the bench into the witness dock. She rose out of her chair, slapping the front of her robe.

"Counsel, in chambers." Aragon's lawyer stood up. "Not you," Diaz said.

"But I'm counsel of record in this case."

"This is another matter. Just those two." Diaz pointed at Fager and Thornton before she disappeared through the door behind the bench. They looked at each other, then followed Diaz while Aragon's lawyer rushed into the hallway, digging her cell out of her purse and shouting, "I'm calling my supervisor."

Aragon helped the bailiff sop up the flood, using the tissues always there on a rail near the witness chair. It wasn't water. She licked a finger. The judge had filled her glass with vodka.

The bailiff saw her do that and shrugged. "She stays awake, at least. I had a judge, he'd doze off, his mouth open. This old lawyer would wave a hand in front of his face, snap his fingers. Yo, judge, you in there? The judge would sit bolt upright. 'Overruled!' he'd shout every time. 'Next question.' I had to make sure he only signed orders first thing in the morning, before the drawer with the bottle stayed open. You could put findings of fact in front of him, up is down, red is blue, he'd sign it you caught him at five."

With a tissue, Aragon picked up the overturned glass and dropped her hand to her side, below the rail. She set the glass out of sight on her chair. When the bailiff bent to drop wet tissues in a can, the glass went into the purse she'd carried over her shoulder to the stand.

The door to Diaz's chambers opened. Only Fager came out, shuffling along, trying to keep the loose plastic slippers on his feet. He'd gone in with pages from a legal pad and come out empty-handed.

"You're deposition is over," he said. "They've had their fun."

The stenographer was packing up.

"What happened back there?" Aragon asked.

"Diaz wanted to know how I knew about Benny Silva. I said I didn't, that's why I was asking. I told her Thornton's been calling the jail, asking around. I asked about Silva's new trial motion growing moss in Diaz's in-basket. Thornton told her, 'Judy, drop it.' Diaz didn't. Wanted to know what I knew about the new trial motion, had I talked to Benny Silva, was he a client? I reminded her I'm disbarred, then asked why she was so worked up. Thornton had her hands on Diaz's shoulders, Diaz's eyes bugging out at me. Made me glad I'd gone fishing with the Silva thing. I caught something big. That's when Diaz said the deposition was in recess and get my ass back to the Santa Fe Country Club."

Sheriff's deputies came into the room and stood behind Fager.

"'I have something for Ms. Thornton before I go,' I told Diaz. I gave Marcy copies of disciplinary complaints filed by nine of her clients, friends I've made in jail. I'd give you copies, but disciplinary proceedings are confidential. Okay, I'm ready, don't rush me."

The deputies pulled his arms behind his back, cuffs jangling as they snapped one wrist.

"The stuff on my table over there," Fager said. "Take care of it for me. These boys are in a hurry to hustle me back to Club Med."

At Fager's table, she saw a legal pad with words addressed to her: *Det. Aragon, Enjoy.*

Loose papers were slotted into pages of the legal pad. She pulled out copies of neatly handwritten documents, each headed *Disciplinary Complaint*, each accusing Marcy Thornton, each signed with a name followed by a prisoner identification number.

She took the glass from Thornton's table before following the deputies and Fager out of the courtroom.

————

Marcy Thornton sat across the coffee table in Diaz's chambers, Judy on the sofa, twisting long black hair round her fingers.

"Now the police will look into Benny Silva. Fager's always talking with them," Diaz said, eyes not really focused on anything. "I shouldn't have dragged things out." Was that a moan? "I got her killed."

"Stop," Thornton said. "Better. That's my girl."

"I should resign. Then they won't have any reason to blackmail me. I'll go to the police, tell them about the blackmail. We didn't know she was lying to us about her age. I admit what happened, take my licks, get on with life. We can practice law together. Civil rights, criminal defense." She tried a smile. It didn't hold. "It would be great."

"How many trials have you done?"

"Hundreds."

"As a lawyer, from start to finish, bringing clients in the door, investigating facts, on your feet examining witnesses? Lining up experts, digging through raw documents? Fighting idiot judges?"

"I went on the bench right out of law school. You know that."

"Keep your day job," Thornton said. "You quit and we have no leverage. That pending motion means Silva needs you with a gavel in your hand. He doesn't get his nine mil, that could make him crazy. He could send the video to reporters. He could put us in one of his dumpsters. Money does that to people. Take it from someone who hears the stories behind closed doors. But there is something you can do. Look at this." She tossed Fager's yellow pages onto the sofa. "Payback. One bitter loser, no problem. But he's got nine and he's only been at the prison a couple days. He's there much longer, I'll be buried."

"But you're a hell of a lawyer, Marcy. You knock yourself out for your clients. I've had a front row seat."

"Two-tiered pricing, two-tiered service. I can't give every client my Johnny Cochrane tap dance. I have to make adjustments, allocate scarce resources. These guys being guilty is the best defense to a malpractice claim. What are the damages? Hell, they did it, they deserve jail. But a coordinated onslaught of disciplinary complaints, that goes to *my* conduct. Nothing to do with what scumbags these men are."

"What can I do? I need you helping me with Silva, not getting eaten alive in disciplinary hearings." Diaz twisted hair around a finger. "I had another e-mail from him. It was a photo of the front of my house. I didn't sleep last night. I haven't slept since I saw the photo of Andrea."

"You haven't been sober much, either. You've been drinking today."

"Only water. And coffee.

"Sure. Give Walter Fager a get-out-of-jail-free card, you want to do something useful."

"Turn him loose?"

"Just get him out of there."

———

At your service, Marcy.

I thought I was the one who issued orders. *Just get him out of there.* Like, *don't screw up anything else, Judy. Because you have "The Honorable" in front of your name, don't think you know what the hell you're doing.*

What I had to do—Judy Diaz wanting to see herself standing, shaking a finger at Thornton—to get to be chief judge, sucking up to the old boys, waiting for them go senior status or drop dead at the their desks. Earning favors in ways I don't want to talk about. Watching you and other classmates post pictures of second homes in Baja, condos in Telluride on your Facebook pages, each of you pulling down more in a good month more than I make in a year.

Because of me. My rulings. Awarding top dollar for attorney fees, approving those cost petitions, denying motions to reduce jury awards so you could scoop your forty percent out of a bigger pot.

For you, Marcy, granting those motions to suppress, reducing bail, throwing out cases for speedy trial violations, granting discovery requests to grind the prosecution into the ground. Mistrials for the asking.

What I had to do to get the party's nomination for that first run for the bench, the September after law school—Marcy, you never asked. It wasn't the envelopes you handed over, cash from lawyers who wanted their support under wraps. You were upstairs in a courtesy lounge, having a time at the state convention. I was in the parking deck under the Eldorado with the man who was chief judge then, in his Lincoln Town Car, the corner away from the elevator, where it was dark.

I came upstairs, needing a drink bad. You took me round for introductions to lawyers from down south, never noticing I'd missed a button putting my shirt back on.

At your service, Marcy. You didn't get those anonymous e-mails, the videos showing what I've become, what the world will see if I don't sell the last scrap of my soul to keep it secret.

I got that girl killed, Lord forgive me.

I hear her laugh, her moans. Taste her. Smell her.

I see her lying dead on roses surrounded by garbage.

You brought her to me, Marcy. Into my house with a camera in her purse watching us, showing everything to men who now think they own me.

Never got out of that Towncar under the hotel. Damn, this bottle's empty. I know there's another around here. Fuck it. So I have a little vodka with my coffee.

Marcy, don't tell me what to do. It's all your fault.

————

"This must be Fager's handwriting on the disciplinary complaints. It's the same on every one of them. Hey, Judy, kiddo, you don't need that."

Plastic crackling and there she is opening a fresh bottle of Absolut, now filling a china tea cup.

"Doan tell mwat to do. Zure fault."

What the hell? She must have been drunk on the bench, couldn't have tied it on this quickly. Damn, she's pouring another.

I've seen enough prisoners' complaints not to take these things seriously. I'll have to put in the hours to respond, but I can handle it. When I question these men it'll be in a closed hearing. Fager won't be permitted in the room. He might be playing jailhouse lawyer now. Outside prison walls, he's just a disbarred attorney.

But Judy, what is she saying, blaming me for not checking out Andrea, getting her into this, putting her head on the chopping block? Jesus, she can put it away. That bottle's going down fast. Why didn't I notice before?

"I should just go to the poleesh. Get them to take out Benny Shilva. I'd get us a deal, we're helping. Providing material ashistance. I am the Chief fucking Judge."

Men shuffling in restraints bitching about doing time for their crimes—that's one thing. If I don't blow the complaints out of the water, hell, I'll get probation, have to report to a supervising attorney, nothing in my life really changing. We'll probably talk cases over steaks and Zin at the Bull Ring.

A suspension at worst. Six months. A year, max. Finally a vacation.

But Judy. She could put us both in jail.

SEVENTEEN

Abel called from the room with the televisions showing what the security cameras were seeing.

"That's them coming in now. Junior and Star. She's as nasty as he says."

Benny Silva looked up from the documents his lawyer had sent over. *Don't tell me I don't know garbage. I'm seeing it right here.* This lawyer was already including "Nine Million Dollar Verdict!" in his TV ads and he wasn't the one doing the hard work.

Benny went from his office and looked at the black and white image showing a trashed Jaguar, hood paint gone, plastic for one of the rear windows, pulling past the last gate, parking in the visitor slot. An unattractive, hell, an *ugly* young woman was driving. The sun sparkled on metal in her face when she got out of the car. Junior stood up from the passenger seat and winked at the camera.

She needs to wash her hair, Benny thought, cover those bony shoulders.

"Bring them around the back. I got the runner from my lawyer in the office, waiting for me to sign papers."

Benny returned to his desk and signed an affidavit to answer another motion in the new trial drama. The runner acted as a notary and Benny gave him a Silva Enterprises ball cap. He waited to see his car pass through the gates onto the street. Then Benny opened the door that led to the windowless room in the center of his cinderblock building.

Up close the young woman looked a little sick. Her color was off. Benny checked her arms. He'd seen this before, his own daughter killing herself. Sure enough, those were needle tracks, very old ones, on the inside of her elbow. His daughter switched at the end to sticking herself between toes. She got tired of Benny always grabbing her arm and turning the inside to the light. With this girl's color, he didn't need to tell her to take off her shoes to know she was still using the heroin.

Junior, already his father's height but minus fifty pounds, said, "Uncle Benny, this is my friend, Star."

"I like your name," Benny said. "There's that."

Star dragged fingers through her hair, each nail painted a different color. The black nails made him think she'd hit herself with a hammer.

"Joon said you might have a job I can do, pay me in cash. Hook me into something big."

"Losing Cassandra spooked her," Junior said.

"You already got work that pays in cash. Sit." Benny nodded at a straight-backed chair, the one the Indian who lost a foot had been in. He pushed it closer to the girl as Rigo entered the room.

Star looked at Rigo, then Benny, then back at Rigo.

"We're twins," Benny said. "Except for Rigo's distinguishing features."

"I never saw old-man twins." Now she was looking only at Benny. "I don't have any job that pays cash."

"Junior, what were you telling me?"

The boy stepped up. Benny could see he was proud to be part of this. Like his father, eager to learn, get his hands on things.

"Star runs girls. She'd stop beatings, chase away bullies, then turn the girls out. Called them the Jags, each getting a crappy tattoo of a Jaguar car on their hip. Cassandra Baca was one. She was doing a judge and a rich lawyer. Lady judge, lady lawyer. That's how Star could buy her own Jag."

"What did Cassandra tell you about the judge?"

Star stared at Junior. "You brought me here saying there was a job."

"There is a job," Benny said. "Look at me. We've got a machine out back that needs attention."

"I don't know shit about machines. That wasn't the kind of thing I thought this was about. I heard about you, you know. I want in."

"You can jump right in. Rigo and Abel will show you. Junior, you can learn, too. This machine, it's the key to this business. Star, I'm ready to feed you right into the heart of the operation if you're up to it. Sit down a while. Consider this your job interview."

Star scratched the back of a hand, letters there Benny couldn't read. She looked behind her and settled her narrow butt on the chair. She pinned her hands in her armpits and bent one leg along the side of the chair, toe pressed into the floor. Benny didn't like her heavy black boots with the two-inch waffle soles.

"She said they were weird, but they paid a lot of money. This last time, she wasn't sure she wanted to go back."

Benny stepped close to the chair, directly in front of her. The tip of his SAS comfort shoe touched her black boot.

"What last time?"

173

"A couple nights ago, right before she, you know. It was on TV."

"She went with the judge and lawyer again?"

"And the lady who picked her up at Pizza Hut. The one who called me."

Benny waved for a chair for himself. Abel brought one and Benny sat next to Star.

"That's something I never quite figured out, how Cassandra got with this judge. You knew the lady who took her?"

"She worked for the lawyer that did my brother's case."

"He shot a kid at a party," Junior said.

"She was the investigator. My brother, he was in jail, said to give her all the guns to give to his lawyer. She wanted to know if I knew any girls liked being with women, or wouldn't mind, what they were paying. That's how I hooked her up with Cassandra. I told her about the kind of money she could make and she said she didn't care."

Benny patted the knob of her knee. The girl could stand to eat a few combo plates. "Did you send this investigator any other girls?"

"No, only Cassandra. She was my best. She was okay, too. Nice. She kept herself pretty."

"This investigator. Was she tall, long arms and legs, a neck like Audrey Hepburn?"

"Who?"

"Never mind. Like a model."

"Oh, yeah, 'cept she's old."

"Abel and Rigo, show Star how that machine works. I'm done here."

"What's the job pay?" Star dragged her heavy black boots to the front of the chair and pushed to her feet. Her hands dug into pockets coming through tears in her jeans, not after anything. Just another place to put them. "Can I start today?"

"You can start right now. Give Junior your keys. He'll move your car around back while you learn the ropes."

"You didn't say what it pays."

"We'll see if you're up to the job first. You finished our interview. Now's the on-the-job training part, where you show the valuable contribution you can make to Silva Enterprises."

Rigo and Abel led her to the door, each taking an arm, bone under skin with that bad color that made him think of ashtrays.

Junior said to his uncle, "How come you never gave me that job? I need to get my own car."

"This kind of job ... " Benny moved the chairs from the middle of the room to a wall. He was thinking about how to put this when the phone started ringing. "Look, you want work that can take you places in life. This one, it goes nowhere. Move that car and catch up with your dad and grandpa. You'll see. Go ahead. I've got a call."

He picked up the phone. The call had come to his direct number, bypassing the number in the Dex for E. Benny Silva Enterprises, Waste Disposal, Recycling, and Sanitation Services. He was thinking who might have this number when he recognized the lawyer's voice saying she wanted to meet him.

"Come by my office," he said, remembering how she moved in the movies.

"Not a chance." A laugh in her voice the same time she was being serious, showing she was sure about things and enjoying herself, all of it, even the danger. Telling him, too, she knew some things about him and his office. Abel had said he thought he saw her circling the block with Frank Pacheco, someone they'd done business with off and on.

"I'll come to your office again," he said.

"I want people around. And I don't want anybody who knows me seeing us together."

"Something you want to keep between us. Tell me where."

"Moriarty."

"That's a drive."

"La Cantina de los Romeros."

"The state senator's restaurant? He's there, I'll introduce you."

"Maybe not. Down the street. Jenny's Truck Stop, I think it's called. It's got a big rig painted on the wall. Meet me at the café inside. I'm leaving now."

"You don't want people recognizing you, meet me at Juanita's on Airport Road. It's full of *mojados* don't know me neither. I don't like to drive so much at night. That's a long way, down and back."

"Divide the distance by nine million dollars. That's what you'll be making per mile."

————

"We've got an Abominable Snowman," Elaine Salas said to Lewis. She sized up Aragon. "What do we call you? A bunny with shoulders?"

Salas was in her own hooded white clean suit. She led them to the sheet of plywood from the dumpster site, now on saw horses inside the evidence room. Spotlights showed it in a pool of harsh white light. With the tip of a surgical knife, Elaine Salas touched a spot circled and marked "#1."

"I found the first tissue here," she said. Six other circles, with matching numbers, spanned the wood. "Tiny scrapings of skin snagged against the grain. I think we can confidently say how Cassandra Baca got those abrasions and splinters on her backside."

She pushed the knife into an unmarked spot on the board and flaked off a piece of wood.

"Plywood's made from particle and fiberboard. I doubt it will have any distinctive signature. But there's glue, waxes, and resins mixed with the fibers. That we can definitely identify with an electron microscope. We find it on the splinters in Cassandra Baca, and a DNA match with the skin on the board, we slide into home plate."

"On to the next question," Lewis said. "Why put her on a board?"

"The Abominable Snowman speaks," Aragon said.

"Why not just heave her into the dumpster?" Lewis tugged at the clean suit where it climbed his chest to pinch his Adam's apple. "It's a lot harder to raise a body on the board, keep it balanced, until you can tip it over the side."

"No splinters in her scalp, right?" Aragon rubbed the back of her own head through the clean suit's hood. "She had the Whole Foods shopping bag on her head when she slid down the board."

Salas wrote numbers on masking tape and stuck them on little packets with wood chips inside. "She went in head first or the bag would have come off. Nate Moss said there was a uniform angle of penetration to the splinters. That should answer it."

"We should get the drag dummy from the Academy," Lewis said. "Load it to Cassandra Baca's weight, get another board like this. See how it might have been done."

Aragon said, "Elaine, can you rig that for us? Something close to a dead body with arms and legs flopping around. A dead weight, as difficult to handle as the real thing."

"Balancing and lifting a body on a board," Lewis said. "We're talking pallbearers. We don't need an experiment to know one person couldn't do it."

"What if they didn't lift her from the ground, but were already higher, closer to the edge of the dumpster? They had her in the back of a pickup. That got the most votes last time we kicked this around."

Lewis said, "You see that a lot. Guys not wanting to scratch their truck. You cut a plywood sheet to fit. A cheap bedliner."

"But she slid off the board, in one direction," Salas said. "She didn't get those abrasions and splinters from rolling around. I would think it requires more force, sudden movement, for wood splinters to penetrate the skin."

Aragon held an edge of the board with white gloves, trying hard to imagine it with a body, raised level, carried to the edge of the dumpster, the end with the feet lifted so high Cassandra Baca slid off head first.

And not seeing it.

EIGHTEEN

THORNTON DROVE EAST FROM Santa Fe and took the US 285 exit south through a sprawling bedroom community. The houses were spread out, on large lots, no tight clusters of lights. Beyond that the night closed in. No houses or gas stations. Road signs coming up fast when her headlights hit them.

She slowed. Last thing she needed was a ticket placing her here on this night. She was driving the Durango. Taking the Aston Martin to a truck stop off I-40, she'd defeat the whole purpose of a hundred-twenty-mile round trip to meet unnoticed with Benny Silva.

Lily had asked her to buy the Durango for work. Her cute BMW three-series was losing its battles with washboard roads and two-tracks when she searched for witnesses on reservations and in the mountains north of Santa Fe. The mileage reimbursement wasn't covering the cost of a new front end every ten thousand miles.

The seats in this thing were huge compared to the Beemer, even the Aston. She'd needed time to get the driver's seat right. Lily had left it way back for her long legs. She had to take it all way to the shortest setting to reach the pedals. Then she needed a couple phone books under her to see over the dash.

Out of the darkness, a sign said "Stanley." For a village of seventy people—no, you couldn't call it that, just a few houses and farms spread wide apart—this place had turned out the state's longest-serving governor and an attorney general, and was the location of a billionaire's ranch. There were lots of very rich people in Santa Fe, but not billionaire sex offenders who chummed around with Bill Clinton and British royalty. Jeffrey Epstein's ranch with its 27,000-square-foot main house was somewhere out there in the dark. Thornton had once hoped his criminal problems would blossom in New Mexico and give her a shot at being local counsel.

Traffic moved in the distance on I-40, nothing blocking the view across open prairie. Soon she was out of the darkness on Moriarty's main street. She'd gotten to know this town from handling cases for drug runners stopped on the Interstate. That had been the route: up from El Paso on I-25 to I-40, left to LA, east to middle America. She hadn't handled an interdiction case in a long while. Most went into the Federal CJA program, appointed lawyers earning a measly hourly rate. She wouldn't take anything now without her full fee paid up front, no refunds for a guilty verdict, no discount for a quick dismissal. When you hit it, that up-front fee could be one huge chunk of money for a couple hours' work, sometimes just a phone call to straighten out an Assistant DA.

Coming down the main street, she saw gas pumps and "JENNY'S" in red letters. There, painted on a cinder-block wall, was the mural she remembered, a cartoonish big rig and a Route 66 sign. She got down from the Durango and started to the door, surprised to see Benny Silva at the wheel of an Oldsmobile, a much younger man in the passenger seat next to him. She tapped on the window. It came down.

"Let's talk inside," she said.

He had the black hair of Benny Silva, with a lower voice and more mass in the upper body. And a face that made her step back, like it had been cut in half then sewed back together, but they couldn't get the lips to line up right.

"I'm his brother," the almost-look-alike said. "Benny's inside." The young man next to him, now that she was closer, could be this man's son.

She heard "La Tierra Encantada," and the men in the car laughing as the window went up.

The lights inside the doors showed what could be any convenience store, but this one had a restaurant in back. She stepped past the register and saw Benny Silva at a table with a Mexican combo plate, red and green chile, steam rising from refried beans. She pulled out a metal chair and sat across from him.

"Juan de Oñate came through here on his way to Kansas," Silva said, mixing chile into his beans. "Imagine riding out across the plains, not knowing where the next water was, land like an ocean. He got all the way to what's now Wichita before he turned around. You want something?"

She waved for the waitress while Silva tore apart a tamale. Coffee would be good, she told the middle-aged woman wearing a *Jenny's Truck Centers* tee.

"We're here." Silva was now onto an enchilada, melted cheese oozing from the folded tortilla. "Something you want to say you couldn't in Santa Fe?"

Her coffee arrived. She took her time bringing it to her mouth, putting it down. She'd been working on how to say this as she drove across the dark prairie.

"You haven't thought it through. Without me, you'll lose your nine-million-dollar verdict. Even if Judge Diaz denies the motion for new trial, enters those findings of fact you want, you'll get reversed in the Court of Appeals. That's where I can help you, but you'll have to hire me as your lawyer."

Silva wiped his mouth and rested his hands out of sight in his lap. Done eating, ready to talk, but he'd missed some red chile in his mustache. "No dancing around," he said. "You get right to it."

"Dancing. Is that what you call it, putting that photo under my wipers? The e-mails to Judge Diaz?"

"I was saying hello, I know you. Now you know me. Tell me why it is I need you?"

"Your lawyer—does he realize what you're up to?"

Silva touched his mustache, felt the wet chile, wiped his mouth again. "He's a choirboy. He looked pretty in front of the jury. We knew the *abuelas* would love him. He thinks he won with his smooth talking. Hasn't once wondered how come the other side had nothing. Maybe we could use new representation."

"I know most of the Court of Appeals. Well. Very well. Beyond them is the Supreme Court. It's in their discretion to take an appeal from the Court of Appeals. You have to petition them for what's called *certiorari*. I can make sure that doesn't happen."

"You know them, too."

"Most have been elected in the past ten years. They remember how much I did to give them their jobs."

Thornton rotated her cup in its saucer, back and forth, putting her nerves somewhere. Underneath the table, she was curling and uncurling toes inside her shoes.

"I already got a deal with the boy lawyer. He gets twenty-five percent."

"That's all?"

"He was doing slip-and-falls before this. Now he'll get better cases, riding his rep. The big gun who shot down the Hollywood fat cat. What I'm saying, I'm not anxious to cut any deeper into my take."

"The other thing I'll do is hold Judge Diaz together so she can enter that ruling you need. You've pushed her over the edge. She may not make it to the finish line. She's talking of resigning. She steps down, your case goes to a new judge."

"Who doesn't have a thing for teenagers."

"She's talking about going to the police. She blames herself for Andrea getting killed."

"Who's Andrea? Oh, Cassandra. Terrible news. Somebody does that to a pretty girl, what's wrong with people?"

"If Judy Diaz unburdens herself to the police, they'll learn about your movies. Those e-mails you sent to get kiddie porn on her computer—the police will be very interested. They can find out the computer they were sent from."

"No, they can't. I guarantee it. That computer was crushed inside a car now the size of a mattress."

"She'll tell them about your case, the blackmail, they'll be setting up cots in your office. They'll dig into why all the defense witnesses disappeared. The insurance company's investigators will now have a grand jury doing their work. You'll never see a dime, even if they don't nail you."

"You want this taco?"

"You understand, any good I can do you will end if that video surfaces, or Judy talks, or anyone else who knows what happened in her house."

"That lady with the long legs, the number three in your triple team on Cassandra." The taco shell crunching, ground beef spilling on Silva's plate. "The Audrey Hepburn neck. You know, I said that to someone today, they said, 'who'?"

"My friends on the Court of Appeals, the Supreme Court, they'll forget they ever knew me."

Silva got the waitress's attention, held up his cup.

"You'll have some houseguests, too," he said. "Cassandra was younger than you thought. Maybe you knew and it made it better. You watch the movies, Cassandra with you and your friends, you can see how young she is. Can't miss it. A little half and half, hon," he said as the waitress refilled his cup. "And more honey for my sopapillas."

Thornton waited until the waitress walked out of earshot. What was Silva thinking, talking like that in front of her? Then she got it: he was showing he had nothing to worry about.

"That birthmark you got down there," Silva said as he tore open a sopapilla and poured honey inside. "You know it's the state symbol?"

"Here's what I propose," she said. "You retain me as appellate counsel. My fee ... hold on." She saw he was about to object. "My fee is five percent, to come out of your trial lawyer's cut, which leaves him at twenty. I'm certain you can persuade him 1.8 mil is still adequate compensation. You have your scary counterpart outside pay him a visit if he gets prickly. Your twin brother, what happened to his face?"

Silva chewed, brown eyes looking happy as he pushed the fried bread soaked with honey into his mouth.

"Now you got me worried about your friend, the judge." Silva talking with cheeks full, pushing the tips of his white mustache forward. "She's how close to going to the police?"

"I keep her from falling off that cliff for a while. She denies retrial, gives you rock-solid findings of fact. You get all she can give, then take it from there. I can't keep her on that cliff edge forever. Her drinking, it's out of control. She comes to one morning, hung over, feeling scared and guilty, blaming herself for a girl in a dumpster, it may not be me she calls for help. Is it your business practice to trust everything you have to drunks? It's not mine."

"You want to explain what you mean by that?"

"I don't think I have to." She held Silva's eyes while he licked honey from his fingers.

"These are good. They say when you break a sopapilla open a fairy comes out. How they got in there, they never say. I got something to ask you."

He poured more honey into another fried bread pocket and took a bite. Golden drops clung to the tips of his mustache.

"That other lady in the movie, with the legs. And the teeth. Jesus. Who is she?"

Thornton reached into her purse and took out a folded sheet of paper. She dropped it next to Silva's plate.

He waited until he finished eating, then tried to wipe honey from his fingers with a paper napkin. It came apart and stuck to his skin. He dipped his fingers in his water glass, then dried with a fresh napkin. He unfolded Thornton's piece of paper. "Lily Montclaire, Loco Lobo Outfitters, County Road 24, Pecos."

"That's where she is," Thornton said, "when she's not with the police."

Silva refolded the note and slipped it into his shirt pocket. He used the last sopapilla to mop chile from his plate. "We got routes out there. Private contracts for what the county won't handle. We're always looking for new accounts. I could have a service rep drop by."

NINETEEN

The fire was eating the mountains. A wall of flames twenty miles across now, towns evacuated, every hotel in Santa Fe booked, people filling RV parks and campgrounds at the city's edge. Today the wind had died. The black smoke was churning straight into the blue sky. The view from Rivera's window, up on the top floor of the FBI offices, showed wet clouds loitering to the south, but not coming closer.

What looked like orange and red mosquitoes spun around columns of smoke, old 747s blitzing the fire, getting in close to drop their lakes of slurry.

"Good day to bomb the beast," Aragon said. "They can get smoke jumpers in with this break in the wind."

"It looks like Desert Storm," Rivera said, "when the oil fields were burning."

She didn't keep photographs in her office. She didn't want the critters she brought in learning anything about her life. Rivera probably never brought murderers and rapists here. He had a photograph of himself in desert camos, lean and tanned, his name on a patch on his chest, pants tucked in the tops of boots. Pancake-flat sand stretched behind him, the only other thing in the frame the barrel of a tank poking in from off-camera. On a bookshelf, framed photographs of a large family, three boys, two girls surrounding a smiling man and woman. The man had the same widow's peak she'd noticed right away the first time Tomas Rivera looked down at her.

"My brother and his family. They're in Maryland."

Rivera pulled out a chair from his desk and took a seat. The desktop was cleared of anything but a pen holder and calendar. So different from her work space, coffee stains on a blotter, cigarette burns left from previous occupants, yellowed bits of tape where she'd held articles about crimes so she'd see them every day, stacks of office memos she hadn't read, an empty box for .40 caliber slugs in which she kept a toothbrush and a small tube of paste.

"Breskin," she said.

Rivera tented his hands, elbows on the desk. This was different, sitting with office furniture separating them. Different than the team around a conference table, kicking a case back and forth, digging fries out of bags. Different than the back seat of Javier's truck.

"It's a dead end. I found the roses Daniel Breskin purchased. Those in the dumpster with Cassandra Baca weren't his."

"When were you going to let us know?" Was he talking down to her? What was under the words?

"It took some time with Sunny Breskin," Rivera said, chin on the steeple of his fingers. "I made a judgment call. It played out."

Rivera pushed his chair back. She was expecting his feet on the desk, showing her the soles of his shoes. Not knowing why, but feeling that it was coming. Instead, he rested a foot on one knee and folded his arms.

First looking at her over his hands. Now folded arms. She was missing something.

"Five dozen roses in a garbage can outside that guest house he uses as an office." Rivera scratched his cheek. "Sunny thinks Daniel used them for a photo session. She saw him come to the house with a group of people, and later flashes going off. She didn't go out. She doesn't want to know more. They stayed until early morning, then everybody left. She saw the flowers scattered on a bed when she went in after we talked to her. She didn't tell me until today."

"You were there yesterday."

"Yesterday I told her the truth of why we were asking about the flowers. I know we haven't released that information, but I thought it important. Today Sunny called, after talking to her lawyer who said it was best she cooperated. She doesn't like her husband's business but she likes him being under suspicion for murder even less."

"You got the flowers?"

"On their way to Quantico to eliminate any possibility they have something to do with those around Cassandra Baca. I retrieved the plastic wrappers as well, with the bar code on the price stickers. The Whole Foods manager confirms they correspond to the bunches purchased on Breskin's credit card."

Anything she was picking up from Rivera was replaced with questioning herself. Maybe her instincts about the roses had been wrong. Maybe they should have used that time on Silva, or Thornton and Diaz. Or Star Salazar.

"So Tucker can redirect his attention from the glamorous world of adult entertainment?" she asked.

"Not completely. He's working the Backpage angle, the dregs of that world. We need that ad. A subpoena came back negative for any payments received from a Cassandra or Dolores Baca."

"The mother?"

"We gave it a shot. The daughter was using her trade name."

"Dolores is still missing." A thought hit her. "Ask him to try payments from a Star Salazar."

She spent the next twenty minutes bringing Rivera up to date with the information on how Star Salazar saved, then used, Cassandra Baca. The ankle-over-the-knee, arms folded pose was gone. He leaned across his desk, getting pulled in. Then he stood and paced, thinking aloud.

"We see something like this in prison populations. A newbie shielded by a stronger, more-feared inmate, only to find themselves exploited by their protector for sex. You're thinking Star Salazar was pimping Cassandra Baca?"

"I'm feeling certain Star Salazar at least knew what was going on and helped Cassandra Baca somehow. Maybe she drove her to the Pizza Hut and waited until Montclaire arrived. I'm pretty certain Cassandra walked to Star's house after, got a ride home from there."

"Maybe Star Salazar had the Backpage ad. Montclaire said Cassandra Baca once suggested involving her, but Montclaire found her repulsive. Maybe the initial contact came through Salazar."

"She's missing, too. Everybody we want to talk to takes off. Can I use that?" Aragon pointed at a white erasable board on the wall to the side of the desk. "I was doing this last night, trying to get a handle on this mess. It's simpler now Breskin's out of the picture."

Last night she'd put *CB* for Cassandra Baca in the middle. Now she wrote those letters to the side. In the middle she wrote initials for Thornton, with initials for Diaz and Montclaire next to that. At the top she wrote *Benny Silva*.

"I was getting lost putting Cassandra Baca at the center of everything. She's just a girl. She's not the center of anything. Now look."

She drew a line from Thornton to Silva. "We know from Fager that Thornton's very interested in E. Benny." Now a line from Silva to Diaz. "And he has this big freaking case in front of Diaz." Now she wrote in Star Salazar's initials, with a line back to Silva where she added *Abel Jr.*

"There's a circle closing here. Breskin was messing it up for me. I couldn't see where he fit in."

"I don't see the circle," Rivera said.

"You will now."

She drew a line from CB to Salazar. "That closes the circle. I may have some of this wrong, but look, we can now see that all these people are connected, with Thornton at the very center. With her in that position, we see everything line up."

"May I?" Rivera took the marker from her and switched Silva for Thornton. "It works this way, too. Silva at the center ties it as neatly."

"Crap." Aragon dumped her ass in a chair. She thought she'd had it. Maybe she only had what she wanted to see. "Do you at least agree we're starting to see the outlines of something that fits together?"

Rivera studied the diagram on the board, then switched out Silva for Diaz. Then he put Montclaire in the center. Then Cassandra Baca, back where they started.

"It's here. I agree it doesn't feel right with Cassandra Baca at the center. We can make connections off her, but 'at the center' implies she is the driving force of all this."

"She's dead and I feel things are still happening."

"It could be something random, people crossing paths by chance."

"I don't buy that." Aragon popped out of her chair and touched a name on the board. "We can't find Star Salazar. Let's talk to her connection to Benny, Abel Jr."

Going down the stairs to her car, she realized Rivera hadn't touched her. Not his hand brushing her arm, his hip against hers, the little things he did to make contact that looked innocent to other people. She'd taken the touches for granted, sometimes resented him pressing it, risking someone truly seeing what was passing between them.

Like sitting across his desk, something had gotten between them.

The heat was brutal, rising off the sidewalk, cooking the branches of ornamental trees dying without rain. It was worse in the parking lot. She opened all the doors of her car to let out the superheated air and shielded her eyes as she looked into the sky, urging forward the distant clouds she'd seen from up in Rivera's office.

Not a chance.

Clear blue. Perfectly, brilliantly, blazingly ... sunny.

TWENTY

SERENA AGREED TO MOVE Montclaire to the closest bunkhouse, where she'd be easier to protect. It stood in the open, the approaches cleared of underbrush and the pines limbed up. The gravel off the county road ran for miles with no other ranches along the way. That was the only way in here unless someone crossed the mountain behind the house. Javier said that looked easier than it was. You couldn't see the deep canyon at the foot of the mountain until you were right on it. Even in daylight that was killer country to cross.

"We'll set up after dark," Aragon said, Lewis with her on the porch, deciding how they would do this. "With Thornton knowing where Lily is, she's not safe. We need to be out here every night. You'll sleep when you're dead, remember?"

"Daytime?"

"We have to figure something out."

"Let's use the top of that rise down the road. We'll see headlights coming before they're close."

"Thanks for helping, Rick." He didn't like going twenty-four hours without seeing his family. He'd arrived after swinging home with groceries and a promise to be back to cook breakfast. Aragon was glad to have him. It would be a long night in the woods.

He said, "I got an update from Rivera. Tucker came through again."

She saw Lily Montclaire moving behind a window inside the bunkhouse. It was hot out here on the porch with the western sun cranking up the temperature in the tinder-dry woods. The bunkhouse was probably an oven. All the windows were open but one, the bathroom with three shower stalls. Serena had caught Montclaire standing in the window, naked, taking her time drying herself, watching Javier as he groomed the mules. She'd nailed boards over the window so that wouldn't happen again.

Lewis said, "Backpage is now cooperating without needing subpoenas. Tucker just had to mention the grand jury the Feds always have working in Albuquerque."

"We could use something like that." Aragon put her feet on the railing, an iced tea by her feet. Lewis had his tea resting on his thigh, leaving a ring on his jeans.

"There was an ad placed by an Andrea in Espanola. She'd meet up in Santa Fe, but she was over forty years old. Somehow Tucker learned she was that teacher, the one who nodded off in her car during lunch hour at the high school with the needle on the seat next to her."

"With her head on the steering wheel. I remember that. Kids found her, thought she was dead."

Montclaire came out of the bunkhouse with wet towels in her arms. She crossed to the clothesline Serena used for the family and draped them over the cord.

"But he also got ads paid by Star Salazar. They were for different girls. None for herself except the oldest, which ran only once. She showed her face in that one, the metal ring in the nose for those who like that. It ran under 'Freaky Latina.' The ones for the other girls, there's no faces, just hips, tight shirts over boobs, and thighs. A couple with sports car tats. One might be Cassandra Baca but Tucker couldn't be certain."

Montclaire was watching them, a towel obscuring her face as she raised it over the line, then her eyes again looking their way when the line sagged under the weight of wet cotton.

"Tucker says the numbers from the ads matches the number found on Montclaire's phone. She was texting Star Salazar."

Montclaire had finished with the towels and was coming their way.

"That woman," Aragon said. "She said she only met Star Salazar once in the Pizza Hut." Aragon dropped her feet and sat forward, her forearm on the top railing. "Lily, get up here."

———————

Serena grilled elk burgers topped with her red chile, loaded with oregano and cumin. Aragon and Lewis waved off beers. Serena talked about where Javier should be right now, camped inside the boundary of the Pecos Wilderness along a stream without a name. The other guiding services were steering customers to peaks and mesas. He'd found a valley that years ago had been cleaned out of elk and deer and written off by local hunters. The animals were responding to pressure in the famous high country by returning to the old range.

"Denise, you should come with us." Serena dished posole onto plates. "Help with camp. Get yourself a cow elk. You can keep the meat in our freezer. We'll get to see you whenever you're hungry."

Lewis should come, too, bring his girls. They ever been on a mule?

Aragon's mind was on what Montclaire had told them before Serena called dinner: she'd never seen the girl she thought was Andrea with a phone.

The time you called about the Backpage ad, she'd asked Montclaire, *who answered? You got to know Andrea's voice. Was it her? How about the other times?*

Montclaire had shrugged. *I did most of the talking, asking about dates, can you do tonight, how much? It was yes or no on the other end, and a number. We always texted after that.*

Tucker had seen something in the video. He passed it to Lewis to ask Montclaire: *What did you leave on the seat in the Pizza Hut?*

Montclaire had pretended the question puzzled her, came back with *Nothing. Why do you think I left something?*

Serena told Montclaire to clear the table. They'd eaten outside under the trees. Montclaire carried dishes into the house, not having talked during the meal, by herself on the end of a bench.

"We're going to lay in the dirt in the dark all night long for that woman," Aragon said to Lewis when Montclaire was out of earshot.

"I'm laying in the dirt in the dark all night long for Cassandra Baca."

Serena reached into the cooler by her chair and cracked another beer for herself. "Javier has a pair of night-vision goggles," she said. "They're fun."

"That's how he's able to shoot mountain lions in the dark." Aragon wanted one of those beers to chase the red chile taste in her mouth. Instead, she'd be drinking coffee at midnight. "And here I thought it was his mountain man skills."

"Isn't that illegal," Lewis asked, "using night-vision goggles to hunt?"

"Who's hunting?" Serena took a long drink and wiped her lips on the back of her hand. "He's protecting his family and property."

———————

A little after one a.m., headlights showed the underside of trees across a little valley from where they'd set up. Aragon removed the night-vision goggles. She'd been getting a kick out of seeing deer, then a bear moving under the trees, coming straight at their position, pausing, sniffing the air, then swinging wide around them.

The light reappeared, topping out on the opposite hill, then angling down the dirt road.

They heard the engine as it climbed toward them. Headlights. A car stopped at the tree they'd dragged across the road.

They came out of the woods on opposite sides of a Crown Victoria. Dashboard glow showed two people inside.

"Police! Get out of the car and turn around, hands on the roof." Lewis taking charge on the driver's side, a big flashlight lined along the barrel of his Glock.

Aragon did the same, holding her flashlight along the barrel of her gun, and saw the face behind the window on her side. "It's Pork and Sauerkraut."

The doors opened. A foot came out. A man stood.

"What the fuck? Is this how you welcome fellow officers come to your aid and assistance?" Albert Fenstermacher unfolded himself from the passenger side, his hand shielding his eyes from the flashlight's beam. Darrel Park came out the driver's door.

"Sergeant Perez told us you might need help protecting your witness," Fenstermacher said. "We needed to talk with you anyway. We've been calling for hours."

"There's no signal out here."

"Would you put that down, for Christ's sake?"

Aragon lowered her flashlight and holstered her weapon.

"We brought sleeping bags." Fenstermacher nodded over his shoulder at the rear seat. "We can spell you guys. Maybe all of us can get a little shuteye."

"Much appreciated. Help us move this tree out of the way. We'll walk ahead. My sister-in-law was going to bed, but she's probably on the porch with a rifle across her knees. You drive up alone, she'll be wondering what happened to us. You don't want to learn what an Annie Oakley she is."

As they dragged the tree back into the forest, Fenstermacher talked about their investigation of the dead Indian without a foot.

"You'd given us the name E. Benny Silva, that photo of the copper cable in his scrap yard. We asked him about it. He pulled out this book from under the counter. 'Sorry, no copper cable this week.' He held it open for us to see. 'I got rainspouts, pipes from a hotel downtown they're renovating. No cable.'"

"You show him the photo I sent you?" Aragon asked.

"He said that wasn't copper, that's why it's not in his book. But it looks just like the copper cable round our Indian. PNM matched it with their stock, some alloy so they can trace anything that gets ripped off."

They got the tree into the bushes, Fenstermacher having a hard time with it. "How did the two of you get that thing into the road?" He was bent over, hands on his knees.

Park took over while they waited for him to catch his breath. "Guess what? Silva lives in that neighborhood that lost power the night before the Indian turned up dead. We went to his street, talked to this old guy with a walker putting out a soaker on what's left of his lawn. You know, the air's getting pretty bad in the city? The wind shifted. He had a handkerchief over his face. We asked him about the power outage, what he'd heard. He'd heard Mr. E. Benny Silva saying it would never happen again."

"El Patron," Aragon said. "Defending the pueblo."

"So what we wanted to run by you, your thing with the girl in the dumpster. Sarge let us see the photos. Don't want to step on toes, but maybe because we have the footless Indian on the brain, it looks staged. Like ours. Why go to all that trouble, severing a foot, wrapping him in wire yanked out of the transformer that cut the neighborhood's AC, unless a message is being sent? Nobody's gonna touch that transformer again except the PNM crew supposed to work on it. Your thing, you think maybe a message, too, in Mr. Benny's dumpster? Yo. What's that?"

Headlights lit up the underside of branches across the valley, then disappeared.

"Someone's coming," Lewis said, already moving. "Let's get this tree back in place."

They dragged it out of the bushes and again blocked the road. The headlights lit trees on the opposite hill, then swung into the little valley.

Aragon said, "Guys, act like you were coming in here and this tree stopped you. Try to see who's driving. We'll be in the woods. Don't let them know you're cops. You're lost, looking for the Interstate."

She and Lewis melted into the darkness. They watched a vehicle approach, a pickup truck. No, it was a cargo van sitting as high as a truck, full size, headlights on high beam. Fenstermacher and Park stood at the back of their car, Fenstermacher waving, friendly, fully lit in the van's headlights. The van stopped twenty feet away.

The driver's window came down. Fenstermacher stepped closer. The taillights on his car showed his shirt lifted in the back above his pistol, riding in a holster inside his pants. Park stepped left for the angle on the passenger. He had his gun behind his thigh.

"Tree fell down," Fenstermacher said.

A voice spoke inside the van. Aragon couldn't make out words.

"We have to turn around anyway." Fenstermacher looked behind him briefly as though he was trying to get a fix on Aragon and Lewis in the darkness. "This isn't the way to the Interstate, is it?"

Park had begun walking down the side of the van toward the rear. The van began backing up, slowly, keeping pace with him.

"Hold on." Fenstermacher said. "Can you help us out? There's no signal for our GPS in here."

Park lengthened his stride. The van picked up speed. Now it began to pull away. Park gave up hiding his gun and ran. The van swerved as it accelerated, then straightened and moved faster down the hill and disappeared in the dip. When they saw it again, the van had turned around and was moving up the far slope and out of sight.

Aragon and Lewis met the other two cops in the road, flashlights on, no need to hide any more.

"I might have done that, too," Fenstermacher said. "On a dark road, middle of nowhere, a car blocking the way, two guys walking toward me. I got a look inside. Driver: Hispanic, thirties, clean-cut. A boy, teenager, in the middle. In the passenger seat, an older Hispanic guy, heavy-set."

"I could almost read something on the side of the van," Park said. "Before it moved off I got 'enterprises.'"

———

They left the tree in the road for the rest of the night. One team grabbed sleep in the Crown Vic while the other kept watch from the woods. No other vehicles appeared out of the night. Shortly before dawn, Aragon stiffened at the sound of branches snapping. Something large moving through the woods. She unholstered her gun and racked the slide.

"Elk," Lewis said. It was his turn with the goggles. "A big bull, a beaut, leading his harem. He's veering off." An eerie, stressed bugle split the night, followed by a bizarre huffing. "Listen to that. He's pissed we're here."

At dawn they cleared the road. Aragon walked ahead of the car carrying the three men. Serena was in the corral, a rifle slung over a fence post. She reached for it when she saw Aragon stepping into the clearing. Aragon realized how it looked, like she was being marched ahead of the car.

"Good guys," she called out. "Cops."

She introduced Fenstermacher and Park and handed back Javier's goggles. "Man, these things are awesome. Rick saw a bull and cows this morning. I saw a bear."

Serena said, "There's carne adovada and scrambled eggs on the stove. I'll be right in to make some more."

The four of them split what was ready and brought their plates onto the porch. Serena was backing a pickup to the corral. She climbed out of the cab and into the bed and heaved bales of hay over the corral's top rail.

Aragon stopped eating and watched. "Look at that," she said to Lewis. "You see it?"

"Look at what?"

"How you can get a body into a dumpster. Serena couldn't throw a hay bale into the corral if she was standing on the ground. From the back of a pickup, it's just another chore."

TWENTY-ONE

THAT WAS IT FOR hiding Lily in the woods.

Aragon borrowed Javier's truck, leaving Lewis with the department car. He arranged for a buddy with State Police to patrol the road into Loco Lobo ranch several times a day. Last night's visitors might return with Serena out there alone. They might not be quick to accept Serena's word that Montclaire was not there.

Lewis was now heading to District Court for the latest filings in Silva's case while she took Lily by her house to grab clean clothes. At the door, Montclaire stumbled through her security code.

A laugh, the first Aragon had heard. "Only a couple days and already I forgot," Montclaire said.

When she got the door open she headed to the bedroom. Aragon walked through the low-slung adobe, checking the location of windows and doors. There was a sliding glass door at the back overlooking a hill that could be climbed in the dark. The walls along the sides of the house would let someone get within a couple feet of a window before being seen. And three separate doors into the house, not including the one from the garage.

She called Rivera to prod him on getting Montclaire into witness protection. As she was waiting for him to answer she wondered why he'd given Lewis, not her, developments in Tucker's work. Now that she thought about it, he hadn't been calling her directly for two days, since before the visit to Sun-Hi Breskin. She got his voicemail and left another message.

"I'm ready."

Montclaire emerged from a bedroom with an overnight bag and roll-on suitcase. Framed in the doorway, she was an older version of the young woman in the poster under glass on the wall, in a yellow bikini, the bottom riding below hip bones, a parasol tilted over her shoulder, not doing any good, not the slightest shade on her face.

"That's you," Aragon said.

"Seventeen years old. The Bahamas. I was right on the edge of making some big money, the next Evangelista. Where are you taking me?"

"Lewis wants to charge you and let the detention center take you off our hands. Screw this headache getting you into witness protection. Maybe I'll agree with him before the end of the day. I want to hear what you have to say after we watch a little movie."

She'd been focused on doors and windows and hadn't noticed the large black portfolio taking up the coffee table in front of a low couch. It probably had Montclaire's career in there, all her different phases, things Lily hadn't shared with them.

She wished Montclaire had taken longer getting her stuff together.

She called ahead for Tucker, not bothering to go through Rivera. She drove to the FBI's offices. Rivera's car was not in its spot. Tucker was waiting in the media room. She skipped introductions and told Montclaire to take a seat.

He ran the Pizza Hut video of Montclaire coming to the booth where Cassandra Baca and Star Salazar were sitting, the flash of an envelope in her hand, reaching for the back of the booth, her hand coming back empty. Then Cassandra Baca leaving and Star Salazar going around to where Montclaire had been. Sliding out with an envelope pressed against her thigh.

Tucker froze the image.

"What was in the envelope, Lily?"

"Money."

"You paid Star Salazar for the time with Andrea. Up front."

"That was the arrangement."

"It tells me something else," Aragon said. "The way you left the envelope, Star not counting. There was some trust between you and her. More than I'm feeling between us right now."

Montclaire did that thing with her hands, laying them flat along her neck, fingertips on the line of her jaw.

"I call bullshit," Tucker said.

"You call it right," Aragon said. "Lily, you didn't want us knowing about Star Salazar. Explain that for us."

"That's how Marcy does it. She said if you give the cops everything right away, they'll still want more. So instead of making stuff up that they'll find out was a lie, you hold things back and play it out a little at a time. Always keep something in the bank, Marcy said."

"Maybe you shouldn't be playing lawyer," Aragon said.

"There's not a lawyer in this town I would trust. Marcy's screwed half of them. The rest won't cross Judge Diaz. I'm doing the best I can."

"I'd say your best is coming up way short."

"I paid Star Salazar fifteen hundred dollars the last time." Montclaire put her hands under her thighs. "I'd started at four hundred. Marcy gave me the money. I put it in an envelope from Judy's office, it was all I had in the car. Star kept it. That's how she knew Andrea was seeing the Chief Judge."

"Why did you have an envelope from Judge Diaz's office?"

"Marcy had been helping her send out invitations for a fundraiser."

"What else are you holding back?" Tucker said. "The federal government doesn't play hide and seek with people who want our protection."

Aragon was on her feet.

"It's more than holding back, Lily. It's lying. You denied passing anything to Star Salazar until you saw we had it on film."

"I'm sorry for that."

"Save 'sorry' for sentencing. Come on."

"Star probably still has the envelope. That's something else you can use."

"Star's missing. No help for you there."

She marched Montclaire to the truck and drove in silence out of town, under I-25 onto south 14. Montclaire could see where they were going from miles away. Aragon turned into the parking lot of the Santa Fe Detention Center and parked at the sign pointing visitors one way, prisoner deliveries the other.

"I'm thinking Rick Lewis is right. Not babysitting you, I could get real work done."

She circled around so the jail's walls and fences were on Montclaire's side of the truck and stopped at the gate for prisoner transports. A van was coming through, heads above red jumpsuits in every window.

"It was Marcy who put me onto Star Salazar," Montclaire said. "She'd handled her brother's case."

Aragon called Lewis.

"Meet me at the office. Grab an interrogation room. We're starting over."

Star Salazar's brother had a different last name. Griego. Victor Griego had been charged with second-degree murder. A party in an apartment gone wrong, shots fired, young men who'd been friends before the PCP kicked in trying to kill each other.

Montclaire had interviewed Star, then brought her to Thornton. Star said her brother had been sitting across from a boy named Stalker, she didn't know his real name. Two kitchen chairs facing each other, pulled close so their knees almost touched. Each tranked, each wearing a Kevlar vest. Each with a mouse gun in the hand dangling at the end of an arm. Mad-dogging in silence, other kids around them choosing sides, passing bottles and joints. Some loud rap music shaking the walls.

The joint in Griego's hand without the gun had been dipped in liquid amp.

He took a hit, staring at Stalker through the smoke. He held out the joint, Stalker reaching to take it, making sure to keep his gun arm limp.

"What was the game, Lily?" Aragon asked, back with Lewis in the same cold interrogation room where Montclaire had first started talking.

"To see who could be the coolest," Montclaire said. "They had to control their nerves, looking into the eyes of someone with a gun in their hand, the PCP kicking in, the kids urging them on. If a muscle twitched, that was it. Fair game. Quick draw with no chance of missing."

"And so the small guns. It wouldn't be fatal unless a lucky head shot. The vests would stop the small slug."

"But when Stalker was taking a hit, Griego shot him point blank in the eye. He killed Stalker right there in front of all those kids."

They left Montclaire to find the file on the shooting. After reading it together Aragon said, "Thornton pulled it off. Witnesses tripping over each other, changing their stories, saying they were hallucinating. Some key witnesses refusing to testify."

"And no weapon. That killed the case. They couldn't even put a gun in Griego's hand."

The DA sought sanctions, claiming Thornton was obstructing justice by withholding the gun that had killed Stalker. She claimed attorney-client privilege. Not saying her client had given her anything, but if he had, just revealing the weapon had come from him would divulge confidential information.

Back in the room Aragon asked Montclaire, "You said mouse guns. Where'd you get that?"

"It's what Star called them."

"What kind exactly?"

"Those little pocket Berettas," Montclaire answered, hugging herself against the cold air blasting from the vents. "The ones where the barrel pops up in the back. The front stays down, the bullet flies out the back. I think .25 caliber. No, I'm sure of it. I'd never heard of that caliber before."

"And you gave these guns to Thornton."

Montclaire nodded.

"Okay. You bought yourself another night out of jail. How do you feel about staying here? We'll bring in a cot. You can order delivery for dinner. Let's talk about that gun."

Montclaire chafed her bare arms. "You can turn down the AC. I can't talk with my teeth chattering."

"In a second. What happened to Griego's gun?"

"Marcy has it. Star gave it to me. I gave it to her."

"So that's why you didn't want us to know about Star. And the Backpage ads had nothing to do with it. Something else I want to know. Did you ever hear the name Benny Silva?"

Montclaire's right arm came under her left, her hand reaching up, the pinkie hooking under the thumb of the other hand. This was a new pose.

"No."

"You do that with your hands, I know you're not giving me the truth."

"I'm just cold."

"So I'll get you a sweater and ask again. Benny Silva. I'll be right back."

TWENTY-TWO

"You should come to my Krav class." Aragon swallowed the chunk of Lotaburger in her cheeks. "We can't keep big guys around."

"Because you bite them," Lewis said.

"Only when we can't break a chokehold."

Aragon tore into her burger, Lewis into something green from Whole Foods. They had the windows down, the AC noisy, the nose of their car at the locked gate leading into the Salazar family compound. On the other side, dogs launched themselves at the chainlink. They'd been doing that since Aragon parked the car to block the gate. If anybody wants out, she said, they have to talk to us.

"There's eye gouging." She chased the burger with iced soda. "If you're not into biting."

Lewis forked salad into his mouth. She didn't see how he could settle for that, the kind of energy it took to push the weight he moved in the gym.

"Have some fries." She nudged the Blake's bag toward him.

His hand in the bag, he said, "Maybe you should try meditation. Having to get your face punched to clear your head, it might be the easier way to go. But I'd miss the black eyes. They tell me you've worked something out."

A Rottweiler crashed into the gate. The posts sunk in cement shivered.

"I did meditation once." Aragon tossed a fry into her mouth. "My friend the Roshi. I used to call her Buff."

"From the Buddhist temple. The woman in the black robe with no hair, like you."

"An introductory session. Nothing woo-woo. No heavy incense, no kowtowing to statues of men with beer bellies."

"That's not meditation. Not what I was talking about."

"That was what I expected." She finished her soda, crumpled the cup, and flipped it out the window with her burger wrapper.

"Yo, Detective Aragon," Lewis looked at the window where the litter had gone. "Toss *no más*. My kids would be on your ass."

"Listen. I'm telling you about my great meditation adventure. 'Just sit and be with whatever it is that arises,' the Roshi told me. Okay. So the room is dark, not completely black. Quiet, even with Airport Road just over the wall from that temple she has behind razor wire. She goes, 'You're in a beautiful garden. The flowers are blooming. Feel the soft wind, you can sense its freshness. All is peaceful.' I'm going along with it. A nice ride. 'There's a door. Open the handle. It pulls outward toward you. A wooden door, heavy, solid. The doorknob is brass.' They want you to see things. She's good. 'Inside there's a hallway leading down steps. You go down. There's a light at the bottom. You step into a lit room. There's a table before you.'"

The Rottweiler hurled itself again at the fence. It bounced back onto a shepherd cross. The two dogs started fighting, circling, snapping at each other, driving the other dogs crazy.

"That's what I was talking about," Lewis said. "You go someplace in your head. What was on the table?"

"Roshi Buff says, 'Walk around the table first. Just look. Don't touch anything. There will come a time for that.' She gets me to see a gold plate painted with white flowers, a beautiful necklace of white pearls, a Chinese kind of fan with pictures of women playing musical instruments, a figurine of a parrot perched on a tree branch, a piece of white cloth, it looks out of place, a little frayed, maybe a little dirty. 'Now choose one. Take it in your hands.' I don't know why, I chose the piece of dirty cloth."

"It was out of place, like you said. Your police brain talking to you, saying something's not right here. We might have to call animal control. Jesus."

The Rottweiler had a mangy terrier thing on its back, its hind leg in its maw, flinging it around like a squeeze toy.

"You'd think someone would come out of a house to stop it. It probably goes on every day."

The Rotty released the terrier thing and suddenly the fighting stopped. The dogs laid down in the dust, forgetting the two strangers parked at the edge of their territory. The terrier limped off to the shade under a trailer.

"So I've got this cloth," Aragon said. "I tell Roshi that. She says, 'where did it come from?'"

"How would you know?" Lewis dropped a plastic fork in the empty plastic clamshell and put it on the seat behind them.

"I'm supposed to find that answer within myself. And I did. It was one of my first cases. A baby buried in a back yard, by the charcoal grill. It was wrapped in a dirty white cloth."

"Your police brain, like I said."

"But then I flashed to something else. It was my shirt. I'd taken it off and folded it up for a pillow. I didn't want Miguel's head on the concrete basketball court." She felt Lewis looking at her but kept her eyes on the top curve of the steering wheel, below the glare on the windshield. "He was dying. The boys that shot him, they weren't done with me, I didn't care. They were laughing. I put my shirt under Miguel's head. I told him how beautiful he looked running to save me, how much I loved him, I wanted to spend my life with him. Raise a family there at Killer Park, show the world it didn't have to be this way."

The dogs started up again. A woman had appeared on the stoop of a trailer in the back of the compound.

"I told the Roshi I didn't like this. She said, 'Stay where you are. Now what do you see?' I said, I see myself running back up those stairs, out through that garden and I'm on a hot sidewalk. Cars flying by. Across the street is the police department. I told her I've got work to do and felt a lot better."

"At peace with things?"

"Hell, no. Tensed up. Ready to go. Shit, stronger than that. Locked and loaded."

"That's not how it's supposed to work."

"She said at the beginning, be with whatever arises. Well, that's what rose up. Who do you think that is?"

The woman was now at the gate, slapping dogs away. She undid the lock with a key and left it open as she stepped to Aragon's side of the car. The dogs milled at her legs. The Rottweiler growled. She kicked it in the head and it settled down with its snout between black and brown paws.

"You're looking for Star," the woman said.

"Who are you?"

"Her aunt. Her mother thinks she ran to Mexico because you want to put her in jail for the rest of her life. She thinks Star's a good girl, the police framed her for that robbery. I see what she doesn't. And I don't think she ran to Mexico. I think she's in real trouble. That Junior, I don't like him."

Aragon looked from the shade of the car into the sun, the skinny woman blocking it, her pinched face backlit.

She shielded her eyes. "Junior who?"

"He's a Silva. Abel, like his father. Her mother thinks he drove with her in that old sports car of hers to Juarez. That car couldn't make it to Albuquerque."

"You get the hell away from them!"

They looked up to see a woman shouting from the plywood landing of the nearest trailer.

"That's Star's mom," the aunt said. "I don't want a fight about helping police so I'm gonna scream at you now."

And she did. Five ways to fuck themselves. They rolled the windows and backed away as Lewis's smartphone gave them an address for Abel and Angelina Silva. It wasn't far away.

His mother was home but not Junior. No, he hadn't gone to Mexico. He was in the mountains with his father learning the business.

———

Serena pried off plywood and looked through the window of the bunkhouse, where Lily had stood naked watching Javier brushing mules. She was glad that woman was gone. A darkness followed her. Standing in full sun, even, there seemed to be shadows all around her. Only during the photo shoot for the catalog did any kind of light come from inside.

The State Police car had just left after its third visit, turning around in the dirt yard until she'd called out and asked why he was here again. The Black officer, in a black uniform, knee-high black boots, said he was doing a favor for Lewis, keeping an eye on the place for today. She sent him off with a Styrofoam cooler of burritos in aluminum foil for the barracks. He said he'd be back in an hour or so. She said don't think you're getting more burritos each time you show up.

That was three hours ago.

Sweeping the floor, she found an earring. None of their hunters wore big silver loops.

She stripped the bed clothes and tossed them into the basket on the back of the ATV parked outside. She would walk miles over mountains and ford rivers tracking a wounded elk. Around her place, she rode the Yamaha everywhere.

From the main house, she called the police station and left a message with a detective who said he'd pass it on to Denise. Next stop, the laundry room. Standing at the window adding detergent to the washer, she saw sunlight flash on the windshield of a vehicle on the straight length of road out of the woods. It wasn't moving. She wondered how long it had been there and why.

The glare off the windshield blinked. It was a van. Coming closer.

The phone was ringing. She took the cordless outside and watched the van pull to the bottom of the stairs. She could now read the lettering along the side. She hit talk. It was Denise calling back. She'd been away from the office but was back now.

"Tell Lily I found her earring. I'll bring it when I come into town. Hey, I've got someone here from a garbage company. Later."

"Shit. Silva's van is there with Serena. Right now. What happened to the State Police?"

Lewis was up and moving, his cell in his hand. "I'll call the sheriff. They're closest."

"And get State Police down there."

Heads turned as they ran the hall to the stairs.

Sergeant Perez was coming toward them, a cup of coffee in his hand and a question on his face.

"My sister-in-law is in danger," Aragon said as she blew past. She raised her voice and didn't stop running. "Get Pork and Sauerkraut. They know where to go."

They flew over the stairs. Lewis hit the crash bar at the bottom and they were in the heat and white sun. The car was an oven. Lewis jumped behind the wheel and put the red and blue light on the roof and was on his horn pushing the car into traffic. He pounded the horn, coming up fast on cars not getting out of the way fast enough.

He was easing back from a hundred starting up the ramp to I-25, the car's weight on the two outer wheels, Aragon's shoulder against the door, when his phone rang. He dug it from his back pocket. Aragon answered, his State Police buddy calling, saying he'd been pulled away to an accident scene, a drunk driving the wrong way on I-25. A family, four kids, wiped out.

Aragon flattened her hand on the window like she was touching the landscape flashing by: rough brown hills dotted with pinyon and juniper, jagged cliffs with red clay tumbling onto the highway shoulder. Above, lazy white clouds in a pale sky.

"New Mexico, I love you," she said, now curling her fingertips against the glass. "Goddamn, why make it so hard?"

Now it was her phone ringing. Serena.

Aragon put the phone to her ear. "Are they still there? The garbage people?" She looked at Lewis. "They're gone. Tell me what they looked like, how many." To Lewis again, "A man and teenage boy, could have been father and son. Another one who didn't get out. Wanting to know if she'd like garbage pickup instead of hauling trash to the dump."

Lewis slowed to ride the bumper of a Suburban blocking the passing lane, both vehicles doing over ninety, the driver in the Suburban now looking back into the mirror, easing over.

"Serena," Aragon said, "those are the men we were worried about. Yes, I'm sorry. They probably think Lily's still there. I'll take care of that. We're coming out. The sheriff will get there before us. Tell them to wait."

Aragon gave the driver in the Suburban a hard look as she passed, then dropped her eyes to her phone and searched the directory. She tapped a name. She waited until she heard a sparkling female voice, "Law offices, Marcy Thornton and Associates."

Thornton was in conference. Aragon told the receptionist to give her this message, word for word: "We moved Lily. Call off your dogs."

She explained it to Lewis. "I want to make sure Thornton gets the news. We'll see Serena's safe, then I'll head back to deliver the message personally. She forced me to reveal Montclaire's location. It was supposed to be a closed hearing. Last night, a van probably belonging to Silva tried the road. Today, a van we know for sure is Silva's rolls up. Maybe it's not a coincidence Cassandra Baca ended up in one of E. Benny's bins."

The circles she'd been drawing on paper taped to walls were starting to close.

————

Rigo and Abel ordered the tamales at the café in Pecos, twenty miles from the outfitter's ranch. Rigo remembered the tamales here. They'd stop in when he took the family to the campground way up the road, dead-ending at the wilderness boundary. Three days of fishing and getting away from the smells and noise of Silva Enterprises.

The place was empty, too early for lunch, the breakfast crowd gone. When the waitress had left with their order—Junior going with beef tacos despite his grandpa saying tamales all around—Rigo talked about bringing Abel through here when he was Junior's age. Outside of town they'd turned from the pavement onto a dirt road winding for miles through a subdivision of undeveloped forest parcels spilling down slopes facing the wide-open country to the east. Rigo had someone to see and it was time Abel learned more of the family's business, just like this trip with Junior.

He'd let Abel pull the trigger, a guy who'd crossed a client of Silva Enterprises. They'd wrestled him into to a chair and tied him down with bungees from his garage. Someone was shooting somewhere, hunters maybe, no, too many shots too fast. Target practice. Rigo said it was good cover.

They buried the problem in the woods, under the heaviest boulders they could push on top. Animals couldn't dig him up, but there was always the risk of a bulldozer if someone ever built there.

Now with El Puerco in the metal building they didn't have those little worries.

"More chips and salsa." Rigo held the empty plastic basket for the waitress coming to check on their iced teas.

"I think the bunkhouse," Abel said. "You see that woman on the three-wheeler? She had sheets. Someone's sleeping out there. Too early to be putting up hunters."

"Those two guys by the tree in the road last night." Rigo took a fresh basket of chips from the waitress, scooped salsa, and filled his mouth. "I didn't buy their lost traveler story."

"Do you think they were cops?" Junior asked.

"They weren't there today and the tree across the road was gone. Maybe they only think they need to be there at night."

"Because the State Police are watching during the day. That Black statie we saw with his lights going when we were coming in."

Their orders arrived, oblong plates crammed with tamales, rice, and refried beans under melted jack cheese for Rigo and Abel. Three hard tacos leaning against each other for Junior.

"That enough for you?" Rigo frowned at the boy's plate. "Bring him a bowl of menudo," he told the waitress.

They took their first bites, then Rigo laid it out. "We go in heavy. Straight to that bunkhouse, get her, then out the way we came."

"Is she disappearing or dying?" Abel asked.

Rigo waited until he had Junior's attention, looking up with the taco at his mouth. "All this science, you see it on *Forensic Files,* there's a body, you're giving the police a gift."

Junior added hot sauce to the ground beef stuffed into a taco. "Do I come with you?" he asked.

"Why do you think you're hearing this?" Rigo dug into his plate. "Good stuff, huh? These tamales, they make them here. None of that freezer-burned Safeway shit. If the cops are back with their tree across the road, you'll be in on killing your first police. Ready for that? It's a lot different than pushing skinny Star Salazar into El Puerco."

Junior was staring at Rigo, the shell getting soggy, grease sliding down the inside of his wrist.

"Any cops we kill," Rigo talking with food in his mouth, Junior still staring, "we bring them, too."

"Eat," his father said, "before that falls apart in your lap."

TWENTY-THREE

FAGER'S MERCEDES WAITED FOR him in the detention center's visitors lot. He'd had it dropped off, not wanting to ride the prison bus to the center of town and have to walk blocks in the heat and smoky air to his car at the courthouse, sitting there since Judy Diaz ordered him jailed for contempt. He was back in the clothes he'd worn to court, the Hart, Schaffner & Marx navy pinstripe with the black tee and canvas shoes. He couldn't understand why he ever wore wool in this weather.

The cloudless sky was brown with smoke. The jail had its own stink. He was wearing it. But he hadn't been smelling smoke inside the prison. That could have caused a riot, prisoners thinking the place was on fire and they'd burn to death in their cells.

"I don't want to go," he'd told Yago when he got word Diaz had lifted her contempt order. "I've got work here."

The men were enjoying filing complaints against Thornton, something to do and a way to take a shot at a women with everything they'd never have. Fager was enjoying it, too. Not just putting Marcy on her heels. He missed being a lawyer. A part of his brain came awake as he pulled law books off shelves in the prison library. He turned out work no judge would confuse with a *pro se* petition: correct legal citations, perfect paragraphs, an orderly argument progressing to a clearly stated request for relief. Two of the motions were actually righteous. The guys had truly been screwed. The rest, they didn't stand a chance. But he gave it his best shot. And damn, it felt good.

He'd done nothing to purge himself of contempt. Something outside the prison walls had shifted. He started his car and headed to the office. He wanted his desk, his computer and printer. He'd finish the pleadings drafted on the metal table in the pod and mail them back to his clients in envelopes marked "legal mail." The boys could sign them and use the money he'd deposit in their prison accounts for postage to file and serve them on Thornton.

He was pleased to see that her parking lot was as empty as his. Kicking back in the pod, work done for the day, he had talked about Montclaire bringing teenagers to Thornton's office to celebrate wins. Sometimes bringing them to a judge's house, the judge also a woman. That got the men listening to what he wanted them to remember and share with everyone they knew: "She's now talking to police, Thornton's investigator. You think there's anything in that office the cops aren't hearing about?"

It would kill Marcy's practice.

His mail was on the floor inside the slot. He'd let his longtime secretary go even before he received the disciplinary board's ruling. The PO box she'd check in the morning he'd let go, too. Now the little mail he got came through the slot. Between a Joseph A. Banks catalog and a notice of the annual bar convention (let them waste postage) was an envelope printed with Thornton's return address. He slit it open with a finger, read the single sheet of paper inside, and was off running to her office.

He made it to the path from the parking lot to the sidewalk leading to her steps before falling flat on his face.

"What the hell?"

He'd caught his toe where flagstones were missing. He scrambled to his feet and climbed the steps. He threw out a "Hello, darling" to the young receptionist and pushed open the door to Thornton's office. She had her feet on the desk, high heels off, a legal brief opened across her chest. She looked at him over her toes.

"Aren't you the guy who used to be Walter Fager?"

That stopped him. He dropped his eyes, saw his grass-stained, torn pants, blood seeping through the knee. Looking up, he saw the window onto the parking lot and realized she'd seen him taking a fall.

"You scheduled a deposition of Leon Bronkowski," he said. "You didn't think I'd be out of prison in time to do something about it."

"So now you are. Thank me. You're welcome." She raised her feet from the desk and swiveled her chair to let them drop. "It would have been a very short deposition. Now I suppose you'll bulk up the record with objections and speeches."

"He's in a coma. He can't talk. What was the point?"

"He's a defendant. I'm entitled to discovery. Maybe he can hear me. Maybe I'll make him so angry he'll snap out of it and tell me to fuck myself. Maybe he's just not answering any questions. You help shoot America's favorite Indian artist, best move is to get very sick. Like geezer Mafia dons, getting heart attacks and dementia right before trial." She stood and brushed down the front of her skirt. Without her heels she was shorter than he'd remembered. She always seemed so big in court. "Depo's still on. Thanks for reminding me why I scheduled it. File your *pro se* motion for protective order. But take a shower before the hearing, okay?"

He came in close so he could take something away by looking down at her.

"Maybe you don't have time to be harassing Bronk. All those disciplinary complaints, more coming, you're going to be very busy."

She swept a foot under her desk. A black high heel, then another skidded across the floor. She retrieved them and sat at the leather couch to pull them on.

"Nuisances." She stood. That sound of hers he knew so well—heels clacking on a hard floor as she crossed a courtroom to approach the witness stand, or walking away down a courthouse hallway after she made her last offer—it was missing as she walked across a Persian rug to get her briefcase from a leather chair.

Why was he watching her and not talking?

She pulled on a black silk jacket and faced him, a trial lawyer in battle armor, the white shirt crisp and radiant, her skirt stopping mid-thigh to show the curve of muscle, the briefcase like a war club.

"Walter, for those complaints to go anywhere, those broke thugs you've stirred up need an expert witness or two to testify they've examined my work and found it fell below the standard of practice in some specific, material respect. Those losers couldn't pay my copying and postage charges. Where are they going to get an expert witness? It has to be a lawyer or a law professor. It will take days to prep, and then they have to sit through me explaining my reasoning for my moves, my decision to call or not call a witness. Then I get to tear them apart. Who does that for free?"

"You're looking at him."

And she did. Up and down. Her eyes came back to his face and she smiled. "You're disbarred. This could be fun."

"I wasn't disbarred for lack of zealousness. I'll explain why. Which means they'll hear more about your sharp practices. I'll bring up Lily Montclaire destroying evidence under your instructions. You serving a disciplinary complaint on me at my wife's funeral. They'll understand why I lost it."

"Why you choked me in front of television cameras. They'll understand that?"

"So maybe you'll blow every disciplinary complaint out of the water." He turned away, making a show of studying the room.

"What are you looking for?"

"I'm wondering if this was the movie set."

"The movie set?" She stopped moving toward the door.

"Those disciplinary complaints, Marcy." He held up a hand and spread his fingers. He had her. "Nine now, five more coming. All the time filing answers, motions, responding to the board's investigators, the hearings, appeals to the Supreme Court, you won't be heading to court. You won't be billing time. You won't be taking in new clients. Word's already out that anything said in your office goes straight to the cops. Two years of dead time fighting a flood of disciplinary complaints, ouch. Not good for a law practice."

"You're living for this," she said. "What were you saying, the movie set?"

Now he moved to the door, getting himself past her. They were close here, both competing for the same thirty inches separating the office from the reception area and the door to the outside.

He smelled her perfume. Nothing sweet or delicate. She wore fragrance to make you stop and think about her, and lose yourself wondering.

He fought it off.

"Judy Diaz terminated your questioning of me too soon," he said, reaching back to where he'd been going with this. Leave her with wondering what he knew that she didn't.

223

"I got what I wanted."

"You got what Lily said to me. You didn't ask anything about what she gave me."

"Gave you?"

"When your practice collapses, Marcy, you can try porn. I've seen your work. It's good. Judy, too. But you should be more careful about your supporting cast."

He saw it in her eyes. She knew what he was talking about.

He squeezed past her and retraced his steps. At the missing flagstones where he'd fallen he took out his phone and snapped photos. They'd be good exhibits for his lawsuit. A trip and fall, this one truly a nuisance. One more thing on Marcy's plate. One more distraction. Another small cut with many more to come. He could write it up and file before the day was done.

———

Fager was taking photographs of her damaged walkway when Thornton came out the front door on her way to court. What a pathetic sight, the man who had once been her mentor, who cost prosecutors sleep, who made judges sit up, gathering evidence for a lawsuit over torn pants.

Forget all that. How the hell did he know about the videos? What did Lily give him?

TWENTY-FOUR

ARAGON MISSED THORNTON AT her office. Bail hearings, her pretty secretary said. Then she has a meeting with Judge Diaz. So Aragon wrote out the message she'd left earlier: *We moved Lily. Call off your dogs.*

A cleaning woman was there, switching out flowers from vases scattered around the office. Friendly, reminding Aragon of her own grandmother, the woman said, "I take the flowers now." On the side, more workers, a three-man crew setting up sawhorses and flags on string, a stack of flagstones nearby on the lawn. Thornton's Aston wasn't in the parking lot, but Fager's Mercedes was in its spot. She wasn't aware he'd been released from his contempt of court charge.

She called Lewis to check that he was in place. He was a couple miles out but the sheriff said he had a car with Serena, his men wanting to know again why they should unsnap their holsters if a van from a garbage company appeared on the dirt road. Aragon said she'd be right out. The two of them would stay until tomorrow, when she'd beg Rivera to share some of his notorious unlimited FBI resources.

225

Hopefully Thornton would get the message and pull Silva back. Maybe the message, telling Thornton the police had connected to Silva, would make her cautious.

Or maybe I've got this wrong and I'm blind to something, Aragon told herself.

She lost Lewis's call as she walked across the parking lot to the 1930s bungalow that was Fager's office. She pressed the bell and caught a whiff of jail when Fager cracked the door.

"I want to talk with you about Lily Montclaire. And Benny Silva."

"Come in. I'm just finishing my lawsuit against Thornton." He touched his leg and she saw the ripped fabric and bloodstain. "Those guys repairing her walkway? A little late. Lawsuit of the century coming."

She followed him to his office in the back, thinking, *Fager's walking fine.* He couldn't be suing just over ruined pants. But Fager had changed since his wife was murdered. He'd wanted to switch sides, become a prosecutor, dedicate his life to truth and justice. She'd never bought it. It was all about the anger that had driven him for years, nothing close to a change of heart. He was still a prick. Maybe a crazy prick now, obsessed with bringing down Thornton and Diaz.

Finally, putting his talents to good use.

His office was a mess. Coffee cups on every surface. Full wastebaskets, books scattered on the floor, the copier open, the toner cartridge missing. He took a seat behind his desk in a padded maroon leather chair, cracked and worn. He'd cleared a space where he'd been writing on a legal pad. The rest of the desk was buried under food wrappers, crumpled paper, an empty holster.

"Where's the gun that goes in there?" she asked.

226

"In evidence. It was the gun that killed Cody Geronimo. I keep the holster so every day I am reminded of the fact I missed the chance to kill him myself. What do you want to know about Lily?"

"She's playing games with us. I want to know everything she told you to see if it's different than the story she's telling now."

"I miss saying, 'That's attorney-client privileged information.'"

"Get used to it."

"But I can still say I don't want to talk to police. Everyone has that right. You want your question answered, subpoena me."

"That's not helping her."

"Helping her is not my job."

"She's not helping herself, not having a lawyer."

"Not my problem."

"Then let's talk about Benny Silva." Aragon cleared books from the chair in front of his desk and sat. "You called Lewis to say Thornton's been asking about him."

"The nine-million-dollar man." Fager leaned back and laced fingers behind his head and showed stains in his armpits. "He's got other people interested besides Thornton. Word about that award got the attention of the Mexican Mafia. They're waiting for him to collect, then they'll levy a tax, if they don't take it all."

"It could be years before he collects."

"They are very patient people. They'll outlast us all, like beetles after nuclear war. The lowest form of life is the hardest to kill. Why was Marcy asking about Silva?"

"That's what I wanted you to tell me," Aragon said.

"I think it's for Judy Diaz. She's got the motion for a new trial. Everything's political in this town. Maybe she wants to know who Silva is, whether ruling for or against him matters. Maybe she's sizing him up for a big contribution to Judy's re-election."

"He keeps popping up, Benny Silva. In the investigation of Thornton and Diaz. In the case of a dead girl in a dumpster on the south side. In this other thing, a teenage girl named Star Salazar."

"Star Salazar. I know that name. Hang on."

Fager pushed away from his desk and swiveled to file cabinets against the wall. He came back with a dog-eared manila folder. "I bet you already know about this case."

"Let me hear you tell it."

"Sure. I represented the kid charged with supplying the PCP and guns, this crazy game in his apartment. Two boys sitting across from each other with bullet-proof vests and small caliber guns, wigged out on the drugs. One kid, this Victor Griego, broke the rules and simply murdered the other boy for the fun of it. He's Star Salazar's brother. I was surprised Judge Diaz granted bail. The DA had wanted my guy held so he'd be around for trial. He took off first chance. The bail bondsman took Grandmom's house. You know, Marcy represented Griego. Montclaire worked the case for her."

"You return your fee, since the case never went to trial?"

"I kept the kid out of jail, didn't I? I hope he's enjoying life in Mexico."

"That where he is?"

"That's where Star Salazar said he went."

"Everybody goes to Mexico," Aragon said. "Just this week Star Salazar said she was going with Abel Silva, Jr., Benny Silva's great-nephew."

Fager checked the file, holding up a finger while he read.

"How about that? That's the same guy my kid went to Mexico with."

"Where's your guy now? I like to have a chat."

"Beats me. Still in Mexico, as far as I know."

Aragon stepped out of Fager's building to see Thornton closing the door on her Aston and walking toward her office. She hustled across the parking lot. Thornton had reached the front door by the time Aragon got close enough.

"You get my messages?"

Thornton turned slowly around, not fully facing Aragon. "Detective, have you been harassing my receptionist?"

"We moved Lily Montclaire from Loco Lobo Outfitters. The people you have going out there, they won't find her."

Now Aragon was at the bottom of the steps with Thornton looking down at her.

"I don't have anyone searching for her, detective."

"I know who's doing it."

"Then tell them yourself."

"Tell them this: If they go out there again, it won't be Lily Montclaire they'll find. It will be me."

―――――――

Rigo collected everyone's phones and turned them off until the job was over. They went inside a foot of lead pipe capped at both ends. This guy on *Forensic Files* had done everything right but the phone in his pocket was sending out a map of where he'd been when he said he was somewhere else. Rigo called Benny from the pay phone at the gas station in Pecos while Abel let air out of the van's tires. Soft rubber was quieter on dirt roads, he said. Whether that was right or not, it was good, Abel thinking things through, the little details that kept you alive and out of jail.

They'd gone to town and come back with his Olds and the equipment they'd need. Junior would drive the van later tonight. Rigo and Abel would flank it, lights out, rolling quietly down the dirt road on soft tires, at the end the outfitter's place with this Lily Montclaire. They should be back by dawn. The Olds would be lead car on the Interstate into Santa Fe. They'd take the car to breakfast after they'd fed El Puerco and power-washed the van with hydrogen peroxide. Then it would be repainted inside and out. Benny was talking about switching from white to bright green for all the E. Benny Silva Enterprises vehicles.

That wasn't why he was calling. He had the steps worked out. It was the why of this that made him want to talk to Benny again.

"The lawyer," he said into the phone. "We take care of her problem, she got what she wants. When do we get ours?"

Junior came out of the gas station with a six-pack of Mountain Dew. They'd drive into the forest, find a quiet spot, grab some sleep. He'd set his alarm for midnight. The soda would keep them going until dawn. He was thinking maybe breakfast at Los Amigos on Rodeo Road, fried egg over a cheese enchilada, green chile, a side of carne adovada.

"We have the movies," Benny said, making him forget food and see the birthmark by the lawyer's pubes. "And she's looking at money down the road. Just in case, save something off the model to show what happens she gets too smart."

Rigo watched Abel tell his son to get out of the driver's seat. Later he'd drive. Now, in town, Abel was the one to drive them, avoid getting pulled over for something stupid. They'd checked all the lights. Everything worked. Registration and licenses up to date. No unpaid traffic tickets.

"Have El Puerco warmed up," Rigo said. He didn't want to wait around. It could take hours sometimes to get the thing to the right temperature.

"Call me when you're heading back. I'll unlock the gate so you don't have to honk, draw attention."

Benny doing the hard work, unlocking the gate.

Benny was good at the numbers. But sometimes he forgot how he got things to count. They'd been robbing houses for years. It had been a nice business going shopping in rich people's mansions. Standing in one of those living rooms, Benny bubble-wrapping Indian pots, him with a pillow case heavy with jewelry, Benny had said maybe he should run the front office. Benny had caught him at the right moment, wondering how they'd turn the loot into money.

Anyway, Benny said, you don't have the face for dealing with people.

Benny was right about that. Their father got tired of not being able to tell them apart. He flipped a coin and told Rigo to come to the garage, he had something for him. Close your eyes.

Took forty stitches to close the gash from the rug knife, running from near his ear across his cheek. He'd jerked away, dragging the hook across his mouth and toward his chin.

His father had smacked him for that. *Mijo,* look what you done. I was giving you a little notch. Now you're going to scare all the girls.

Feo, fuerte, y fiel. When the stitches came out his mother said he'd grow up to be the ideal man. Ugly, strong, and loyal.

He'd hit all three. Started putting on muscle while Benny read about conquistadors. Loyal, he had that going, too. Same wife since high school, no women on the side, not even test-driving the ones he ran for politicians in the Legislature.

And loyal to his brother. Him and Abel, and now Junior, were the ones who turned jobs into money that Benny could invest in land

231

that could be a Five Guys or a Java Juice. He and Abel paid for the Vactor trucks, the car crusher, dumpsters from mining towns where they weren't needed any more. He'd first told Benny he was nuts but El Puerco had turned out to be a good buy. It made this end of the business easier in so many ways.

How we normally did things, Rigo wanted to tell Benny, was getting paid up front, not trusting a lawyer to keep their word. How we normally did things, we would have hit this woman in town, a lot closer to El Puerco, somewhere we could scout for days, maybe drop a dumpster nearby so it was ready. Having to go down a road deep into woods, not able to know what was in the trees, get up close, look in windows a couple nights, try the doors, listen to sounds in a sleeping house. This wasn't right.

But he'd do it for Benny.

Last night, seeing how close to the outfitter's house they could get, if there were dogs barking, if there were lights to think about, they'd run into those men on the road. Which way to the Interstate, help us, we're lost. Fucking GPS piece of shit.

Normally, after that, we wouldn't be coming back. Not when everything says those guys were cops.

Rigo walked around the van, giving it another look. He opened the back doors and checked the barrels to make sure they wouldn't be rolling around. Abel and his boy had just about laminated the inside of the van, there was so much plastic taped down in there. The guns and night-vision goggles were in the metal trunk, locked with a combination, no way a cop could say he accidentally looked inside if they were pulled over. The drums were black plastic, locks on the lids, marked *biological waste*. Red stencils of biohazard symbols. A skull and crossbones. *Danger* repeated in Spanish.

He came to the passenger side and Junior climbed in the back. He was a good kid. How he got tall like that, no Silva breaking five-six before, Rigo couldn't figure. Maybe it was not growing up on beans and tortillas, getting meat and milk his whole life. But the boy was still hungry, eager to learn the business. The kind of hunger that carried you through life.

"You good back there?"

"It's all good, *abuelo*." Junior cross-legged on the floor of the van, relaxed. He knew what was coming and was holding steady.

"Let's find a place, get some sleep," Rigo said. "It's going to be a long night."

Abel started the van, the even rumble of the engine saying all was good to go.

———————

Marcy Thornton unwrapped a chocolate Buddha as she waited for her private tub. A couple hours at Falling Waters, Rising Sun, outside of town in the quiet of the mountains. A hot bath, massage, hair treatment—the camellia oil so much less complicated than sex—and herbal wrap to finish. She needed this. She'd seen Judy Diaz in the afternoon. Drunk again, straight vodka out of a water glass, unread motions on her desk. Her robe unzipped showing cleavage was becoming a regular thing. She was working on Benny Silva's findings of fact. Why she just didn't take his lawyer's proposed order, copy it into a Word document, print it out and sign, she didn't understand. Judy was handwriting the thing, copying a paragraph from Silva's motion, one from defendants' response, writing one of her own. She said she didn't want to look so obvious.

Right then, Thornton told herself she was doing the right thing giving Judy to Silva.

Diaz had taken a long drink, then got back to blaming herself for getting Andrea killed. Then she was onto Lily, cursing her, throwing things, a boob coming out of her robe, tucking it back in with the hand holding her pen, leaving a mark, a jagged Z on breastbone and tit.

Thornton decided against bringing up Fager knowing about the videos. She still needed to think that through. She'd searched court records, entering Fager's and Silva's names, and found no indication he'd represented E. Benny or the business. She'd been surprised to find no criminal filings against Benny Silva or Rigo.

She'd also been surprised how much property Benny Silva had scattered around town. She'd seen only a sample on her brief tour with Frank Pacheco. Silva had the kind of money that could put him in a trophy house in the hills on the east side. But he chose to live in the single-story stucco and drive that old American car. Working with garbage trucks, dealing with porta-johns, other people's trash, when he could be looking down on everything from up high. It told her E. Benny had discipline. He stuck to a plan, knew how to avoid attention and keep out of trouble.

She preferred stupid clients with lots of money. Or desperate people who'd empty their pockets after she terrified them about the consequences of fighting the DA on the cheap. When it came time to reach out to her friends on the Court of Appeals, she'd have to be careful not to say too much. No apocalyptic stories for Silva. No nightmare scenarios to steer him into the course of action she wanted. She had a feeling all he would want to hear was she'd got it done.

She hadn't passed along Aragon's message about Lily having been moved. On one level she didn't believe Aragon. Cops don't go around telling you things like that. But when Aragon said she'd be waiting if they came again, she saw the Silvas and Aragon shooting it out in the woods. She'd keep the warning to herself. Might as well see how good Silva and his people were. If anybody got killed, there was no one in the mix she'd miss.

Besides, she hated talking to Silva. The way he'd leered at her, like he knew how she looked naked.

Because he did.

A young man in a black robe with Japanese lettering approached and said her bath was ready. She walked a gravel path lit with lanterns to a private suite with two pools. She'd learned about the communal baths. The one and only time she'd made that mistake, a fat hairy man, who took the clothes-optional route, had backed up to one of the jets and leaned forward, eyes closed. Another man had puked into the bubbling water; he'd done his hot tub after eating sushi and drinking too much sake at the restaurant. It was a great restaurant, but that image ruined it for her forever.

Her suite was open to the sky, fenced apart with bamboo walls. She stripped, sat on the wooden stool on the pebbled floor, and rinsed before easing into the tub. Perspiration beaded on her forehead. She wiped it from her eyes and looked up. She was far enough out of the city to see the Milky Way.

Then came the cooling berth. After she stopped sweating came a soft robe and the flat sandals they provided. Down another gravel path to her massage. She'd asked for Evan with the strong hands. She drifted off when he worked her neck muscles.

Colors, white and lavender. Everything soft and melting. Water falling somewhere, singing as it sparkled on smooth rocks.

Lily reaching out to her with bloody hands.

"I'm sorry," Evan said. "Is that too much pressure? You're really tight here all of a sudden."

"No. It's great. Don't stop."

The herbal wrap with Melanie was last and her favorite. She loved how they sold it: *Cocooned in warm herb-soaked linens, the therapist massages your head, neck, face, or your feet. Relaxing music leads your whole being into sighs of relief. Profoundly detoxifying, a wonderful step on a journey to freedom from bad habits.*

Judy Diaz. That woman was getting toxic. Let the journey begin.

Wind caressing chimes, a breathy flute. Fingers in her hair, rubbing her scalp, kneading her temples, rock hard jaw muscles. The scent of herbs calming her, bringing her again to the edge of dreams. A door opening. A man laughing.

She opened her eyes as Melanie said, "What are you doing? Get out."

A guy in a tight polo shirt ignored Melanie and leaned in close, bringing the smell of cigarette smoke with him.

"Marcy Thornton, you've been served."

He dropped stapled pages on her herb-infused pillow, took a look at her ass under soft linens, and left, not bothering to close the door. Cold night air rushed in.

She wriggled an arm out of her cocoon and held the papers so she could read.

First Judicial District Court, County of Santa Fe, State of New Mexico.

Walter Fager was suing her for his goddamn torn pants—one hundred seven dollars—and *physical and emotional injuries sustained, the full extent to be proven at trial.*

She shivered as the damp linen sheet was rolled down her spine.

Melanie said, "I'm sorry. Our time is up. *Namaste.*"

TWENTY-FIVE

"THREE-HUNDRED AND TWO PUSH-UPS nonstop," Aragon said, in the dark woods with Lewis. Pine needles under her chin, Javier's night-vision binoculars on the ground by her hip. In dim starlight she could see her Springfield on the folded towel in front of her. She didn't want to be lying on it when she needed to release the holster. With the towel under the gun, she wouldn't be grabbing up sticks and twigs if she had to move fast.

They lay under the trees by the straight section of road leading to the house. The sheriff's deputies had left. They couldn't wait around on the hunch that guys in a van for a Santa Fe waste disposal company presented a real and present danger to one of their citizens. They had a wingnut in his cabin outside Tecolote shooting at cars on the interstate.

Rivera said if they needed help, give Tucker a call. He'd come himself, but he had meetings running late, then a conference call with Peking, something about espionage at Los Alamos Labs, he couldn't say more.

They talked to stay awake, another night without sleep but needing to be ready, alert.

"On the back of the hands?" Lewis adjusted his body to put the shotgun on a stump by his right shoulder. "That's the top of the wrists."

"That was another woman, three hundred eighty or something in fifteen minutes on the back of her hands. She has some kind of wrist problem, can you believe it? At two hundred she took a deep breath, then got back to it."

"I couldn't do that many push-ups in a day."

"You can lift a mountain over your head, bench press a Mack truck."

"The burn. I get it fast."

"I reached 125," Aragon said. "I was on fire. Drop me in a tub of ice cubes."

"What's the men's record?"

"I heard it was over ten thousand."

"No way."

"Some meatless Japanese guy."

"So he wasn't pushing that much weight. But dang. How long did that take? Not fifteen minutes."

Sometime later, the shadows different now that the stars and slivered moon had moved overhead, Lewis asked, "How far to the closest Blake's? You nail it within a mile, I'll buy breakfast. I'm thinking of their two-pound burritos right now and a hot coffee."

He'd caught her nodding. "It would be the one on St. Michael's." She rubbed her eyes. "From here to I-25, twenty-two miles. I clocked it coming in. Down the highway, into town. Forty-four miles total. I'll have the number one egg and bacon burrito, green chile."

"No home fries?"

"They're inside."

When she caught herself nodding again, the moon now out of the sky completely, she said, "I've been thinking about going to Mexico."

Lewis yawned and stood just to move. Branches broke as he circled their position. "I bet you've accumulated enough time to take a year off."

She stood, her limbs stiff. She put her pistol in its holster on her hip. "These people who just up and disappear. Dolores Baca, Star Salazar, Fager's client, the PCP pusher. That witness against Rigo Silva in the prostitution case. Those Jewish brothers buying real estate in Silva's neck of the woods, back when south of Cerrillos was the frontier. I was in on the search when their wives called us to report their husbands missing. A realtor there to get keys said the place had been bought by locals. He said it was funny, two Jewish brothers switching places with two Hispanic brothers, twins, even. He'd heard the Jews decided to take their business to Mexico."

"Without their worried wives." Lewis groaned. She saw his dark shape bending forward, reaching for his toes. "You don't believe any of those people ever crossed the border," he said with his head by his knees.

She tried for her own toes and couldn't reach them. Damn, was she stiff. She shook her legs, rolled her neck, swung her arms. She tried again and made it.

"Back when the Sureños were moving in." Now she stood tall, stretching arms toward the stars. "A bunch of them on our radar suddenly disappeared. We thought they'd gone back to LA. That was when they were pushing up Agua Fria, into Benny's neighborhood. That had never been gang territory. Not Mann Street, not West Side Locos. Just nice old Hispanic grandpas raking the gravel in their driveways, *abuelas* washing bird shit off the Virgin of Guadalupe in their yards."

"In his lawsuit"—Lewis was out in the road, casting a shadow on silvery ground—"the watchman wasn't available to testify. Defendants could never locate him to serve the subpoena. It was all Benny's show, his story going to the jury without any inconvenient facts getting in the way. You hear that?"

They both stopped moving.

"An engine," Aragon said. "But I don't see anything." She found the night-vision binoculars on the pine needles. Standing in the road next to Lewis, she looked to where the straight section started right after it climbed out of the arroyo. She wished she had the department's military goggles that read heat signatures. These hunting goggles from Javier only enhanced dim light.

"Some kind of vehicle," she said, interpreting the fuzzy green and black images at the limit of the binoculars' range. "Two men walking on either side, approaching our position." The images sharpened as they came closer. "Out of the road, Rick. They're carrying rifles."

———————

"Was that a bear?"

Rigo Silva pushed his Army goggles hard against his face, trying to reclaim the blurred shape that had danced across his eyes.

"I saw it, too," said Abel, walking on the other side of the road, also with night-vision, Junior at the wheel of the van, headlights out, following ten yards behind. "It went into the woods on the left."

"I saw it on the right. There's two."

"Got it." Abel pulled up and Junior stopped the van behind him. "Laying low. I can see its heat in there. It's big."

"Mother and cub." Rigo scanned his side for a heat signature. "Shit. We're between them. We have to drive past. I'm not walking into that." He studied the thermal image on his lens. It wasn't moving. Wouldn't a bear run, climb a tree?

He saw something else. Last night, the maybe-cops, saying a tree blocked the road. They'd passed that spot a half mile back, all clear. Now a tree across their path when they were almost to the outfitter's ranch. He could see the trailer straight ahead in a clearing, heat showing someone floating above the ground, probably on a porch.

There had been no tree here when they scouted earlier today.

The thermal image in the woods shifted, arms in front of a body, holding something long, a black line across a white and gray body.

"Bears don't move like that." He flipped the safety lever on his AK-47, the only thing left from the Sureños who'd tried to bother them once. "That lawyer put us in a trap." Rigo leveled his sights on the person trying to hide, but their body heat was saying *here I am*.

Then he heard it.

Bears don't rack shotguns.

———

She was close enough to see the black rifles in the men's green hands, slung forward from the hip, a wide strap over their shoulders. Lewis must have seen it too, even without night-vision. The two men were on the road, starlight glinting off the windshield of the van behind them, dash lights showing the driver's body, knuckles on the steering wheel.

Fire leaped from the rifles in Lewis's direction. Fully automatic weapons, she couldn't guess the number of shots. His shotgun boomed once. She took aim and emptied her magazine. One of the men went down, but the other swung his machine gun toward her. She saw the fire sweeping in an arc coming her way and threw herself behind a log. The goggles came off when she went down. Branches rained on her back as bullets tore the forest apart. The second machine gun started firing again. She had only wounded the man.

She ejected the spent magazine but was afraid to lift her hip to get at the spare strapped to her leg.

The curtain of bullets dropped lower, found the log and ripped it apart. She pushed harder into the earth, pressing a cheek into the ground, making herself flat. Something dug into her face, needles piercing skin, her flesh on fire. A goddamned cactus. She took it, eyes watering, chewing her tongue to keep from screaming.

A break in the clatter of machine guns, silence, the shower of twigs and branches stopped. Then magazines snapping into place. She rolled, snatched the extra clip on her thigh, and slapped it into place. She armed the pistol and lifted it above her head, the butt on the ruins of the log. She fired without looking. She got off she didn't know, eight, ten rounds, and Lewis's shotgun exploded twice—he was alive!—before the machine guns started again.

It sounded closer. One of them was walking toward her. She was sorry she'd given her position away wasting bullets.

She tilted the barrel at where the shooter would stand when he came to finish her. She might be able to fire once.

Behind her a rifle cracked. More shots. Breaking glass.

It was Serena with a hunting rifle.

The machine gun fire lifted, hitting branches higher on the trees. One gun stopped. Then the other. She heard the van's doors opening and looked up to see a man pushing another man inside, then closing the door behind him. The van backed away fast, tail lights lighting the road and making trees glow red. A gun fired from the passenger window, two, three bursts. She dropped behind the remains of her log. When she lifted her head again the van was pulling a K-turn right before the arroyo. One knee bent, both hands on her pistol, she used her last rounds. Metal pinged down there. Glass cracked. Then the van was gone.

"Denise?" Lewis's shadow stepped from the forest onto the starlit pan of the hard clay road.

"I'm good. You?"

"Standing and breathing. I think you hit one."

"I know I did. Did you hear what they said right before they fired?"

"'The lawyer put us in a trap.'"

"I told Marcy Thornton if they came out here again they'd find me. She must have forgot to pass that along."

———————

Serena showed them the bullet holes through Hunter Hayes and Kellie Pickler posters in her girls' bedroom at the end of the trailer, the last room down the hall from the kitchen. She tugged a mattress off the box spring and put her finger in a tear, a bullet inside.

"Javier may feel guilty for what happened to you, Denise. It makes no more sense than blaming yourself for not saving Miguel. Javier was two hundred miles away. If he'd been there, you would have watched your brother dying next to your boyfriend." She ripped off the posters, revealing the holes in the home's metal wall, the pink insulation inside. "But my daughters don't owe you anything. What do I tell them about why someone shot up where they sleep?"

"I'm sorry, Serena."

"Javier's even now, *comprende*?" Her looks softened. "You've got cactus in your face. Follow me."

In a bathroom, Serena ordered Aragon to hold still as she used a tweezer to pull cactus spines from her cheek. Then she told them to leave, she'd clean up, get new posters from town, lie to the girls she'd redecorated their room as a surprise. She'd plug the walls with extra insulation and find something for a patch.

But it wouldn't work. The girls would want their own posters and take down Mom's. They'd see the holes and ask and she'd have nothing to say.

Aragon used the house's landline to report the shooting to her sergeant, then the Sheriff's Office. There was only one way out of the canyon, the interstate. Travelling east or west, a van with the windshield shot out should be easy to find. She asked her sergeant to get someone at the gate to Silva Enterprises just in case the van got through.

Next she called Rivera's cell. She needed help she couldn't get elsewhere. He didn't answer. She called twice more and settled for voicemail. As she was leaving a message, his number showed as an incoming call.

"Where are you?" she asked.

"I was sleeping. I left my phone in the living room. Sorry it took so long to answer."

She told him about the fire fight. "Machine guns, Tomas. We don't have anything to match that."

"We do. But we don't have a SWAT team on standby. It's a volunteer crew in the Santa Fe office. I'll call them out and get over to Silva's place. Can you meet me there? We're getting the forensics on Cassandra Baca. Some things we really must consider."

"I'm in the truck. Lewis is heading to the office. Our sergeant wants him to brief the chief in person."

"But you're okay? Nobody hurt?"

"One of them is wounded. My sister-in-law is pissed. Lewis is talking to his wife, asking about his girls. I'm still shaking. A machine gun is a very scary thing, Tomas. There's nothing you can do but wait to die."

They found more holes in the mobile home. All the lights on now, even in the barns and bunkhouses. In the wooden deck and stairs at the front door, bullets had splintered steps and railings. The picture window had almost been blown out, three holes near the bottom left corner. An inch higher and Serena would have had shattered glass all over her living room.

With her back to the house, Aragon looked down the straight stretch of road to where the van had been close to two hundred yards away. Serena had fired from the porch. The sound of breaking glass, she'd hit the windshield, the scope worthless at night, using starlight to aim.

"We should stay," Lewis said. "Down around the bend where she won't see. At least till dawn."

"We should stay until Javier gets back. But she won't let us."

———

The damn steering wheel had been slippery with blood. Now the blood was sticky and messed up his phone's screen.

He didn't like using his personal cell phone so soon after a job. Bullshit there were no records somewhere that would put him close just by turning on the phone. And somebody, somewhere was listening, recording everything said. You talked about these things with only people you trusted, face to face, no one else around, with lots of machinery screaming or deep in the woods.

Nothing like this had happened before. Benny needed to know.

Rigo said, "I'm an hour out. Junior's dead. Abel just died next to me. I'll be driving my Olds. The van's shot to shit." The phone slipped from his hand. He found it in his lap, blood pooled under his balls: Junior's from when he got killed driving the van slowly behind him and Abel. One rifle shot through the windshield. Going in at his Adam's apple, tearing all those veins and arteries when it blew out the back of his neck.

Benny's voice down there with the blood, asking, "Junior *and* Abel?" Rigo brought the wet phone to his ear, hoping it wouldn't short out. "Yeah, both of them. That lawyer, she's dead next. Make sure the gate's open."

TWENTY-SIX

BENNY WENT OUT FRONT to unlock the gate. None of the businesses around here were open this late. But cars were parked across the street. A black panel truck drove past. He saw its brake lights before it went dark at the end of the block. Then a light blinked inside. No doors opened. No one got out.

Marcy Thornton had led them into an ambush? She had assets like that? Not likely. Those cars across the street, the black truck, it was police. She was working with them and knew what was waiting at the outfitter's ranch.

He checked the monitors in the room Abel had built, seeing more cars at the back of the lot, a man getting out, walking up to the chain-link fence, rattling it, looking in.

He went out front and locked the gate he'd just opened.

In his office, he got Rigo on the phone. There's cops everywhere. I don't want the gate open, give them an invitation. You'll be okay. They're looking for the van. Flash your lights to let me know it's you, then hit the gas. I'll open and close fast. Drive straight back to the hangar.

The police would be watching all the time now. That had never happened before. Maybe they were outside his house, too. And Rigo's. And Abel's. They'd notice he wouldn't be coming and going. Abel Jr., the school would report him truant.

The future in those two, gone. No one to take over the business, all he and Rigo had built. He sat in the security room, the black and white images of the gate, the fence, the street, and the police cars. Abel's notebook there, he'd been studying on how to do the job better, learning so much from the television shows that showed real cases.

None of that he'd ever use.

Benny Silva ripped pages from the notebook and fed them into the shredder in his office. Above him was the painting of the conquistadors massacring Indians, his Spanish sword on the wall above his desk.

He wanted Marcy Thornton to see that sword shining, him flipping it back and forth, reflected light in her eyes making her bring a hand up. But she couldn't. Rigo would be holding her, her shirt undone showing the ribs and tit over her heart.

Rigo bringing in two dead bodies. Then what? They couldn't do funerals, no way to explain how Abel and Junior got shot. The cops would figure out it had been Rigo blowing past them. After that they'd stop any car leaving the gate with some excuse, maybe have dogs to tell them what was in the trunk.

It would be nice if they could sneak Abel and Junior out so they could be buried somewhere secret. He and Rigo could visit them, maybe once a year on this very day.

But that wasn't going to happen.

Benny went through the door at the back of his office, staying inside the buildings and fences screening him from the cops on the street. He went to the hangar at the back of the lot. El Puerco needed time to warm up.

Aragon tapped on the window. Rivera reached up and covered the dome light in the panel truck he was using as his command post. She got in next to him. The gate to Silva's place was down the street and closed.

"Hey," Rivera said.

She'd expected more. "Anything?"

"Benny or his brother came out," Rivera said. "Jiggled the lock, cover to look around. He knows we're here."

She lifted a water bottle from the console. "I'm really thirsty. Like I ran ten miles in the sun. Drained. I've never been so scared."

He kept his eyes on the windshield. She waited for something from him.

"At least I didn't shit my pants," she said.

The water was good, really good. Something in it. Citrus and sugar.

"We've got all approaches covered, between us and SFPD," Rivera said. "There's a team out back. Still no sign of the van. State Police has choppers over the interstate."

She took another swig. "Any reports from ERs?" What was that on her tongue?

"Nobody coming in with gunshot wounds. How do you know you hit someone?"

"I saw them go down. They got back up firing. Those goddamn machine guns. I don't ever want to face that again. But the way they dropped, I hit something critical. Look."

A brown car, older American model, turned onto the street, moving at about the speed limit, not too fast, not slow enough to look suspicious. Behind the gate inside the business's yard, a man, it looked like Benny, not his more muscular brother, stepped into the light and moved quickly to the gate. The car accelerated, the engine raced. Benny swung the gate open, then threw it shut behind the car. She saw him fastening the lock, looking their way, then heading around the back of the building, following the car that had not stopped out front where the parking spaces were.

Aragon said, "I bet that was Rigo driving. So who was in the van?"

Rivera checked a text message. "They got a license plate. Hold on, yeah, Rigoberto Silva."

Aragon cracked the door, letting the dome light go on, no point in worrying about it. "I want to go in there. Why are all the lights on out back? Is that steam?"

"You can't go in." Now Rivera was looking at her. His eyes were different, not really connecting deep within her. She wasn't sensing Miguel in him anymore. "That's why you're being sued. Entering and searching Geronimo's ranch without a warrant."

"It stopped a killer." She rolled her tongue in her mouth, thinking about the taste of the water.

"If it had gone to trial, it would have derailed the case. Everything you found would have been suppressed."

"Calm down. What was it you said we had to talk about, the forensics that came back?"

"Get back in. This might take a while."

She closed the door. They sat in the glow from streetlights a little distance away.

"They recovered buccal cells from the bite wounds on Andrea," Rivera said.

"That's good, right?"

"They ran the DNA against the samples you collected, from Montclaire, the water glasses in the courtroom from Thornton and Diaz. They got a positive match, ninety-nine-plus percent certainty."

"And? Why are you stringing this out?"

"The buccal cells came from Lily Montclaire."

Montclaire lying to them every step of the way. And she had bought it. The time wasted. Bullets from machine guns sending wood chips into her face, somebody out there shot, maybe dying with her bullet inside them. Her relationship with Serena destroyed, probably Javier next when he returned home and saw bullet holes in his kids' room.

"They can do that, get buccal cells from a bite mark that long after?" she asked.

"They got DNA from Thornton and Diaz on the girl's clothes you secured from the Baca residence. But the DNA in the bite wound, that's all Montclaire."

She pulled out her phone and called Lewis, told him the news, and said he should wake up Lily.

When she was done she turned to Rivera. He was drinking from the water bottle.

"We know she was with Cassandra Baca," she said. "Lily didn't deny that. Why lie to us about the bite? Hell, she admitted to procuring, to everything else."

"Dumping more on Thornton? Maybe shame?"

"Lily doesn't know that word. I think it's the first one, dumping more on Thornton. You want to be in on questioning her?"

"She's screwed for witness protection. It's time we consider her in an entirely different light."

Rigo had Abel and Junior in the trunk of the Olds, wrapped in the plastic they'd intended for the model. Abel had been shot twice,

251

once through the thigh, another in the ass. It was the bullet in the thigh that had killed him, the big artery in the leg cut in two. Junior's head was barely hanging on, just the skin on the side of the neck keeping things together.

Rigo added fresh tape so the sheets didn't open when they lifted them out. He did most of the work. Benny wasn't much help. They got Abel and Junior onto a cart with wheels.

Rigo brushed his hand over the trunk's carpet.

"They always find something," he said. "You can't beat forensics. I like this car. Only twenty thousand on the second engine. But it goes to the crusher tonight."

Benny was able by himself to push the cart to the lift that fed El Puerco.

"There's no other way, Rigo," Benny said. The look on Rigo's face reflected the sadness and anger in his own heart. He saw Rigo's scar as a second frown. "We say they went to Mexico. A trip, father and son. Abel got the idea and just wanted to take off. Fishing season down there, deer hunts on a private ranch, no limit, we'll think of something."

"When they don't come back?" Rigo tugged the plastic and touched Abel's cheek.

"Things happen down there. There's a war, bodies in mass graves, people getting stopped on roads. It's a crazy country."

"That lawyer. We bring her here."

They lifted the plastic sheet with Junior first and rolled him into the broth. Abel went next, pushing Junior below the surface, the boy under his father. They could see the acids already working when bodies rolled and fingers broke the surface.

Benny closed El Puerco's heavy stainless lid, like the top of an enormous pressure cooker. Rigo worked the dials, pressed the red switch. The needle on the temperature gauge rose, steam escaped from a place under the lid where the seal was worn.

The plastic from the trunk went into the incinerator. Rigo drove the car to the crusher. Benny sat at the controls and watched the Oldsmobile turning into a block of metal and rubber.

———————

"Busy for middle of the night," Aragon said into her phone, Rivera listening from his panel truck. She stood at the fence around Silva Enterprises, the front gate a half block behind her, another half block to the end of the property. "Machines turning. I hear metal, glass popping. Lots of chemical smells. And steam out of that big metal building at the very back. It just went rushing up the stack like a pressure valve was opened. I'm going in, Tomas. No, not now. We need to talk to Montclaire. But I'm going when I figure how to do it."

The phone brushed her cheek. She winched. Serena had missed some of the cactus spines. She tried pulling them out and cursed her short fingernails. They'd stay in her face until she got home.

TWENTY-SEVEN

"I DON'T KNOW WHAT buccal cells are," Montclaire said. "I won't argue."

"That's it?" Aragon drummed fingers on the table in the interrogation room, the cot Montclaire had been using pushed to the wall, a sheet and blanket clumped over a pillow.

"Mr. Fager said things would turn up I couldn't foresee and to be ready for bad news."

"Fager?" Aragon felt Lewis's tension, seated next to her, as he crushed an empty Styrofoam cup. Rivera was against the wall, letting them wrestle with Montclaire. "You think he's in this to help you?"

Montclaire had her hands pulled inside the sleeves of a fuzzy sweater. She wore long pants and socks. She wasn't going to freeze while being questioned again. Aragon got a different sense from her, as though Montclaire knew this moment had been coming.

Keeping his shoulder against the wall, Rivera said, "Ms. Montclaire, I previously informed you that if you were less than completely truthful, you would be excluded from the witness protection program. Your life could depend on telling the truth. First, Cassandra

Baca is found dead just as you're revealing how Thornton used her with Judge Diaz."

"That was her real name?" Montclaire's hands emerged from the sweater's sleeves. She laced her fingers together, rested her chin on her knuckles.

Aragon heard that as, *Now you're the ones telling me things.*

"And tonight," Rivera went on, "an attempt was made on your life."

"I heard the party boys screaming when they were shoved into cells. And some guy going on about getting his wife when he makes bail. Nobody else has bothered me."

"The attack occurred where you'd been staying recently. Men looking for you exchanged fire with detectives Aragon and Lewis. They'd tried getting to you before, but a police blockade stopped them. They returned with automatic weapons tonight."

"How did they know to look for me there?"

"Marcy Thornton forced Detective Aragon to disclose that information in a deposition presided over by Judge Diaz. Draw your own conclusions, Ms. Montclaire."

"So that's why you moved me." Montclaire's big eyes took in Aragon and Lewis, hands back inside the sleeves of her fuzzy sweater. "You know, I never said I didn't bite Andrea. Cassandra. Listen to your tape. I didn't lie to you."

"But you've been less than completely truthful." Rivera moved from the wall and stood over Montclaire. "It is very hard to believe anything you've told us, an impossible story about a prominent lawyer bribing a judge through the sexual exploitation of a teenage girl. Where I'm at now, I'd need to see film to believe you. It could have been you enjoying Cassandra Baca on your own. When we caught you destroying evidence, burning down a neighborhood, you put it on Marcy Thornton and Judge Diaz, thinking we'd fall over ourselves rushing to get them in jail. You're still the last person who we know was with Cassandra Baca."

"You want a movie," Montclaire said.

"I'd buy front row tickets."

"They don't sell reserved seating for movies."

"You're sounding confident, Lily." Aragon took it from Rivera. The smart comeback, they hadn't heard that before. "You told us you learned from Thornton to always keep something in the bank when you're dealing with police. Are you about to make a late withdrawal?"

Montclaire hunched her shoulders to her ears, a trim, long body inside a bulky sweater three sizes too big. It was a pose, something from a fashion magazine from years ago. She held it while they waited for an answer.

Damn, Aragon thought. *She's in control right now.*

"Call Mr. Fager," Montclaire said. "He has something for you. You'll be surprised."

"Tell us first. Why the surprise?"

"Mr. Rivera said he needs a movie. Mr. Fager will show it to you. Do you know you've got prickly things in your cheek? Your skin's turning black."

––––––––

Four thirty in the morning. Aragon didn't care as she pressed the buzzer on Fager's front door, then banged with her fist. A light went on inside, a deadbolt slid back. Fager stood there in boxer shorts and a T-shirt that said *Army Rangers*.

Aragon put two fingers into his chest and pushed him into the house. Lewis and Rivera came after her. They formed a semicircle around Fager, his butt against a wall.

"Turn over the video Montclaire gave you," Aragon said.

"You could have called." Fager adjusted his boxers to close the fly. "I would have brought it to your office."

"We saved you the trip. Where is it?"

"In my office. You may watch it on my computer."

"Put something on," Aragon said, and Fager stopped first at a bedroom for a robe.

He was living in his home office. A blanket and pillow on the leather couch, law books on the floor serving as tables for cups and empty plates. The waste baskets overflowed with balls of crumpled paper. The clothes Fager had been wearing before sleep were in a pile on the floor, what looked like a good suit mixed in with sweat pants and jeans.

He pushed away dishes and brought a laptop close to the edge of his desk. From the top drawer, he withdrew a postage-stamp-sized card and plugged it into a port. In a second they were watching a close-up of women's feet, then a room, what looked like diplomas and certificates on a wall, Cassandra Baca's face close to the lens, her nose unnaturally big, then backing away and looking normal. Marcy Thornton and Judith Diaz behind her, Thornton handing Diaz a pair of handcuffs, Lily Montclaire coming into the shot with a bottle and glasses. Cassandra facing the camera, opening her shirt. Then the four went at it until Lewis said, "I've seen enough."

"Where did Lily get this?" Aragon asked.

"This is where I send you back to her." Fager ejected the card and handed it over.

The sun was just rising over the mountains outside when Aragon waved the video card inside a baggie in front of Montclaire's face.

"How did you get this?"

Montclaire had made up the cot since they'd left. Her small roll-on suitcase was packed.

"I found it in Cassandra—Andrea's—I don't know what to call her. I'm sticking with Andrea. I found it in her overnight bag. After the first time, she always brought it. She said she needed to clean up before going home. She always set it in the same spot. Not in the bathroom, but there in the living room. Once I put a bottle in front of it. She got up to pour when we didn't need refills and put the bottle in a different place. When we moved around, she'd dive onto the couch and call us back. The last time, she moved the bag for no reason I could see except it followed us to Judy's bedroom. I caught her in the bathroom when Marcy and Judy were snoring. She was checking a camera."

"But you didn't tell your boss?"

"Things were falling apart. I'm not going to lie to you."

"What, starting now?"

"Look, I held it back as insurance. Something told me Marcy would throw me overboard when the shit hit. Remember how she wouldn't let me see what evidence you had against me, right before I fired her? You know your cheek's looking worse?"

"Where's the camera?"

"I let Andrea keep it. I didn't want it, just the video card."

Aragon made her describe the camera. Montclaire couldn't remember the brand, but said it seemed expensive. Too expensive for a teenage hooker? I did wonder where she got it, Montclaire said.

Aragon looked to Rivera to see if he had questions. He stepped forward and pulled a chair across from Montclaire. Standing, he put

258

a foot on the seat, his arms folded across his chest. Montclaire had her poses. He had his.

"You've played your cards well, Ms. Montclaire. I am prepared to move forward with formally placing you into the Federal Witness Protection Program. We'll be talking a lot more. And I remind you to be always truthful with us. So I'm going to ask a very important question right now. Where are the other videos, of the other times?"

"I can't say for sure."

"Did you ask Cassandra Baca about them?"

"When I was taking her back to the Pizza Hut, I kept thinking she had to be working with someone. The expensive camera. There was that case in Albuquerque, the little judge."

"The little judge?"

"I know what she's talking about," Aragon said. "He was a polio victim, his legs were sticks. He'd been bringing a whore to his house, and she started videotaping him, a camera in her purse. She and her pimp tried blackmailing him. She later said he'd threatened her, raped her. The case got him off the bench but he ducked jail."

"That one," Montclaire said. "I asked who Andrea was working with. It was Star. She got the videos after each night."

"How was Star going to use them?"

"She didn't know. She told me she was going to get in a lot of trouble because I took the last video and she didn't want to ever see me or Marcy or Judy again."

Aragon called Rivera and Lewis into the hall. Lewis anticipated what she was going to say.

"The money under the car, the twenty grand even. That was what Cassandra Baca got for videotaping the parties. No way that came from turning tricks. Are you seeing this, Tomas?" Aragon asked. Years of working with Lewis, she knew he did.

"You're going to tell me," Rivera said.

"Benny Silva was blackmailing Diaz. Through his nephew's son, Junior, he had a connection with Star Salazar. His brother, Rigo, knew Dolores Baca had tricked, maybe also knew Cassandra was doing it. Remember Lily said the first time she handed Star money in an envelope from Judge Diaz's chambers? Benny Silva learned about it and opened the door to opportunity knocking."

"So Silva's been extorting Judge Diaz?"

"With that video," Lewis said, "we can get warrants. The ten minutes we saw will get us into Diaz's house. Lily can identify the location. She used Thornton's car to taxi Cassandra, we get a warrant for that. She said the cuffs are in Thornton's office, throw that in, too."

"Can we get into Silva's place?" Aragon asked.

"I don't see it. We're short of anything solid on him," Rivera said. "But I'm with you, we search every place owned or controlled by Diaz and Thornton. We'll work with Lily to fine-tune the probable cause. By the way, no shot-up van has yet appeared at Silva's place."

"We'll find something through Thornton or Diaz to get to him." Aragon opened the door to re-enter the interrogation room. "I want to be on the search of Thornton's office, okay?"

Montclaire was waiting for them, holding the extension for the roll-on suitcase, ready to go.

———

Fager had watched the detectives in his driveway after he turned over Montclaire's video, busy on their phones, a high-five between Aragon and Lewis. Next they'd be getting warrants, giving Marcy and Judy visits they would never forget. Nothing they owned would escape fingers inside blue latex. He hoped they went for cheek swabs. He'd like to see Marcy being told to open her mouth and don't bite.

But they were fuck-ups, these cops. They'd botched his wife's case. If he hadn't played along with Aragon, sanitizing her illegal search of Geronimo's ranch by playing the private citizen who just happened upon fourteen graves upriver from the compound—just chanced upon depressions in sand at the head of a canyon on the edge of nowhere—the case would have been blown out of the water on the first motion to suppress.

No way he'd trust them to get this right.

He took a sleeping pill. He needed to appear rested and calm tomorrow, not the crazy man stalking the lawyer who had defended his wife's killer, a disbarred shylock bent on revenge. He didn't want to come across like some strung-out pornographer when he played the video for, in order, starting at eleven down in Albuquerque: the investigative reporter from KRQE-TV; then across the street to the other station, a reporter he knew there who used to cover the court-house; heading back north, the station on Carlisle just off the inter-state; mid-afternoon, the criminal reporter for the *Albuquerque Journal* and last, around six, the AP stringer who covered Santa Fe.

The TV people wanted to photograph him here in his house, have him point to things left behind by his wife, connect the audi-ence with his sorrow. The files from her case, the autopsy, crime scene photos, were still there on the dining table from the first day he'd gotten them. That cup, the one from their trip to Alaska, where he'd sat reading the initial reports on the investigation of the man who'd murdered Linda.

They could do that later as the story grew and he had time to straighten things up.

In the hallway to his office, the detectives had stepped around clothes and shoes. Dishes were piled in the kitchen sink. He needed to take out the trash.

The house probably smelled. He hadn't opened a window in months.

He'd wear the somber gray suit, not the navy blue blazer with brass buttons. A plain white button-down shirt, no stripes. Skip the French cuffs and links. Go with wingtips, not the loafers. Make sure he shaved right, put something on his hair to keep it in place. Get it cut, this week for sure.

He'd be sorrowful, distraught at the discovery of disheartening evidence showing the depths to which Santa Fe's legal system had sunk. He'd ask the reporters if they wanted copies of the video, passed onto him by a concerned citizen. He just happened to have an extra with him.

He wanted something done about a judicial system no longer meeting the pledge made to citizens. He wanted reform, improvement, a return to the high standard of ethics justice requires.

What he really wanted to know was how to get the video on YouTube, or that other thing he'd heard about, Tumblr, whatever that was. The television stations would never show all the action. They'd say, *The following report may offend some people. Parental discretion is advised.* Then they'd soften the edges so much, use bland words to describe what you weren't going to see, you'd wonder what the warning had been for.

On the Internet, the world could see Marcy and Judy in all their glory, forever, nothing they could do about it.

Maybe he should pay some kid to set up a website just for the video. MarcyThornton.com.

Yago and the boys in Pod B wouldn't have to use their imagination any more. Somebody could smuggle in screen shots. They'd be taped to walls above beds until the next contraband sweep. Pictures of Judy Diaz would turn up in the men's rooms at the courthouse, be passed around by staff, fellow judges looking differently at her in meetings.

He took another sleeping pill. His mind was taking off and he needed to shut it down for a few hours.

TWENTY-EIGHT

"Put in"—Rivera pacing in his office, dictating in a robotic monotone to Aragon—"the confidential informant, who has established his/her credibility on numerous instances as corroborated by subsequent investigation, states the deceased was transported recently in two vehicles owned by subject, a 2010 Aston Martin and a 2015 Dodge Durango. We can add the license numbers. I'll get them from DMV."

Aragon at Rivera's desktop, in his office with its view of fire in the mountains, black clouds lit from inside, a wall of flame below, orange and bright even in full sun. She asked, "Do we need to include what Lily told us that we couldn't corroborate? She's credible on some things, not on others?"

What she wanted to ask was, how did I get the job being your secretary? More important, she wanted the warrants approved and executed today. It was still early morning after another sleepless night. Rivera said a judge was waiting to meet him over breakfast in chambers in the federal courthouse. He was to bring the warrant application and burritos.

She wanted to get home to get the cactus needles out of her face. Montclaire was right. The skin was turning black, pimples of dead flesh around the places where she still had cactus in her skin.

But she wanted this more.

So she was taking dictation for the first time since riding shotgun, the junior officer in the car, back when Santa Fe police patrolled in pairs, before computers and radios and cameras ate up the passenger seat.

"We show the judge the video," Rivera said. "It will be a tactical nuke and blow away all doubts and questions. Lily is credible for what matters."

"You're the FBI Special Agent, Albuquerque Division, assigned to the Santa Fe Resident Agency, with an MA from Georgetown University, employed as a special agent for twelve years, who has attended numerous seminars on investigative techniques and criminal procedure and has earned the equivalent of one year toward a law degree." She'd written that down in paragraph one.

"The scope of the alleged conspiracy"—the monotone again—"includes bribery, obstruction of justice, and murder. The criminal acts described herein occurred at numerous locations in Santa Fe County, New Mexico, and utilized subject's personal vehicles and law office premises. You paint it broadly like that"—talking now to her, some feeling in his voice—"you can include a wish list for whatever and wherever you want to search. I've never searched a lawyer's office. I'm looking forward to it."

"Separate warrants for Diaz and Thornton?"

"We just cut and paste, but yes, each subject is served with a warrant particular to them. It's their privacy right being invaded."

"I've done warrants."

"This is federal. The rules are different."

Yes, sir.

"I'll summarize our interviews with Montclaire," she said. "More than stating a general belief in the informant's credibility, we can lay out specifically where she's been on the money. The video showing her arriving in Thornton's car, for instance, what I saw standing outside Diaz's house the first time, before we understood what was going on. Me being a fellow law enforcement officer, graduate of Northern New Mexico Community College who has attended the New Mexico Law Enforcement Academy and exactly two seminars at the UNM Law School, qualified in over twenty trials to testify as an expert on various investigative techniques, you may rely on my observations and conclusions reasonably drawn therefrom."

"You've done this before."

Hadn't she just told him?

Something was wrong between them. She pushed it out of her mind and got to work combining her notes. Rivera went down the hall to check on the coffee. You could smell it burning. She looked in his desk for a highlighter. There among the paper clips and Post-it note pads, the ruler and scissors, was a CD case for the country song he'd played for her, about not closing her eyes, looking straight at him, putting her past behind to be with him now.

She opened the plastic case. Instead of a disc matching the cover, she found a CD labeled in black marker. *Yoga Zone: Blues and Greens, Wind and Rain*. She pushed the drawer shut at the sound of footsteps and focused on the keyboard.

He returned with two cups of coffee and placed one by her keyboard.

"Do you have any more of that water you had in the car last night?" She didn't turn from the screen. "It was good."

"Sorry. That was it."

"It had pineapple juice. Where have I tasted that before?"

She heard him moving behind her, pulling out a chair, exhaling a little too loud after testing the hot coffee.

"I'll draft the section requesting a forensic examination of their computers," he said. "It's a little trickier than authorization to search a physical location. As for attorney files, we must establish prophylactic measures to avoid violating attorney-client privilege. It's like minimization procedures on a wiretap."

Prophylactic measures.

"Are you screwing Sun-Hi Breskin? *Sunny*?"

The sighing again, but not because the coffee was hot.

He had his eyes down, thinking what to say.

"Last night, I pull up in the truck," she said. "No reaction. Every time one of us went through something terrible, faced death, dealt with it, I'd bring the truck. It was our signal we needed each other. Now, *nada*. Not even a hug after I was shot at by machine guns. The water, the pineapple stuff, we had at the Breskin place. That flaky music, I remember you said you liked it. Did she burn the CD before or after you finished your list of questions that cleared her husband?"

"Denise, let's forget this for now. We have work."

"We'll get to work. It's what keeps me going. You went out to Breskin's alone. I thought maybe it was some new FBI procedure, letting you guys fly solo. You just wanted to be with her. You were there last night when I called."

Rivera closed the door though they were alone in the building.

"You weren't there for me," he said. "I'd hoped it would get better."

"*I'd* get better. That's what you were hoping. Your magic touch would fix me."

"You have needs. So do I. Maybe you were getting what you wanted."

"I was giving."

"And maybe that's the problem. You were doing it just to make me feel better. To serve and protect, even in the back of your brother's truck. What I needed was someone alive with me in the moment."

"Not closing their eyes, not going back to somewhere else."

"Someone else."

"And that's what you're getting from her? This deep, meaningful relationship? She's married to a porn king."

"She doesn't want to be. She was a programmer, helped him get started, then stepped back from her career when his took off. She's watched him go crazy. She's starting to see a new life for herself."

"She's sexy, with a great body and long black hair, alone in that big house with nothing to do. Why not ball an FBI agent? She ask to see your abs before she went for your zipper?"

"She didn't ask to see my abs."

"She asked to see mine. Hmm. Hey, it just hit me. You could be a star in one of Breskin's movies and not know it." Argon made the shape of a square with fingers from both hands and framed Rivera's face. "Your face and ass already out there on the Internet, making it with Sunny and her making sure you face the camera now and then. An FBI Special Agent's home video on some pay-for-view." She snapped her fingers. "Or maybe you should watch for the blackmail demand. There's a lot of that going around."

"You've got her wrong. She's a warm person who needs to talk. We talk about how we feel, Denise. Everything about you is hard, your body, your heart. I just bounce off."

"Go to hell." Aragon held his eyes until she felt him folding. "We need Thornton's smartphone as well as her hard drive. Diaz, too. Can you handle that?"

"She's not available," Aragon said. "She's married." On the phone in her car outside Rivera's office, guessing he was probably where she'd left him: at his desk, where he'd been trying to discuss business, explaining the difficulties of getting into a lawyer's communication channels. But the both of them knowing that it wasn't what they were talking about.

She started the engine, put the transmission into reverse and then back into park.

"And one more thing about your fuck buddy." She waited for him to say *Do you have to use that language?* Even better: *Don't talk about Sunny that way. There's more to our relationship than you know.* That would have gotten them talking, her for sure. But nothing came back. Rivera had stopped talking in the office and she couldn't get him going again.

She ended the call and looked at her phone, needing to talk to someone. Serena? Maybe if this had happened last week, before bullet holes in her daughters' bedroom.

Javier? He'd be there for little sis. He'd come straight out of the mountains but was way the hell the other side of Santa Fe Baldy, deep in the wilderness, one of the blank spaces on the Verizon coverage map.

Lewis? Couldn't do it. Dead girls, drive-bys, serial killers . . . they could talk for hours. Not this.

Roshi Buff? Christ, she'd light incense.

No, that wasn't fair. Buff would listen. She was good at that. But talking about losing Tomas to the easy-lay Asian wife of a porn pig living in a white castle like the queen of Santa Fe? Seeing herself telling it at Buff's place, the Buddhist temple and its meditation garden of smooth stones, gangbanger music thumping beyond the walls on Airport Road? No way. She'd be thinking about what those kids were up to in their war wagons ten yards past the cinder blocks instead of what was going on in her heart.

Shit.

Lotaburger time. Make that a double order and throw in a chili Frito pie.

———————

Fager, in charcoal wool-blend pants, sharp crease, pale yellow shirt, maroon tie, no jacket in the morning sun, set up a card table and stretched an extension cord to power a thirty-cup coffee pot. He asked a uniformed cop to let him get his car out of the parking lot. The police had secured it, Thornton's Aston and Durango parked in there. The cop called Lewis over. Fager said he was going out for pastries while the coffee brewed. Lewis let him through. While he was gone, the number of federal and state vehicles outside Thornton's law office grew. Lewis went back to discussing with an Assistant US Attorney how to handle the search of Thornton's file cabinets.

Aragon was inside, following Elaine Salas collecting fingerprints in the hope that they'd find proof Cassandra Baca had been here, though Montclaire hadn't mentioned it. Aragon went straight for the dressing table next to Thornton's desk.

She came outside with handcuffs in an evidence bag.

Fager had returned, a cardboard box now on the table next to the coffee pot. He was setting a folding chair when he saw her.

"Find something good?" he called across his yard.

She ignored him and told Lewis to spread the word no one was to step over there. Fager would pump them for information. At trial, Thornton would be wailing about cops being bribed cheap for a cruller and cup of joe.

A station wagon with two men and woman arrived. Aragon thought they were reporters as they unpacked video cameras from the back.

"They're mine." It was Thornton on the front step, emerging from the conference room where she'd been busy on the phone, while a young female officer watched her from the door. "I want my own record of this invasion of my rights and the rights of my clients."

"Morning, Marse." Fager, seated, legs crossed, raised a pastry and took a bite. Powdered sugar on his fingers, jelly on his lips. "O'Hori's coffee, croissants, napoleons, and Danish from the French Pastry Shop in La Fonda. Join me watching the police dismantling your office and your life. C'mon, where's that Marcy Thornton smile we've come to love?"

"I don't have to let your team in during our search," Aragon told Thornton. "You personally have the right to be present. It's your property. You could have your lawyer inside. Too bad you got Walter Fager disbarred. He was damn good and he's right over there, dying to be part of this."

Aragon looked to the DOJ lawyer, the only person in a business suit besides Fager with his treats and coffee. The lawyer nodded his agreement and Aragon ordered two SFPD officers to block the video crew's entry onto the property.

"You just made your second mistake, detective." Thornton crossed her arms and waited for the obvious follow-up.

"Okay, I'll bite." Aragon said. "Tell me my first mistake."

"I'll save that for pre-trial motions."

Aragon dangled the baggie with the handcuffs in front of Thornton's face. "You use these on clients while you empty their pockets?"

"Where did you get those?" Thornton was holding it together, tucking her chin, trying to look puzzled and not pulling it off.

"Your dressing table."

"Bullshit. I don't keep handcuffs in my dressing table."

"The search video will show you did. I'll bet we find some interesting things on here. Your fingerprints. Judy Diaz's, too. And probably Cassandra Baca's DNA. You knew her as Andrea."

That hit Thornton. "You found those in my dressing table?"

"With Chanel and Aveda eye cream."

"And this is about Andrea? You think I had something to do with killing her?"

There was a look on Thornton's face Aragon had never seen. In court, bluffing a plea deal, Marcy Thornton had never shown that look, not even when things came at her she never could have seen coming. This time the case was about her, not something she could pack away in a file cabinet and forget until tomorrow.

Maybe Thornton was thinking, *I need a lawyer right now.*

Aragon left her on the sidewalk with her look and went to Lewis. "Rivera's at Diaz's house?" she asked her partner.

"Roger. He's in. But the FBI boys at her chambers are looking at a locked door with Diaz on the other side. They put one of those fiber-optic cameras under the door to watch until they get it open. She's getting sloshed, hitting a gallon jug of vodka in a dressing table just like the one in Thornton's office. She takes a slug, puts it back. Closes the cabinet door like she's done. A second later she's at it again."

"Half of Thornton's office is a dressing room. A closet full of silk suits, racks of shoes with heels, a full-length mirror she can see from her desk. Clients telling their tales of woe, getting the bad news on what it's going to cost, she's looking past them at herself."

"Takes work to always look great."

"I've got a hair trimmer and Ivory soap in my dressing room, the shoe box by the sink."

They walked together to where Elaine Salas with the FBI's Evidence Recovery Team was blowing black fingerprint dust on the Aston's expensive leather. "We should find Cassandra Baca's latents in the Aston," Aragon said. "I'm more interested in the Durango. If you're moving a body around, backing up to a dumpster, which would you use?"

"Something I noticed standing here." Lewis nodded behind her, and she turned to face the State Capitol. "See all those cameras on the Roundhouse?"

"I like it. We might get Diaz coming to Thornton's office, Thornton's cases pending before her, opposing counsel nowhere to be seen. Maybe match the visit to a ruling Thornton wins the next day." Aragon rubbed her face. "Man, I'm beat. How are you holding up?"

"The shade and grass under that tree look good."

"I gotta keep moving or I'll fall asleep. I'm going to swing by E. Benny's place, check in with—who's outside?"

"Rivera put Tucker there. I'll get going on Thornton's filing cabinets with the AUSA."

"Let me know when the vehicles are ready for us."

Lewis's face told her someone was coming behind her. It was Fager, walking up with the pastry box.

"Look, guys. These are going to waste. I've PR work to get to down in Albuquerque."

"PR work?" Aragon squinted at Fager. "You don't need to advertise a law practice anymore."

"I think the term is 'earned media.' Here. Have to run."

She took the box. What the hell? The guys would love these. Ham and cheese croissants. And chocolate. Things with raisins and jam. It looked really good. But she had a bad feeling about what Fager wasn't telling them.

"Employees arrived," Tucker said, eating the pastry Aragon brought him. "Trucks going out, the kind that pick up dumpsters and turn them upside down. An empty flatbed coming in. Contractors are returning their rented dumpsters, those smaller models, stacking them outside the gate. Every once in a while a big forklift comes out to get one. We haven't seen the Silva brothers."

She was in the backseat with one of Fager's ham-and-cheese croissants, steering clear of sugar and caffeine, knowing that meant a hard crash and burn later today.

"No van, shot up, the windshield blown out?"

"State Police are all over the Interstate and side roads in the canyon. Zip."

Tucker's partner in the passenger seat was a Chinese woman, short, round cheeks, hair pulled back tight. She'd declined Fager's goodies. She was drinking from a tall, narrow bottle, one of those designer waters. Aragon thought of Sun-Hi Breskin and her pineapple water and was glad Rivera was somewhere else.

"How are you covering this?" She finished her croissant and dropped the wrapping on the floor.

"Six-hour shifts. Rivera's on tonight."

They watched one of Silva's trucks stop at the gate. The driver put a cell phone to his ear.

"It's always locked," Tucker said. "The driver calls. Someone comes out to let him in, then locks it again."

"We could pull over a driver, ask a few questions. It would get back to the Silvas, but so what? What's in those dumpsters outside the gate?"

Benny Silva saw the bald lady detective getting into the brown Ford that had been sitting at the corner all morning. One of the cameras Abel had set up showed that part of the street beyond the gate.

He and Rigo needed to get out of here. The van was in the woods, safe for a while, Rigo said, at the end of an old logging road he'd blocked with branches and rocks. That's where they'd parked his Olds, what he was going to drive back, Abel and Junior supposed to follow in the van, a father-and-son team finishing a night's work. Instead, he'd returned with his son and grandson in plastic in the trunk.

Rigo came in and they watched the Ford together.

Then Rigo said, "Time to go."

The flatbed was pulled into a garage so they wouldn't be seen climbing into the cab. Rigo and Benny curled on the floor and passenger seat. One of their guys, he'd been with them for years, a straight-up sanitation engineer, no idea of the company's other interests, took the wheel. At the gate another of their guys was waiting to let them out. No doors in the truck had to be opened, risking the people in the brown car seeing inside.

Rigo gave directions, head near the floor, talking to the driver's shins. After twenty minutes the truck stopped on an open stretch of Old Pecos Trail.

"Anybody following?" Rigo asked.

"We're alone."

"Go the other way now, to the casino. We'll pick you up later. Here's a hundred bucks for slots."

That's how they worked it. In the lot of the Camel Rock Casino west of town, Rigo got behind the wheel. He backtracked again, took

St. Francis to St. Michael's to Old Pecos Trail and got on the interstate heading east into the mountains.

Benny had been quiet, looking out the window, watching the smoke from the Los Alamos fire, trying to remember the last time he and Rigo had gone out on a job together.

"This truck, when did we buy her?"

Rigo drove with an elbow out the open window, the wind flapping his short sleeve. "So long ago they didn't come with air conditioning."

"When we were always looking to the future. Now I think we're only going to look back. Abel and Junior, they were the future."

"I still got something to look forward to. Killing that lawyer."

"I been thinking about how you were ambushed. It had to be police, but they never identified themselves? And three against you?"

"The two in the woods we saw with the goggles. And a sniper. Whoever put that shot from nowhere right through Junior's head."

"I'm trying to figure who all we need to kill. That's Aragon's brother's place. It was probably her in the woods, and her partner."

"A mama bear and her cub. That's what I thought we were walking up on."

"We'll find the police sniper's name. They have to report these things. That woman you saw cleaning the bunkhouse? Probably Mrs. Javier Aragon."

"Anybody had anything to do with this, they're on the list."

"She has kids, I think."

"I didn't see any kids when we checked it out."

"They might be there when we go back to finish this."

"I lost my son and grandson."

"I hear you."

Benny had no idea how Rigo found the van. They left the interstate at Glorieta and wound around dirt roads for forty-five minutes.

Then even worse roads, the truck lurching from side to side and Benny wondering how Rigo got his Olds in here.

"This is it," Rigo said when a pile of brush and rocks blocked what little was left of any kind of road.

They cleared the way, then drove for another half mile. The van was there, nose in. When Benny came around the front he saw the blown-out windshield and bullet holes in the front. There was blood on the seats and floor mats. Flies were having a field day.

Rigo found a way to turn the flatbed around, then backed to the van. He pushed out a metal gangplank that fell with a heavy thud. With Rigo driving and Benny shouting if the wheels were going the right way or the wrong, they got the van on the flatbed. They stowed the gangplank and covered the van with tarps held down by chains.

Back on the gravel road and picking up speed Benny looked behind to make sure the tarp was staying put. They stopped twice to tie down flaps the wind pulled loose.

On the interstate, Rigo kept his speed down, but not so they'd get pulled over.

"The only thing keeping that lawyer alive," he said, watching a State Police cruiser pass them, "is nine million dollars. When are we going to see that?"

"It could be some time. I'm letting Judge Diaz know we're done waiting for her part to get done."

"We kill the lawyer now, what difference does it make?"

"There's the appeal. She said she can fix it."

"Why can't we fix it ourselves? Those appeals judges, they have families. We send them pictures of their kids at school, the wife shopping, getting her hair done. We find out they like whores, or boys, they do drugs, gamble too much. All the time it's going to take, we can find something."

"There's no guarantee."

"So we put a gun in their face, tell them we'll be back they don't rule the right way. How would you like to find your kid in a dumpster?"

"We get Diaz's ruling," Benny said, "we can go for a settlement, avoid an appeal. But it won't be the full verdict."

Santa Fe was coming up, they'd be taking the next exit, heading to the plant.

"What are we going to do with all that money?" Rigo asked. "There's no one to pass the business to. Your daughter in California don't want no part of it."

"She'd take nine million dollars."

"You haven't seen her in how long? Your Millie and my Barbara, they'll be set, between what the plant is worth, all the properties. There's enough for Abel's wife, too."

"You're in a hurry."

"We do the lawyer—it's telling the judge she's the one needs to hurry."

Now they were in town, moving through traffic, not far to go. Benny called ahead to have someone at the gate.

"These streets," he said, "the conquistadors laid them out. Where the interstate is, that was how they got to the Great Plains. All the way to Nebraska. That was Don Juan de Oñate, the last conquistador."

"You and the conquistadors."

"I'm thinking he wasn't the last. That's you and me. Five hundred years ago the first Silva men came into this country. They never stopped conquering shit. We're the end of the line. My daughter in California, she married a gringo, goes by Smith now. Doesn't even speak Spanish."

"Schmidt. Her name is Schmidt."

"Anglo names, I can't keep them straight."

"What are you saying?"

"Don Juan, he didn't do it right, how he went out. Hauled back to Spain, people pissing on him for doing what none of them had the guts to do themselves. Put on trial. Disgraced. Wasting away his last years."

"Maybe he went back to pig farming."

"That was Pizarro. The pig farmer who conquered the Incas. That was the way to go. Pizarro dying with his sword in his hand. He got fat at the end. Look how far he'd come, he had a right. But he never stopped being a warrior."

"That time comes, it won't be a sword I'm holding." Rigo being Rigo. Benny knew where this was going no matter what he said.

"Let's get this van in the crusher. Then we're done."

"No, we're not," Rigo said.

"Right. The lawyer."

TWENTY-NINE

THE BLACK FINGERPRINT DUST would get into every vent and hand-sewn seam in Thornton's Aston. The techs had used a ton. Elaine Salas, just eyeballing it, was confident they had recovered three distinct sets of latents.

Something interesting in the Durango, she said. At the back, the tailgate down, Salas plucked tiny splinters from the carpet.

"And look at the edge of the tailgate. The vinyl. Something rough was dragged across it."

Aragon leaned in close with Salas's magnifying glass. The scratches were clear, all running in the same direction, almost at right angles to the tailgate. "Like a wooden board that gives off splinters?"

"Like a wooden board that gives off splinters. I'll get this under a microscope, see what we've got. Look here."

They closed the tailgate. No scratches in the paint. But at the window, rubber looked like it had been torn.

"Could that board we found by the dumpster fit in the back?" Aragon asked.

"Sure could. Keep the magnifying glass. Come around the side." Salas had her lean over the seat and shone a light on the carpet. Soil, blades of grass and fine, tangled pale roots were matted into the fabric. "Something heavy ground that dirt into the carpet," she said.

"What did you get in latents?"

"One set on the passenger side up front, two on the driver's. I can't say yet if they match any from the Aston Martin, but I'd bet on it."

Aragon snapped on a double set of blue latex gloves and began with the compartment for the spare. She removed the tire and felt around in areas she could not see. She worked her way forward, shoving hands between the rear seats of the Durango and reaching up and underneath. She checked door sashes, then the glove box. Registration in Thornton's name, insurance papers, maintenance records, owner's manual, road maps for the Navajo reservation and northern New Mexico.

She reached under the front passenger seat into the springs, then moved to the driver's side. In the door sash were pens, a hairbrush—"You want this, Elaine"—and loose change. The seat was all the way forward and she thought of Thornton's short legs. She reached under to probe the springs and couldn't get her hand high enough in there. She pushed the seat back and tried again. Something that did not belong to a car seat came out with her hand. She didn't need to see it to know what it was. She was just glad she hadn't pulled the trigger.

It was a Beretta Tomcat, .25 caliber. She ejected the magazine. The numbers by the holes told her it could take eight rounds and currently held five bullets. This kind of gun, you could carry one chambered. The barrel popped loose and tilted forward. There was a bullet ready to go.

Two short of maximum capacity.

Thornton was watching from her doorstep, arms crossed, looking twitchy. The fingers of one hand drummed the other forearm, rolling from pinkie to thumb.

Aragon held the gun for Thornton to see. Thornton's fingers went still.

Lewis saw the gun and came, almost running. She extracted the cartridge in the barrel and handed everything to Salas, who dropped it in a bag.

Lewis said, "All we're missing are Thornton's prints on the trigger."

Aragon sat in the driver's seat and tried to reach under to the spot where she'd found the gun. She couldn't do it. "You can't reach it if you need it in a hurry."

"Why didn't Thornton dump it?"

"Maybe she thought we had surveillance. It's not a bad hiding place. I almost missed it."

"So why not get rid of it immediately after she shot Cassandra Baca, if she was the one?"

"Nerves. The mind skips. The heart's going like crazy. Things you planned ahead of time get lost in the rush. Good thing, or we wouldn't catch a lot of killers. And people like Marcy Thornton would have a lot less to do."

"Marcy Thornton and nerves," Lewis said, squatting to look more closely at the floor of the Durango. "Do they go in the same sentence?"

————

The first three attorneys Thornton called wanted a hundred grand up front. Two quoted a flat fee of half a million bucks. The third would work hourly and bill monthly. But he wanted an additional hundred grand now toward expenses. She asked if he'd take jewelry and guns. She had a safe deposit box with necklaces, rings, loose gems, rare coins from cash-poor clients, an arsenal in a storage unit.

He said he'd take a real estate contract on her office property. He'd always liked her space across from the Roundhouse.

Aragon and her marauders were all over the office. They let her have the conference room after a brief sweep, nothing in here but two empty flower vases and a station for coffee and water.

She locked the door and tried calling Judy's personal number on a prepaid cell she'd used to talk with Lily about things she didn't want on her business lines. A man answered and identified himself as Special Agent Tomas Rivera. She hung up fast.

Accepting property from clients who didn't have cash had been smart business. She'd sold dozens of mobile homes and beat-up cars over the years, sometimes selling them back on contract at double-digit interest rates. Real estate contracts she loved. The client could pay for all but the last month's installments. They'd default, start over at zero, all that interest and principal turning into rent.

Now she was in their shoes. She'd have to liquidate to come up with half a million. She had some Cody Geronimos in the office. They'd shot up in price right after his death. She would look at them and feel rich. But when buyers realized he really had killed fourteen women, and what he'd done with the body parts, the market for his work tanked.

She got to thinking about the guns. They were in a storage space, some in steel cabinets that had come with the weapons. Most just in boxes or wrapped in oil cloth. Some had come as evidence in a case. The client would tell her, the gun's buried behind the shed, or in the freezer in my Mom's house. Lily would get it. It would go into the safe or the storage unit. One or two she kept around the office, loaded, within reach when she gave clients bad news.

A knock on the door to the conference room. Aragon stood there with a woman in a white bunny suit, one of the people who'd been making a mess of her office and cars.

Aragon had the little Beretta in a plastic bag.

"We were wondering if you'd care to tell us anything about this number we found under the driver's seat in your Dodge. Or the handcuffs recovered from your office. Take your pick."

"I'm invoking my right to speak with an attorney. End of conversation."

She closed the door in Aragon's face and returned to making calls.

Somebody out there must be willing to take her case for under half a million.

Maybe she could interest them in a mint condition Aston Martin, low mileage, just a little fingerprint dust in the seats.

―――――――

Millie asked why the gate was locked when she arrived with her enchilada casserole and had to be brought to the office by a Mexican. Benny told her it was the copper thieves. They were in the neighborhood.

She asked, is that copper thieves or police over there in the brown car?

Police, Benny said. We're working together on this.

Maybe I should take them some enchiladas. I made extra.

That's okay. I saw them with bags of Lotaburgers.

When she was gone, he and Rigo sat in the security room and turned on the television that showed real programs. Dr. Oz was talking to women about their butts. How could he get away with that? Then the news came on, teasers of the top stories before the show started.

"That's the judge," Rigo said, pointing a fork dripping red chile and melted cheese.

A quick black-and-white photo, Judge Diaz's face, naked shoulders, the rest of her body under a black square. The setting looked familiar. They'd seen it in the videos.

There was Marcy Thornton, a black square over her body, too.

The anchor, a white guy with a horse face who'd been on air since Reagan was president, the whole state watching him get old, said police are investigating the sexual abuse of a teenage girl, recently found murdered, who appears in videos with the judge and lawyer. Then a school photo of Cassandra Baca.

They weren't hearing anything they didn't know until a man who could have played Don Quixote, pointy white beard and eyebrows, a spokesman for the Supreme Court, said the justices had suspended Judge Judith S. Diaz from acting in any official capacity.

Millie's enchilada casserole got cold while they turned to the other stations. Judge Diaz was on all of them, and the Supreme Court Don Quixote delivering the announcement that her days as a judge were about over.

Benny was thinking, there goes nine million dollars.

But Rigo said, "What are we waiting for?" and Benny knew exactly what he was talking about.

————

"You committed a felony," Aragon said as soon as Fager picked up.

She'd been at home, waking up on the sofa, groggy and stiff, the TV on while she'd slept. She'd readied the Mr. Coffee and headed for the shower, three days now just changing her shirt. She could smell herself. She was stepping into the spray when she heard Diaz's name on the news. Back to the living room, leaving the water running. She stood there naked watching until the anchorman's last words: "Police representatives declined comment, citing an ongoing investigation."

She'd checked her phone to see if reporters had called while she slept. They'd done that to her before. Call right before broadcast when they knew they wouldn't reach her, then report she'd clammed up.

Lewis had tried to reach her, and Sergeant Perez, a heads-up to expect her case on the news tonight. And Rivera and Tucker.

She'd thought about the report while she stood under the shower. The hot water ran out and she toweled suds off her legs. Then she called Fager, standing in underwear by the little Formica dinette.

His voice said, "How have I become a felon?"

"You said you didn't have any copies of the video."

"When you posed the question about copies, I responded, 'who's asking?' You answered, 'Me, Detective Denise Aragon of the Santa Fe Police Department.' Remember that?"

She did, but let him talk.

"Now, if FBI Special Agent Tomas Rivera had said it was him asking, I would have unequivocally stated that I had copies. Intentionally providing false information to a federal law enforcement official is in fact a federal felony. But there is no law against snowing a Santa Fe cop."

"You're having a good time, aren't you?"

"Marcy Thornton and Judy Diaz are having a very rough time. That's all that matters."

"Agent Rivera will call and ask if you have any copies left, and any other evidence Lily Montclaire gave you."

"You're upset the story's out there."

"It's making things happen, huh? Faster than the criminal justice system. Diaz off the bench, Thornton on the run. I can't say that pisses me off. But don't expect to hear 'good job' from me. This game

286

you're running with Montclaire, it's not getting us closer to whoever killed a teenage girl."

"Enjoy the rest of your evening," Fager said.

She opened the voicemails from Rivera and Tucker and learned a lot once they got past venting about Fager leaking the video to media. With the chance of nailing a chief judge and a lawyer that everybody on the blue side of the line hated, the scientists had pushed other work aside. They now knew:

- The bullets inside Cassandra Baca's brain were fired from the Beretta .25 recovered from Thornton's Durango.

- Cassandra Baca's fingerprints were found in the Aston, the Durango, and Diaz's house. Around the passenger seat in both vehicles. In the house, on the leather sofa, the glass coffee table, the bathroom closest to the living room.

- Cassandra Baca's DNA was recovered from the handcuffs seized from Thornton's dressing table.

- The wood particles in the back of the Durango were pine and aspen, same as the splinters in Cassandra Baca's back. Same as the plywood board found at the scene. Better yet, traces of a binding compound used in a particular type of plywood manufactured by a specific wood products company were detected in all samples.

- Diaz's office computer had e-mails with video files of the Gang of Three, as Tucker was calling them, and Cassandra Baca. The setting was Diaz's living room. Five videos, all different from the one Montclaire had turned over.

She tried Lewis, got voicemail, and said, "Tag, you're it." She dressed, foraged from the refrigerator, and poured coffee into a travel cup Javier had brought her from the Las Vegas SHOT show.

Lewis called back before she reached her car. She wanted to know when he was going to grab some sleep. He said he couldn't sleep, thanks to the boys and girls in the Crime Lab pulling an all-nighter. The test bullets fired from Thornton's Beretta scored a hit on the ATF's National Integrated Ballistic Information Network.

"I should try sleep more often," Aragon said. "Things happen while I'm out."

"That case where Montclaire crossed paths with Star Salazar, the two idiots on PCP mad-dogging with vests and mouse guns? Lily got the murder weapon? Bingo."

"She said she gave it to Thornton."

"I showed Lily the Beretta you found. She remembered the wooden grips and the funny little barrel. Last she saw it, Thornton was putting it in her desk."

If Fager thought today was good because it had been miserable for Thornton and Diaz, he was going to love tomorrow.

THIRTY

THORNTON REACHED FOR THE cord on the shade of her office window. Fager was at his window across the parking lot, the only car parked there now his Mercedes. The police had loaded her Aston and Durango on flatbeds and hauled them away.

He waved as the shade came down. Bastard. Those news stories, her face above a black rectangle but leaving no doubt she was naked. Judy, too. He had something to do with it. That wasn't a move the cops would pull. It would blow up on them at trial, demonstrate malice, unprofessionalism. No law enforcement agency had offered any comment. But Fager had been in the stories, talking about the search of her office, how shocked he was seeing it happen. "A prominent attorney," he'd said, the same line in every report, "subjected to the humiliation of police intruding into the space where she practices her profession. I can't imagine the humiliation."

She got back to what she'd been doing before she'd felt Fager's eyes on her. She had bank statements, a print-out of her mutual funds and brokerage accounts, and a handwritten list of her other assets on her desk by a coffee mug holding red wine. This was something she told her clients to do: decide what you can turn to cash, fast. Be ready if your best option is running.

She'd thought she was worth a lot more than what she was seeing. Knock taxes off the mutual funds and brokerage accounts, it was even less. She could get a second mortgage on her house. The office she owned outright. It would sell fast. But there were realtors' commissions, closing costs, and taxes on the appreciation. And the depreciation recapture, don't forget that. She'd probably have to put on a new roof and fix the sidewalks before it went on the market. When they got to inspection, the things she knew about the plumbing and foundation would come out.

She'd open the safe deposit box in the morning and start selling the jewelry and coins. The guns in the storage unit, the best she could do was call Frank Pacheco and agree on a price. Sight unseen, but a lot of guns, all kinds, she told him. I'm not vouching they're all clean. I got them from clients, you know.

He said, "I get the picture," and gave her a price that factored in the risk he'd be buying weapons that could be traced to crimes. He'd pay in cash, right after he moved the guns to one of his places.

She wanted him to do it tonight. The police would learn about the storage unit from the bills they'd rifled. They could be there before him. She gave him the code for the key pad at the entrance to the facility and the combination for the lock on her unit.

He called back not much later. He got past the gate, but the combination to the lock wouldn't work. In fact, the lock needed a key.

She didn't remember switching locks. She hadn't been to the unit in a long time.

She told him to use bolt cutters. He had to go home and would hurry back.

Those news broadcasts ... Benny Silva certainly had seen them. He'd be wondering how his movies made it to the small screen. The Supreme Court immediately suspending Judy, Silva would know that meant the end of his blackmail scheme.

The bungalow shook a little. That happened when the garbage trucks came. She wasn't sure if this was pick-up night. The last thing on her mind.

Pacheco called again. He was inside the storage unit. He needed to give her more money. He didn't want her resentful next time he might need her speaking in court for his family. Where'd she get the Barrett fifty caliber? Three Uzis? And that old Colt with pearl grips, Wild West stuff. Cherry. He knew a crazy Texan who collected and had too much money.

Someone was at the back door. She told Pacheco to hold.

She opened the door to two Benny Silvas in brown coveralls, caps on their heads saying Silva Enterprises, black hair sticking out above their ears. No, the one in front wasn't Benny. That scar running across his face, no mustache where his lip was patched together. You could see teeth in the gap, though he wasn't smiling.

"Mr. Silva, what—"

His hand came up. A gun pointed at her chest.

The ugly Benny said, "Now we know what it takes to make a lawyer shut up."

————

Fager felt like drinking. One thing he hadn't done after his wife's murder was get drunk. He'd held it in, packing it down deep, thinking he was turning grief into strength, coal into diamonds. Maybe if he'd gotten drunk he could have cried. And if he'd cried, maybe he wouldn't have tried to strangle Marcy Thornton in front of news cameras and he'd still have a law practice.

Tonight's drunk wouldn't be about grief. He felt like he'd just kicked ass in court when all he'd done was leak Montclaire's video. Not one of the reporters had said turn it off before they watched to the end. A couple said, "Run it again." He reached for the bourbon in the bottom drawer. It made him think of the old days, setting up glasses for staff, sometimes taking everyone out for steaks to celebrate. Marcy, too, when she was a baby lawyer, his only associate attorney back then.

A cigar would be great. He had one left in the box under the picture of Winston Churchill, bulldog face scowling and chomping a stogie. He snipped the end, wet it in his mouth, and fired up, sending smoke circles toward the ceiling. Then he leaned back in his old-style oak lawyer's chair, feet on the windowsill, facing the parking lot, Marcy's shiny red Aston no longer out there sneering at him.

The garbage truck cut off his view of her window where her shadow had been. It rolled to the back of her office and parked at the end of the walk where he'd tripped and fallen. He saw her shadow again, rising, then moving toward the rear door. A garbage man was there. Now another, rolling one of those oversized black cans on wheels, laying it on its side.

That wasn't what garbage men did.

He didn't see the door open, but he saw them pulling Marcy outside, one stuffing a rag in her mouth. They looked alike, those two. They dragged her toward the garbage can, pushing her feet in first, punching her to stop kicking.

Fager swung his heels off the windowsill and reached for the phone to call 911.

Benny-with-the-scar grabbed her in a head lock. Benny-without-the-scar shoved a sock in her mouth. She tried scratching the one holding her head and he punched her in the nose. They say you see stars. She saw galaxies.

She blinked her eyes clear. Her feet were about to go inside the garbage can. She kicked and the real Benny punched her in the stomach, right under her ribs, knocking the wind out of her.

She felt the black plastic edge of the garbage can scraping her ribs as they pushed her deeper. She threw out her arms, catching an edge in her armpit. They pried the arm loose and the scarred Benny hit her in the back of the head.

The black plastic was up to her chin. One arm inside already, the fingers of her other hand being twisted to make her let go. The garbage can was moving, turning her around, a last glimpse of the parking lot before the lid came down.

There was Walter Fager in his window, standing, a phone to his ear, looking her way.

She tried screaming: *Get out here and help me, call the police.* But the sock was so far back in her throat she gagged.

For a second, Fager met her eyes.

The hand with the phone dropped to his side.

With the other, he closed the shade.

THIRTY-ONE

ARAGON PARKED THREE BLOCKS from Silva's business and avoided street lights as she worked her way closer. The brown FBI Ford was there, two heads backlit by a portable billboard down the street. Farther back was Rivera's command post in the black-panel truck.

Only a single light above the gate glowed outside Silva Enterprises. The rest of the street was dark. No one lived here. The other businesses, a car painting shop, a pool supply warehouse, were shut for the night. She smelled chlorine coming from the warehouse and the odor of sewage crossing the street from Silva's.

Stronger than anything was the smoke. An inversion, they said on the weather report. All that ash from the forest fires riding winds above Santa Fe was now settling on the city. The streetlights were gauzy halos. Her eyes watered. The back of her throat burned.

A car passed. She waited until it disappeared and sprinted to the stacked dumpsters outside Silva's gate. She knew the FBI people had seen her. She turned under the weak light to let them see her face, then lifted a heavy rubber lid and climbed up and over into the nearest dumpster. She fell onto plastic bags. Her fingers broke through and she touched something damp.

The phone vibrated in her pocket. In the pitch black of the dumpster she read a text from Rivera: *Wht u doing?*

She texted back: *Going in. Legal this way. I think.*

Brilliant.

Official FBI OK?

No follow-up came.

She had a pen light and could have learned what she was sitting on. The smell was a mix of sheetrock dust and rotting garbage. She wiped her damp hand on her pants. The smell was no worse than a horse barn, what she called the heroin trailers in the woods, where junkies sprayed blood from syringes, cruised in their own shit, nobody giving a damn about the toilet backed up.

She texted Lewis to forward reports from the scientists and drafts of the warrants he was preparing. She might as well work while she waited. He wrote back *roger* and asked where she was. She sent him a photo, the flash showing what she really didn't want to know. She got back a string of question marks.

Something hard hit the side of the dumpster and it shook. Heavy machinery groaned. The dumpster rose, the lumpy bags under her shifted and threw her on her side. Maybe she hadn't thought this through. Maybe the dumpster was going to be lifted high, tilted, emptied into the belly of a bigger truck. One with a hydraulic compactor.

But the dumpster returned to level, then landed hard. She risked lifting the rubber lid. She was on a low boy, other small dumpsters being parked in rows, a man in a hard hat operating a forklift and wearing a mask against the smoke. She was knocked backwards when another dumpster banged against hers. She found a seat and pulled up Lewis's draft of arrest warrants.

The sounds of the forklift stopped. A truck engine fired up. The dumpster jerked backwards, then she felt motion. She was going in. She slipped her phone into her back pocket, the side away from her gun. The dumpster lurched harder and she fell onto her face, thankful to hit a clean plastic bag.

She couldn't hear anything but the sounds of the truck engine and metal straining. It got quiet when they stopped.

"That does it. We got this." An older man's voice with a Northern New Mexico accent. He sounded like her grandfather, a light voice dancing between high and low notes on alternating syllables. "You boys go home. Your wives miss you and I'm sick of your whining."

Then other male voices. Feet tromping, car engines starting, the sound of the gate at the front opening and closing.

"What's wrong with people?" She knew that voice: Benny Silva. "All that overtime, you'd think they'd be happy. All I heard was bitching about working in the smoke. You want to do it now?"

"Let her hang, think about what's coming." The first voice. She'd guess a man about Silva's age, who almost sounded like him.

She waited until she felt safe they'd moved away. A quick look, the heavy rubber weighing down her head, her eyes just above the edge. She was alone, deep inside the business's yard. She made sure her phone was off and climbed out, letting the lid down gently. She dropped to the ground and made her way to the front of the truck. Some kind of heavy machinery was gearing up behind a corrugated wall, metal screaming, glass exploding.

She jogged to a door, sheet metal on hinges, and inched it open. Benny Silva, wearing orange plastic ear muffs, had his back to her watching a white cargo van getting smaller. Another man was at the crusher's controls. She saw the old man's shoes under his coveralls, the crepe soles, the ventilated arches, the same kind of shoes she'd

296

noticed on Benny Silva. Killers wearing SAS comfort shoes. That had to be a first.

She wondered how the van got here, then thought of the flatbed the FBI had seen coming and going. It had carried rows of dumpsters. It could transport a van under a tarp.

She backed out and worked her way deeper into the compound, planning on climbing over the fence at the rear when she was done looking around.

Rows of blue and white porta johns. Two honey-dipper trucks, a pickup, more forklifts, a front-end loader. A mountain of broken glass, bins of cable and aluminum. A metal hangar off by itself, a single bulb over the port burning orange in the smoky air.

She used an aisle between the porta johns, then ran across open ground to the hangar's door.

Different sounds here. Like a huge hot tub, jets gurgling and churning. That smell, strong chemicals. She thought of salt. How can salt have a smell?

The door slid on rollers. Her eyes traveled across a concrete floor to a circular mound of stainless steel, rings upon rings. Gauges, valves, mist rising from a bubbling surface of green liquid.

Marcy Thornton hanging by her wrists, naked, one foot in the green broth, her other leg bent, tied back, heel against her ass, stretching the thigh like some yoga pose. That birthmark by her black pubes, damn if it didn't look like the New Mexico state symbol.

Thornton's eyes came around, her face bruised, a little blood under her nose. She spat a rag from her mouth and screamed.

"The lawyer's calling," Rigo said, coming down from the controls of the crusher. "They don't stay quiet for long."

Benny said, "We could take her hands while the foot's melting. Oñate cut off hands. People forget that. People forget a lot."

"He wanted them to live. How'd he do it?'"

"Put a sword in fire till it's white hot. Then press where the hand or foot used to be. Burns everything closed. Smells like a *matanza*. Pig skin on hot iron."

"Lawyer *cicharones*. We're not gonna do that. She doesn't tell us who shot Abel and Junior, we drop her to her chin while El Puerco does his thing. I suppose she'd keep living until he ate her lungs and heart. No, her throat would go first. Six hours later, we can flush her down the toilet." Rigo hung his ear protection on a hook and unzipped his coveralls. "And away go troubles down the drain."

"I'll get my sword," Benny said. "Something to wake her up if she passes out again."

———

Aragon was trying to understand the winch controls, not wanting to hit the release switch instead of the one that would raise Thornton, when she heard voices at the hangar's door. She searched for a place to hide. Barrels marked *Bioliquidation solution / Caution: caustic contents* formed a wall. She got behind in time to look back and see two Benny Silvas walking into the hangar, one carrying a sword.

The other one must be Rigo. One hell of a scar, the mangled lips. Lewis had called him zipper face and said she would understand if she saw him. He went to the winch controls and hit a button. An electric motor churned. He leaned into a lever and Thornton rose, what was left of her foot rising from the broth.

Thornton dropped her eyes, her chin on her chest. Then she looked at the twins.

More panting than talking. "It was Aragon." She focused beyond them at the barrels where Aragon was listening. "She said if you came there again you'd find her. That's who killed your people."

Benny touched her nipple with the tip of the sword.

"What you haven't explained is why you didn't let us know she was waiting."

"I tried to warn you. I called. No one answered."

"There's an answering service, I don't get to the phone fast enough. Lower this time, Rigo. Dip her to the knee."

Aragon came out from the barrels, her gun on Rigo.

"What you want to do is swing that boom around and bring her down, here on the floor. Gently."

Benny pushed the sword through the nipple into Thornton's breast. She screamed again.

"You shoot Rigo, this goes through her heart."

"Okay, I shoot you first."

And she did, hitting Benny dead center, sending him backwards, the broth splashing all over Thornton, she was sorry about that.

Rigo spun toward her, a gun coming under the arm that had been on the winch controls. His first shot hit one of the barrels. A spout of liquid leaped into the air and splashed her face. Aragon hit him with a double-tap, bam, bam, one above the other along the buttons on his shirt. He stood there, already dead, before his legs folded and he went down on his face.

She turned back to where Benny should have gone under. But there he was, bobbing at the surface, trying to swim, face down, arms thrashing above his head, legs kicking. Not getting anywhere. That damn sword had fallen hilt first, all that metal heavier than the tapered tip. He landed on the point and it held him up. The more he struggled the deeper the blade went.

"Stop moving." She searched for something to pull him over so she could drag him out.

He turned once to her, his mouth open, struggling for air. Instead he got a mouthful of broth. She wondered what that was doing to his tongue, her own face and arms burning. The tip of the sword came out his back, through his kidney. Then he was gone.

Aragon pulled out her phone and called Rivera, the closest backup, as she studied the winch controls. She saw Thornton watching her.

"I'm not going to mess with this," Aragon said. "I hit the wrong button, you'd probably sue me."

THIRTY-TWO

"Not even a thank you." Aragon put her feet on the dash inside Lewis's car. Through the windshield, she watched the ambulance with Thornton pulling away. "We had a couple minutes alone, she's hanging by her wrists, me checking Rigo's pulse. Don't ask me why."

"Tell me again what she said."

"Tucker figured out the winch thing. They swung her around, brought her down into my arms."

"Now you've got burns to go with the black patches from those cactus needles. You know that's oxalic acid killing the skin. You're a mess."

"Whatever ate her foot, man, it's nasty."

"You should let them work on you."

"I'm all right. No worse than splashing hot grease."

"So what did she say?"

"I've got her in my arms, all limp. She's having trouble breathing, must be hurting really bad. I said we'll do a televised arraignment from the hospital. We know you killed Cassandra Baca. That's when she said, short legs. I said, I've got them too. Strange, huh? She was out of it."

"One leg's going to be shorter. She'll lose that foot. Don't scratch." Lewis pulled her hand from the burns on her cheek. "You're worse than my girls. I'm taking you to the ER."

"Benny, he's still in there, you know."

"Rivera's trying to run down the manufacturer to learn how to drain that thing. By the time they pull the plug, they won't know what's Benny and what isn't."

Aragon got the standard suspension with pay and temporary loss of her official firearm for officer-involved shooting while the incident was investigated. The only eyewitness was Marcy Thornton and she wasn't talking, not even crazy stuff about short legs. Surgeons took everything below the knee. The DA was ready to hit her with state charges after she was released from the hospital, giving her more of a break than Aragon wanted. The US Attorney was presenting a RICO indictment to the grand jury, with murder, bribery, and obstruction of criminal investigations as predicate acts.

Judy Diaz was arrested at home, arraigned, and bailed out to be met with news the Supreme Court had permanently suspended her and a full investigation by the Disciplinary Board was underway. All her cases were being reassigned. *E. Benny Silva Enterprises v. Jeremiah Kohn Productions* was going to a judge from Lea County, over three hundred miles removed from Santa Fe's politics. The FBI had found Diaz's work on an opinion denying the motion for new trial on her desk with margin notes *check with Marcy*, leaving everybody puzzled because Thornton didn't have a dog in that fight.

Aragon lay in bed, sleeping late—*sleeping!*—feeling her burns, listening to traffic sounds outside her apartment, people heading down the stairs, doors closing, music thumping somewhere below.

Someone pounding on her door.

She took a Smith & Wesson .38, Chief's Special, from the night-stand and pulled the curtain aside.

She relaxed and opened the door.

"I came to get your ass out of bed and on the range."

It was Tommy Arenas, her instructor from the Law Enforcement Academy.

"You're supposed to refrain from handling firearms during this time of introspection and inquiry. Bullshit. Best thing you can do is blow up a couple hundred rounds. You don't want the memory of shooting someone in your head next time you need to use your weapon, seeing someone dying, your brain working on that instead of the threat in front of you. You're going to shoot so many guns today, you won't remember pulling the trigger last night."

He hadn't come empty-handed. He walked past her and put a bag from Blake's on the dinette.

"The perfect meal, I know you say. Every food group in each Lotaburger."

"Tommy, you mind if I dress?"

"I was going to suggest that. Nobody may recognize your face, but a block of Latina muscle in panties hitting bull's eyes, they'll know who's under the bandages."

————

It turned into a glorious day. The first thing Tommy had her shoot was a Smith & Wesson five times the size and weight of her Chief's Special.

With both hands, he gave her a Model 500 Magnum, .50 caliber revolver, fifteen inches total length, the bullets so big they reminded her of acorns. After just one trigger pull, the feel of the Springfield firing at the Silva brothers seemed like a nervous twitch, not recoil.

She had fun with the revolver that could take down an elephant. Arenas moved her to a semi-automatic shotgun, this crazy Kel-Tec thing, like something from *Star Wars*. It was fun, too.

An M1 Garand next, heavy like a war club, then an antique .44 that kicked like one of Javier's mules. The Webley Bulldog, an ugly gun with a short, flat-sided barrel, kicked even more. It split the webbing of her gun hand. She didn't mind that Arenas lacked bullets for a reload. He said it was hard finding .454 slugs.

He worked her down in size until he handed her a Springfield XDM, same as official carry. She understood what he'd been doing. When she fired, all she noticed was the metal disc at twenty-five yards. All she heard was the lovely pinging of rounds striking its target.

Her hand was sore, she had to admit. So instead of shaking Tommy's hand at the end, she gave him a hug.

She hit the gym after, not giving a damn about her bandages. The women's world record for a bench press, she'd read and never forgotten, was 264 pounds, set by a nurse in Oregon weighing in at 130 pounds, five-foot-one, an inch shorter than she was. Holding twice her own body weight above her face, that was something to think about.

Lewis joined her and filled her in while he spotted. She had to rack the bar to take it in.

"Thornton's office safe, we got it open. The AUSA wouldn't let us look at hardly anything, but the one piece of paper he let us see was enough. It was a screen shot from the Cassandra Baca videos. Fingerprints for Marcy Thornton and Abel Silva, Jr. And on her phone, calls to and from E. Benny Silva Enterprises."

Aragon swung her legs around and sat up. One of the bandages on her arm had come loose with perspiration. She tore it off and let it fall between her feet. The arm didn't look too bad. It would heal. She hoped the same for the burns on her face. And the dead black spots on her cheek. Lewis had her worried about oxalic acid.

"Get this." Lewis sat on the opposite bench, both of them wearing SFPD tees, white letters on navy blue. "Diaz blurted out she was a victim when we arrested her. Blotto. Vodka in her orange juice for breakfast. She said she was being blackmailed by Benny, they killed a girl to scare her. Why weren't we doing anything about that?"

Aragon peeled another bandage off her arm and saw blistering she couldn't pretend didn't look serious.

"Did we have it wrong that Diaz was doing favors for Thornton out of, what the hell would you call it, friendship?" she said. "Was Thornton working with Silva, setting up the blackmail? Maybe she was going to get a cut of the nine-mil verdict."

"And they were renegotiating, hanging Thornton above the tissue digester?"

"That's what it's called?"

"Large animal alkaline tissue digester and sanitizer system. It's the piece of crap that never worked for the State of New Mexico. Silva picked it up cheap, and somehow it works for him. The manufacturer is out of business. Benny's still in there while the FBI calls other companies to see if they can help."

Aragon pulled a set of dumbbells off a wall rack and got to work on alternating shoulder presses, her mind working better while she moved.

"Where did the Silvas grab Thornton?"

"Those cameras on the State Capitol." Lewis stood next to her, with dumbbells twice what she was pushing toward the ceiling. "We have a Silva truck going behind Thornton's office, coming out a little later. The lights were on at Fager's, his Mercedes in the lot. We asked if he saw anything. He said he was too busy working on his lawsuit against Thornton to be gazing out windows. He gave us a copy, stupid thing about falling on her sidewalk on account of missing flagstones. Exhibits, A, B, and C, photographs of the empty spaces where the flagstones were supposed to be, his bloody knee, a rip in his pants. He's looking forward to her deposition. Says he's going to serve her in the hospital."

Aragon moved up ten pounds on each hand. Lewis went up twenty but cut back on reps.

"Did he turn over other copies of the video?"

"Rivera went with me this time and did the asking. Fager had a couple more. Rivera grilled him about other evidence he was withholding and he said no. He knows the law. He wasn't going to lie to a federal officer."

"How far back can we get film from those Capitol cameras?"

"They're digging it up. Might take a while. Not exactly the Smithsonian archives over there."

Aragon dropped back five pounds. Lewis moved to cables.

"Cassandra Baca weighed about a hundred pounds," Aragon said. "I don't see how Thornton could have done it. All these connections to the Silvas, maybe they helped her."

"And not use the digester? Why? We're back to sending a message."

"To Diaz, dragging her feet. Thornton couldn't persuade her to move faster. So scare the crap out of her with a dead girl in a dumpster."

"Abel Junior's prints on that screen shot." Lewis was talking with arms stretched wide, curling the cable grips to the sides of his head.

"Him and Abel Senior haven't been seen. Mom's not worried. She's sticking with they ran down to Mexico. They'll be back when they have enough fun." Lewis finished, walked one cable, then the other, to their seated position. "You want to come for dinner tonight? No excuses now. We'll get some green stuff inside you. I'll bake fish. Unless you've got plans with Rivera. You guys still a number?"

"The Silvas aren't the only thing that died this week. What time?"

———————

She was up early next morning, watery coffee in a travel cup, leaning into the curves on the winding road to the trailhead for the seven-mile climb up Santa Fe Baldy. She parked in the lot where she'd met Rivera on the Cynthia Fremont case and impressed him by nailing where Fremont had been killed, a lake off this trail she knew from fishing trips with Javier. She'd seen Miguel in him then, the same widow's peak, thick black hair, the way he held his head, making her think of a boy she'd loved grown into a man.

She reached the trailhead while the sun was the other side of the mountains, still cold enough up here for a jacket and wool cap at the start. She was going to move fast and didn't want her gun bouncing on her hip. The .38 went into a mesh pocket outside her daypack. She headed out, picking up speed and peeling off clothes as the trail grew steeper, taking no breaks, pushing her heart and lungs hard.

Jogging on level stretches, concentrating on her feet so she didn't trip, she forgot the job. She loved it here, the trees changing as she climbed higher, the air clean, none of the smoke and exhaust clogging Santa Fe's air. But it was scary dry. Her feet kicked up dust. The ground was cracked. The trees looking weary and stressed.

God, she hoped this never burned.

She finally took a breather where the tree line ended at a ridge, giving the first views inside the Pecos Wilderness. Below her the rising sun bounced off the smooth surface of a tiny lake, someone camped down there, smoke curling through the trees. Idiots. The last section of the climb up Baldy was to her left, only a half a mile to the summit. She went straight, running now, heading for the campfire.

A mile later she was there. No one around. They'd burned their garbage and left embers smoldering after breaking camp. She carried water from the lake in a charred tin can. Six, seven trips and she had it out. She stirred the ashes, then kicked dirt over the fire pit.

The climb back to the ridge was the steepest of the day. She'd trashed her quads running downhill and took her time. Her second wind came when she reached the ridge. She covered the remaining open ground in a steady jog.

She had the summit to herself. Santa Fe spread below. The Rio Grande, a strip of green against parched brown, wound its way south from Colorado. When she turned she saw the sharp point of Truchas Peak, and behind that Wheeler Peak, almost 14,000 feet, just outside Taos. The Pecos Wilderness was a green oasis between the dry Rio Grande Valley and the brittle, arid plains disappearing on the eastern horizon.

Turning back west, she watched a thunderstorm building over the Jemez Mountains, lightning flashing in black, boiling clouds above the wall of flames eating mountain slopes. Rain, she prayed. Drown us. Flood the arroyos. Kill the fires.

The storm was moving straight at her. She couldn't wait for it to hit.

She pulled a PB&J sandwich from her pack, not her favorite kind of food. It made her feel juvenile. She compensated with a fistful of elk jerky. She watched the storm opening up, dumping sheets of water on the Jemez fires, and fell in love with New Mexico all over again.

Heads appeared on the far ridge. They grew into bodies. Over a dozen people swinging walking sticks and trekking poles. The first one—you've got to be kidding—was wearing lederhosen. They were singing. The hell was this, *The Sound of Music*?

She'd been seated on a mound of rocks with her daypack at her feet. When they drew close they stopped singing, stared, then mumbled among themselves and moved away, glancing back over their shoulders as they retraced their steps off the summit.

Her hand went to her cheek. She'd forgotten the bandages on her face and the black dead flesh from the cactus toxin. She didn't think she looked bad enough to scare anyone. She crumpled the wax paper from her sandwich and bent to put it in her bag. Her pistol showed through the mesh in the pack's outer pocket. That's what drove them away.

She couldn't see them when the singing started again. It drifted on the wind, voices rising and falling like eagles riding thermals. They must be from the Santa Fe Opera, it was that good. Now a woman's voice, slicing the sky, men's deeper voices giving her a platform to reach for the darkening clouds.

Aragon soared with the music, a small bird drafting behind eagle wings. Now a man and woman singing a duet, voices intertwined. Silk cables.

And she thought she hated opera.

On her way down, the singers shifted closer to each other when she passed by. She said, "Thank you," and floated down the mountain, their music deep inside her.

Seven miles later, her clothing heavy with sweat, her lungs working overtime, legs screaming from running downhill, she reached her car. In the last mile, flying through the switchbacks, hikers coming up getting out of her way, her mind had swung back to work.

She saw what she'd been missing: she should have stayed on the roses.

THIRTY-THREE

"I'm a zombie cop," Aragon told Lewis. "Just one look at me sends people running."

She'd asked to meet at the Blake's on St. Michael's. She'd had a good day at the office on top of the mountain and wanted to tell him. And she was starving, three thousand calories burned so far.

"You could get a role on *The Walking Dead*," Lewis said. "Play a cop who won't die until she solves every murder. She's been gored by cactus, burned by acid. Nothing stops her. There's always murders, so she can never rest. She eats the killers. Hell, you already bite. You'd be a natural."

"I need you to talk to some people." Aragon scratched a red splotch on her arm, the burned skin already peeling away. "We can't wait till I'm off suspension."

"You'll be command central, the wounded zombie general, sending zombie troops into battle. Me, your first wave of shock troops."

"I'll be in the car, waiting for you to come back and tell me."

"No you won't. You'll be at home taking care of yourself. You need to change those bandages. Half are falling off. People are staring." He pointed at the bag on the table, the lights bouncing off the surface, the sun pouring through windows that needed to be cleaned. "For your fries, I'll march where you order as long as you stay home and don't move for a couple days."

"I'll go nuts in my puny apartment."

"You'll have time to relax. Remember what that was?"

She asked him to find the cleaning woman she'd met outside Thornton's office, the one taking flowers out the back.

"She said, 'I take the flowers *now.*' Does that mean she's taking flowers because Thornton's done with them now, or now she's the one taking the flowers? Did she take the flowers *before?* Did someone else take the flowers?"

"You want to tell me what you saw up there in the clouds got you thinking about flowers?"

"Not ready. I want it to make sense when it comes out."

She was a good girl and went home to shower and remove her soiled bandages. The dead skin and redness on her face scared her but the cactus devastation looked better. She applied more of the salve prescribed in the ER and left her skin exposed to the air while she called Elaine Salas to talk about roses.

Salas said, "I should be earning credits toward a degree in horticulture."

"Tell me."

Most of what Salas had to say, the genus of the roses, their likely source of production, how they're transported and kept fresh en route, the wholesalers for New Mexico, did not interest her. But two things did.

"The stems were shorter than what I thought you'd see in a store. I compared them to fresh roses at Whole Foods."

"Why Whole Foods?"

"Just did. Maybe the bag on Cassandra Baca's head. Anyway, the stems were about six to eight inches shorter than what was on sale."

"Any idea what that might mean?"

"Flowers wilt, their petals drop because the stems get clogged, they can't take up water and nutrients. You keep them fresh by cutting the stems an inch a day, misting them, using a preservative."

"So these could be six days older than what comes out of a store, not one day like we thought."

"You thought that. I never said."

"I don't know shit about flowers. I only ever bought them for my mom. Never grew them. Don't keep any around. Coming home late at night, alone, to dead flowers in beer bottles, I don't need that."

"Takes being splashed with flesh-eating soup to keep you home."

"Didn't keep me from climbing Baldy today."

"Why am I not surprised to hear that? Back to what you said. With the high level of sucrose in the stems, definitely, they could have been out of the store for a week."

"Explain that."

"Plants need food. When you cut stems from the mother plant, trim the leaves, you deprive them of nutrition. The sucrose level drops. But we found good sucrose levels in these roses. Somebody was using a flower preservative. There's also a biocide for fighting bacteria."

"You never looked away from the flowers, did you?"

"They bugged me."

"Bugged me, too. I just got distracted with little things, like people trying to kill our witness."

———

She was out of the house as soon as she'd changed bandages and found clean clothes in the back of her closet. She took Javier's truck to Home Depot and had a clerk cut a sheet of plywood, three-quarter-inch thickness, the same as the plywood recovered from the crime scene. With the board in the back of the truck, she drove around until she found an E. Silva Enterprises dumpster the size of Cassandra Baca's tomb.

She hadn't forgotten watching Serena using the truck as a work platform.

She backed in and laid the board against the edge of the tailgate, making a ramp to the dumpster's edge. That didn't look right. Too unsteady. Then she tried it with the tailgate down.

That could work. The board took care of wrestling with a dead body, always harder to lift than the weight alone. Still, it was the same as a hundred-pound clean and jerk, getting your fingers under the board, legs bent, pushing up from your heels and lifting the board above your head so a body would slide off.

But she knew she was close.

She played with the board, pushing down on the end extending over the dumpster. The board came up an inch off the truck bed.

A counterbalance. She pushed the board out farther. The same pressure brought the back end up higher. A counterweight on the end of the board would make it even easier.

Okay, a counterweight? What was it and where did it go?

Probably into the dumpster. It would be on the end, the first thing to fall off, Cassandra Baca coming next, sliding along the board head first.

She called Lewis. He wouldn't talk to her, she'd broken her promise to stay home. He must have heard sounds suggesting she wasn't in an apartment. Maybe all the traffic from the streets around here and the dogs barking in the mobile home park. She said she was on the balcony getting air.

She told him, e-mail me what the academy cadets found in the dumpster.

"You want to read about Q-tips and dog food cans and pizza boxes? Soiled diapers, how many, what brands? Nineteen banana peels, various states of decomposition, sixteen lime halves, nine empty jars of salsa. Cat litter, the clumping kind, collected and weighed. Denise, enjoy the time off. There's cage fighting on the tube tonight, the girls coming up after Ronda Rousey and Holly Holm."

"You find that cleaning lady? It's been two hours."

———————

Rivera asked how she was feeling, but that wasn't why he'd called.

"One side of the equation for wit sec is the witness's cooperation, how valuable and critical their information. Montclaire meets the grade. The other side, the threat evaluation, just fell out from under her."

"No Silvas, no threat," Aragon said. "And Thornton and Diaz are out of action."

She was on her sofa bed, the mattress pulled out, pages from the inventory of the dumpster on her chest. She'd printed out the attachment Lewis sent, pulled together a plate of what food she had in the fridge. The stale, leftover fries were hard like nails. She'd settled on plastic cheese, crackers, and a mushy apple. Somewhere down the list, in the middle of a tally of broken dishes, a busted microwave, a cardboard box containing ninety-one hangers, ripped sneakers, shoes without mates, a tube of furniture polish, and a dented frying pan, she stopped reading to pace her efficiency apartment, stare out the window at the parking lot, the street beyond the dead landscaping.

She'd been told something to her face, what was it? Why had she let it slip?

Because she'd wanted to hear something else.

"The bean counters," Rivera was saying, "won't let me keep her in the hotel if she's not in the program."

Sergeant Perez had told them he needed the interrogation room. The FBI had helped out by putting Montclaire in the Days Inn. She'd have to go home now or pay her own hotel bills.

She was surprised how easy it was talking with Rivera, as long as they kept it on the job. She said, "Funny how her play with Fager holding the video backfired. She thought he was helping her. Instead, he played her ace for himself. Benny, he still in the bath?"

"We tried fishing him out with nets. Just soup bones."

"Nice way to remember the old guy. Look, I don't want her taking off. Lily's figured out where she stands if she's been watching the television in her room. One more day, Tomas."

"I can do one more day. Outstanding work, by the way. I haven't had a chance to say that. I get the feeling the Silvas were a lot worse than we knew. We've got a lock on the surviving members of the cast."

"Do we?" Aragon picked up the pages listing each individual item of trash in the dumpster. She needed to get back to this.

"Diaz is through as a judge forever. We'll get conspiracy to obstruct, bribery, maybe more. And on Cassandra Baca, Thornton's going to take a very hard fall."

"No doubt. Thanks for calling. Really."

Krav Maga was out of the question. Aragon hit the gym and pushed herself to failure on every major muscle group. She needed to do this more often, destroy her body, get it out of the way so her mind could work.

She was on the calf machine, a stack of forty-five pound plates on the fulcrum, thinking about counterweights. She dropped the bar with a clang and got her phone from her pants in the locker. She stepped into the gym's lobby to call Lewis.

"I thought you were taking it easy," his voice said. "I know that headbanger music. You're at the gym."

"Can you meet me at Thornton's office? Bring Fager's lawsuit."

"Give me an hour. My turn to clean up after dinner."

"Did you find the maid?"

"I know where she'll be tomorrow. When you're home recuperating."

Then she called Elaine Salas.

"Can you meet me at Thornton's office, bring your field kit?"

"This suspension of yours, it's kind of rough on the rest of us. Hang on." She heard Salas yelling something, someone yelling back, the phone being put down, a television playing. Kids whining. Footsteps getting louder. Salas's voice returned. "On my way."

————

Aragon angled her headlights to cover the walk from Thornton's parking lot to the office door. The work had been finished, the sawhorses and string with flags removed. The crew had done a nice job fitting flagstones into the missing spots, getting everything tight and level.

Salas arrived first and Aragon showed where she wanted soil samples. Lewis rolled up next. Together they read Fager's lawsuit against Aragon and studied the exhibits, photographs of the missing flagstones.

"Seven stones, it looks like," Lewis said. "Good sized. What, about ten, fifteen pounds each?"

"We can weigh them and know for sure." Aragon pulled out the detailed inventory of the contents of the dumpster. "I had to get to the end before I picked up on what I was reading." She'd circled seven items, scattered throughout the inventory, listed by different cadets sorting the trash on different shifts. Only one was identified as *flagstone*. The others were *two pieces of rock*, *slate*, *granite slabs 2x*, and *stone shelf*.

"I have a feeling they're the ones that were missing from here. Look at Fager's photos. See how the shapes of the missing flagstones are marked where grass had grown between them?"

"Thornton's flagstones thrown in the dumpster way out on Jaguar Road?"

"It's how a person without much arm and leg strength could have raised Cassandra Baca high enough to put her in the dumpster. Elaine, did you ever build that dummy we asked, to resemble a body the size and weight of Cassandra Baca?"

"It's been waiting," Salas said, "for you to get done shooting people and bathing in alkaline hydrolysis solution."

"That's what splashed on me?"

"Be glad you didn't get it in your eyes. Meet me around the back of the evidence locker so no one sees you, you being on suspension and all."

It worked. The seven stones came to a total weight of eighty-one pounds. They did it on a wall outside the evidence locker, not sure the height matched the tailgate of a 2015 Dodge Durango backed to a Silva Enterprises dumpster. But with the counterweight in place, Elaine Salas, who said she couldn't do a single chin-up, was able to lift the end of the board with the dummy's dead weight equaling that of Cassandra Baca.

"It wasn't a bed of roses," Lewis said. "It was a bed of stone."

"It makes me wonder," Aragon said, "if Cassandra Baca was killed inside Thornton's office."

"In a hurry, grab what's close at hand. So where did the board come from?"

"It could have been taken off a construction site. All around there, houses are being remodeled constantly."

Salas said, "We should go back and look for blood evidence. The warrant didn't cover that."

Aragon looked to Lewis. "You always say, 'I'll sleep when I'm dead.'"

"Right," he said, "I'm on it. I'll get started on the application. Most is already done. What are you doing?"

"Finally remembering I'm on suspension. 'Night, all."

———

She didn't go home.

She stood again in the night where the dumpster had been, Cassandra Baca's last resting place above ground. She was trying to see Marcy Thornton here, bringing a body in the Durango, sliding the board from the back over the edge of the dumpster, getting Cassandra Baca on, weighting the other end with the stones.

How high would the end be in the air, how far would Thornton have to reach, arms extended straight out from her shoulders, to stack flagstones on the end of the board?

Short legs.

Maybe she stood on something to make it easier, or balanced the flagstones on the edge of the dumpster, slid them up the board, nudged them out to the end.

Was it Thornton who'd thrown it in her face, the key to all this? That would be like her, convinced she was smarter, enjoying the risk, the challenge. Aragon tried to replay every conversation she'd had with Thornton, searching for what it was she'd said.

Her mind was still doing reruns when she got to her apartment. She brought the last beer in the fridge to the bathroom while she examined her face in the mirror. Her skin was red right to the corner of her eye. She'd been lucky.

She drained the beer and flopped on the sofa bed. Enough thinking about Marcy Thornton. She called up the dream that always made it easy to sleep and never want to wake. A gun in her hands, killing the gangsters aiming at Miguel, blowing them off their feet, exploding their heads, more and more coming, emptying from low-riders pulling to the curb, her gun never running out of bullets, her aim never failing.

But what she saw was Cassandra Baca lying naked, dead, on the plywood board, minutes from being thrown out like trash.

Forget sleep.

THIRTY-FOUR

SHE SAT WITH THE street people in the main library on Washington Avenue, smelling them, a man next to her with his head in a skullie bloodstained above the ear. A fresh gash peeked through greasy hair. He nodded like he knew her, this nearly bald, brown woman, face in gauze and tape, huddled over old magazines staring at pictures of girls.

She'd asked for decades-old *Cosmo* magazines. The reference librarian brought boxes from the basement. Aragon was lucky they had them, the librarian told her, so much of the library's collection had been scanned and digitized to save storage space. In another couple years, there would be no paper under this roof.

Aragon took a quick look and came to the counter with something she'd found just under the top layer of magazines. Old *Hustler* issues. Somebody had kept the boxes for reasons other than a backlog in digitizing.

She had twenty years to look through, knowing this was a long shot and there had to be a better way. Certainly not every issue would be here. Rivera could probably get a rookie agent in DC to go to the Library of Congress and make sure they weren't missing anything.

Was *Cosmo* in the Library of Congress?

The street people around her changed. The odor did not. She dragged the boxes to a carrel and used them to wall herself off.

This wasn't her world in these pages. "*Look sexy now: make them obsessed with you.*" And "*What he's really thinking when you talk dirty.*"

The magazines on the floor by her toilet had articles like "*Boobs: A Girl's Best Friend for Concealed Carry.*" Or "*Mother's Day for Moms Who Love Guns.*"

Aragon searched the *Cosmo* back issues for the photos Lily said she did when her modeling career was hot. She found lots of tall, thin blondes with almost-uniform face, eyes, and cheekbones. No Lily yet.

"You done with these?"

It was the street guy with the head wound, squinting at the boxes.

"You wondering what are the ten secrets to every woman's wildest fantasy?"

"The boxes," he said. "I could use them. I already know the secret to every woman's fantasy. It's only two."

"Tell me, two what?"

"Love. It's that simple. And respect. The hardest things to give, the hardest to get. Who needs a magazine subscription to learn that?"

"I like the way you think." She peeled off a twenty and handed it to him. "Buy yourself some Neosporin for that head," she said and hoped she wouldn't see him drunk later on the Plaza.

She got a text from Lewis to call. She went outside and found a spot away from the tourists moving between the Plaza and Marcy Street.

He'd just spoken with Thornton's cleaning woman. Caught up with her at the last job for the day. You need to hear what she says. And don't worry how you look. Just get over here.

Ermelina Garza waited with Lewis inside the front door of a place called Great Adventures Family Dentistry. Garza wore a flowered smock tied in the back, a purple clip holding white hair, hands as red as Aragon's burns.

"Some name," Aragon said before she saw the African safari motifs, the life-size plastic animals kids could climb, a fort of plastic logs under fake palm trees. The receptionist wore a safari shirt with epaulets and a pith helmet. "I get it."

"Mrs. Garza, I want to show you a photograph," Lewis said. "Denise, your phone? I don't have the photos on mine. Step over here in the shade so you can see better."

They moved from the front door to stand under a sign listing the dentists' names.

"Yes, that's Miss Thornton." Garza settled glasses on a chain on the bridge of her nose. She reminded Aragon so much of her grandmother, around sixty years old, wide hips from bringing children into this world, wide shoulders from carrying a family on her back. "And that's Miss Lily."

"Which one of these women would take flowers from the office?"

"Miss Lily. But now she's gone, Miss Thornton lets me."

Aragon said, "That's what she meant by 'I take the flowers home now.'"

"Always the roses," Garza said. "She likes roses."

"Flowers in five places in Thornton's office," Lewis said, "twice a week. Reception, Thornton's credenza, the conference room, Montclaire's desk, and the main hallway. Mrs. Garza doesn't know how many in each vase, but says there were a lot. We can get the quantities from the florist."

"When was the last time there were roses?" Aragon asked.

Garza squinted an eye, furrowed her brow.

"Last week? Miss Thornton won a case. Roses when she won."

"We didn't go back far enough," Lewis said.

Aragon felt momentum building. "How do you know when she'd win a case?"

"Oh, the mess in the morning. Bottles, clothes, spills. They'd call, because I usually came evenings. Come now, what's her name up front, Maria Nicole. She'd say, clean up before we open. Hurry. I work all night, so I'm up. But I double my hours. Missus Thornton tells me do that."

"And was there a mess last week?"

"Like it was Cinco de Mayo."

Aragon showed another photo, of Judith Diaz. "Did you ever see her?"

"I clean her house. And Miss Lily."

"How do you get in to Miss Lily's house?"

"I have a key, and the codes."

Aragon stepped closer to Garza. She added a serious tone to her voice.

"Miss Lily is with the police. She's helping us on something very important."

"She's very nice."

"Yes, she is. She needs clothes from her house."

"Denise." Lewis was giving her a look. She ignored him.

"She asked us to get the clothes, but her keys are in the house. We were going to call a locksmith. You could save Miss Lily some money."

Lewis, stress in his voice this time. "Denise."

"Why were you in Miss Thornton's office making a mess? All the police. That black powder everywhere, I don't know how to clean it up." Garza pulling back a little, a hand shielding her eyes from the sun. "Why is Miss Lily working with you? I don't know."

"Why is Miss Lily working with us?" Aragon opened her palm to take her phone back from Lewis. She scrolled through files, searching for another picture. "She's helping us find the person who killed this girl." She turned the phone so Garza saw a photo of Cassandra Baca, the one of her dead, in the dumpster. "We have to stop that person. They could hurt another child. They need help themselves."

"Roses." Garza extended a finger to touch the image. "So many roses. *Dios mio.*" She chewed a knuckle. Aragon kept the screen in front of her face. "That poor child. Let me get my purse."

––––––––

"When was the last time you solved a crime without breaking the law?"

Lewis stood behind Aragon at Montclaire's front door as she punched in the code Garza had written for them.

"You don't have to come in." She used the key and the door popped open, swollen in the frame from heat blasting the wood, stale air rushing out.

"I'm as good as in already." Lewis checked the street on the other side of a low wall made to look like adobe. The houses in the hills here, north of downtown, were on larger lots, most with elm or pine trees blocking their view of each other. "I don't stop you or run straight to Sergeant Perez … You're doing this to me again."

Aragon left the door open for Lewis. She heard him close it behind her, saw the light from outside shut out.

"All right, what are we looking for?" Lewis asked.

She tapped a wall switch with the back of her hand. Track lighting under thick, rough-cut timbers showed a Mexican tile floor, a

Navajo-style rug, low leather furniture. Dust on everything. It was cool in here, the thick walls doing the job of air conditioning. A bookshelf ran along the wall opposite the couch, photos of a much younger Montclaire in frames on the shelves. No books. Just dozens of framed photos of young Lily.

"Are we digging through panty drawers?" Lewis hadn't come very far from the door.

"We're looking for pictures."

"There's pictures." Lewis swept his hand toward the bookshelves. "Lily likes to look at herself, doesn't she? She hasn't aged too bad."

"Models have portfolios. At Santa Fe University, you see girls with the big black folders walking around, the ones who want to break into movies. Lily's always going on about her glory days in front of cameras, marching down catwalks. Pedaling a bike through sand and posing on a seesaw. I want to see if she's been lying to us, or not telling us everything. So much of what she's told us, we can't take to the bank."

"That check would bounce. What's a model's portfolio look like?"

"Like this."

On the coffee table, alone, lay the black, oversized folder she'd seen before when she brought Lily to collect clothes. It was closed with a string wound around a black leather tab. Aragon sat on the couch and brought the portfolio onto her lap. Lewis joined her, his weight on the cushion leaning her toward him. Under the cover were loose photographs of Montclaire holding an umbrella in rain, sprawled on cascading marble stairs, and a sheet of proofs, close-ups of her face from different angles.

The first mounted photograph showed Montclaire on a stool, hands under her thighs, stretching her long arms, heels on the highest rung, bony knees wide. It was the only photo, centered on the page of stiff, heavy paper.

"Look how young she is," Aragon said. "Barely a teenager."

"The camera's looking straight up her dress. It's almost kiddie porn."

"This is."

The next page, black-and-whites mounted on the corners, Montclaire in the exact same pose as the first shot. But naked.

Aragon felt something right then. Montclaire had been abused like herself, by a camera instead of a gang pinning her to a hot sidewalk. She concentrated on Montclaire's eyes. In the early photos there was a spark, a girl setting out on the rest of her life, excited, having fun. Even in the early nude photos there was life, a challenge to the camera, determination overcoming fear.

More nude shots, getting more graphic, the look of determination fading, then Lily in a fur, a dead animal around her shoulders, ice and snow in the background. Older, more cleavage than the first shots. The dead eyes showed up for the first time. At a distance, the clothes, the colors, the setting made her. Up close, it was all the eyes and the dark light inside.

Aragon felt Lewis tense on the couch next to her, their thighs touching as they looked through the portfolio. His breathing grew shallow. The hand on his knee balled into a fist.

"Rick?"

"They killed her." He'd seen it, too. "This is a dead woman in designer clothes, all these glamorous locations. Look, her arms and legs, you start seeing the bones, more and more every year. This one of her and the ravens, she's in black. This one, on her back, just bones under the skirt, laying back, like, come on in."

"Her face in that one, pasty. Like ash."

"Those eyes aren't seeing anything."

"'When dead girls were in,' Montclaire said once."

The next shot showed Montclaire clearly posed as a corpse, the skeleton under her skin so close to the surface, shadows making it jump out. Eyes painted black, lips, fingernails, hair. The tip of her tongue, too, between white teeth.

"On a bed of roses." Aragon exhaled it more than said it. Surrounding a dead Lily Montclaire: red, red roses, the only color in the shot matching a drop of liquid in the corner of black lips.

The house was quiet, cool, in shadows except for the light they'd turned on. They sat in silence. They'd seen so much together. They were sharing something else they knew would be with them the rest of their lives. Something no one would ever feel the way they were feeling it now.

Aragon was the first to move. She turned the page. More dead Lily shots. That was Notre Dame in Paris behind her in this one, on her spine, the back of her hands splayed on the ground, legs hooked over the stone wall, her pelvis thrust toward the thousands of statues and faces on the church front. This was Times Square, dead Lily in a gutter, tourists snapping photos. Nobody on a cell calling for help. Was that staged, the tourists actors, or did the photographer stand back to catch the crowd's reaction? Maybe disguised as another fascinated passerby?

Dead Lily in a folding seat in a football stadium, a beer in the holder on the back of the seat in front, half-eaten hot dog by stiletto heels, other trash around her feet, a team practicing on the green rectangle below.

Dead Lily in an airport waiting area.

Dead Lily at Mardi Gras, a string of beads, a naked pale chest, nipples—shit, painted black—poking at fat men with mouths gaping, drinks in plastic cups spilling on polo shirts.

"What were these photos advertising?" Lewis's hand was shaking. He'd seen a girl die in the past minutes as they turned pages. He was probably thinking of his own girls, how they could go from the pure, happy child in the first photos—a really pretty girl—to this. Like that.

"Nothing I'd want to buy."

The last page had the cover from an old *Cosmo* issue. The stupid headers: "*Twelve ways to enjoy dangerous sex and laugh afterwards.*" Jesus. "*Eat your way to power orgasms.*"

"You could write that one," Lewis said, pointing. "The hidden power of Lotaburgers. The green chile G spot."

He was trying for something to lift the shadows. It was okay.

Two small photos were taped to the bottom corners of the magazine cover, the ones Lily had told them about: her in a sundress pedaling a bike across a sand dune, and her on a seesaw. Her face in *Cosmo*. The high point in her career.

Or the end of it.

The one of her on a seesaw was not the way Lily had described it. It was two Lilys: on the low end, a dead weight, the ashen skin and black makeup; a living, breathing Lily in a yellow sundress and hat suspended in the air at the other end of the board.

"I found this magazine at the library. I remember the stupid advice columns. There were no photos of Lily Montclaire. That was her fantasy."

"These photos are all of a sudden different." Lewis turned back to the one right before, dead Lily in the passenger seat of a convertible, an expensive car, a bottle of Champagne in a lifeless hand. "She's alive again." He returned to the sunny photos.

"Except for her double on the seesaw."

"These are taken from a distance. You can't see her eyes. On the bike she's looking away. On the seesaw, she's looking toward the sky."

"Dead Lily's looking straight at the camera." Lewis returned to the nude photos at the beginning, then closed the book, rewound the string around the leather tab, and settled it in the dust-free square on the coffee table. "This what you wanted to find?"

"More than I expected. But something else I want to check."

She pushed herself off his leg to stand and entered the hallway to the back of the house. Bedrooms on the right, the bath across the hall. Dark in here, only clerestory windows up high above a modern, European-style shower stall of slick stone. A showerhead as big as a sunflower.

Lewis, behind her, said, "I don't understand these designs, no shower curtain, no door. They remind me of outdoor showers at the Jersey shore. With my girls, we'd have a flood every night. I guess that's why there's a drain outside the shower on the floor, too."

"Lily did it here."

Aragon saw it: Cassandra Baca showering after a rough party with older women. Facing the wall and showerhead, her back to the bathroom.

"Cassandra never finished rinsing," Aragon said. "Lily killed her where the body wouldn't gather trace evidence and clean-up was easy."

"Shit. The caked shampoo in her hair. She threw her wet into the dumpster."

"Those movies, they don't show every second, I know, but they don't ever show Lily biting Cassandra. She brought her here afterward, driving the Durango that night. Maybe she paid Cassandra for an extended one-on-one, suggested the shower before she headed home to that filthy bathroom her mother trashed. Freshen up, let me give you some tips on makeup and hair. I was a fashion model by your age, you know, with my own agent, flying all over the world, limousines from the airport. New York, Paris, Rome. It's something you might want to try. With your looks and body, you could make a lot of money. And then she shot a girl washing her hair and dreaming."

"Let's get out of here." Lewis was already moving into the hallway. "I want to stand in the sun."

———————

They walked streets, letting their minds work, keeping thoughts to themselves. Lewis's phone rang. It was Elaine Salas. She wanted to see them. They returned to their car and drove to Salas's office.

"You found something," Salas said. "I see it in your faces. I did, too. But it confuses the hell out of me."

She'd found blood in Thornton's office, under the sofa. She showed them a fleck of dried blood on a microscope slide, held down with another slide on top. But something wasn't right. It was drops of blood, hard to see on the Persian carpet. Distinct drops of blood. No spatter. No spray. No blood anywhere else in the office, including the sofa above.

It looked like it had coagulated before it hit the carpet fibers. It hadn't been absorbed. In other words, it hadn't come straight out of a body.

She ran the samples fast against Cassandra Baca's blood type and DNA and got a nearly perfect match.

How'd it get there?

Aragon said, "I think I know. But we'll never prove it."

THIRTY-FIVE

They needed Rivera.

"That's history, you and him?" Lewis asked while they waited for an answer to Aragon's call. "You said the Silvas weren't the only thing dead last time the two of you came up."

Rivera came on. She said, "Tomas, we want to work something with you. I'd say trust me, but that word between us, it's not what it was." She met Lewis's eyes, telling him, there's your answer. "All we share now is a case. And it's going sideways. You file charges against Thornton for killing a federal witness, you'll be sorry you didn't go with this."

To Lewis she said, "Someone with him. He'll call back."

They had transcripts of their sessions with Montclaire on their laps, cold drinks in cups on the floor between their feet. They'd parked in a piece of shade by the Basilica of St. Francis.

"What was it that made you see?" Lewis asked.

"Everything pointed straight at Thornton. Everything. We were swept along. I wanted her to be good for killing Cassandra Baca."

"Nailing Marcy Thornton for murder. Yeah, I was running straight at it just as hard."

"It was Thornton. Hanging there, a foot gone, Benny floating below her, her boob bleeding from his sword. Not 'get me out of here.' Not even 'help.' What she tells me is 'short legs.' Then the gun. I replayed finding it."

"The Beretta under the driver's seat."

"Thornton was telling me it wasn't her who put the gun there. Not someone with short legs who pulls the seat close to reach the pedals. I had to push the seat all the way back to get to the gun." Aragon lifted the transcript. "Working the rez, running up to the villages in the mountains for Thornton. The Durango was Lily's ride for work. She only used the Aston to taxi Cassandra."

"But Thornton's prints are on the Dodge."

"Lily would have known that. It was Thornton's property. You're going to say something about the prints on the gun next. Lily gave it to Thornton, watched her handle it. We were eventually going to learn how Montclaire could have got to it and planted it for us to find. Thornton gave us that one thing, the short legs. The rest she'd hit us with at trial."

"We'd tie the roses to Thornton. More evidence piling up against her. But Lily didn't think about the cleaning lady seeing her take the roses home."

"The invisible woman. Nobody sees the Mexican with the vacuum cleaner."

Lewis reached down for his drink and stirred ice with the straw. "What we don't have is a motive for Montclaire to kill Cassandra Baca."

"Lily already told us. She saw things going south and knew Thornton was hanging her out to dry. The way she killed her, the staging, that was about something else. She was going to plant blood evidence in Thornton's office. But she saw how the blood had started to dry and didn't soak into the carpet. She moved the couch over what she'd started planting, Cassandra outside in the Durango. She remembered the seesaw, something never far from her mind."

"The bag on Cassandra's head?"

"Maybe Lily couldn't handle seeing her face. She did shoot her from behind, those little bullets like pressing a button and making a dead girl, as neat as you can get."

Lewis shifted his weight in the seat, wanting to cross his legs but the steering wheel was in the way. He pushed the seat all the way back, caught what he was doing, and shook his head.

"You want to psychoanalyze," he said, "maybe Lily was seeing herself on the seesaw, and covered Cassandra's face to help along the fantasy. Maybe this is all about Lily's revulsion for herself."

"I hate wasting time on that kind of crap. Lily killed her. If it doesn't help us nail her, I don't care about it."

"You think we're ready to take a run at her?"

"We're almost out of time when she'll talk without a lawyer. After she's charged, she'll be arraigned, the judge will lean on her to get representation, assign a PD for the meantime."

"What really creeped me ... " Lewis rolled down the window and emptied the dregs of his cup. "That portfolio front and center on the coffee table. She brings a guy home, or a woman, take a seat, I'll fix us drinks. Hey, what's this, they ask, and open the thing. Page one, gee you were a cute kid. Page two, Lily fourteen years old with her legs spread. And Lily calling from the kitchen, I've got white wine, I could open a red. There's a beer in here somewhere."

"I see Marcy Thornton sitting there, Lily's book open on her lap, a glass of wine in her hand."

Aragon's phone rang, Rivera calling back.

She told him, "Time to bring Lily home. You know the address?"

————————

They waited for Montclaire to punch in her security code. Rivera stood behind with her suitcase, Aragon and Lewis to the side, knowing it was a six-code number, not helping Montclaire when she got it wrong the first time.

"Numbers," Montclaire said. "I don't know why I have trouble."

She got the door open and took her suitcase from Rivera. "Make yourself at home."

Lewis followed her in, leaving Rivera and Aragon on the doorstep.

"Where's Tucker?" Aragon asked. "You look smaller without him."

"Contrary to popular belief, FBI agents don't always do things in pairs. He's at Diaz's office, talking to her secretary about the private meetings with Thornton."

"And you're playing chauffeur for a washed-up model and child molester. The worst you don't know about yet."

"What are you up to, Denise?"

"Taking our only shot at getting this right."

She stepped inside. Montclaire was opening shades, the level of light coming up with each uncovered window. They watched her move around the furniture, then get her suitcase and head for the bedroom.

Lewis took up a blocking position at the front door. In a second Montclaire was at the sink pouring herself a glass of water.

Rivera looked from Aragon to Lewis, got nothing, then nodded at the bookshelves lined with photographs from Montclaire's past. "Lily, you were something to look at." He stepped to a photo apart from the rest.

"I caught your use of the past tense," Montclaire said, the edge of the glass at her lips. "I was sixteen in that one. I'd already seen Tokyo, Jamaica. A week in Paris being taken everywhere except restaurants."

"Was this before or after your shoot for *Cosmo*?" Aragon moved toward the coffee table.

"I did *Cosmo* when I was nineteen. This one"—Montclaire took a framed photo off the shelf—"I was fourteen. My first job, for a photographer in New York. He said I had a glow about me, innocence under a knowing smile."

"What's this?" Aragon sat on the low couch and pulled the portfolio toward her.

"That's private. I'd rather you don't look."

Aragon already had it open. She turned straight to the nude black-and-whites.

"The guy who got you started, nice of him to let you have some of the shots he took. Fourteen years old, innocence under a knowing smile. Even when you're grabbing your ankles."

Rivera was behind the couch in five steps.

Aragon turned pages. "Ah, here you are with clothes. I like it, all the light on your face. Man, the long neck."

"It was one of my strong features." Montclaire put her glass down and stood with hands on her hips. "That's enough. You can stop."

Aragon looked up, studied her neck, and said, "We all get that sag, Lily." Back to the photos. "Here's another nice one. You had the legs going on. Two miles long. Me, I've got short legs. Like Marcy Thornton. I get in a car someone else drove, I'm always sliding the seat up so I can reach the gas. Tomas, wasn't Lily beautiful?"

She angled the portfolio so he could see the page she'd turned to: the first of the dead Lilys, a pale corpse on a bed of roses.

Montclaire had edged closer, but still couldn't see what photograph they were looking at.

While Aragon turned the page to show Rivera more of Dead Lily she said, "You look great in pants. You had it, the way you'd lean against something. Like you were dancing with whatever was there, a chair, a doorframe, a car."

Now it was obvious they were at the end of the book. Montclaire started backing away when Aragon flipped to the last page, the dead girl on the seesaw.

"I'm going to unpack," Montclaire said, "and freshen up. I could use a shower. Please close the door when you leave."

She left them.

"These pictures from *Cosmo*," Aragon called out, getting to her feet and dropping the book on the coffee table. Rivera was ahead of her, following Montclaire. "They're the ones you told us about, when I promised if you weren't telling the truth about anything, our deal was off."

Now they were in the hallway, a light on in the first room. Rivera entered first, Aragon right behind. Montclaire had her suitcase open on the bed. She was moving underwear and bras to the second drawer of her dresser, folding them, laying them in neatly.

"I went looking for those shots you bragged about." She and Lewis hadn't got this far into the house before. She looked around as she spoke, Montclaire not always in her line of sight, sometimes Rivera in the way. "The one of you on the bicycle, the one of you on the seesaw. I found that *Cosmo* issue. Lily, you weren't ever in *Cosmo*. Those photos in your portfolio, the very last entries, they were rejected. You were rejected."

Montclaire shook out a camisole, refolded it, placed it in the open drawer.

"They couldn't use me."

336

"You did the dead girl thing," Aragon said, "and never came back to life." Rivera slid closer to Montclaire. Aragon wished she hadn't laughed off Lewis's crack about digging through Montclaire's underwear. She didn't like not seeing her hands when they went in the drawer.

"I was ahead of my time," Montclaire said. "Female corpses are back. There's nothing more beautiful than a dead girl."

"How much did you hate Andrea for being young and pretty?" The question made Montclaire stop, a bra strap dangling loose from her hand. "As much as you hated Marcy Thornton? Or was it all just a calculated play when you saw the cards going against you?"

Montclaire balled up the bra and tossed it in the drawer, no longer careful to fold everything.

"You broke into my house when you were holding me." Montclaire tried a fierce look but failed. "You saw my portfolio before. All this time, me thinking I was helping you, you were after me. You can never use that, anything you saw in here. I know about fruit of the poisoned tree, how an illegal search taints everything. You thought you were so smart. But you screwed yourself."

"Lily, I never saw your photos before. You let us in, just now. The portfolio was in plain sight. You explicitly said, 'Make yourself at home.'"

"I heard it," Rivera said.

Aragon might tell him one day that's why they wanted him along, to witness Montclaire inviting them in so they could use what they already knew was inside. An FBI agent backing up two detectives, hard to beat.

Lily reached into her suitcase—how much underwear did this woman have? She held up a red negligee, shook it loose, drawing Rivera' eyes as she tossed it on the bed. Aragon was wondering why she would have packed something like that for a stay at the police station when Lily's hand came out of the drawer.

A little gun pointed at Rivera's face. Montclaire fired.

THIRTY-SIX

LEWIS CHARGED THE BEDROOM. His shoulders swept pictures off the narrow hallway walls. He came around the door frame gun first, the side away from his heart exposed.

Blood seeped from Aragon's fist. She had her bloody hand over Montclaire's, a polished wooden grip and thin black barrel showing between their fingers. Aragon had Montclaire's other arm by the wrist as she twisted and turned. Rivera was behind, trying to get his arm across her throat.

Montclaire kicked Aragon's leg. Aragon kicked back, a knee to the top of the thigh, her foot raking Montclaire's shin, slamming onto her instep.

The gun hand swung his way. Lewis stepped out of its path as Aragon drove her knee into Montclaire's groin. Montclaire folded, a sick groan replacing her shrieks. Aragon backed away with the gun, a small Beretta, a twin to the one found in Thornton's Durango.

Rivera pulled Montclaire's hands behind her back and pushed her to the floor.

"I never thought that worked on a woman," Lewis said. "Jesus, your hand."

Blood pulsed from a hole between the bones for the ring and pinkie fingers. The flow increased, blood spurted. Lewis took the Beretta and lifted Aragon's empty hand above her head. His thumb pressed the hollow on the inside of her wrist.

"Does it hurt bad?"

She shook her head. "I grabbed the gun right as she fired." Blood now flowed down her biceps and reached the shirt sleeve. "She couldn't fire again. The spent brass couldn't eject. That barrel has to pop up."

"I told you I didn't like those things."

"I love them. Any other gun, someone would be dead."

"You saved me from getting shot in the face," Rivera said, his knee in Montclaire's back while he dug plastic ties from his rear pocket.

Aragon looked at the hole in the back of her hand, then the ceiling. "It went somewhere."

Lewis stripped a pillowcase from the bed and wound it tightly around her hand. He told her to keep it high. Instead, she kneeled to bring her mouth close to Montclaire's ear.

"You just made the case for us, Lily. Those creepy photos, they weren't enough. But with you trying to kill an FBI agent, and actually shooting a Santa Fe police officer … Let me just say, thanks for your invaluable cooperation."

Lewis reached to help her to her feet but she pulled away.

"What's that, Lily?"

"I said—" Rivera's weight on her back, Montclaire spoke into the carpet. "I can give you more on Marcy. The things she had me do. You have no idea."

"We don't trade a girl's murder for piling on a dirty lawyer. Thornton's through without your help."

Aragon let Lewis pull her up. She leaned into his arms.

"Okay, now it hurts," she said and began shaking and couldn't stop.

———————

"You know what you did?" Rivera at the foot of her bed, a private room at Christus St. Vincent. She was still groggy from the stuff they'd slipped into her blood before surgery, a man behind a light blue mask saying softly, "You might like this."

"Don't you see it?" Rivera tried again, and she still didn't know what he was talking about.

Cards and balloons taking up the space along one wall and the dresser top. She'd requested no flowers, especially roses. She couldn't force Tomas to leave and didn't want to start anything with Sergeant Perez in the room. Soon a captain would join them, standing in until the chief got back from the border law enforcement conference to check on his wounded detective.

Rivera was on the other side of her bandaged hand and the arm with the feed to the tube running to a bag on a hook. Her hand was suspended above, her body in a thin blue robe tied in the back, riding up her thighs, ankles locked, wanting a sheet to cover all of her. They said the hand had stopped bleeding, but it throbbed like a beating drum. The little bullet had cut through small bones that would take a long time to heal, then plastic surgery after this first round of cutting to re-attach ligaments so she'd have some grip and strength. Months with a physical therapist getting muscles to work, fingers on her good hand crossed, like her ankles. Hoping.

"I did my job," she said, her voice scratchy from the tubes shoved down her throat when they'd put her under.

"You saved Miguel," Rivera said. "The barrel was pointing at me, but it was Miguel you jumped to save. Now you can put that behind you. You don't need to blame yourself anymore."

She saw the look on Sergeant Perez's face. *Who's this Miguel?*

"I don't want to talk about it. Get me a blanket, so everybody isn't looking up my robe when they come in the room."

Rivera left. She heard him calling for a nurse in the hall.

Sergeant Perez said, "You were talking about a Miguel when you were out in surgery. The doc told me it was about a rape and shooting. Another Silva we need to worry about?"

"Nobody you need to know about."

"Rapes and shootings, that's police business."

"It's personal, from when I was a kid." Rivera was back with an ugly orange blanket. Maybe they used that color so nobody would want to steal one. "Tuck it under my feet," she told him. "Here." She grabbed a corner and pulled an edge to her waist, catching Rivera's eye as he worked around her feet. Wanting to chew him out for mentioning Miguel in front of Perez, knowing the sergeant would always be wondering.

And then she saw that Rivera was right. She had saved the life of a man who loved her. Her nightmare with Miguel relived, but coming out different, the way she'd wanted to turn those dark dreams around. Yeah, she felt it. Rivera did love her. He'd never told her, but she was sure he'd said it to himself, maybe catching it later like she had, surprised, hearing it inside her head.

Does this make up for Miguel? Will all of that stop?

"You guys want coffee?" Perez asked and they shook their heads.

Never gonna stop. That day on her back watching Miguel die at her feet was in her, always would be. It's what made her, drove her forward, forced her to be always stronger.

When they were alone, Rivera said, "I want to do something to thank you. I know you like the fights. We could catch a big card in Vegas, see the next women's championship."

"I hate Vegas. You know how many times I've gone there to bring back someone's daughter, or return with worse news?"

"The opposite of Vegas, then. Disneyland."

"We're a little old for Mickey and Cinderella, don't you think?"

"Just trying here. What about Nashville? You love country music."

Every one of these an overnighter—how many nights?—going through the trouble of insisting on her own room when they checked in. No, before she even agreed to go.

"Or a Sandals resort in the Bahamas." Rivera not giving up. "Sit back, be pampered. Somewhere exotic, an island with white beaches and palm trees. You told me once you'd never seen the ocean."

"You want to do something for me?" Her toe peeked out under the orange blanket and she thought for a second of what Marcy Thornton was going through in another room in this hospital. "Check the bull riding in Farmington."

"Farmington? You want a date in Farmington? Pump jacks and cowboys?"

"I like Farmington. It still feels like New Mexico, more than what's happened to Santa Fe. Regular people at regular jobs. No New Yorkers or Californians claiming they discovered the Land of Enchantment. Those Navajo boys come in to show how crazy brave they are, bull-fighting teams getting between horns and riders when they hit the ground. You've never seen fearless until you see a skinny Indian pulling the tail on a one-ton steer named Red Rock Assassin."

"Farmington?"

"Yes, Farmington."

"Is there anywhere to eat out there?"

"We'll eat in the stands. Navajo tacos and mutton stew. Then we can drive back home. After that, maybe I'll think about some place on a beach, as long as it has a weight room. You can get your daily dose of iron, too."

THIRTY-SEVEN

ARAGON ADMIRED THE T-BONE, its juices pooling on the plate, long, thick scallions across the top for the extra kick. This restaurant, almost a part of the Roundhouse it was so close, had great steaks, but the green chile—wrong part of town for that. Too bad. The high temps and dry weather during a long fire season gave this year's chile crop sweat-popping heat. Still, she wished the monsoons had come sooner. A fire in the Pecos Wilderness had charred a stretch of aspen she loved to run.

More than autumn was in the air. She was smelling roasting chiles everywhere outside the tourist sectors. Farmers sold them out of pickups, searing them on the spot in homemade steel mesh turbines spun over propane flames. She'd bought a bushel, roasted, of Chimayos, dumped into a plastic fifty-gallon bag almost melting from the heat. A week later, she still had to let down the windows when she drove to work to keep her eyes from watering. Her car would smell like roasted chile until Thanksgiving.

Lewis leaned forward with a knife and fork. "Should I cut it for you?"

She said thanks and reached for her beer while he sliced her steak into fork-sized pieces. She still couldn't hold anything in her right hand. She was getting better shooting with her left, working up from a .22 revolver, fighting the soft-wrist issue of shooting with only one hand. She was finally able to work a semi-auto without a misfire.

"You sure tuned up Montclaire's insurance company." Lewis pushed her plate back to her.

"They're going to pay policy limits," Aragon said with a mouthful of rare beef. "Who's going to rely on a child molester, murderer, lying monster to make your defense? Intentional infliction of emotional distress on top of physical injury, making me see Cassandra Baca in the dumpster. It will always be with me. PTSD for life, you know."

"Yeah, you're damaged for life. You're looking happy."

"Three hundred grand can do that."

"I thought Montclaire had a half-mil policy."

"Lawyer's cut, costs. You should have sued, too. You saw the body, something you'll never get out of your nightmares. You were traumatized by Montclaire waving the gun around, seeing yourself killed, your daughters without a father. You could be buying this dinner."

"That case would have been fought to the bitter end. Every cop who sees a body, who has a hard time with a suspect, from now on getting to sue?"

"It's our turn. Everybody's always suing us."

"You got yours because you got shot, and Thornton didn't want your claim hanging over her while she's fighting criminal charges. Hey, the damages you claimed for not being able to use your hand. I wanted to ask about that."

Aragon chased beef with the last of her beer and looked to the waiter for another round. "Hedonistic damages," she said. "Loss of life's pleasures. Shooting is what I like to do. And Krav Maga. Can't be blocking punches with a hand that leaks doing push-ups. And working out. *No más*, for a long time."

"Your legs, though. What are you squatting?"

"Over a hundred pounds more than before. But only on the machines. I can't handle a bar. My left arm's getting stronger. Lots of curls and extensions."

"Don't build up too much while your right side's out of action."

"I'm freaky enough, huh? The docs say I'll have scars from that acid, here, near my eye. But it's all right. I never saw myself as a fashion model. Man, this is a good piece of meat, even without green chile."

"Check out Hop Along."

She followed Lewis's gaze. Marcy Thornton had entered the restaurant. Black leather pants, black boots, a black cane, one with the three prongs on the end like old people use so they don't fall. Thornton was scanning tables, searching for someone.

"Crap, she's coming over." Aragon hunched her shoulders and burrowed into her meal.

"Detective Aragon, nice to see two of Santa Fe's finest enjoying the good life."

Aragon looked up from her plate. "We were just trading jokes about one-legged whores, but we'll stop." She jabbed a cube of bloody meat and pulled it off the fork with her teeth.

"I've never fully thanked you for saving me."

"It's my job."

"My I sit? Unless you object to speaking with someone like me."

"Talking to people like you is how we detectives gain insight into workings of the criminal mind. Pull out a chair."

"My date should arrive shortly." Thornton moved slowly when she let go of the cane. It remained upright on its three feet. She settled into her seat and turned to Lewis. "Detective Lewis, good evening."

He nodded and drank beer so he didn't have to say anything.

"What I want to say"—Thornton now giving all her attention to Aragon—"is I never should have confronted the Silvas alone about their extortion of Judge Diaz. That was insanely foolish. When I learned what was going on, I should have gone directly to the police instead of trading calls with very evil men."

Aragon said, "Start over. You were confronting Benny and Rigo Silva. That's what you call hanging by your wrists over a vat of flesh-eating soup?"

"I'm sorry about your face. It makes you look tougher, scars on the outside to match those on the inside."

"I was enjoying my meal here."

"We understand much about each other, don't we? I was going to say, Judy Diaz came to me for advice on how to handle the blackmail attempt. I told her, don't give in. Once you do, they own you. I believed since I've represented so many individuals like the Silvas, I could convince them they were headed for more trouble than their scheme was worth. I'd suspected, but not until Benny Silva told me did I know, that Lily Montclaire had been working for them, setting us up. She told us Andrea, Cassandra Baca, was a friend, well, lover, attending community college."

Aragon and Lewis stopped eating, Thornton talking now to the space between them, not making eye contact.

"She showed us an ID once. A community college student card. I wanted to be assured she was old enough to drink legally. I suppose that fake ID is with her clothes, whatever happened to them."

Aragon folded her arms and leaned back in her chair.

"I get it. You're breaking radio silence. We're getting a preview of what we'll hear in your lawyer's opening statement."

"Oh, you'll hear it tonight if you watch the news. I was saying, on the Griego case, the one with the misguided young men facing each other with bullet-proof vests and those little guns. I forget what drug they were using."

"PCP." It was Lewis, beer glass out of his hand. Balled fists on the table.

"Thank you. Lily brought the two guns to me, and insisted I hold one. She told me, press that black button, look how the barrel pops up."

"Why weren't her fingerprints on the gun?"

"I've thought about that. I remember she put it on my desk in a plastic bag. I took it out. I don't remember seeing her handle the gun with bare hands."

"Where were the guns all this time?"

"I presume in Lily's house. I'd instructed her to return the weapons. It wasn't our job to warehouse weapons for clients. That could be misconstrued as obstruction of justice."

"Sure you did," Lewis said.

"She ignored my instructions."

"So you were being a hero?" Aragon rocked in her chair. "That's the story you've cooked up these past months?"

"No, you were the hero, detective. I was the fool. Arrogant, naïve, believing my status as an officer of the court meant anything to Benny and Rigo Silva. I think my only heroic moment was when I used my last ounce of strength and willpower to overcome the pain. When I told you I had short legs. I couldn't finish the sentence. I used the Durango once, after Lily. The seat was way back. I'm glad you discerned what I was trying to explain under severe duress."

"You could have told us when you were recovering in the hospital."

"By then I was a criminal defendant. My advice to clients is never talk to the police. You're never helping yourself."

"You're talking now. You've worked out your script."

"The heart of all the charges against me, state and federal, is Lily Montclaire, who will disappoint everybody but me when she takes the Fifth. For now I'm enjoying my suspension from the active practice of law, for which I should thank Walter Fager. He and his gang of bitter losers gave me the vacation I would never give myself. All I have to do is report to a supervising attorney and pay my bar dues." She waved across the room, silver and turquoise bands jangling on her wrist. "There's my date. Let me introduce you. Fred!"

A portly man, silver hair swept back on his head, white pants under a navy blue blazer, returned her wave. He wore one of those dress shirts with a solid white collar, though the rest was striped in tones of blue.

Thornton struggled to get up. Aragon and Lewis didn't move to help her. Fred came to the table and steadied her with a hand under her arm until she found her balance with the cane. She introduced him, Fred Norman, her supervising attorney.

"My probation officer." She beamed, and he beamed back.

Norman stuck out a pudgy, pink hand, French cuffs at the end of his sleeve, a blue stone in the cuff link.

"You were the detective who rescued Ms. Thornton. I'm honored. She's looking terrific, isn't she?"

Aragon eyed Thornton's black leather boots, a fake foot and calf in there, the tight leather pants showing off her thighs. "Not bad. But I bet she holds up the line passing through courthouse security."

Aragon and Lewis watched them take a table against the wall, the most secluded spot on the floor.

"He's banging her," Lewis said.

Norman pulled out a chair and helped Thornton sit. As he was pushing her in, his hand trailed along her upper arm.

Aragon looked at her steak, now cool, in a shallow pond of blood. "Let's get out of here, grab some beer in cans. And find somewhere with a better view."

———————

It took some talking to get Javier and Serena out of the mountains for the 305th Santa Fe Fiesta. She'd tried the "C'mon, it'll be a blast" approach, saying their children could march in the Desfiles de los Niños, dress up however they wanted, bring any kind of animal, see what Santa Fe kids were like. She took a run at family pride, reminding Javier the Aragons had entered New Mexico in 1598 with Don Juan de Oñate, his full name ending in "y Salazar," something she'd learned from Benny Silva.

"Denise," Javier said, "it'll take more than ancient history to get me into Santa Fe."

And Serena was still angry. She was an Armijo. They'd arrived on the Camino Royal when New Mexico was a US territory. If her kids wanted history, she'd take them to the Alamo.

"You can advertise." That earned quiet on the other end of the line, Javier waiting for her to explain. "Bring your mules, your rifles, a banner saying 'Loco Lobo Outfitters.' Plumbers do it. Politicians out the kazoo."

That worked. They came from the mountains towing a horse trailer, inside mules for everyone. Javier dressed as a settler, an axe over his shoulder, muzzleloader in the crook of an arm, old bear traps lashed to the pommel. Serena wore a tiara in her black hair. The camo gown she'd sewed for herself was a nice touch. The kids wore buckskins and sneakers and held between them a banner with the family business name.

They joined the Historical/Hysterical Parade forming up at the DeVargas Center. A man in a lined cape with high velvet collar, sweat pouring down sagging cheeks, told them to get in behind a float with women in bikinis wearing Day of the Dead masks—wrong festival, but nobody seemed to mind. Behind the Loco Lobo ensemble came the National Guard Humvee.

Aragon walked the route as a conquistador, sweating as her father had under the same mail corset and *morion*, the foot soldier's metal helmet, the hammered tin a dome over the head with a crescent brim swooping to a sharp point over her face. She wore cross-trainers; the route was too long for authentic hob-nailed boots.

It had felt good pulling the armor from her closet, so many years since anyone in her family had last marched.

"Nice sword," she heard from a *caballero* on a grand horse, decked out in red cape and shiny boots, his own sword in a scabbard along the horse's flank. She could see his was fake, with a rubber handle to make it easier to hold. Hers was real and it weighed a ton. The blade alone was over four feet long. With the hilt, the two-handed sword was almost as long as she was tall.

The parade got under way. Serena and the girls tossed elk jerky strips into the crowd. Javier and his mule were the largest living things moving. She could imagine how pueblo people felt looking up at terrifying giants with thick black beards on strange animals they'd never seen before. She marched in front of the mules, keeping the blade straight up, aimed at a blue sky, the smoke gone, aspen on the high peaks turning gold. Her wounded hand hurt but she held on. She pressed her elbows against her ribs to help steady the weight.

People cheered. She saw cops she knew. They cheered even louder when they recognized her inside the armor. The sun on her face irritated the new skin over her burns. She ignored it and marched past the Basilica of St. Francis and out along the route following what had been the city's early fortifications.

At the end, she fell out and accepted a cold drink from Spanish grandmothers. Javier and Serena, their girls capable of handling their own animals, stopped to say they were heading back to the horse trailer.

"Before you go—" Aragon dug into the pocket of the vest and withdrew a folded slip of paper and set of keys. "This is for you. A double-wide to replace the one I got shot up. I can't say I'm sorry any other way. This is the address where you can see the model. They'll deliver. It's all taken care of."

They argued until she walked to Serena's mule and shoved the keys and paper into a saddle bag. She left them before they could say any more and moved through the crowd, the sword resting on her shoulder, seeing another side of the city she loved. Boys who looked so much like Miguel, dozens of them, dressed as young colonial soldiers. Beautiful girls in colorful, flowing dresses, their shining black hair combed for hours into perfection.

"That's the real thing isn't it?" It was the horseman in the red cape, now dismounted, the top buttons of his uniform open, perspiration beaded on dark chest hairs. "Can I hold it?"

"Careful, it's sharp."

He got a grip then raised it above his head. She stepped back and checked around them. Kids were too close.

"How'd you carry this for the whole parade?" The blade wavered above his head. "It's like a piece of train track."

"Fun's over." She stepped right into him and held his wrists, easing the sword down and into her own hands.

He dug a smartphone from his costume.

"Lift it up high." He stepped back to take a photograph. The crowd parted, people watching, pulling out phones to take their own photos of the short, powerful woman in ancient armor with the enormous sword. "Yeah, like that. With one hand even. Damn, girl, look at you. The last conquistador."

ACKNOWLEDGMENTS

Is it beyond strange to feel gratitude toward a character of one's own imagination? Is it vanity to say I really admire Denise Aragon, a fictional character whose life I control? Yet that is the truth. I am quite interested in this woman and I find she takes me on unexpected journeys through a Santa Fe you don't find in tourist magazines. What the heck: thanks, Denise. It's always a blast.

Of course, my deepest-felt thanks go to the real people in my life. First and forever, I owe so much to my wife, Kara. She reads the initial draft of every book. If the stories are good and true, it is because her insights kept me from running off the rails.

Thanks to my agent, Elizabeth Kracht of Kimberley Cameron & Associates, for always cheering me on. Thanks also to my editors at Midnight Ink, Terri Bischoff and Sandy Sullivan.

Last, many, many thanks to my readers. The way you have talked about Denise Aragon when we correspond or meet at book signings reassures me she is every bit the powerful, determined, irreverent, and fearless woman I encounter every time I sit down to write her story.

© Deja View Photography

ABOUT THE AUTHOR

James R. Scarantino (Port Townsend, WA) is a prosecutor, defense attorney, investigative reporter, and award-winning author. He lived in New Mexico for thirty years before trading high desert for Pacific Northwest rain. His novel *Cooney County* was named best mystery/crime novel in the SouthWest Writers Workshop International Writing Competition.